USS Hamilton

OTHER BOOKS BY MWM

USS HAMILTON
IRONHOLD STATION

Mark Wayne McGinnis

Published by:
Avenstar Productions

ISBN: 978-1-7350108-1-6

To join Mark's mailing list, jump to:
http://eepurl.com/bs7M9r

Visit Mark Wayne McGinnis at:
http://www.markwaynemcginnis.com

chapter 1

3rd Fleet, USS Hamilton—Approaching Auriga Star System

XO, Commander Galvin Quintos

If I had known what would be happening within the next fifteen minutes—that our fleet of eight powerful U.S. warships, the pride of U.S. Space-Navy, a part of Earth's United Nations Forces, *EUNF*, was about to be surprise attacked, decimated, with the death toll over ten thousand—I wouldn't have been languishing now in self-pity. This was supposed to be a laid-back run to the Auriga Star System. But I'm getting ahead of myself.

I was already three minutes late for an officers' meeting as I hustled down the wide passageway, my hurried footsteps echoing off the blue-gray bulkheads. Massive structural over-head girders spanned the passageway's width—commonly referred to as *Whale's Alley*, since it looked a hell of a lot like a whale's internal ribcage structure. I should have been long past brooding about my latest deployment, but seriously, how many times would I be posted to one of these lumbering old space buckets? I'd been here about two years. And that was about my limit for any assignment. What can I say? I get antsy. Sure, I'd heard the same words uttered by my mentor and, dare I say, *friend*, Admiral Block, over the last couple of months: *Yes, Commander, I'm working on a new post for you, son ... soon. The paperwork is in process. Just be patient.* And Block had been true to his word. He'd pulled the necessary strings, using his substantial clout to get me reassigned. Hell, right now, I was supposed to be five light-years away from here, the XO of a sleek, brand-new Light Battleship, the *USS Truman*, coming out of Earth's Lunar Halibart Shipyards. But there'd been a last-minute change order. I'd been held over for one more deployment on the *USS Hamilton.* There had been no explicit reasons for the duty alteration—although I'd heard rumblings that I was being preened for a Captaincy slot on another ship altogether, which didn't interest me in the least. Look, I've been aboard enough military warships to know that that level of responsibility was far more than I was capable of handling. Hey, we should all know where our personal competencies lie, as well as knowing where our *incompetency's* lie. For me, that meant knowing I had already reached the pinnacle of my military career. When it came down to making one of those *really* big, perhaps life or death decisions, one requiring me to be selfless and objective, I just didn't think I could be that altruistic. It's good to know one's limitations, I always say, and I know mine. So, no, being elevated to a U.S. Navy warship's skipper? No thanks. Don't get me wrong, I'm a qualified ship's Executive Officer. I make it a point to get to know the crew and, for the most part, I think I'm well-liked—if not, at least appreciated for not being a total tool. Anyway... I was ready to keep doing what I do best—*moving on*. Be nice to find a post on a vessel not built so many decades before I was born. Still, it's an honor to be posted aboard such an iconic vessel. The *USS Hamilton*—once the epitome of raw combat prowess of all existing Earth space warships—is a three-kilometer dreadnaught built to withstand even the most hostile enemy attacks.

Anyway, back to our present mission. Earth's nations jointly support thirty-six foreign, interstellar embassies within Orion's spiral arm of the Milky Way. The exo-planet Bon-Corfue, lying within the Auriga Star System, was one of our earliest important strongholds within that sector. When word came of discord amongst that twelve-world star system—that the Grish were making serious and persuasive inroads into the already capricious parliamentary government there—our battle group was dispatched with haste. While the Grish and Earth were not at war, per se, for decades now, the tension between our two civilizations had been escalating. Losing the Auriga Star System to such a powerful, barbaric, enemy—one this close to the Sol system, to Earth—would be... well, unthinkable. Although arriving with considerable force—the entire U.S.

3rd Fleet—this was expected to be little more than a diplomatic mission; a means for Earth's diplomatic envoys to quell local ruffled feathers. Perhaps to extend promises, perhaps do better supporting their technology-stunted (although exotic) mineral-rich system, with both financial and military-aid enticements. At least, that was the story for why we'd been deployed here. This was merely a show of force. And this being a time when Earth's intergalactic presence was being pulled to a number of other hot spots around the sector, we'd left port with just enough of a crew—about half of what was typical— to maintain operational status. Again, this was little more than a diplomatic mission—a show of force.

My wrist began to vibrate. To communicate with one another, all Navy crewmembers utilize an integrated comms display system called *TAC-Bands*. The device encircled one's wrists with a projected virtual display sleeve that had a tactile interface. The brains of our TAC-Bands stem from a device no larger than a grain of rice, called a *T-bead*, embedded just below the skin. The tiny device is packed with an immense amount of Thine technology, providing for a variety of visual communications whereby an integrated halo-projector allows the host to view incoming or make outgoing video calls. The virtual display also provides for touch responses—like tapping out text messages and such. Optionally, the virtual displays can be seen by others or can be hidden from other's view. Of course, our TAC-Bands are integrated with our auditory implant devices. Our TAC-Bands also allow for crewmembers to be tracked within the confines of any given ship; that is unless one knew how to disable that feature like I do from time to time when necessary. A quick glance at the text on my forearm informed me Captain Eli Tannock would not be extending the meeting start time for me.

Capt. Tannock: Will you be gracing us with your presence anytime soon?

I slowed, catching my breath, before entering the captain's conference room. I made a swiping waving motion at the door—it swooshed open, and I hurried in. The conference table, one of the captain's prized additions to the ship, was a continuous four-foot wide by twelve-foot-long, slab of translucent Jinhong crystal. Eight irritated-looking faces turned to look in my direction.

"Sorry, everyone . . . got held up on the Bridge," I said, taking the closest available open seat.

Captain Tannock, a stern man of medium height with salt-and-pepper short buzzed-cut hair, stood at the far end of the table. Clearly, I'd interrupted his dissertation. At sixty-four, Tannock was a fine commanding officer, yet, in my opinion, he was too *old school*—a little draconian in how he managed the crew. Not strict so much, although he could be that too, but pretty much always by-the-book regulations follower. For me, that was the rub, since I'm far more of a situational, *gray-area* kind of officer. That's why the captain's seven a.m. sharp officer meeting time meant *seven-ish* to me.

The captain glanced up at an old-fashioned analog clock

on the wall. He continued, "We're entering Auriga star system space now . . . Our diplomatic envoys are scheduled to meet on Bon-Corfue, within two hours . . ."

"Will we be granted shore leave, sir?" I asked. Several others around the table nodded their heads in approval, as I'd asked what they were undoubtedly too hesitant to ask themselves.

"We'll be making spaceport within the hour," he said, sending an admonishing glance my way before continuing, "Although shore leave will be granted, off-ship crewmen must abide by strict curfew rules—be back onboard this and every evening by 2100 hours, not a minute later."

I hardly listened as the captain's voice droned on and on. Across the compartment, beyond the far side of the table, what seemed to be a large window, with a view into space, was actually a live, high-definition video feed coming off the ship's outer port side. Thousands/millions of stars twinkled against an obsidian background. An occasional starship came into view, then was gone quickly due to our high relative speed. Lowering my gaze, I noticed Major Vivian Leigh, the ship's Chief Physician, staring at me with a less-than-congenial expression. Her eyes conveyed: *you might want to pay better attention to this, asshole.* Rolling her eyes, she refocused her full attention back on the captain. It wasn't that the Doc and I were enemies so much as we just didn't get along. I can't recall the last time she and I agreed on anything. Other attendees around the table were Chief of Engineering Craig Porter; Chief of Security Alistair Mattis; Science Officer Stefan Derrota; Ensign Lucas Hughes; Lieutenant Wallace Ryder; and the captain's friend and confidant, Chaplain Thomas Trent, who, for some unknown reason, would be joining the diplomatic envoy, along with the captain, as they headed down to the planet. *Better him than me.*

The captain, moving to the next item on his agenda, spoke of replenishing the *Hamilton's* waning supplies stores once docked at port.

"All section-heads should have amended their department's logistical stores requests by now."

To my right, Chief of Engineering Craig Porter, an officer with sandy-blond hair, a strong cleft chin (and in his late twenties, like myself), leaned in and whispered, "Ever been to that little place in old-town Calihoo ... you know, the pub with that chick riding that Aurigan creature in the window?"

I thought for a second. Clearly, Aurigans weren't unduly concerned with modern-day political correctness. Sure, I remembered—the ultra-real looking robotic woman riding the robot creature—a bronc riding cowgirl with all her, um, attributes in full view. "You mean Hobo Thom's?" I whispered back. Typically, Bon-Corfue establishments were known by their *unpronounceable* alien names, as well as by their Earth English name equivalents, posted on signage.

Hanson nodded, then smiled at me ruefully. "Meet for a drink later?"

I shrugged. "Let's play it by ear ... I'll be battening down the hatches here until at least 1600 hours."

"I'll wait for you. I'll be the one at the bar ... probably listing a bit to starboard by then."

All of a sudden, the ship's emergency klaxon began to wail. Everyone around the table jumped to their feet. My TAC-Band began to ping and vibrate, as did everyone else's. But I wasn't looking at my forearm—across from me on that ultra-real-looking window display, I saw exactly what the issue was. No less than a hundred incoming missiles made visible by their fiery blue aft thrusters—all inbound toward us. My heart skipped a beat and my stomach sank. *We're so fucked.*

MATHR, pronounced Mother, the *USS Hamilton's* Artificial Intelligence system, squawked out an announcement: "Battle stations! . . . Battle stations! All crew make haste to your assigned battle stations!"

The captain yelled, "Move it, people! Stations . . . Now!"

As we quickly funneled out into Whale's Alley, the first impacting missile strikes could be felt, rumblings rising upward through the deck plates. A forlorn sound—like a painful wail—emanated somewhere deep within the old warship's bowels.

Captain Tannock, Science Officer Stefan Derrota, Ensign Lucas Hughes, and I all turned left, sprinting toward where we needed to report—the *Hamilton's* bridge. Fortunately, it was relatively nearby.

As the captain turned the next corner, I heard him yell something unintelligible.

Then I heard an explosion and a concussive blast threw me backward off my feet. Next came nothing but blackness.

I awoke, probably a couple of minutes later. Lying in a crumpled heap on the far side of Whale's Alley, my head hurt—and the still-blaring emergency klaxon wasn't helping. With still-blurry vision, I saw fuzzy undefined shapes running back and forth along the corridor. MATHR's announcements didn't make much sense—something about ice cream being rationed due to rainfall on Deck 22 . . .

With considerable effort, I got myself up on my feet and staggered forward. Black smoke billowed forth from a number of compartment entrances along the corridor, including those leading from the Bridge. I stopped at its entrance and gasped aloud. It was nearly impossible to hear over the klaxon's blare. MATHR was still rambling on incoherently, and there were the cries of men and women—those still conscious—yelling within the damaged compartment. The first thing I noticed was that a portion of the ceiling had collapsed, along with one end of a support girder. Above me, through a ragged opening in the ceiling, I could see what remained of a charred compartment on an upper deck. As more black smoke billowed down through the opening, I assumed the striking missile had actually detonated somewhere up there. Multiple consoles around me were fountaining sparks up into the air. More than one fire was being attended to by surviving Bridge crew. Amazingly, the forward halo-display, still active, did not appear to be damaged. Bodies lay inert on the deck. The typical Bridge crew consisted of some thirty officers, along with a support crew. My guess was that at least half of them now were either seriously injured or dead.

"XO! XO!" someone yelled off to my right. Ensign Hughes, who'd entered the Bridge in front of me, along with the captain, said, "Captain's down!" He gestured toward a crumpled, uniformed man lying next to the fallen girder. "Orders! Sir, the ship is yours!"

The ship is mine? I staggered, struggling to see clearly. "Someone give me a damn situation report! . . . who's attacking us? What's happening to the rest of the fleet?"

Shaking my head in an attempt to clear it, I made my way forward, toward what commonly was referred to as the Captain's Mount. A silly, historical, reference back to a period when officers on horseback, usually atop a hill or ridgeline, observed an ensuing battle below. On this ship, it referred to a raised captain's chair, positioned mid-section within the bridge. I literally fell into its cushioned seat. Gaping at the forward display, I yelled out, "Who's on Tactical? Leave the dead and injured for now . . . someone get on that station . . . hurry!" My mind raced—*I can't do this . . . someone else needs to be sitting here.* My eyes roved across the deck to where the captain's inert body still lay. *Get up, you old son of a bitch!*

Young Lieutenant Gail Pristy, waif-thin and typically timid, on taking her assigned seat immediately began tapping at the tactical controls. The halo-display quickly segmented into multiple feeds.

I watched as Ensign Hughes ever so carefully pushed a deceased Bridge officer off his seat in order to sit in front of the helm station. Another officer, Crewman Grimes, positioned himself at the weaponry station.

"I still need a sit-report!" I yelled.

"All mid- and aft-shields are holding . . . forward shields

are still down, but Engineering reported they'll have them up within ten minutes, or so," Lieutenant Pristy said.

"Tell them we'll be glowing space scrap by then ... they need to do better than that. Show me the enemy's position, Lieutenant ... and someone get me that fucking *sit*-report on the fleet's current standing!"

Lieutenant Pristy rapidly tapped away at her station for several more seconds. "XO, the fleets taking heavy damage ..." Raising a hand up to her mouth, tears brimming in her eyes, she added, "It's the Grish," she gestured to the display. "Six enemy battle cruisers, sir, and four of our fleet have lost propulsion although all our warships are fully engaged and now returning fire."

Christ! How? How could we have been caught so unprepared? My heart sank. *No time to think. Just act!*

"The enemy's attacking from all sides ... they've surrounded us ..." Lieutenant Pristy said.

"Jump us out of here!" I yelled. "Order the rest of the fleet to jump away!"

I caught sight of Science Officer Stefan Derrota. The man was of Indian descent and spoke with a pleasant sing-song accent. He was a bit chubby and always a tad rumpled-looking. I liked him, but the man was a worrier, the kind of person that wrung his hands and rubbed his forehead at the slightest sign of unrest or tension. With that said, I liked Derrota. Currently, his left cheek was bloodied. Standing over the Sensor's Array board, he shook his head. "There are overlapping saturating grav-fields . . . they're restricting any of the fleet from jumping away."

Jumping into a manufactured wormhole required the bending of the local space/time continuum. But with a little pre-planning, an enemy with sufficient advanced tech can blanket spacecrafts and their surrounding space with gravitational disruption fields—making the creation of jump wormholes—*impossible.*

Derrota continued, "Laid in wait . . . cloaked . . . this was a total ambush attack. Fucking animals!" He nervously rubbed his face with his palms and let out a defeated breath.

"Two of our warships have been destroyed, obliterated," Lieutenant Pristy said, glancing over to me. "The Federal and the Republic, sir . . . We're being outgunned."

"Lieutenant, I want visuals on every enemy position. Deploy sensor-drones."

"On it, XO. Um, this isn't good . . . seems their ships are cloaked—"

"Best guess then. Track weaponry flares . . . heat signatures, radiation wakes, whatever gives up their rough position."

"Grimes, weapons status!"

"Most weapons are online . . . Rail Guns online and firing; Phazon Pulsars online and firing. Smart Missiles are offline . . . MATHR handles those, and she's . . ."

"I know, I can still hear her rambling on, something about bats in the laundry chutes." I thought for a long moment. Sure, the *Hamilton* was big—its shields robust, she could take a licking like few other ships. But what we needed was to find a way to get on offense—not simply to hold on. We were losing this battle, and no one would be coming to rescue us out here. Then something occurred to me. "Talk to me about the Broadsides, Grimes," I said.

The crewman stared at me blankly, as did most of the others on the Bridge.

Broadsides. Let me quickly inform you about these colossal cannons. First of all, only three USS warships were ever fitted with these monster-size weapons everyone refers to as Broadsides. The *Hamilton*, along with her two sister ships, the *Washington,* and the *Adams*—all built more than sixty years ago—were all outfitted with twelve of these behemoth weapons, six cannons per side. Each cannon fired twelve-hundred-pound *bowlers*, nicknamed for their visual similarity to massive looking bowling balls and their strategically placed circular finger-like holes. Prior to impact, these holes were the dispersal element for magnesium scatter frags, which effectively weakened enemy hull armor plating a nanosecond prior to impact and allowed the giant explosive cannonballs to decimate anything, everything, they came into contact with. The problem was these *big bad boys* were found to be somewhat unstable. More than a few bowlers, would sometimes, *though rarely*, go off-course. In one such case, during spatial wargames close to Earth, a British Frigate was destroyed with all hands lost. Needless to say, these big weapons were then deemed too dangerous—even for wartime use. Subsequently, newer warship construction did not include Broadsides. Instead favored were more advanced energy weaponry, such as the newer Phazon Pulsar and railguns.

Yet the simple fact remained that the *USS Hamilton,* and her sister ships also, still had bowler munitions stored onboard. Removing them from their onboard magazine compartments had been deemed far more expensive and labor-intensive than deemed practical.

"Helm . . . get us into that fight. Put us right in the middle of the enemy's position! I want optimum firing attitudes for those Broadsides . . ."

Young Grimes, not much more than a lad, maybe twenty-one or two, sat wide-eyed, like he was ready to pee his pants. "They've been mothballed . . . trying to get them prepped for battle—"

I held up a hand to shut him up. "Whatever it takes . . . get every available crewman on that task, as well as all those busy doing something else. Have them report to each of the twelve Cannon Silos!"

"XO . . . got latest situation report," Lieutenant Pristy interrupted. "Mid- and aft- shields are taking a beating, yet still holding. Forward shields have been brought back online, although Chief Porter reported they are barely being held together with baling wire and duct tape. Propulsion is failing."

So much for meeting the Chief at Hobo Thom's later. For some completely illogical and ill-timed reason, I thought about that naked robotic gal, riding that lizard-like thing in the window he'd mentioned earlier today—and how life can turn on a dime.

"Silo crews reporting in . . . think they have three Broadsides almost operational, one portside and two starboard, sir," Grimes reported. "Crews still working on the others."

"Enemy ships no longer cloaked . . . visuals updating now," Pristy said, sounding a little more confident.

I never actually had the pleasure of utilizing these big guns before. Hell, no one had in over fifty years. What I did know was the tracking and targeting for the gargantuan weapons was done locally, within each respective Cannon Silo. Unlike our other weaponry, like Smart Missiles, which were plotted, targeted, and often fired from the *Hamilton's* Combat Information Center (CIC), which functioned as our tactical center. The CIC also housed the ship's AI, or 'Main Artificial THought Resource'—commonly referred to as MATHR. The CIC compartment, situated directly adjacent to the bridge, is accessible through a wide passageway. Looking off to my left, what I could now see inside the CIC was in as much disarray as the Bridge. Some movement in there, but the lingering dark smoke made it hard to see inside.

"Lieutenant Pristy, relay to each silo to go ahead . . . mark their targets and fire at will."

"I will, sir . . . they're . . . um, still trying to figure out how to work the cannons. Bowlers are being loaded, via their individual ramp-injectors now."

Okay, whatever those are. Suddenly, the ship shook—dust and debris drifted downward from above. "We get hit again?" I asked Lieutenant Pristy, expecting to hear the worst.

"Um . . . no, well . . . yes . . . we're still taking fire, but our shields are holding. That was one of the Broadside cannons going active."

The deck shook again and again. I now discerned that distinct shaking pattern as the powerful individual broadside cannon recoils. We turned toward each other. No one said anything, but what was happening now felt good—felt awesome! "Status?" I asked.

Lieutenant Pristy altered the main halo-display—concentrating instead on the feeds that showed the two Grish battleships. One was port, one starboard. Apparently, the *Hamilton* was situated directly between both enemy warships. The deck continued to gyrate as the Broadsides roared. On the halo-display, I watched via active drone feeds the two flanking Grish Battle Cruisers being pummeled—turned into heaps of scrap metal. Grish shields, it seemed, didn't have the means to compensate against those thundering, sixty-year-old explosive bowlers. Multiple locations on both Grish ships began to geyser out great spews of venting atmosphere, along with mangled bodies and other internal debris. Billowing balls of fire erupted up and then just as quickly flared out as the vacuum of space-starved flames of oxygen.

Science Officer Stefan Derrota quickly reported from the Sensor's Array console, "We've certainly gotten their attention, XO. Three of their warships have made definitive course changes . . . they're directing firing on us as they head out."

Lieutenant Pristy chimed in, "Mid-ship shields are fluctuating . . . the aft-shields not far behind."

Ignoring her comment, I asked, "Helm . . . what can you

do to get us turned around, get optimum Broadside firing attitudes for those new targets?"

Ensign Hughes squinted at me; his face drained of color. "Sir ... *Hamilton's* Reactor Core One is dumping plasma ... HyperDrive Alpha is winding down."

The ship had three reactor cores, and four drive engines— HyperDrive Alpha, HyperDrive Delta, HyperDrive Omega, and HyperDrive Beta. "Damn it," I shouted, "someone tell me we can jump away from here!" Glancing toward the CIC, where such jump wormhole functions were plotted and initiated, I saw a crewman in the haze negatively shake his head. *Fuck!*

"Incoming! Smart Missiles ... they appear to be fusion-tipped," Derrota announced.

The *Hamilton* was jolted so hard I was thrown from my seat. Glancing around me, most everyone experienced a similar fate. Derrota, lying on the deck in front of the Sensors Array Station, moaned and clutched at one elbow.

"Suck it up, Derrota ... we need you!" I ordered. "Everyone, back to your stations! Lieutenant Pristy?"

Now resituated at her tactical console, Pristy cut me off: "Major damage! We're venting on decks 12, 13, 23, and ... oh shit, we just lost the *Hamilton's* aft dorsal rail cannon."

"I got us turned around!" Ensign Hughes yelled victoriously. "Broadsides are resuming their firing gauntlet."

I watched the updated display as the three-kilometer-long *Hamilton* turned into a more optimum firing position. As the deck below us began to gyrate again, everyone, including myself, let out a cheer. "Yaaa!"

My left forearm was practically numb from the constant, vibrating, hail prompts, which, until now, I had ignored. Stealing a glance, I saw this one was from Frank Mintz, Chief of Flight Bay, and pilot crews. I tapped my TAC-Band, "Bay-Chief . . . a little busy here . . ."

"Gotcha . . . just wanted to relay portside bay port doors are now operational. We can deploy close to a full wing on your command."

"Thanks, Frank!" Truth was, I hadn't considered the flight bay ports being inoperable. *And that's why you're in way, way, over your head.* The flight bay was immense; spanned the entire width of the ship. Access bay ports out to space were situated on both port and starboard sides of the ship. Since the enemy hadn't deployed any fighters yet, I was reluctant to do so myself. This battle would be over, one way or another, in just a matter of minutes. "I'll get back to you, Bay-Chief," I said, terminating the connection.

"Getting updates from several silos now . . . we're running low on bowlers, XO," Pristy said, looking concerned.

From what I could see of these last arriving Grish Battle Cruisers, we wouldn't be needing much more in the way of bowlers. Two of the four remaining enemy warships had been decimated by our broadsides—were down for the count.

Science Officer Derrota clapped his hands so loudly I jumped in my seat. "And there they go!" he exclaimed. "The last two Grish ships . . . just jumped away!"

chapter 2

At the moment all was relatively quiet here within Auriga Star System. There were no enemy vessels within local space—not even those damaged during the battle. Seems those two surviving Grish battle cruisers had done a bit of house cleaning, firing upon their own ships—*atomizing them*—just prior to jumping away.

The ambush had caught us totally by surprise. Within a timespan of twenty-eight minutes, the pride of the EUNF—U.S. Navy's 3rd Fleet was reduced from an impressive, substantial eight warships, down to a mere three. The first surviving warship, the *USS Union*, a small frigate, sustained heavy damage to its propulsion and environmental systems, its crew currently forced to float around in a zero-G environment. The second surviving warship, the *USS Colorado*, a destroyer, sustained two breached decks and damage to its RSM, Relational Stability Matrix, resulting in the warship constantly tipping back and forth—side to side—as if perpetually floating upon stormy seas. And the third surviving warship, the *USS*

Hamilton, our sixty-year-old dreadnought being the hardest hit, sustaining catastrophic damage to virtually all its primary ship systems. What the three warships now had in common was none would be making a jump to light-speed anytime soon. That, plus a still-climbing death count on each vessel. Ship officers stationed amongst the three warships had not fared well either. The highest-ranking officer onboard the *Union* was, Lieutenant Randy Cobb, and Lieutenant Brian Giar, aboard the *Colorado*. Captain Eli Tannock, yes still alive, although currently unconscious within the *Hamilton's* HealthBay, was the highest-ranking officer of the three wrecked ships. Myself, I was a commander in rank and the *Hamilton's* XO—and I was the highest-ranking *still-conscious* officer between any of the three warships. *Shit!*

Word of the attack would normally have been automatically conveyed back to Earth via MATHR sending light-beam communications routed along a network of one-hundred-and fifty-two fortified repeater stations. But with the *Hamilton's* damaged AI, her still acting sketchy, and long-range transmitters on the *Union* and *Colorado*, damaged and currently incapable of sending a signal, I knew Earth would still be in the dark as to our predicament. FTL comms were commonplace amongst Twenty-Second Century starships—taking place via leap-frogging micro-wormhole laser transmissions. Still, intergalactic text/voice/video-feed messaging was by no means, instantaneous. Back-and-forth conversations could be exercises in patience—often, delays waiting for replies could be infuriating and even dangerous in those cases where desperate crews were awaiting new orders. And the sobering fact that the Grish could jump back here at any moment with reinforcements, finish what they had started, was not lost on me or anyone else here on the bridge.

So, my first post-battle decision was to directly contact Command back on Earth—inform them of our devastating Auriga Star System battle and the current disposition of our three remaining damaged warships. It took close to an hour before a viable micro-wormhole laser transmission could be established. Admiral Cyprian Block, having been jostled out of bed, acknowledged our situation with both dismay and shock. Earth, in all most likelihood, would now be at war with the Grish. *This changes everything.*

Currently, the admiral was conferring with his ranking officer peers on the next moves to be taken. We were told to hold in position for now, attend to our dead and injured. Do what we could to isolate any still-venting decks—get active in making repairs.

EXHAUSTED, FIGHTING THE EFFECTS OF WHAT I SUSPECTED was a mild concussion, I was currently assisting others in pulling crewman Cara Robinson, a forty-three-year-old Czechoslovakian immigrant, out from beneath a stacked food replicator located at the far end of the Mess Hall. Four other helpers—groaning and cursing from exertion—hefted up an end of the metal tower just far enough for the whimpering

Galley Assistant to be fully excised and brought to safety. Although emotionally shaken, her injuries seemed to be minor.

With one of her arms draped over my shoulder, I was supporting much of her not-insubstantial weight. "Can you walk, Cara . . . do you think anything's broken?" I asked.

She replied back in broken English, "No, I fine . . . ohh . . . my ankle . . . hurts . . . very sore."

"That's okay . . . just lean on me."

Together, we headed out of the Mess Hall. Cara, trying to be stoic, sniffed repeatedly, fighting back tears.

Hearing running footsteps behind us, I glanced back over my shoulder and saw Ensign Lucas Hughes—who was still a good distance down the corridor.

"XO! There's damage to LabTech . . . atmosphere's venting. We have science officers and crewmen getting sucked-out through a hull breach," he shouted.

Trying to redistribute Cara's weight to a different area on my aching shoulders, she winced and stifled a groan. "Sorry, Cara."

Reaching us, Lucas slowed then came to a stop. Bending over, his hands on his knees, he struggled to catch his breath. "We can't get the AI to activate the emergency doors into the lab. I was on my way to the CIC . . . maybe figure out what's wrong with MATHR."

I pivoted around, still balancing Cara's weight, and brought my TAC-Band up near my face. That one action alone—detection of my direct gaze—initialized the comms device. I said,

"MATHR... Emergency protocol... you need to provide access into those LabTech hatchways immediately!"

MATHR's voice, bypassing my ear implants, emanated from the acoustic speakers above us. Sounding more nurturing, schoolmarm-ish, than in her typical, flat-toned—personality-void—AI voice, she said, "It is best to wash one's hands after use of the toilet; use liberal amounts of soap and hot water—"

"MATHR... damage report!

The AI instantly changed back into her normal-sounding voice, giving us momentary hope. "LabTech...vent...vent... vent."

"MATHR stop! Run a self-diagnostic! And be prompt about it!" I said.

Lucas peered at me with nervous eyes—a trickle of sweat emerging at his hairline.

"Shit! Help me, Ensign," I said. "Let's get Cara over to the elevators."

Hughes, moving across to Cara's far side, tucked his shoulder under her arm, and together we hefted her body up between us. We reached the bank of elevators just as three crewmen rushed out, their faces covered in soot. All were coughing. I quickly scanned their embroidered identification rank and name I.D.'s: Crewman White, Crewman Lasalle, and Crewman Richie.

"Where you three coming from?" I asked.

Lasalle said, black, muscular with broad-shouldered said, "We're SWM," which meant Ship Wide Maintenance. "We

were helping out on 23 . . . it's bad, sir . . . really bad up there."
Doubling over, he coughed into filthy palms.

"Why are you here? Why aren't you on 12, heading to
HealthBay?"

"We're here looking for you, sir. Comms are squirrely."
Pointing to one of his ears, he added, "and MATHR's not
responding." Crewman Richie violently coughed into his
elbow. "Need help getting access to LabTech . . . get those
people out of there."

I slapped the call button and the elevator doors opened
right away. Thankfully, the empty car hadn't moved off yet.
"Everyone in!" I shouted, far louder than I probably needed
to. We rode the lift from Deck 10 up to 12. En route, several
TAC-Band messages appeared on my arm.

"Looks like we have visual comms back online," I said, as I
read one dire damage report after another. When the elevator
doors opened, I turned to the three crewmen, "Out!"

Crewman White said, "We're going back with you, sir . . .
we're fine."

Lucas and I extricated our shoulders from Cara's weight.
"Can you make it over to HealthBay, Cara . . . we have other
injured—"

Cara cut me off, hobbling from the elevator car. "You go . . .
I'm fine . . . it not far."

The doors slid shut. As the elevator began its ascent, I texted
Doctor Vivian Leigh and was surprised when we connected.

"This better be important!" she snapped, sounding out of
breath.

"Doc Viv, Cara Robinson . . . she's a Galley Assistant, is on her way to you—"

"You mean the poor woman I just found sobbing on the deck outside HealthBay? The same woman you abandoned there?"

"Look, people are dying all over the ship! Right now, I'm attending to a deck breach on 23. LabTech is venting scientists out to space. So, let me see . . . should I have stayed and helped the woman with a sprained ankle, instead of trying to save others from dying? Hmmm . . . what to do . . ." I cut the connection.

Ensign Hughes made a face. "A little harsh, sir?"

I shrugged, "Maybe." More to myself than to Hughes, I added, "That woman really knows how to get under my skin."

The elevator doors opened, and I Immediately felt the icy-cold chill of a deck losing its atmosphere. The klaxon above continued to blare as all five of us ran down Deck 23's passageway toward LabTech. Being the first one to run in through the open entrance door—which I noted should have been sealed—what I found was even worse than I'd expected. LabTech, was the *Hamilton's* expansive science and technology center, comprised of nine, individually, sealed compartments. The whole department, typically pristine white—a *cleanroom* environment, with floor-to-ceiling glass walls separating various areas—was now in total disarray and soot-covered. It looked ruined. Only a few of the inner glass walls remained intact, the rest were indirectly destroyed by one of the missile strikes. In the distance, I noted that three outer compartments were even more blackened, void of their long lab benches. All the high-tech equipment, which once occupied those spaces, was gone. Beyond any doubt, the personnel stationed here had been sucked out. Through the still intact, but seriously fractured, glass wall nearest us, we could see the ragged opening along the far outer bulkhead where the hull breach had occurred. The only good news was this must have been an exploded missile's errant fragmentation breach, versus being a direct detonation—whereby nothing would have been left of this part of the ship.

"XO . . . over there!" one of the three SWM crewmen said pointing.

Catching movement behind one of the few intact inside glass walls, I counted six men and women wearing lab coats. Muffled yells for help were barely audible over the klaxon's penetrating shrill. The farthest glass wall had tiny fractures and little openings along with a serious crisscrossing of spiderwebbing cracks. Papers and other debris circled above in the troubled air—everyone's hair buffeted about in that swirling, venting, atmosphere. Those trapped inside were frantically pounding on the glass walls. *Shit! That's a bad idea.* Concentrating—I mentally pictured the path I'd need to take, in order to reach that lab area. A sealed door stood between the lab and us.

"What specific area is that over there?" I asked no one in particular.

Hughes brow furrowing, said, "Um, that's . . ." he rubbed at his chin.

"Hurry, Ensign!" I spat impatiently.

"I think that's the Genetics Lab. Yeah, pretty sure."

Lasalle nodded. "Most definitely, sir . . . it is the Genetics Lab."

Since these SWM guys knew every nook and cranny of this old ship better than anyone—I took his word for it.

I intoned a silent prayer and spoke into my TAC-Band: "MATHR! Open the inner Genetics Lab door!"

"Hull breach detected . . . all compartments are sealed—"

I was momentarily relieved on hearing our ship's AI sounding a little more coherent. "Command override code 523. MATHR, open the inside Genetics Lab door and hold open for seven seconds . . . do so now!"

I saw the inside glass door wobbling in place but was obviously jammed. I said, "I need to get in there!"

"Not a good idea, sir . . . any glass remaining in there could crumble away . . . get you and the rest of us sucked out to space," said Crewman Richie warily.

"Just be ready to move those trapped inside off this deck. Got that?" I said, staring at each of the SWM crewmembers. "Be ready to move fast!"

I looked up. "MATHR . . . can you hear me?" hoping to find she was capable of conversing normally, rather than exclusively via my TAC-Band.

"Affirmative, Commander Galvin," I heard her reply above the noisy klaxon.

"Open the glass door in front of me. Do it now!"

It took a moment, but the glass door—streaked with cracks—slid to one side. The cold air hit me as if I'd jumped into an Arctic stream. I ran my previous envisioned route over to the Genetics Lab door, where the six scientists sat huddled together on the other side. Shivering, their skin had turned ashen blue. Seeing several of their mouths rhythmically gape open—I flashed back to my childhood, momentarily recalling a handful of wide-eyed bass flopping around on the floorboard of my grandfather's old fishing skiff.

"MATHR, try it again! Open the inside Genetics Lab door!"

Once again, I saw the door wobble in place—*still jammed.* I placed my palms against the glass and pushed sideways, using all my strength to get the thing to slide left. One by one, I watched as three scientists locked within dropped to the deck unconscious. I could still feel MATHR engaging the door servos unsuccessfully. I was well aware the six men and women had mere seconds to live.

Suddenly, Ensign Lucas Hughes was by my side. Then the three SWM crewmen were there too. I yelled, "On three! One, two, three . . . push!"

That did the trick and the door shot sideways. I wasn't pre-pared for the bone-chilling cold. Even though the openings in the far outer glass wall were relatively small, the tempera-ture in here had easily fallen fifty, *hell*, a hundred degrees or so, below zero. Then I remembered. Had almost forgotten, I'd given MATHR a mere seven-second countdown for the door to remain open. The five of us quickly moved, physically drag-ging everyone from the Genetics Lab. No sooner had the last one been pulled through—an unconscious middle-aged man, with a circular crown of gray hair—the glass door slid back into place, its seal making a loud sucking sound in the process.

Everyone was uncontrollably shivering. Those who'd previously dropped down to the deck unconscious were coming around, attempting to stand. "Ensign, this entire deck isn't safe . . . you, along with the other SWM guys here, need to get these people into the elevators and down to HealthBay."

I didn't need to prompt them any further, as they were already on the move—helping one another to move as far away from the precarious LabTech area as possible.

"Sir?" Hughes queried, looking back at me. "Aren't you coming?" he said as he assisted two women. I lunched and with arms clutched tightly around themselves, they hurried toward the bank of elevators.

"I need to clear the rest of this deck before locking out any further access to it. Go . . . I'll be fine." I watched the group funnel their way into an elevator car. Just before the door shut, crewman Lasalle managed to shoulder his way out through the narrowing gap.

He ran toward me and shouted, "We'll clear the deck together, sir . . . ain't safe, you wandering around here by yourself. My SWM guys will be back up here too, just as soon as they deliver those six *eggheads* into HealthBay."

chapter 3

We approached one of the Deck 23 Vac-Gate, basically a reinforced, emergency-deployed bulkhead. Made of some kind of iridium/tungsten composite—these bulkheads, half a meter thick, are virtually indestructible. Strategically situated around the *Hamilton*, they automatically close, sectioning off entire passageways, when serious hull breaches were detected.

A small data display was flashing red, just to the right of a narrow hatchway, built into the structure. Crewman Lasalle tapped on the display with the gnarled forefinger of a man who'd undoubtedly worked a lifetime with heavy machinery of one type or another. He spoke with a southern, maybe Louisianan, accent. "Sir, I have no idea how heavy the damage is on the other side of this Vac-Gate..." and gestured to the flashing data display. "Sure, I can override the locking security bolts at this hatch, but we may be walking into a shitstorm. Might be best to return back with protective environ-suits..."

I'd been tapping away at my TAC-Band receiving status

reports, also directing five other rescue teams that were far better equipped with personnel and equipment than the two of us were. The death toll kept climbing. In most cases, the best thing a team could do was to flag any of the dead, the corpse's, locations for later retrieval, then move on—find crewmen still alive. Each rescue team had been designated an alphanumeric code name. I updated the other teams on our code name change. Crewman Lasalle and myself would now be designated Team HF. After listening first to other team leaders' situational reports, I informed them of what had transpired with LabTech and the six survivors. I also learned interfacing with MATHR was still hit or miss.

Looking up, making eye contact with Crewman Lasalle, now waiting for my reply, I said, "According to our illustrious ship's AI, if we can believe her, there's still enough atmosphere inside there to breathe. What she can't tell me is if there's one or multiple life-readings ... any more folks trapped in there. So, let's open it up, Crewman Lasalle." I took in his smooth relatively unlined face, his salt and pepper close-cropped hair and estimated his age to be early to mid-fifties. And at the moment, I was glad to have him along with me.

"Let me go first, sir," Lasalle said, then entered several strings of code into the datapad. I heard the telltale sound of locking bolts being withdrawn deep within the Vac-Gate. Lasalle lifted a manual latching lever up then shoved the hatch open several inches.

I peered in over his shoulder. Smoke-filled warm air wafted out from deep within. "Let's move, Crewman," I said, patting his back. We crossed over one after the other to the other side of the Vac-Gate, where Lasalle quickly re-secured the hatchway behind us. The overhead lights in this part of the ship were out, with only sporadically working emergency lights providing dim illumination. The farther in we walked, the cooler it got. An unnecessary habit—but one virtually everyone onboard a naval space vessel was guilty of—I looked up unnecessarily before querying the ship's AI: "MATHR . . . you now capable of locating any injured personnel for us on this deck?"

"There are multiple types of goldfish . . . the "standard" version of this variety is best known as the American Shubunkin. Interestingly, the little fishies are almost identical to one called the Comet goldfish. Now, the Wakin goldfish . . . is a strange variety, with large bubble-like eyes—"

"MATHR, stop!" I said with annoyance. I next TAC-Band -texted Ensign Hughes to go over to the CIC and ensure that Stefan Derrota, our Science Officer, was still working on getting MATHR fully back online.

I said, "Let's keep going," and continued on down the corridor. When my wrist vibrated, I saw Doc Viv's face icon being displayed. I rolled my eyes as I answered her hail.

"Where the hell are you?" she demanded. "You do realize you are now in command of this ship . . . that the crew needs a commanding officer—"

"Is there something specific you need right this second, Major Leigh?"

"It's *Doctor* Leigh, and . . . you . . . needed . . . HealthBay . . . strange . . ." the garbled connection suddenly terminated. In that moment, I better appreciated MATHR's technical issues; anything to avoid speaking with that interminably annoying woman.

"XO . . ." Crewman Lasalle said, pointing. He'd moved toward a portside diamond-glass window. Glancing out, I could see what had captured the crewman's attention. From here, we had a clear view of Deck 23's Maintenance Dome. Each deck had a number of them—diamond-glass semi-circular domed airlocks—used primarily by maintenance crews to access the growing number of old and failing components outside.

We could see the ship was a damaged mess out there—tubular conduits splayed open, ventilation ducts torn away, electrical conduits sparking—clearly, those high-power-lines were still live and dangerous. Donning a full, hardened space-suit, someone out there was flailing, frantically waving his arms to get our attention. I caught the problem—one leg was tightly wrapped, held immobile within an ensnaring cable.

Crewman Lasalle said, "That guy's got himself in a whole world of trouble."

I agreed. "Shit! How the hell did he get himself all tangled up like that? Think he was already out there . . . prior to the battle? Maybe doing some maintenance or repairs?"

Lasalle made a face. "While this ship was underway? Unlikely . . ."

"We'll find out soon enough," I said. "Let's move on over to that airlock." We entered the sealed, pre-access safety-zone. Above the closed hatchway was stenciled:

Deck 23 Maintenance Dome A15

Directly above the metal hatch was a lone, brightly lit, green strobe indicator that told us there was sufficient atmosphere present inside the airlock dome, making it safe to enter. We still could see the entangled crewman flailing about outside. A two-way intercom unit was mounted on an adjacent bulkhead. I suspected that it was rarely, if ever, still used, since the standard issuance of integrated T-Bead implants decades ago. But I gave it a try anyway and pushed the button. "This is Commander Galvin Quintos, you copy me out there?"

Sounds of static erupted from the intercom's speaker holes. We heard a distant voice, perhaps yelling, was too faint to make any sense of. I wasn't sure if it was a technical problem with the ancient equipment or a problem with the spacewalker. His voice seemed to be fading and I considered that he might be losing consciousness.

Hurrying, I tapped in the necessary code on the adjacent datapad to the airlock's inside hatch. As it slid to the side, we hurried in before the hatch sealed behind us. I noticed this particular curved high-domed airlock was one of the larger ones. Easily, ten people could have fit inside here with us. Integrated lockers lined the inside back wall, while the other side was curved diamond-glass. We had crystal-clear views to open space beyond. I eyed the ensnared still-flailing spacewalker several meters beyond the dome. *Idiot... he should be conserving his air supply.*

Lasalle, opening and closing lockers, finally said, "Sir...

seems there's only this one, old, environ-suit. No hardened spacesuits. That numskull out there seems to have the only one."

I studied the drab, brown, hanging environment suit stowed within the open locker. The thing could have been hanging there since the ship first launched, some sixty years prior. I joined Lasalle—opening then closing more of the lockers. Sure enough, there was only the one, clearly ancient, limp-looking environment suit.

"No, sir . . . these things are pieces of crap. Better for internal ship emergencies only. Just look at this fabric," he said, pinching a pant leg between two fingers.

Today, any crewmember traveling into deep space, be it on an exploratory vessel or a military vessel such as the *Hamilton*, must go through basic astronaut training. Perhaps not as thorough a training program, say, as those provided by our forefather astronauts some two-hundred years earlier, but even today, crewmembers would have learned basic maneuvering and survival techniques. That, and to competently operate within a variety of different spacesuit models. Truth is, general spacesuit architecture hasn't changed all that much from those early days. They still consist of a pressurized enclosure, a thermal micrometeoroid garment, as well as a separate liquid cooling and ventilation component. The main difference today is that the inner high-tech fabric materials are far thinner and more pliable, while there's usually a composite outer layer resistant to extremes in temperature and accidental piercing. Hey, deep space environments can reach the unholy temperature of -450 degrees Fahrenheit. Cold enough to turn any—even partially-exposed—human body into a block of ice within a matter of minutes. For those needing to work outside the safety of a spacecraft, their spacesuits are constructed with an added outer-shell layer of *kamacite,* an incredibly hard alloy. Even harder than diamond, this alloy was discovered originally within a Russian meteorite, back in the 21st Century. The *kamacite* is manufactured and used for countless items on a space vehicle, including outer hull plating, diamond-glass windows, and yes, spacesuits.

"I'm pretty sure even that old thing had to have been rated for space . . . for sub-zero environments," I said with a shrug, gesturing to the ridiculous, limp-looking suit.

The SWM crewman continued to study the suit with a dubious expression. "You won't have any kind of MMU," he said, looking about the airlock.

Lasalle was referring to a Manned Maneuvering Unit, a jetpack that would allow me to move about in open space. "Just help me get suited up," I said. "Five minutes out there is all I'll need."

"I should be the one to go out there, sir" Lasalle said.

I grabbed the spacesuit from Lasalle and began putting it on. "You can help me by grabbing that helmet off that shelf."

Several minutes later, wearing the clearly inadequate, unprotected environment-suit, and with Lasalle standing outside of the dome, I triggered the airlock's outside hatch to open. For one full minute, an alarm sounded as red lights flashed around me. I heard the dome's atmosphere vent into its dedicated storage tanks. At some point, the dome's gravitational generators switched off and I began to float about. The helmet's Heads Up Display, or HUD, seemed to be operating as it was intended to. I glanced at the readout showing my physical stats: body temperature, heart rate, and respiration. I was breathing way too fast. *Shit, I need to relax!* Next, I noticed that my oxygen level was already half depleted! *Hadn't anyone ever checked this damn suit? Weren't there maintenance procedures for doing that kind of thing?*

"How you doing, XO?" came Lasalle's concerned voice within my helmet. He was using the old intercom unit.

"Fine. Heading out now." Clipped onto the framework inside the dome, I had forty-five feet of coiled combination safety/comms line available to me. I figured that should be more than enough line to reach the entangled crewmember.

I was surprised how effective the spacesuit was at keeping the cold at bay—maybe I'd needlessly worried. Perhaps this suit was fine after all. I heard my own *far too rapid* breathing inside my helmet.

"Sir . . . how you doing?" Lasalle asked again. He sounded concerned.

"Fine," I grunted, being careful not to tear the spacesuit on any of the jagged metal fixtures along my chosen route.

"Did you know, sir . . . that Alexander Hamilton was the last statesman to correspond with President George Washington prior to his death?"

"Um . . . no, but that's an interesting bit of trivia," I said. Finding new handholds wherever I could, I crab-crawled toward the entangled crewman. His movements had become far less frantic now. I wondered if he'd expended his air supply. Speaking of which, I saw that my own air supply indicator visually lessened in just the few minutes I'd been out here in space.

"No sir . . . there's no one onboard this fine vessel who knows more about our ship's namesake than me. Just two days before Washington, America's first president, died, he'd sent a dispatch to Hamilton, his former aide and cabinet member."

"That dispatch, what did it concern?" I asked, thankful for the distraction, which was, of course, Lasalle's obvious intention.

"Well, Hamilton had recently argued that here in this new country, new Federation, that there was need for a regular military academy . . . and that one ought to be established soon. Washington wrote him back, praising the idea. This was in 1799. That letter would be Washington's final dispatch to anyone. The elder statesman told Hamilton that such an institution would be of primary importance to this country."

Feeling lightheaded, I wondered if I'd be able to reach the spacewalker in time. His arms and legs were no longer moving. *Damn it!* I'd taken too damn long getting out here. He might already be dead. I was forced to stop and catch my breath again. Clinging to a ventilation exhaust, I was now mere feet from where he floated—immobile. I took a closer look at the cable entangling his leg. Yup, it was a multi-strand laser-fiber braid. These things were used all over the ship. Reaching out I got ahold of the braid and, hand-over-hand, began to pull the spacewalker closer. Once near enough, I grabbed his shoulders and pulled him into me. His body was positioned with his back and MMU facing me. I noticed that his tool caddy was filled with electrical metering devices, a few old-fashioned wire snips, and crimping tools. The guy was a ship's maintenance electrician. I briefly wondered if Lasalle knew him. The back of his helmet was mere inches from my own. Awkward, maneuvering the lifeless suit in zero-G space, I was finally able to get him turned around; we were pretty much face-to-face at this point. Beyond the bright reflection of the *Hamilton*, mirrored on the faceplate of his helmet, I could just make out a younger man's face—perhaps not much older than Ensign Hughes. That, and he was dead. His eyes wide open and glazed, his mouth agape.

"Sir . . . how about an update?" Lasalle said.

"Sorry to say, I've reached him too late. Crewman's dead."

"Your own breathing, sir . . . it's sounding a bit ragged. Can you give me your heart rate and respiration numbers?"

I looked . . . tried to make sense of the HUD display readings, but the numbers were blurry. In fact, everything now was coming in-and-out of focus. "I can't read . . . and that sound . . . that *damn* sound."

"Sound? Sir?"

"Hissing . . . like a fucking hissing cat . . ."

"Try to tell me your oxygen level, sir . . . you should be able to see the indicator, the graphical meter. Is it in red, sir?"

Everything seemed to be happening in slow motion, like I was operating within a vat of thick gooey syrup. Even moving my eyes had become difficult. "Um . . . yeah . . . I see a smudge of red there. Is that bad? I can't remember." Struggling to breathe, I said "Green, red, yellow . . . so many colors . . . they're supposed to mean something . . . right?" It was then that I realized I was no longer holding onto the dead crewman. That he was now floating seven or eight feet away from me. I also realized, there'd be no way I'd be able to make it back inside the airlock. I had no energy, no will. Struggling to breathe, I gasped like those who'd been suffocating within LabTech. Once again, my mind flashed back to my childhood. I was six . . . no seven. Wearing wet sneakers, brine-colored lake water slopped beneath my feet. A handful of wide-eyed Bass flopping around on the bottom of my grandfather's old fishing skiff.

Sleep, I just need to sleep now. I heard Lasalle's voice from far, far, away—like I was submerged within deep lake waters, ever sinking, and he was yelling something incoherent down to me. But it didn't matter. All was fine now . . .

Blurry movement nearby. Huh . . . will you look at that . . . a small spacecraft of some sort. Maybe an alien has come to watch this dying Earthling wearing his ridiculous environ suit. "Hi aliens . . ." *Wait . . . I think I know that face . . . Wallace Ryder, hey, old friend.* "What are you doing flying around out here with the aliens?" *Sleep . . . I need to sleep.*

chapter 4

I awoke in a daze—incoherent—not knowing where I was. After a few shallow breaths, a throbbing pain in my head was becoming all too apparent. Some part of me wished I'd stayed asleep. I tried to swallow and grimaced. A blur of yellow came into focus above me. Several soft, wavy strands of golden locks had strayed loose from her upswept ponytail. I reminded myself not to be fooled—not to be drawn in. Sure, she had the face of an angel. But looks were all too often deceiving. To say her eyes were simply blue was like saying the sun was simply yellow. Her eyes were the azure blue of mountain lake water; so deep one would be leery jumping into it, albeit tempting. Her facial features were small—some would say perfect, almost doll-like. *Huh*... I'd never noticed the almost imperceptible dusting of freckles across the bridge of her nose. But then again, I'd never been this close to her before. Yet, this woman was far from angelic—much too often she was the bane of my existence.

"I guess you're going to live," Doc Viv said, moving the

flashlight's beam from one eye to the other. "You in any pain?" She almost looked concerned.

I shook my head, then wished I hadn't. "No, I'm fine," I lied. "The ship, what's the status of the ship?"

"Same . . . death count rising, hundreds injured. The ship is heavily damaged and unable to maneuver. But at least we're not under attack. Local Auriga System vessels are hailing us, offering medical and other assistance."

I shook my head and winced. "No fucking way we're letting them anywhere near us . . . good chance they were counting on the other side to come out ahead in that battle."

She nodded, "Craig is on it . . . feels the same way."

I said, "Craig?"

She looked at me with a mixture of sympathy and disdain. "The highest-ranking officer still conscious. He's on the Bridge, where you should have been all along."

Through the swirling mental fog, it now made sense. Craig Porter, Chief of Engineering, was one of my best friends onboard the *Hamilton*. Doc Viv sat up straighter and I felt the warmth of her backside pressing against my legs. "You were carried here by a very worried Lieutenant Ryder and Crewman Lasalle. Apparently, it was a miracle that Ryder was even there . . . making some kind of external damage assessment of the *Hamilton* from within a shuttle. He said he pulled right up next to you . . . found both you and SWM Crewman Darren Clyde just floating out there . . . like two mindless sacks of potatoes."

Flashing back, viewing Clyde's dead face within his helmet,

I wondered if I'd looked similar to him when they dragged me in here. Had Doc Viv witnessed seeing me like that?

Again speaking, she said, "...you know, Lasalle hung around here like a lost puppy for several hours—"

I cut her off. "Hours ... how long have I been—"

"You were out close to eight hours," she said. A pregnant pause followed, and I could tell she needed to attend to other, far more needy, patients.

"Anyway...I heard what you did. Going out there in that broken-down environ-suit. Really? You have some kind of death wish?"

"Seems like it."

The smirk on her face, there just a millisecond earlier, disappeared. "You know, that was beyond selfish of you. *We*, and I mean the collective *we*," gesturing around the HealthBay, yet meaning the entire ship, "need a leader right now ... a commanding leader. What you did, tells me that's not you." She reached for a nearby squeeze bottle, then I felt a straw being positioned between my lips. "Take small sips."

I swallowed a little liquid and felt somewhat better.

"Look, a commander's true character matters. And a good commander, or a captain, whatever, possesses a stable nature. He's comfortable delegating crucial responsibilities out in times of emergency. Sometimes, those decisions will be difficult to make ... but a captain secure in his judgment knows how to balance the vessel's needs above any desire to be personally liked. The ship captains I've most respected in my career had the confidence to assume full responsibility, balanced with the ability to admit making mistakes along the way. But never, ever, should the fate of the entire crew run second to his, or her, personal agenda."

"Thank you, O enlightened one . . . I'll keep all that in mind the next time we are surprise-attacked by the Grish," I croaked, gesturing with my chin for another sip. As she gave it to me, I felt her incriminating stare on my face. I said, "Please! Tell me the captain has come around, that he's back on the Bridge doing all those commander-like duties you so admire . . . things, clearly, I am not capable of performing."

"You really are such an asshole, Galvin . . . you do know that, right?"

I nodded back and regretted doing so. Glancing around the compartment, I noticed every bed was filled, with cots set up to handle the overflow of injured crewmembers. Medical personnel hurried about from one patient to another. A drab, green, spindly-looking medical bot was administering oxygen to a woman in the next bed over. I recognized the patient as one of the scientists from LabTech.

Doc Viv asked, "What are you looking around for?"

I glanced up to her. "Just looking to see where you keep your broomstick."

"Ha . . ." she replied, almost smiling. "The captain's still in a coma. So, for the time being, it's all up to you, Galvin. God save us all . . ."

Ignoring the jab, I said, "So, am I cleared to go back on duty now, Doc?" I asked, struggling to rise up onto my elbows.

"First, let me get you something for that blaring headache you say you don't have."

I watched her stride over toward a cabinet. She couldn't hide her lithe athleticism beneath her baggy pink scrubs. As she rifled through the contents of a drawer, I managed to rise into a seated position. As the room spun around me, I felt I might hurl. Taking a few deep breaths, I stood up and made a beeline for the door. Out in the corridor, I heard Doc Viv say, "Damn it, Galvin!"

I checked my TAC-Band. Doc Viv had put it in a temporary standby mode—pretty much telling anyone trying to reach me that I was *unavailable* until further notice. Resetting it to normal online status, I headed for the bank of elevators and listened to one frantic message after another. Things had not only *not* calmed down—they may have gotten worse.

By the time I'd made it to the Bridge and listened to most of the more critical messages, I came to the realization that Doc Viv was one-hundred percent right—no way was I qualified to be the active senior officer in command of this vessel.

I spotted Chief of Engineering Craig Porter, sitting up on the Captain's Mount. Looking out of place there, he appeared completely overwhelmed. Catching sight of me, he rose.

"Thank God . . . the way the Doc described your condition, you were dying."

"No, Craig . . . she only wished that were the case."

What remained of the Bridge crew hungrily flocked around me like a school of rabid Amazon River piranhas. I raised my palms and said, "I know each of you has important questions to ask or information you need to share . . . One at a time, starting with the Chief here."

Porter nodded, momentarily recollecting his thoughts. "All three reactors are still down, but we're hopeful . . . we should get at least sub-light propulsion within eight or nine hours . . . my Engineering team knows this is a priority."

"Yeah . . . that might be useful when the Grish jump back into our system," Head of Security Alistair Mattis said, in an antagonistic tone. Clearly, Mattis and Porter had been at each other's throats of late.

Noticing the Chief was ready to spiel-off his own snarky retort, I said, "I need a status report on MATHR, as well as one on the *Hamilton* . . . not to mention, the *Union* and the *Colorado*."

I spotted Ensign Lucas Hughes exiting the CIC and hurrying to join our impromptu meeting. He said, "Good to see you're back on your feet, XO!"

"Thanks!" I gestured toward the CIC. "MATHR?"

"She's still . . ."

"Off her rocker," Lieutenant Gail Pristy interjected while sending a scowl overhead, as if the ship's AI somehow was watching us from above.

"Anyway," Hughes continued, "Science Officer Derrota is in there now trying to restore MATHR with the most recent backup copy of her software . . . but, by the number of curse words he's been spewing, I don't think he's having much luck."

"I'll check in with him in a minute. Rescue teams? How are we doing on the ones still trapped and injured?"

Pristy said, "Decks 12, 13, and 23 have been sectioned-off with Vac-Gates. Also, they're closed to elevator access. Repair teams are making temporary hull breach repairs as best they can. There is an issue on Deck 5 . . . one of the starboard Phazon Pulsar cannons is actively overheating."

That item was one of the messages I'd listened to on my way to the bridge.

"Problem is, that cannon is adjacent to the ship's armory and a munitions magazine," she said.

"What kind of munitions?"

"Smart Missiles . . . rail gun spikes. The same magazine that supports the big guns positioned there along the starboard side mid-section. Right now, crew members stationed around there think they'll be able to get things under control pretty soon."

"Shit," I muttered. "Okay . . . I'll get over there." But as the words tumbled from my mouth, Bridge crewmembers started shaking their collective heads.

"I promise . . . no more spacewalks or taking undue risks. I only want to make an assessment, see if there's any possible danger to the ship," I said, looking around for Crewman Grimes who'd been filling in at the Weapon Station. Seated nearby, he had turned toward us, listening intently. His direct, next-level-up officer had been Lieutenant Aries—killed during the attack. At least for now, Grimes was my "go-to guy" for ship-wide weapon status.

"Crewman Grimes, report on our weaponry readiness in case those piglet friends of ours come back for round two."

Okay, let me pause to expound on a few things, put our

current situation into a better perspective for you. By the mid-21st Century, Earth's scientists were still hundreds of years away, if not longer, from developing any kind of feasible interplanetary travel. Much longer for FTL, *faster than light*, space travel capability. Sure, back then, NASA had multiple development teams tinkering with various concepts—a myriad of ideas for Star Trek-type warp drives or Alcubierre propulsion systems. But it was all speculative, since the amount of energy—more accurately, negative energy, or *anti-matter*—required to proportionately bend time/space, propel a starship far into the universe, would be beyond anything feasible—anything realistic. How planet Earth catapulted into interstellar space travel was partially by accident. To say the right technology practically fell into our scientists' laps would not be stretching the truth. Whoever would have thought that Earth's closest neighbor within the cosmos would be dropping by for a visit one late September afternoon, in the year 2048? They came from the Alpha Centauri star system, a mere 4.37 light-years distance from Earth, arriving on planet Earth aboard a lone starship. Highly advanced, they had the capability to eradicate all humanity if they had wanted to. But, interestingly enough, they arrived on our *proverbial doorstep* desperate for human help. As it turned out, space—even relatively local space—was, and still is, extremely dangerous. These neighboring alien visitors were called the Thine, their home planet was Morno. It was estimated that the Thine were a thousand years or so more technically advanced than us Earthlings. As it turned out, what human beings once thought were the definitive laws of physics were pretty much laughably inadequate. Actually, we were out-and-out wrong, and the Thine enlightened mankind as to what was really true. What the Thine did have going for them was *smarts*—cognitive reasoning on a whole higher, different level. Comparing human intelligence to chimpanzees was comparable to how the Thine's intelligence exceeded that of ours. But they possessed very little in the way of physical prowess. Picture a snow-white worm-like being with tiny nubs for arms and legs. Basically, a five-foot-long maggot, but one with an expressive and friendly face. Also, picture the least intimidating being to inhabit neighboring space. From what I understand, the Thine once possessed little legs and arms, but over the course of a few million years, mechanical bots were pretty much doing everything for the Thine on planet Morno. Hence, they evolved into their current, um, physical condition. So, what the Thine needed from Earthlings was twofold. First, they needed our physicality; our ability to manufacture *things* relatively easily, beyond what their personal bots could achieve. Second, they need to survive within an oxygenated atmosphere. As it turned out, those maggot-like alien beings required environments both thick and viscous, more like mud, than water or breathable air. All these factors led to the Thine being ridiculously smart, yet wholly inadequate at manufacturing galaxy-crossing spaceships. Arriving anywhere, ambulatory issues were a real problem for them. The one spacecraft they managed to build, with help from their droids and bots, was filled to the brim with that breathable mud-like substance—something called Ambiogel. Earth was their first intergalactic destination to look for assistance.

Studying humans from afar for many years, they'd watched as our civilization progressed. What got them most excited were our war-faring ways, our compulsion to head blindly into battle. Thine travelers, desperately seeking to build a local alliance with a neighboring world, felt they'd hit proverbial pay dirt when they landed on Earth. Almost immediately, they began what at first seemed altruistic: a fervor-paced-transfer of both knowledge and technology. Earth's scientists, of course, were ecstatic—if not overwhelmed—by the mind-bending amount of information being shoved down their collective throats. Although the Thine didn't provide too much detail about their chief motivations, eventually Earth's primary governments were brought up to speed on others existing in nearby space. More specifically, those who wouldn't be thrilled to learn of our newly-formed alliance with the Thine. As it turned out, another interstellar society, one suspicious that the mud dwelling organisms may have well-hidden technology, had invaded their world twice in recent years.

Think of the Grish as a neighborhood gang of thugs... bullies. Aggressive and threatening—no one wanted them for an enemy. From what I've discerned, Earth's few intergalactic neighbors, living within our sector of space, had simply rolled over—giving the Grish pretty much whatever they wanted. This often meant open access to mining and agricultural resources. The Grish took what they wanted, sometimes leaving barely enough behind for the host world, or star system, to survive on. Thus, came the Thine's delight in finding a neighboring world that not only wouldn't roll over so easily, but actually *relished* the prospect of picking a fight with the Grish. The Grish, like humans, are bipedal—having two arms and two legs—although they tend to walk around on all fours just as often as they walk upright. Standing up, they are about four feet tall. Totally hairless, they have a pinkish cast to their fleshy hides. The *piglet* reference relates more to their round, piggish, snorting, snouts.

The biggest mistake the Grish made, some one-hundred-and-thirty-years back, was not viewing the *barbaric* Earthlings as a possible threat. Sure, the Grish had come snooping around—orbited Earth—even landed several scout ships. But after five days investigating, perhaps disappointed at what Earth had to offer, they lifted off and didn't return for another seventy-five years. By that time, Earth had a good number of crude, but effective, spaceships patrolling local space. We also had Thine technology, Phazon Pulsar energy tech—something the Grish did not have. A powerful weapon that Earth's warships, although limited in number, were adequately prepared to use to send the little piglets packing. But Earth's benefactor race of intelligent maggots, the Thine, were careful not to provide too much in the way of technological advancement capabilities. From their perspective, which was totally understandable to me, the greater need was for a balance of power within the sector, not development of a new, perhaps bigger, neighborhood bully—Earth. Earth's humanity was given just enough *smarts* to keep the Thine safe, and, by default, Earth's citizenry as well. Since Earth's introduction to intergalactic space travel, some one-hundred-and-fifty years ago, humanity has become *a small-fry force* within our own little corner of the Milky Way. Using baseball as an example, think of humanity as, say, a Double-A (AA), minor league team. The Grish would probably fall into the Triple-A (AAA), minor league team classification, as they are a tad more powerful, more advanced, than us mere Earthlings. And sure, there are classifications lower on the power scale than humans' Double-A rating, like those in Class A (the classification for rookies.) But there also are far more experienced, more powerful forces in the sector, equivalent to the all-powerful Major League teams. The Kaviacts, the Pleidian Weonan, and the Mowerstrah come to mind. Over the years, Earth's humanity has encountered a few of these "Major League" superpower societies. Humans, the Grish, and even the Thine make a concentrated effort to keep clear of any of them.

Anyway, getting back to the here and now, Crewman Grimes was still thinking about my question concerning the *Hamilton's* weapons readiness, in case our *piglet* friends returned for round two.

"Sir, if we were attacked in our current condition, we'd be in big trouble. Although there are sufficient, intact, Phazon Pulsar cannon platforms, the raw power we need to drive those big guns just isn't there. Those weapons require fully operational reactors. Currently, one reactor is heavily damaged. Two others are off-line, being modified to better distribute and make up for the loss of that third reactor. Our Rail Guns are in good shape, and we have an excellent supply of rail spikes in our magazine compartments distributed around the *Hamilton*. We also have an ample supply of various smart missiles, both fusion and nuclear-tipped, but because of MATHR's issues, they are mostly inoperable. Oh, and we also have the resurrected Broadsides . . . although we're running short on bowlers, as you well know."

Chief of Engineering Porter added, "Back to the reactors. It is imperative we get those three systems up and running. Without them, even sub-light propulsion will be impossible."

"ETA on those repairs?" I asked.

"At least the rest of today, maybe most of tomorrow, too."

I said, "And jumping to lightspeed—"

Chief Porter, waving away my intended question, said, "No . . . HyperDrives are still down until further notice. And remember, we'd need MATHR to make any kind of jump wormhole computations."

Shit! I kept my facial expression neutral. Expecting the worst, I said, "MATHR, connect me to Bay Chief Mintz . . ."

To everyone's surprise, the ship's AI not only understood my request but opened the channel.

"Mintz . . . go ahead, XO."

"Frank . . . I'm here with what remains of our Bridge crew. Talk to us about the flight bay and fighter readiness."

"As reported earlier, the portside bay port is open and fully operational. We're still working on the starboard bay port, which is where we were hit. We lost half of a Group complement. Flight Barracks C was hit, too. Lost some good pilots . . ."

"I'm sorry, Frank. I'm getting similar reports from all over the ship." I attempted to do some quick mental calculations. I knew that the *Hamilton* had one of the largest contingents of battle-ready Arrow fighter craft of any U.S. space vessel. A full Group comprised several Wings, each consisting of three squadrons.

"Wait . . . half? Christ, Frank . . . how many Arrows was that?"

"From the original Group of roughly five-hundred . . . we have two-hundred-and- sixty viable, operational, Arrows at the ready. But, Galvin . . . that's the least of our problems."

My head began pounding again. I knew I wouldn't like hearing what the Bay-Chief had to say next. "Go on . . ."

"Losing Flight Barracks C . . . hit by that Smart Missile, left us with a mere one- hundred-and-twenty-two pilots capable of piloting an Arrow. Another thirty are still in HealthBay. They may return to duty, eventually."

His update left me speechless. The fact that we'd lost hundreds of good men and women in one well-placed missile-strike. The loss of life was truly catastrophic, as was the loss of life aboard the other five vessels totally eviscerated by the Grish. Cumulatively, I knew the number of souls lost had already crested ten thousand. But now wasn't the time to deal with that; I couldn't allow it to interfere with the command decisions needing to be made for those who'd survived.

"Thank you, Bay-Chief. Until the *Hamilton* can get underway, it's best your pilots are on standby on a moment's notice."

"We're always ready, XO . . . but, as a pilot yourself, you already knew that."

"I'll get back to you, Bay-Chief," I said, terminating the connection.

chapter 5

I headed for the closest bank of elevators. All lifts on the three-kilometer-long seventy-five Decks *USS Hamilton* were required to travel horizontally, vertically, as well as at forty-five-degree slant angles. Hurrying into an open car, I headed aft toward the supposed overheating starboard Phazon Pulsar cannon on Deck 5, which was in Zone F. The dreadnaught's superstructure was sectioned off into seven zones, A to G, with A the most forward aspect of the vessel, and G the farthest aft, where the ship's Engineering and Propulsion departments were situated. Sections like the Bridge, CIC, and HealthBay were situated mid-ship for easiest access no matter which direction someone was coming from. At close to three kilometers in length, the *Hamilton* would be a beast to transverse without the use of crisscrossing elevators and lifts. Alone, I stood within the jerky, clattering, lift car, taking in, and letting out several long breaths. The problem with having several minutes to stand alone, with nothing to do but wait, was the time it allowed one to think. Muse about those who'd lost their lives in the midst of what was supposed to be little more than a diplomatic mission.

Depending on the Captain's prognosis, and being the acting skipper of the USS *Hamilton* and senior officer of what remained of the 3rd Fleet, I would be the one writing obituary letters—informing wives, husbands, mothers, and fathers that their loved one had died bravely defending the United States of America, and Earth itself. To convey how proud and honored I was to have served with each of them. More than ten-thousand letters would require my personal, from-the-heart, condolences. There would be no place for pre-written form letters when giving loved ones what just might be the worst possible news they would ever receive.

Stepping off the elevator, Crewmember SWM Lasalle was there waiting for me. Earlier, I'd requested his presence, considering his proven track record—knowing the *Hamilton's* complex inner workings like he did. He looked as tired as I felt.

"Yeah, so, XO . . . I've already been over there. That Phazon Pulsar cannon still hasn't shut down yet. Things don't look good."

Together, we scurried down a narrow passageway that provided access to a number of aft ship cannon embattlement enclosures. We passed several crewmembers, their hair moist with perspiration, each looking like they'd been through the wringer.

"We've been sending in hardened maintenance bots, trying to physically decouple that activated cannon from the power conduit inside," Lasalle said.

"Sounds reasonable . . . so, what's the issue?" I asked.

We'd reached a section of the passageway that had broadened out into a kind of wide vestibule that accommodated the Phazon Pulsar cannon compartment. To say it was hot in there would be a gross understatement. To our right was a heavy metal hatch-door, one that seemed more likely to have been found on an old 20th Century submarine than on this 22nd Century starship. Four scuffed and burnished robots stood idly by, as did exhausted-looking crewmembers, of which there were three men and one woman. Standing there huddled together, I recognized the woman. Gunny Zan Mattis—our Chief of Security Alistair Mattis's daughter. She was short, attractive, with large penetrating brown eyes. Her non-regulation hairstyle was buzz-cut on one side, while worn long, to her shoulders, on the other side. All four crewmembers, wearing heavy gloves and heat-resistant overalls, looked grimy and were dripping in sweat. They were conversing, if you could call it that, with raised, nearly desperate, voices. Glancing up at our approach, they stepped apart from one another.

"Talk to me . . . what's the problem. What have you tried so far, and what do you recommend we now do to alleviate the situation?" I asked in a rapid-fire approach.

No one spoke. I signaled out one. His embroidered identification told me he was SWM Crewmember D. Dipper. I had little doubt he'd paid a heavy price for that name growing up. "Go ahead, Dipper?"

"XO . . . problem is we can't turn the *MFing* cannon off. Can't go back in there anymore. It's burning too hot inside . . .

hot enough that the Zone F Armory," he gestured down the passageway, "is in jeopardy, as well as the magazine compartment over there." He pointed to another metal hatch door on our right.

"A munitions magazine that stores Smart Missiles. I understand," I said, and all four, actually five, if you included Lasalle, nodded their heads.

I strode across to the magazine's outer bulkhead and lightly held my palm above the metal. It was blazingly hot. Inside, beyond any doubt, it was much, much hotter. "I asked what you've tried so far. Those robots over there ... they weren't effective?"

Gunny Mattis said, "Nah, XO ... three of them shit the bed. Got halfway in there and became all sluggish. Totally forgot *what the fuck* their directive was and began bumping into bulkheads and one another. At one point, we had three ass-fucked robots roaming around in there ..."

Momentarily taken aback by her use of such colorful language, I had to force a smile from my face.

She continued, "This last robot," gesturing to the only robot still standing erect and appearing to be functioning properly, "was sent in; pulled the others out one at a time."

"Gunny ... what I need to know is how likely is it that one, or more, of those Smart Missiles in this magazine will ... go boom?"

She shrugged. "Not likely ... I imagine any of those fusion or nuke reactor ordinances would need to be electronically detonated. Heat alone, Nah ... I don't see it. But there are barrels filled with explosives, mainly . . . rail spike belt-windings inside there; if those go up, we're all *fucktapated.*"

"Recommendation on how to alleviate this situation? Anyone?" I asked.

No one spoke. I paced the passageway trying to think. Unfortunately, there wasn't enough time for idle pacing. If the *Hamilton* wasn't in enough of a pickle already, this dire situation could literally end her existence—and all of us with her. I pointed toward a series of three heavy brackets on the deck, also to three above our heads. Each bracket was bolted into place with a large, three- to four-inch sized, metal nut. "What are these?"

"Brackets," D. Dipper answered back.

"Gee, thank you, Dipper. I can see that! What do they do . . . why are they here?"

Gunny said, "Every one of the *Hamilton's* Phazon Pulsar cannon enclosures around the ship can be swapped out if necessary. But we already thought about that, XO . . . it's a space-dock job. We'd need a ginormous crane to pull this heavy mo'fo of a compartment out of here."

I tapped at my TAC-Band. A moment later a voice said, "Hey, XO . . . a little busy, here."

"Too bad, Ryder, this is more important . . . I guarantee it." This was the same pilot—Lieutenant Wallace Ryder—who'd rescued me, saving my life earlier today. Or, was that yesterday, now?

"Go ahead, Galvin . . . tell me what you need."

Ryder, like the Chief of Engineering Craig Porter, was among my better friends onboard the *Hamilton.* It wasn't uncommon for them to drop any formality—rank designation. "Tell me what's left in the flight bay that has ample pulling power, has real thrust."

I pictured Ryder doing a visual inventory of undamaged, still space-worthy, aircraft in the bay. I'd been tempted to ask Bay Chief Frank Mintz, but he'd take too long to make a decision. He'd want to ensure the right forms were all filled out in triplicate before actively doing anything.

"I've got just the *bird* for that sort of thing," Ryder said. Tell me what it is you want me to do."

I gave Ryder the lowdown of the situation and cut the connection. I asked Lasalle, his hands currently inside the back panel of one of the maintenance bots. "How fast can you get those brackets unbolted, Crewman?"

The heat had already risen another ten degrees in the past few minutes, and I knew our time was running out. I tried to stay calm, at least look somewhat collected.

"Me . . . never," Lasalle said. "But that bot? It can probably do it." Lasalle strode over to the lone, still operational robot and began speaking to it. Most of the *Hamilton's* bots and droids took verbal commands, although this particular maintenance bot looked to be as old as the vessel itself. One of the original TL-MAX series bots.

The MAX bot went right to work. These bots had human-like, five-fingered mechanical hands. The bot bent over the nearest bracket and positioned four fingers over the nut that was securing it to the deck. The sound made was like that of a pneumatic power wrench. The bot's hand began twisting around at its wrist joint—slow at first, then faster and faster until the hand became a spinning blur of motion. *Ping!* The nut flew off the stubby end of the bolt and clattered across the deck.

"One down, five to go," I said, conscious that this was taking far too much time. Using the sleeve of my uniform to wipe the sweat from my forehead, I said, "Why don't the rest of you head away from this area. Get a few bulkheads between this *run-amuck* Phazon Pulsar cannon and yourselves. No sense anyone else getting—"

"Uh, thank you, *shmank* you... but that's not going to happen, XO," Gunny Mattis said, an exaggerated bewildered expression on her face. "We're the expendable ones here. Truth is, you shouldn't even be here. Don't we have a ship's Bridge that's missing its captain?"

Tempted to ask her if she'd been exchanging views with Doc Viv lately while doing my best to keep my temper in check, I said, "Not that I have to explain myself to you, Gunny Sergeant... but right now I *do* need to be here. I need to ensure, after surviving such a devastating battle with the Grish, that the *Hamilton* won't be blown *the fuck up* by an out-of-control energy weapon. Something I cannot do from the Bridge. So, is that alright with you?"

Gunny's breath visually caught in her chest and her eyes immediately brimmed with tears. Watching her, now paralyzed... not knowing what to say, or do, I felt both guilty and angry at myself for such a stupid, knee-jerk overreaction. Sure, she was a smart-ass; she was disrespectful and irreverent, but she was also young. Trying to show how tough she was within a mostly male-dominated crew. In one reckless moment, I'd crushed her young, fireball spirit. *Fuck!*

"Gunny, I apologize. You didn't deserve any of that."

She shrugged it off like it was no big deal and offered a lopsided smile back.

Fuck!

The maintenance robot had moved over to the last deck bracket. *Ping!* Another nut rolled onto the deck. My TAC-Band vibrated—it was Lieutenant Ryder.

"We're here . . . got a two-man team running cables out to the exterior of that . . . *whatever* that thing is. Man, it's glowing red hot. Is it going to explode while we're out here? Geez . . . this ship's been ape-fucked to the point we're all screwed."

Behind me, Gunny Mattis snorted. I turned to see her covering up her mouth. "Sorry, XO. But, *ape-fucked* . . . it's just funny."

Before I could comment, Crewman Lasalle tapped my shoulder before he walked farther down the passageway and knelt down. Something liquid could be seen oozing out beneath the bulkhead. He reached out, about to touch the yellowish liquid—

"Don't touch that!" Gunny yelled. Crouched down now next to Lasalle to get a better look, she said, "Shit, it's Flash Soliniam and maybe polymers." Looking up to blank-faced stares, she added, "The modern 'big brother' to nitro-glycerol trinitrate, TNT . . . I think it's from the stacks and stacks of over-heating rail-barrel munitions in there. Everything's melting." She stared over her shoulder at me. "We're in big trouble, XO."

chapter 6

Flash Soliniam... That wasn't the first time I'd heard of this highly explosive compound. Unlike TNT, it was relatively stable if kept away from moisture—good ol' H^2O. The eight-inch long brass, compartmentalized, *rail spike* munitions contained ninety-eight percent H^2O, and five-percent Flash Soliniam. Upon impact, these explosive rail gun munition's two components join together in a flash *fulmination*—combustion—with enough effusion force to breach an enemy's hardened hull plating. Now standing there, staring at the yellowish goo oozing out from beneath the bulkhead, I wondered just how those many thousands of individually contained rail spikes could be leaking?

Gunny Zan Mattis must have read my expression—my momentary dismay. "It's at the tail end of the spikes... the primer hole linings. They're made from lipid-derived polymers. The big containment barrels in there are also made of lipid-derived polymers."

I knew that seventy-five years had passed since plastics had become a serious environmental hazard; so threatening, global laws made the use of any kind of petroleum-based plastics illegal.

"It's the intense heat, or maybe the radiation, XO ... the polymers are breaking down causing the Flash Soliniam within them to leak all over the place."

"And the water component of those rail spikes?" I asked.

Gunny shook her head. "Nah, water's sealed in metal ... that shouldn't be a problem."

Crewman Lasalle looked up to something overhead. "Oh shit, there's a problem all right. A real big problem ... won't be long before the heat in there reaches a certain threshold."

The rest of us followed his upward gaze to a series of overhead pipes and strategically placed fire suppression sprinklers. Lasalle said, "This zone of the *Hamilton* uses a wet chemical fire suppression system ... I think it's potassium bicarbonate."

"That's good, right? At least it's not water," I said, like I knew what I was talking about.

"It's fine ... but beyond this section, Zone F, it changes. Fire suppression water sprinklers are used for most of the ship's other zones."

The yellowish goo had already made a river—a river that meandered all the way across the passageway, pooling along the opposite bulkhead. I said, "These bulkheads are supposed to be air-tight. Vacuum-safe in case of a hull breach."

Crewman D. Dipper laughed out loud. "This old bucket? Air-tight bulkheads? Seriously?"

I ignored him. Fortunately, my TAC-Band vibrated—it

was Wallace Ryder. "Give me some good news, Wallace," I said. "Where are we at with those cables?"

"It's done... all connected. But you better hurry. That Phazon Pulsar cannon enclosure is virtually melting the adjacent areas of the hull."

I checked the status of the TL-MAX series bot, now working on the last one of those bracket nuts. Then we all heard it; that telltale, high-pitched sound of zero resistance when metal threads have become irreversibly stripped. The robot stopped and stared at me with its pathetic looking, expressionless, face.

I wanted to shout, 'What else can go fucking wrong here!'

All eyes had focused on me. It was up to me to come up with some kind of decision. Wondering, I spoke into my TAC-Band. "Ryder... what spacecraft did you end up with out there? Specifically."

"Uh... It's the Hub Gunther."

I smiled. As a young pilot, I'd flown just about every spacecraft in circulation on Earth. I lived to fly... there was nothing more important to me than flying. Hell, I still missed it. The few ships I hadn't flown, I still wanted to. One of those that I thought would be a *gas* to operate was one of those old, big Hub Gunther mining beasts. The Hub Gunther, which is actually the name of the corporation that makes this particular space-faring vessel, is the only craft kept in the flight bay that's not military-grade in origin. It's an ugly, fifteen- to twenty-man mining craft. The aft hold, with its big metal overhead doors, is used for hauling mineral deposits. Basically, it's like an outer space dump truck. These craft were built to handle brutally rough conditions, its propulsion system crazy powerful, too. Certainly, necessary when attempting to lift off an alien exoplanet, its hold full of rocks and gravitational properties that might be seven times greater than those on Earth.

"This area . . . Zone F . . . you say it's sealed? We can close it off?"

Lasalle, D. Dipper, and Gunny Mattis nodded their heads in unison. Lasalle said, "We'd need to close the passageway's Vac-Gates."

"Can you do that from here?"

Lasalle, already tapping at his TAC-Band, said, "On it right now."

"Lieutenant Ryder," I said, "give us two minutes. Then I want you to put *pedal to the metal*. Burn rubber. You got that?"

"Copy that, XO, *pedal to the metal* . . . Ryder out."

Gunny Mattis asked, "And that still-attached bracket up there?" She pointed to the overhead bracket with the stripped bolt.

"Won't matter. Go! What are you all waiting for? Out of here!" I ordered.

By the time we'd hustled the four robots—of which three were practically comatose—through the Vac-Gate hatchway, a full minute-and-thirty seconds had elapsed.

A flurry of negative thoughts raced through my mind. *What if that attached bracket holds? What if the outer hull is irreparably damaged? What if that Flash Soliniam shit somehow erupts and blows the Hamilton into oblivion?* And then I both heard and felt it—*CLANG!* The ship shook so violently I had to reach out for a bulkhead to remain up on my feet. The sound was loud enough to cause physical pain within my eardrums.

"Talk to me, Ryder!" I said. "What happened out there?"

"Well . . . I have some good news and some bad news."

"Start with the good news," I said.

"We got that Phazon Pulsar cannon enclosure yanked right out of the ship."

"And the bad news?" I asked, bracing myself for the worst.

"First, let me ask you this, XO . . . have you ever flown one of these Hub Gunthers?"

"No."

"You know that they're mining vessels, right?"

"Yes . . . already know that. What's the bad news?" I asked, getting impatient.

Ryder said, "I'm just going to rip the bandage off here, fast . . ."

"Ryder!" I yelled.

"Okay . . . okay! We took more than the cannon enclosure . . . we also took off the Zone F armory and the munitions magazine. Not to mention a substantial section of the surrounding armor plating. This entire area of the ship will be vulnerable to attack, to say the least. I'm sending you a TAC-Band snapshot now . . . picture's worth a thousand words."

I only had to wait a few moments before the image appeared on my TAC-Band. Lasalle, D. Dipper, and Gunny Mattis, all listening on the open channel, crowded in close to see too. Taken from the perspective of the Hub Gunther, we saw multiple heavy cables tied to a free-floating rectangular block of three of the *Hamilton's* compartments. Torn, jagged sections of the ship were bent outward, while sparks sporadically flared. Vented debris continued to spew out where the compartments had so violently been ripped away from the vessel.

"Sweet mother of God," Gunny said. "Hate losing that cannon, not to mention the munitions stores and armory weapons... but that sure did the trick. One crippling, devastating, ship-wide explosion averted—guess that's why you make the big bucks, XO..." she said.

"Glad you approve, Gunny. Lieutenant Ryder, good job out there. Go ahead, jettison that section of the ship, and head for flight bay."

"Copy that. Glad to have been of service."

By the time I reached the bridge, I already had checked in with all the other officers and section chiefs. Four rescue squads were still at it; getting more injured and dead cleared away from damaged areas. The repair teams, deployed to Decks 12, 13, and 23, were currently shoring up breached sections of the hull. Everyone understood these temporary patch jobs would have to suffice until we reached a suitable spaceport.

Entering the Bridge, I sensed things were even more intense than when I'd left. What I didn't expect to see was Admiral Cyprian Block's craggy old face staring down at me from the main halo-display.

I knew Chief Porter had returned to Engineering, where

he was desperately needed if even limited, sub-light propulsion could be brought back online. Lieutenant Gail Pristy and Chief of Security Alistair Mattis, in the midst of conversing with the admiral—while coping with the long comms delays back and forth—glanced back as I entered the Bridge. I wondered if Mattis knew how close he'd come to losing his only daughter—Gunny Zan Mattis.

"Here he is now, sir," Lieutenant Pristy said.

"Good . . . good," Admiral Block nodded back. "I was just getting an update on your situation out there, Commander. The lieutenant tells me you averted an explosion due to an energy cannon malfunction . . ."

"Aye, sir. Things got a bit closer than I wanted, but we're out of danger . . . at least in that regard."

The admiral's expression turned more serious. "Commander, it is imperative you get the *Hamilton*, *Union*, and *Colorado* moving. Get them out of that system immediately."

"I assure you, Admiral, we are making every—"

"The Grish are coming to finish what they started," the admiral interjected. "Intel tells us you have mere hours. Maybe less."

"I understand. We'll double our efforts."

"Now I'm going to tell you something you're not going to like." The admiral, choosing his next words carefully, added, "If it comes down to it, you must leave the *Union* and *Colorado* behind and let them fend for themselves. The *Hamilton* must reach Earth . . . and certain, um, passengers must not be seized by the enemy . . . not taken alive."

"I'm sorry? Which passengers are these?" I asked, having no clue who he was referring to.

"Both Diplomatic Envoys—Coogong Lohp and Milo Wentworth."

I'd known about Coogong Lohp, a Thine diplomat, due to the fairly extravagant preparations required to house one of these worm-like aliens—providing a compartment filled with that putrid-smelling Ambiogel shit. But I had not been told about Milo Wentworth. I knew he was a wealthy British businessman, a real dealmaker. But just why I hadn't been informed of his presence aboard this ship, I had no idea. Hell, I was the Chief Executive Officer—second in command to Captain Tannock. I inwardly cursed the captain—*what else have you kept secret from me?*

The admiral must have observed my irritation. "It was my directive that no one, other than Captain Tannock, was to know of Wentworth's inclusion to the Envoy team. Let's just say his business ties have not always aligned with others within the Auriga Star System."

All this was beyond my pay grade. Frankly, I had far more important things to deal with than being concerned with a spoiled businessman who was looking to exploit the resources on another exoplanet, or perhaps several exoplanets. Then, it occurred to me that it was strange the Grish would give two shits about a human capitalist. Who the hell was Wentworth to them?

"Sir, can you tell me where Wentworth holding up on-board the *Hamilton*?" I asked. "As you know, this is a big ship."

The admiral looked momentarily stymied. "I honestly don't know. You'll have to ask Captain Tannock ... when he awakens. Perhaps your MATHR system can be of help."

I nodded, exchanging a furrowed glance with Mattis and Pristy. The captain might never wake up, and MATHR was less than useful right now.

"Sir ... what about sending assistance? The 4th Fleet, or, maybe an assigned battle group?" I asked.

"I've deployed a Space Carrier strike group. Embarking later today will be the Prowess, one of our newer carriers, along with two cruisers, three destroyers, and one frigate, deploying from the Lalande System."

"That's farther away than Earth, sir! We're talking weeks before they'd be able to reach us!"

"I'm sorry ... but we have our own *issues* to contend with, Commander," the admiral said sternly. "Earth's space resources have all been activated. It's not just the Grish. The Borno ... even the fucking Sheentah ... are currently on the move. Seems to be a concerted uprising across the sector."

"Aye, sir."

"Again ... I want you out of that star system within the hour. Make whatever repairs necessary for that to happen. Then set a course for Earth ... the *Prowess* group will intersect with you en route. Where, will depend on whether you can get the *Hamilton's* Hyper Drives online, and if you can start making some jumps. And Commander ... find Wentworth; keep him safe. Admiral Block out." The feed went black.

chapter 7

Back within the confines of another lift heading aft, I hailed Doc Viv.

"What is it? I'm super busy," she said.

"I'll make this quick then, as much as I enjoy hearing your oh-so-pleasant voice."

"Again, what is it you want? I'm heading into surgery."

"I'm looking for someone, a Milo Wentworth—"

A moment passed. "That obnoxious tycoon back on Earth?" she asked.

"Yeah."

"He's here on the *Hamilton*?"

"Apparently so. So that's a no, then?"

"I can check, but I don't think so. We have beds set up in seven different holds. Other holds, down on Deck 1, are makeshift morgues, set up as freezers . . . you're free to wander around and take a look. I'd bring a jacket."

"Maybe later. One more question."

"Come on, Galvin . . . surgery."

"How about the alien? The Thine passenger. You're aware he was onboard."

"Yeah, heard something about that, although I probably would remember, seeing a four-foot white maggot lying on a cot. Just saying."

I had to bite my lip. This woman was the queen of snark.

"Just let me know if you see either one of them."

"Uh huh, yeah, I'll do that," she said, and cut the connection.

I ARRIVED IN ZONE G—ENGINEERING AND PROPULSION. The area was a madhouse. Crewmembers running here and there—a number of bots clomped loudly above on the metal crisscrossing catwalks where an open, multi-deck section of the ship loomed high overhead. I descended down two small metal flights of stairs and turned a tight corner, heading down a passageway plastered on both sides with hanging 3D images of Chief Craig Porter's wilderness adventure travels over the years. I recognized several of the locations since I'd been there with him. Proceeding down this memory lane of sorts, just as I had countless times before, I slowed and took in a few of Earth's most amazing remote locations: Machu Picchu, the Galapagos Islands, Iguazu Falls, Rio de Janeiro, and finally, the Amazon rainforest—easily the most biodiverse place on the planet and home to an astounding array of flora, mammals, birdlife, invertebrates, and marine species. I stopped to look at one image where Porter and I were standing in a long fishing canoe along with our native guide, Hector.

I found Chief Porter in his office, which also doubled as his quarters. As with the passageway outside, the compartment was an homage to his worldly adventure travels. I think Porter saw himself as a modern-day version of the twentieth century Indiana Jones character. In addition to hundreds of books, various shelves displayed stone statues that at least looked to be ancient in origin, and a brass sextant I knew was from a British sailing ship from the late 1700s.

"Man, it stinks in here... a cross between old socks and rotten eggs."

He gestured with a raise of his chin, "It's the mummy."

I knew about the mummy. From the exoplanet Niminor XX4, it was a foot-long, wrapped in something black, a juvenile Molskie—which to me looked like a kind of baby monkey. On his desk was a kerosene lantern that had been rewired for modern illumination.

"You know, I do have things to do, Craig..." I said. "Like captaining a dreadnaught."

Porter, not looking up as he tapped at his terminal, said, "One more sec... almost done here." Behind him, a large metal birdcage gently swayed back and forth upon it's hanging chain. Atop the cage, sat Millie—a nastily-dispositioned Scarlet Macaw. The talkative bird, *I think*, actually liked me; I was one of the few people within Porter's circle of friends who hadn't been bitten by it. I wandered around the quarters, picking up various items—I examined a rock that had an angry face chiseled onto one side.

Without looking up, Porter said, "That's incredibly old ... a relic. Please don't touch my stuff."

I put it down and picked up what looked to be an opalescent gem of some kind.

My friend and fellow on-leave adventurer gave one last exaggerated tap upon his console and looked up. "For God's sake, put that down."

I did as he asked.

"Thank you ... Hey, I'm glad you're here. Come on, let me show you the problem over at Propulsion."

Two minutes later we were standing outside a diamond-glass, safe access perimeter to the *Hamilton's* three anti-matter reactors. Inside were several maintenance robots not doing very much of anything.

"*MF*rs ... look at them in there," Porter said, blowing a defeated breath out puffed cheeks.

"What are they doing ... supposed to be doing?"

"We still need two operational reactors to do ... well, anything. Reactor one, in there, is pretty much scrap metal. We might get the other two reactors operating minimally. The three stooges in there had to insert a couple of Hafnium carbide shunts, basically radiation limiters."

"So, what happened?"

"You've heard the expression, 'if you can't stand the heat, get out of the kitchen'?"

"Yeah, sure."

"These robots were pretty much standard issue when the ship first exited spaceport some sixty years ago. They can't stand the heat anymore. And, of course, no human, even someone wearing an environ suit, could be inside with those reactors due to the radiation heat."

I glanced at the three, *wavering/teetering,* bots. "What if I can get you an extra- ordinary maintenance bot, one that could get that job done for you? Could you then get minimal sub-light propulsion going . . . like, within the hour?"

He rubbed the scruff on his chin. "Suppose I could get a bit of thrust going. Be better, though, to shut everything down for a spell, even for a couple of days, and make some much-needed repairs."

"We don't have a couple of days. We don't have a couple of hours," I said.

"Grish?"

I nodded.

"So, no shore leave . . . no Hobo Thom's?" he asked with a smile.

"Uhh, no."

"Okay . . . you have . . . like a super bot somewhere?"

I held a finger up and texted Crewman Lasalle.

"Lasalle. Yes, XO."

"I need you in Zone G."

"Where? Propulsion?"

"Reactor platforms, safe access perimeter. Um, and can you bring along that TL-MAX bot?"

"Can do . . . see you in ten."

I smiled at Porter. "I'm out of here. Keep me informed." I turned to leave.

"XO . . . Galvin, I can't promise anything. We're a long way from any kind of jump capability."

"Just get us moving. For now, we need to get into neutral space at the very least."

Heading out from Zone G, I reached out to Lieutenant Ryder.

"Go for Ryder . . . What's up, XO?"

I recognized the soft humming background sounds on his comms; knew he was in an Arrow Fighter. "Those vented dead crewmembers you've been . . . um, collecting out there."

"Yeah . . . significant number of them. Several hundred."

"You're doing what with them?" I asked.

"Bay Chief's got three shifts going. Eight Arrows are out on patrol at any one time. We locate the dead, then *spatially digi-tag* their locations, and move on. That shuttle you saw me in comes around and does the actual retrievals. From there, Doc Viv's got us storing the *popsicles* in Hold 253 and Hold 254, adjacent to HealthBay's actual morgue."

"Copy that . . . keep at it. Be aware we're moving out of this system within the hour."

En route to the *Hamilton's* mid-ship zone, I got a text message from Doc Viv.

Doc Viv: An assistant found your tycoon. Galvin. There's something irregular about the body that you need to see.

Before I could respond back, I was hailed. Lieutenant Pristy on the Bridge.

"Go for XO."

Her voice was just above a whisper. "XO . . . he's back."

"Who's back?"

"Captain Tannock! He's on the Bridge. Can you get back here?"

"On my way."

I replied back to Doc Viv.

XO Galvin: It'll have to be a little later; putting out fires. By the way, thanks for the heads up, that Captain Tannock is back on the Bridge.

Doc Viv: Oh yeah, he suddenly woke up. Against persistent medical advice, he insisted on going to the Bridge. I'd watch him . . .

I thought about that. I had pretty much done the same thing, too—awakened in HealthBay then rushed off to the Bridge. So, this really was good news, wasn't it? Time to let Captain Tannock take back the reins. Everyone, including myself, knew I was in way over my head.

I looked up, "MATHR, conduct a physical health-scan on Captain Tannock."

This was not an uncommon request, typically someone would do this to get a rudimentary assessment of one's own overall physical health status. Check to see if any viruses or infections were detected, or even a disease, that sort of thing. But having the ship's AI run a physical scan on another person— well only three people onboard the *Hamilton* had clearance for such an action: Captain Tannock, Doc Viv, and the XO—*me*.

"This function is currently unavailable . . ." MATHR came back.

Of course, it is. I made three more stops along the way to check out the most heavily damaged areas of the ship. The *Hamilton* was still in bad shape; just not as bad as it was several hours prior. Heading for Zone E elevators, I was aware of a familiar, and very welcome, sensation. Coming up through the deck plates—through the soles of my boots—I felt faint propulsion system emanations. Apparently, the two reactors had been brought back, at least partially, online.

Ten minutes later, upon entering the Bridge, what struck me first was how ominously quiet things were. I immediately recognized the back of Captain Tannock's head. He was sitting ramrod straight within the Captain's Mount, the local star map feed on the main halo-display. The star map indicated the *USS Hamilton* was in the process of now changing course. Both the *Union* and the *Colorado* were still maintaining their previous course out of the system. What was strange was the direction the *Hamilton* was now heading—not towards Earth, as the admiral so vehemently demanded, but going back further into the Auriga Star System.

As I approached, Science Officer Stefan Derrota stood at the captain's side. Derrota's jaw was set, his eyes boring into the skipper's. He had started to wring his hands, unconsciously.

I cleared my throat before stepping into what was clearly a tense conversation. I listened quietly for a moment.

Derrota said, "Sir . . . of course, I understand your orders. I just wanted to bring you up to speed on—"

The captain erupted, "How dare you question my orders! Until the day comes you are sitting here, wearing these U.S. Navy collar devices," he gestured to the silver eagles pinned to his shirt collar, "I suggest you stand the hell down!"

Tannock was a mess. His head bandaged—a spot of rust-colored dried blood had seeped out on his forehead. His uniform was wrinkled and stained—his trousers' fly splayed open at half-mast. Refocusing his attention back on the halo-display, his momentary confusion turned to something else . . . perhaps fear. Abruptly, the captain turned his attention toward me. "Where the hell have you been, Galvin . . . the ship's been attacked. The whole fleet's been attacked! Executive Officer, *pffft!* You've never taken your responsibilities seriously. Young man, I have a good mind to make you spend the rest of the day in the brig." Next, he stared down at his hands, as if he'd only then discovered he had these two strange appendages. He peered up, "Where's my sandwich?"

I shrugged, attempted to appear concerned. Casually, I took several steps back. Lieutenant Pristy and Science Office Derrota huddled in close to me. "Was he like this when he got here?" I asked them, keeping my voice down.

"No,' Derrota said. "I got a heads-up from a crewmember.

Found him in the Mess, sitting on the deck in front of an open refrigerator, eating an egg salad sandwich."

Lieutenant Pristy said, "Sir . . . he's totally unfit to be sitting in that chair. We tried to tell him that Admiral Hughes wants us to make haste in returning to Earth." She shook her head. "It's like he doesn't hear us."

"Either that or he doesn't understand us," Derrota added.

"He needs to be removed—"

"Careful, Stefan . . ." I said. "You're talking potential career suicide if things don't go down exactly right. Look, he probably has a severe concussion. Blows to one's head can be serious."

"Then what do you suggest?" the Science Officer asked. "Lock him in his quarters?"

"That's crossing a line I'm not quite ready to cross. I suggest we get him *situated someplace* where he can't cause trouble. Give him a chance to clear his head." I looked up at the halo-display and nodded my head. "How about we give him a mission . . . something that will keep him off the Bridge?"

"Can we do that? Won't that get us into even more hot water?" Derrota asked.

"Let's be clear. The three of us never had this discussion," I said, matter-of-factly.

The corners on both the lieutenant's and science officer's mouths turned upward. "Can we really do this?" Lieutenant Pristy asked nervously.

I suspected that the young officer had rarely, if ever, done anything in her short military career that wasn't totally on the up and up. She took pride in being the quintessential *good* girl.

Today would be a baptism for her—moving more into my world. I said, "Okay, we'll need help. Someone to, um . . ."

"Babysit the captain?" Lieutenant Pristy asked, smiling even more broadly now.

Both Derrota and I replied at the same time: "Ensign Hughes!"

"Speak of the devil," Derrota said, looking over to the CIC. Ensign Hughes had just emerged. Making his way to where the three of us stood, he first glanced toward the captain then back to us. Assessing the situation, he leaned in and spoke conspiratorially, "What's happening here?"

I placed a hand on the young officer's shoulder. "Lucas . . . we have a super important job for you."

Derrota said, "It's top secret . . . the ship's been infected."

"Infected?"

I said, "Yeah . . . Wonkies . . . they're all over the place, in sub-deck crawl spaces, bulkhead ventilation ducts . . . lighting fixtures. They love lighting fixtures."

"Crap!" he said, looking up, then all around the Bridge. "Um, what exactly is a Wonkie, sir?"

I ignored the question. "You and the captain, seated over there, will be spending the rest of the day looking for them. Leaving no stone unturned, as they say."

"Me and the captain?" his shoulders slumped.

"Here's the thing. The captain needs to accept the search is a priority. That it demands his full, *personal*, attention. He's disorientated, won't get up off that chair for just any reason.

Can you head back into the CIC, have MATHR make an announcement that's heard exclusively here in the Bridge?"

"Sure . . . shouldn't be a problem. That aspect of MATHR, I think, is still functioning."

"Now, Lucas, on your trek around the ship, seeking out these elusive Wonkies, you need to keep steering the captain away from here. You got that?"

"I'll try . . . for sure, I'll do my best."

"That's all I can ask," I said.

It took a few minutes for us to come up with something appropriate for Lucas to have MATHR vocalize. When the announcement came, the captain, who'd settled into some kind of stupor, perked up and listened intently.

"EMERGENCY PROTOCOL . . . EMERGENCY PRO-TOCOL . . . THE *USS HAMILTON* IS UNDER ATTACK. ALIEN INFESTATION DETECTED."

The same message was repeated several more times. Captain Tannock, standing up, looked about the Bridge, like he wasn't buying this bullshit ruse. In retrospect, it really was somewhat lame. We watched from the CIC as Ensign Hughes approached the captain. Appearing despondent, Lucas—wearing a sidearm *Tagger,* pistol—held up a deactivated plasma rifle, a *Shredder,* to the captain. "Sir . . . there's no one else to help me. No one to stop this infestation!"

"Infestation? What the hell are you talking about, Ensign?"

"The Wonkies, sir . . . they're all over the ship." Lucas handed the captain the weapon. "We need to go, now, sir!"

Lieutenant Pristy, Science Office Derrota, and I watched as

Captain Tannock and Ensign Hughes hurried from the Bridge. Within moments, I had crewman Grimes, positioned now at the Helm Station, re-heading us on a course out of the system.

chapter 8

"NO... not to add to an already desperate situation, we're running low on fuel," Grimes said spinning his chair around from the Helm Station. "Have had half-dozen updates from Chief Porter over the last hour. Says getting the reactors online was only half the problem. With what was emergency-expelled during the battle with the Grish, we're now operating on fumes."

I'd had some of the same messages from Porter. That, and thanking me for the MAX-TL robot which saved the day. Unfortunately, the old bot had not survived its time in such close proximity to the *Hamilton's* massive reactors. For some reason, I felt a bit of sadness at losing that mechanical man. Anyway, the plan had been, on arrival, to get fueled up in high orbit above Bon-Corfue. That was no longer an option—the Bon-Corfue Trentiant Space Station had been destroyed by an errant Grish Smart Missile during the battle. FTL capable starships, such as the *Hamilton*, utilized antimatter drives. The fuel, an Exotic-Derivative Antimatter Proton *(ADAP)* kind of soup, was beyond rare within the known universe. It was typically mined from what are called *Vortex Dark Worlds;* these hard to find, strange, and uninhabitable exoplanets have unique atmospheres. Atmospheres typically rich with antimatter—basically the mirror image of ordinary matter, thus, the electrical charges of antiparticles are reversed. For instance, an anti-electron would have a positive instead of a negative charge. When antimatter meets matter, the result is an explosion. Both particles are annihilated in the process, and their combined masses are converted into pure energy—and there you go—powerful electromagnetic radiation thrusting outward at close to the speed of light. Containment for EDAP fuel was complicated, dangerous, not to mention, expensive. There were a number of EDAP fuel Space Stations within the sector. The problem was finding one close enough that we could reach with our current reserves and one that was not already under the control of the Grish or one of those all-powerful and unfriendly major league super-powers.

Lieutenant Pristy had the star map feed up on the halo-display. There was nothing within our direct route. It was clear we would have to venture into Pleidian Weonan space, where there were several fueling space-stations.

"I know what you're thinking, XO, But the Pleidians would just as soon atomize us as to allow us anywhere near any of those stations of theirs," Chief of Security Mattis said. He looked thoughtful for a moment then shook his head.

"What is it?" I said. "At this point, no idea is too stupid."

He looked at me, "Yeah? How about too dangerous?"

I splayed my hands, "Tell me."

"Gail, zoom in on this quadrant here..." Mattis said, pointing to a section of the map that wasn't all that far from the *Hamilton's* current location. She did as asked, and the star map was instantly filled with three smaller star systems, each having a small unimpressive, red dwarf star. There wasn't a planet amongst them that would be capable of supporting life. Mattis said, "Now, zoom in here..."

What appeared on the halo-display now was a kind of shanty-space station. A discombobulated clutter of ill-fitting parts.

"What am I looking at, Alistair? Looks like a space junkyard."

"You're not far off," the Chief of Security said. "It's called *Ironhold Station*... actually surprising that the low-life proprietors of this, um... establishment, haven't been driven off by the Pleidians yet."

"Who are they?" Gail Pristy asked.

"It's more like, what are they? Called *Pylors*... Cluster of them are all over this part of the galaxy. They're clan criminals. Space desperados and pirates."

Pristy laughed, but then saw Mattis wasn't kidding. "Really? What? These Pylors hold up the rickety stagecoaches on their way into Tombstone?"

"What's the ETA for reaching that...um, station?" I asked.

Lieutenant Pristy pursed her lips while she tapped at her console. "Twenty-eight hours, based on our current sub-light rate of speed."

All eyes turned to me.

"Helm, go ahead and set a course for Ironhold Station. In the meantime, if anyone's looking for me, I'll be in HealthBay."

THE AUTOMATIC DOOR SWISHED CLOSED BEHIND ME AS I stood, taking in the disheartening scene before me. The first thing that hit me after entering HealthBay was the smell. The overwhelming acrid sweet scent of decomposing bodies. To my left, down a narrow passageway, was the Surgery Center and beyond that, the ship's Morgue. Undoubtedly, that was the origin of the bad smell.

The illumination within HealthBay had been turned down—and as earlier, all the beds were full. All the temporary cots were also full. Off to my right, I spotted Chaplain Thomas Trent. Dressed in his long black clerical cassock, he was leaning over one of the patients lying on a cot. My guess, he was administering last rites to a sleeping. or maybe unconscious, crewmember.

Now, I have to be honest with you, I don't really like Chaplain Trent. I've never gotten any sense of any real authenticity from him. Like he was always playing a part in a movie.

The Chaplain stood up, crossed himself, and closed the Bible he'd had open to one particular verse or another. Trent looked unremarkable in every way. In his late fifties, his hair was snow white and parted to one side. Liver spots, like faded drops of ink, stained his forehead. His mouth conformed into a frown and, as if he had a perpetual itch there, he constantly pulled and pinched at his nostrils. He turned and saw me—his expression mimicked my own. His dislike of me was as readable as any of the words written within that Bible of his, now dramatically clasped tight to his chest. We approached each other, meeting halfway across the dreary space.

"Chaplain," I said.

"Commander Quintos ... may I help you?" he said in a hushed tone.

That was not the best way for him to start. First of all, this was not *his* space. As if he held some kind of dominion here. The Vestry Chapel was two decks up and where I wished he'd stayed. "I'm here to see how our injured crewmembers are holding up," I said, glancing around. I furrowed my brow. "The lights being dimmed ... was that your doing?"

He raised his chin a few millimeters. "Why, yes ... it's for the calming effect. It's done to provide a more peaceful, soothing atmosphere."

"No. It's depressing. In fact, it provides the opposite effect as needed. These people don't need to feel that they're waiting to die, they need to feel they're getting better ... that they're still among the living. And to be honest, you ... lurking around in here, well I think it's a bad idea. Gets people wondering when you'll be stopping by their bedside to offer last rites."

The Chaplin plucked at his nose twice. He swallowed, and his jaw muscles tensed. "You are an intolerable man. I warn you ... if the Captain, a dear, dear friend of mine, should hear of your—"

"Spare me the lecture, Chaplain," I said, no longer speaking in my own hushed voice. "Feel free to go tattle to the captain . . . good luck finding him. Anyway, I don't really care. What I do care about are those that have been stuck in here with you. Please, feel free to come back if anyone requests last rites . . . other than that, make yourself scarce."

A few of the patient's heads turned our way. I turned my gaze to the exit. "Please . . . leave."

Chaplain Trent's angry eyes narrowed, as if sending laser beams into me. He turned and stormed out. I said aloud, "MATHR increase HealthBay illumination to seventy-five percent."

Now that I could see actual faces, I saw that there were a cluster of fighter pilots in adjoining beds, deeper into the HealthBay. Approaching, Fighter Pilot Lieutenant Akari James offered up a weak smile. Above her, on the bulkhead, was an array of halo-screens with a myriad of physiological indicators and readouts.

"Lieutenant James . . . how are you holding up?" I asked. I noticed she had a bandaged left shoulder and some facial scrapes and bruises.

"My injuries aren't so bad, XO . . . Doc Viv says I should be back in service in a few days."

"Good . . . we'll be needing every able pilot back on duty."

She said, "I heard you were lying in one of these beds recently," somewhat disinterested.

I didn't take offense; all these people just wanted to get out of here—get back to their jobs. "Yeah, well, if it hadn't been for Ryder, I'd be in a cold locker next door."

"Wallace saved you?" She said, now perking up. "How did he . . ."

It was no secret that young, pretty, Akari James had a crush on Lieutenant Wallace Ryder. If it was reciprocated, I had no idea. Ryder was a bit of a player; keeping track of his off-duty conquests would be exhausting. I said, "He was piloting a shuttle . . . was at the right place at the right time. Out of air and unconscious, Lieutenant Ryder dragged my sorry ass inside and, ultimately, got me here."

A male nurse was attending to several of the other pilots in the area. I read his embroidered identification, Crewman Morgan Cooke. Fluffing a pillow, and without looking at me, he said, "You looking for Doc Viv, sir?"

I waited for him to actually make eye-contact with me before answering. Then I remembered why I was here—Doc Viv had found Milo Wentworth, had requested me to come see something out of the ordinary. "She around?" I asked.

The nurse, now giving me his full attention, said, "The Doc is in the morgue, sir."

I spent another ten minutes making my rounds within HealthBay. I stopped to chat with the injured, thanking them for their service, and letting each and every one of them know, no matter what their condition was, that I expected them back on duty as soon as they were cleared. I reminded myself to speak with Doc Viv—ensure there would be no more of the hovering death watch by the Chaplain.

Leaving HealthBay, well into the narrow passageway, passing by the Surgery Center and heading toward the ship's

Morgue, I now had to fight the urge to cover my nose and mouth with a palm. I suppose one would get used to the smell, but this was bad. I made a swiping motion and the double doors opened before me.

I stepped inside and immediately my gag reflex had me looking for a sink, or a bucket, even an open drain on the deck. But I held my stomach in check. Busy men and women attendants in scrubs milled about. I scanned the brightly lit space. Four tall inactive *cutters*, the term used for dedicated autopsy bots, stood idle next to four tables, their mechanical heads lulling to one side, arms drooping, as if these mechanical men were amongst the dead, themselves. There were ten stainless steel autopsy tables in all—cadavers in various stages of examination lay upon three of them—each of their chest cavities splayed open.

A woman attendant, the front of her scrubs splattered with something dark, hesitated on her way past me. With a bemused expression, she said, "Lost, XO?"

"Uh . . . no. Um . . . is the Doc around?"

She gestured to an area off to the left. A bank of stainless-steel refrigerator doors filled the far bulkhead. Doc Viv was in the process of sliding a sheet-covered corpse inside one of the opened one. She looked up and saw me.

chapter 9

Major Vivian "Viv" Leigh — Ship's Primary Physician

Doc Viv looked up to see Galvan Quinto's, the *Hamilton's* Executive Officer, standing there with that stupid expression of his. He was looking at her. Just seeing him was enough to make her blood boil. She inwardly counted to three. That was usually enough time for her to calm herself—keep herself from saying something regrettable. He was, in fact, her superior. She unconsciously swiped at a stray lock of hair on her forehead and thought she felt something gooey up her gloved fingertips. *Fuck! Did I just wipe blood onto my face? What is he doing here, anyway!?*

She raised her chin and strode toward him. This was her area of the ship—she didn't need to make excuses for anything. "What do you want, Galvin . . . you can see I'm pretty busy."

"What's with that smell?" he asked making a face.

"Power in here was out for a stretch. Refrigeration was off."

He raised his brows, "So, you asked me to come look at something . . . um, Milo Wentworth's body?"

"Oh . . . yeah, the tycoon guy. Sorry. Things are still crazy," Viv said.

"You don't have to explain. I know you have your hands full. You're doing an amazing job, Doc. And everyone . . . I, appreciate all that you do here."

Asshole! Don't you dare start being nice to me, she thought. She let out a breath and with it, some of the animosity she felt for him. God, why did he have to be so good looking—and fit—and that rueful half-smile.

"That was, like, hours ago!" she said. Before he could protest, she held up a palm to hold off a rebuke—and then she saw it now—there actually *was* a bit of blood on her fingers. "Look, I don't know if it's all that strange, considering how much battle damage the ship's incurred. Come with me." She led the way back to the two rows of square stainless steel doors. She used a pointing finger moving from one to the next, "It's this one, I think." She reached for the latch and then stopped. Looking back at him she said, "Maybe I should be talking to the captain about this since he's awake now."

"Sure. There's plenty of other things I could be doing," he said looking perturbed. "You and I both know he's . . . uh, a bit impaired, right? Maybe not to the point we have him deemed unfit for duty? Maybe give him some time to . . ."

"Gain his wits?" she said.

Quintos shrugged and nodded.

"Where is he, anyway?" Viv asked.

"Let's just say Captain's on a special mission . . . ship's been infested with Wonkies . . . he and Ensign Hughes are tracking those little pests as we speak."

She tried to stifle a laugh but was unsuccessful. "Fine, let's you and I discuss my findings. It's probably nothing, anyway." She unlatched the door and pulled the drawer out on silent rollers. A sheet covered the corpse. She looked up to Quintos. "You're not squeamish, are you?"

"Me? Hell no . . . show me what you have here."

She pulled the sheet away, exposing the entire body.

Quintos took an involuntary step back. "Good mother of God!"

Viv crossed her arms over her breasts as she reassessed the remains. A blackened husk—sure you can tell there were two arms and two legs, a featureless head—but the body looked like it had been put through a blast furnace.

Quintos said, "He's little more than . . . charcoal. Electrocuted, right?"

"Uh huh, that's right. But it's rare, this kind of injury onboard a starship."

"Why's that . . . there's no shortage of high voltage conduits—"

She cut him off, "He's a businessman, not someone typically climbing around high voltage lines."

"Never know how an exploded section of the ship might come in contact with someone," Quintos said.

"But that's what's strange. Yes, this man was electrocuted, clearly, but it was from the inside out!"

He stared back at her. "You can tell that?"

"Of course, it's what I do. Look, I'm not saying this absolutely couldn't have been some kind of battle-related injury . . . but," she shook her head, "I don't see it. Would have to check out where the body was found."

Quintos made an exaggerated eye-roll. "Come on. What other explanation could there be?"

She held her tongue. Then with raised brows, she shrugged.

"No!" he said adamantly. "No, no, no! You're not throwing that out there. Not now, not when we're in the midst of this shitstorm."

"I didn't actually say that he was murdered."

"There you go . . . You had to say that word, didn't you?" Quintos said accusingly.

"Alistair certainly thought it was worth looking into," she said. "But he said he had no time for it."

"You spoke to Mattis about this? Involved the Chief of Security before talking to me?" Quintos asked, getting mad.

She supposed she may have overstepped. But it was too late now. "I also went to Stefan." She captured her upper lip between her teeth and tried to look innocent. "Sorry."

"Why'd you go to Stefan Derrota?"

She said, "He's our Science Officer . . . guy knows his stuff. I'm a doctor, not a physicist . . . he *is* a physicist. He doesn't see any possible way Wentworth here could have been electrocuted from the inside out unless foul play was involved."

"Foul play?" Quintos said, looking exasperated. He raised his hands, "Just stop talking. Please." His eyes lingered on the charred remains. "Promise me that you won't talk to anyone else about this. This stays between you, me, and Derrota."

She was already nodding enthusiastically, "Of course. The three of us will investigate. In secret. A crime scene team." She huffed, "Hmm, what if the captain does regain his wits?"

Quintos said, "Let's cross that bridge when we get to it . . . for now, it's just the three of us."

"And if there is a . . . *killer* onboard?" She asked.

"There isn't. There can't be . . . this can be explained, I'm sure."

Viv tilted her head, still looking at Wentworth's remains. "Maybe it had something to do with *who*, he is. His secret mission back in the Auriga Star System?" She looked up, "I think it's time we talk to our Thine passenger . . . he, too, is one of the secret envoys."

Quintos was getting messaged. He glanced at his TAC-Band and then back to her. "Give me an hour to put out several new fires . . . We'll meet at his quarters."

AN HOUR AND TWENTY MINUTES LATER, DOC VIV WAS waiting outside the Deck 19 Zone D, cabin 1944's closed door of the Thine envoy, one Coogong Lohp. Prior to disembarking from Earth, she had been alerted to the alien's existence onboard the *Hamilton*. In case of an emergency, she had been given medical supplies and MATHR was provided basic Thine anatomy and treatment protocols. But that was the extent of her involvement. She had been told that these quarters were off-limits to anyone but the captain.

Viv leaned against the passageway's bulkhead and tried to relax. Something she was nearly incapable of doing. Perhaps it was her upbringing, a young girl brought up away from the U.S., Viv had grown up in a military family. She had one sister, a year older than she was, her mom and her dad were Jackie and Don. Her memories of that time were sparse, her being so young. She remembered an exciting life—they'd traveled all over the world. When she was five or six, they'd moved to China. That's where it happened. Where everything had fallen apart. There was an epidemic—what she would come to learn was called the Borallovirus. Viv's dad was on base, a pilot, her mom was a pediatrician, both working in Beijing. Viv had been home with her sister, Sky, along with their Nanny, Daphne. Sky had been the first to get sick. She remembered her and her sister being hurried off to the ER. Mom and Dad had met them there. Sky was confirmed with the deadly virus. It wasn't long before mom and then dad, and even the Nanny, contracted the Borallovirus. The virus rapidly broke down their arteries and soon their bodies became bloated—filled with their own blood. Eventually, those stricken with the virus literally drowned from the inside out. Somehow, as her own family succumbed to the virus, as well as millions of others, Viv had been immune. She eventually was adopted by a wealthy Chinese American man, *Bohai Chin,* who heard about her plight. A strict and impersonal man, an investment banker, he'd raised her as his own daughter. She'd wanted for nothing, other than the affection she pined for on a daily basis, that of her deceased family. Bohai Chin and Viv moved to the states when she was in her early teens. Initially, Viv was sent to the best schools. Then, Bohai Chin lost his fortune with several bad investments—had become depressed and somewhere along the line, lost his will to live. It had been Viv, herself, who had found his body hanging from a tree branch in the back yard. Even now, she could see that toppled over footstool lying on their manicured emerald green lawn. It was then, soon turning eighteen, she'd decided to follow in her mother's footsteps—become a EUNF—U.S. Navy physician—become a doctor, so she could help people like that of her stricken family.

Rumpled looking Derrota was the first to arrive. "Hey, Doc," he said in his pleasant accented voice.

"Hey, Stefan . . . thanks for coming."

"No, I should be thanking you. I'm a scientist . . . to actually observe one of these elusive Thine beings . . . well, that's simply fine with me." He looked up and down the passageway. "Where's the XO? He's still a part of this—"

She cut him off, "Yes, I guess. He's just late. But that's typical for him."

"Are you two going to be . . . alright working together? It's no secret there's a bit of animosity between you two."

About to answer, she spotted Quintos hurrying their way.

"Sorry . . . got held up on the bridge." Quintos nodded to Stefan and then to her. "I only have a few minutes, so, let's get on with this."

"We're all busy, Quintos . . ." she snapped back—*God, he's already getting under my skin.*

"I tried to wave the door open . . . it's locked," she said.

Quintos moved to her side and waved his hand, the door made a melodic sound and swooshed open. He said, "Stopped by the CIC and with Mattis's help got my security permissions raised to that of the captain's. Took a bit of time . . . why I was late."

"Shall we?" Stefan said as the three of them stared into the murky darkness within the quarters beyond. No one moved.

"Oh, for goodness sakes, I'll go in first," Viv said. She moved passed the threshold and said, "MATHR, lights on."

Overhead panels gradually increased the illumination to where they could see the entire quarters.

"Fascinating," Stefan said, stepping closer.

"Reminds me of a kid's ant farm," Quintos said.

Viv agreed with both assessments. What they were looking at was a deck to ceiling glass enclosure that took up two-thirds of the compartment. Considering this was one of the larger passenger quarters, fifteen-feet by twenty-five-feet, the enclosure was about 10 feet by 15 feet and maybe twelve feet tall. Within the dark substance, there were crisscrossing impressions, like trails, from where the Thine had traversed within.

"Looks like it's full of dirt or maybe mud," Quintos said.

Stefan said, "It's called Ambiogel . . . required environment for our Thine friend to breathe."

Quintos tapped on the glass with a forefinger.

"Hey, what are you doing?" Viv scolded. "That's incredibly rude."

"How else are we going to get his attention ... maybe he's in there watching a holo-movie or brushing his teeth."

She fought back a smile. She said, "Maybe we just talk to him. His name is Coogong Lohp."

Quintos tapped on the glass with a forefinger a few more times, "Uh, Coogong Lohp ... you in there? Sorry to disturb. Hello?"

Viv shot Quintos an annoyed look. Turning back to the enclosure, they waited. Nearly a minute had passed when Stefan said, "Maybe we should come back later—"

Suddenly, a white face appeared on the other side. Pressed up against the glass, two oversized, expressive, brown eyes, a flattened nose, and a small mouth were right there. Viv's first impression of the Thine being was how friendly and, well, kind of cute the creature looked. More of the Thine's body came into view as the rest of it pressed in closer to the glass. It was somewhere between four and five feet long, white and segmented. There were nubs where arms or legs maybe would have been present somewhere along its evolutionary past.

"Step back, Quintos ... he's communicating!" Viv said.

chapter 10

Executive Officer, Galvin Quintos

I took a step back and saw what Doc Viv was talking about. Somehow the worm was projecting reversed text, in English, onto the glass from within for us to read.

Hello . . . please tell me what is happening? Has there been an attack on the Hamilton? My communications with your ship's AI have not been fruitful. I do hope all is well . . .

Both Doc Viv and Stefan looked to me, so, I guess I would be the designated spokesperson here. "Yes, we've been attacked . . . by the Grish. Much of the fleet has been destroyed, a terrible loss of life." I let that sink in for a moment.

The Thine's features expressed his true sadness—his eyes moistened. Eventually, he replied.

I am so sorry for your loss, Executive Officer Quintos. As well as for yours, Doctor Leigh, and your Science Officer, Stefan Derrota.

My people will be devastated upon learning of this … and that they, we, may have been in some way responsible.

"You know who we are?" I asked.

Of course, … I know of every crewmember on this vessel, as well as those upon the other vessels within this fleet. This is a terrible loss … terrible. Commander, you must leave the Auriga Star System at once.

I said, "Coogong Lohp, our jump capacity is offline. And we have minimal sub-light propulsion … but we *have* already left the system, I assure you. We're doing all we can to put some distance between us and the Grish."

Doc Viv said, "Wait … why is it you think the Thine would be responsible? Does it have something to do with you being here? Onboard the *Hamilton?*"

My informed assumption? Yes, partially. Again, my connection with your MATHR AI is no longer functioning, which hinders my ability to acquire updated information.

Stefan said, "AI's been having trouble … damaged during the battle. We're working on it. But I'll make sure your connection is reestablished as soon as it comes fully back online."

I would be most appreciative of that. May I enquire about Captain Tannock? I do hope he has not been injured or killed.

"He incurred a head injury but we're hoping he'll recover soon," I said.

Doc Viv said, "Can I ask you something else?"

Yes, of course, Doctor.

"You and Milo Wentworth … what exactly were you two doing together here on this ship? I understand you're both some kind of envoys . . . were you to meet with the Aurigans on Bon-Corfue?"

I suppose there is no longer the same need for confidentiality . . . but, please know, Milo Wentworth and I were not here together . . . if anything, our intentions were diametrically opposed.

"In what regard?" I asked.

This meeting on Bon-Corfue, was to culminate an accord between Earth and the inhabitants of a world you call Juno 5. This recently discovered world, much of it uncivilized, is within fron-tier space and less than two light-years from Earth—and has been determined to be an area of space rich with rare exotic minerals— many used in the manufacture of jump drive engines and artificial wormholes. Thus, the reason for Milo Wentworth's presence here was potential investment . . . to increase his corporate holdings. Meeting on Bon-Corfue, the Aurigans were merely playing host for the negotiations. It was them that had requested that a Thine presence, specifically me, be there to ensure balance . . . to ensure that the Junops, what the inhabitants are called on Juno 5, are not taken advantage of and that their world would not be, what you would call, ravaged . . . strip-mined.

"What does all this have to do with the recent attack? Doc Viv asked.

The Juno 5-star system is closer to Earth than even Proxima . . . Alpha Centauri. Earth is making the claim this area of space is within Earth's own space territory . . .

"I can see why our galactic neighbors, namely the Grish, might feel a tad threatened by this. Thus, the disruption of these negotiations," I said.

"Explains why Earth sent the Hamilton's Dreadnaught group here for what was deemed little more than a diplomatic mission," Stefan added.

I flashed back to something Admiral Block said—"...*we have our own issues to contend with ... Earth's space resources have all been activated. It's not just the Grish. The Borno ... even the fucking Sheenah ... are currently on the move. Seems to be a concerted uprising all across the sector.*"

I said, "So, Earth is making a stand. We've sent resources to maintain dominance over that Juno 5 system?"

The Thine being merely blinked his large brown eyes.

"You, the Thine, support this move?" I asked.

Yes ... it is in both Earth's and my world's, Morno's, interests. But we will not be a part of violent invasion practices ... or the raping of one's resources ... one's lands. My presence here was to ensure measures were in place to protect the Junops throughout the process.

Doc Viv said, "Well, that explains a lot. I certainly don't like the idea of Earth's United Nations Forces, EUNF, going to war for what seems to be purely economic reasons ... although Juno 5 being so close to Earth, I guess it makes sense. It being more or less in our own back yard. We'd certainly want to keep our enemies at arm's length. Anyway, can we get back to Wentworth? It is my opinion his death was anything but accidental. That he was electrocuted ... murdered. Can you tell us anything about that? Who would benefit from his death? And do we actually have a murderer onboard the *Hamilton*?"

Coogong Lohp seemed to chew on this a moment before

answering . . . *Quite possibly.* He turned his gaze towards Stefan, *Please, ensure my connection with MATHR is reestablished. I may be able to help. Your largest, most immanent concern should be the Grish. Having a murderer onboard, that too could be catastrophic. Would you like me to join you with your investigation?* He brought his gaze now over to an area of his quarters which had stayed fairly dark.

The three of us now saw there were two large items looming there. One was an advanced bipedal robot. The compartment's illumination now increased—easily seven feet tall, its mirror-like reflective surface literally gleamed. The thing silently screamed ultra-high-tech. Its head was tear-dropped shaped with its back coming to a point. There were no eyes, no nose or a mouth, only a circular array of silver sensors. As if on cue, the head turned in our direction. I figured the bot must have some kind of wireless comms connection to Coogong Lohp. Right next to the bot was a hardened space suit—but not like any space suit I had ever seen. This one was black, and, primarily was shaped like a stout canister. An unwieldy canister with short stubby legs and arms. Multiple tanks encircled the main torso area—my guess was that those were filled with that mud-like Ambiogel atmosphere.

New text appeared upon the glass. *The robot's name translates to LuMan . . . Thousands of these ChronoBots were purchased from the Sheentah some three-hundred years ago, back when relations between our two civilizations were better.*

"You name your bots?" I asked.

Although not fully sentient, these mechanical beings are far

*more than mere machines. They have rudimentary emotions . . .
morality centers within their computational centers. Look at me,
Commander Quintos . . . I am intelligent, yet totally defenseless . . .
LuMan will protect me with his life, if need be.*

Is that why you brought, um, him onboard with you?"
Stefan asked.

*Yes, that, and only with LuMan's help was I able to get sit-
uated within the environment suit and then transferred into my
habitat here. I am fond of this ChronoBot more than you can
imagine. I depend on him for my very survival.*

I wasn't exactly sure why Coogong Lohp was telling us all
this.

*Commander Quintos . . . you will take LuMan with you when
you leave here, soon.*

Ready to object, I said, "Thank you for the offer, but I
assure you we have plenty of bots aboard the *Hamilton*—"

*No . . . you have nothing like LuMan. This ChronoBot may
not have the AI capacity of your MATHR system, although that
is debatable . . . it does have phenomenal strength and is highly
resourceful, and again, there's the loyalty factor. LuMan will be an
integral part of your team.*

I objected, "No, you need, um, *LuMan*, here with you. In
case you need to uh, I don't know, get up and move about in
that suit of yours over there. We're fine—"

*No more discussion, Commander. I insist. You see, I have been
entrusted with the fate of the Junops. My life is inconsequential
compared to their future wellbeing.*

I was still looking at the ChronoBot.

Please, Commander, look at me.

I did as he asked. "Sorry."

While we have been speaking, I have also been communicating with LuMan. Other than myself, LuMan has now aligned with you . . .

"Aligned with me? What does that exactly mean?"

In the event something happens to me . . . LuMan will migrate his total sole obedience over to you, Commander. But you will take him with you, now . . . utilize his abilities to find this potential killer. If for some unexpected reason I require his assistance, he will return to me.

Doc Viv said, "Coogong Lohp, why would *something* happen to you? Do you feel you are in some kind of imminent danger? Maybe related to Wentworth's death?"

That is unknown. Go, now . . . although I do ask but one favor of the three of you.

"Sure, anything," I said before thinking.

The fate of the Junops . . . these people must be protected at all costs. I fear there are dark forces at work here upon this vessel . . . as well as our enemies in space beyond.

Before I could clarify just how limited our abilities would be to protect anyone but our own crewmembers for the near term, Doc Viv spoke up first.

"You have our word on that . . . we'll do all we can to keep the Junops safe."

Both Stefan and I glared at the good doctor. She ignored us, placed her palm on the glass, and said, "Be safe, Coogong Lohp . . . we'll keep in contact with you."

On our way out of Coogong Lohp's quarters, about to admonish Doc Viv for making promises we in no way could keep, I received an Emergency hail on my TAC-Band.

"XO . . . we've got company!" Lieutenant Gail Pristy said.

"On my way."

chapter 11

I entered the Bridge with both Derrota and LuMan, the ChronoBot, mere steps behind me. The Doc had returned to HealthBay. All eyes nervously went to LuMan. Until this moment, I hadn't feared for the safety of the crew or ship, regarding the striking, towering, robot. My trust of Coogong Lohp had been that absolute—but right at this moment, I was having second thoughts as to why.

But seeing the forward halo-display reset my priorities. Two vessels were approaching. "Pleidian Battle Cruisers," I said aloud. Normally they would be no match for the *Hamilton*, but in her current condition with many of her big guns off-line, MATHR unavailable to plot smart-missile weaponry fire, and the big one—our inability to maneuver anywhere fast—we could be in trouble.

"Distance?" I asked.

"Two-hundred-thousand clicks," Lieutenant Pristy said. "You're looking at a direct forward feed, sir. They've been using active scans to take our measure."

Shit! Using active scan versus using passive scans meant they didn't care that we knew they were giving us the once over. And right now, they'd know we had been heavily damaged.

"And the *Union* and *Colorado*? They still behind us?"

"Yes, sir ... two-hundred and five-hundred clicks, respectively."

"Orders, sir? Shall I lock Phazon Pulsars ... let them know we mean business?" Crewman Grimes said from the Weaponry Station.

"Tempting, but no. This is their space, we're the trespassers here." I looked to the Communications Station—empty. I now remembered Officer Leo Briggs had been killed in the battle. As were many of the other stations on the damaged bridge, we were dangerously shorthanded.

"I will man the Comms Station, Executive Officer, Quintos ... came a deep, electronically synthesized, male voice behind me. I wondered, *who, what, onboard had that kind of voice?* I turned to see LuMan poised to move over to the nearby open station. Normally, MATHR would have been more than capable of handling this situation. But I had no confidence the AI would handle such important communications. *Hell, she may decide to offer the entire enemy crew grilled cheese sandwiches and tomato soup.*

"Everybody, this is LuMan," I said.

"I am fully acquainted with all EUNF, as well as U.S. Navy, communications protocols and hailing practices," the robot proclaimed.

"Bad idea, XO," Chief of Security Mattis said, eyeing the

sleek-looking reflective robot. "Who knows what that . . . whatever it is . . . intentions are?"

It was true, I didn't know. And it got back to my trust of the Thine being. I nodded to LuMan, "Take your seat at the Comms station." I myself had yet to take a seat at the Captain's Mount. "Send a broad-channel voice message. Keep things friendly. Ask permission for temporary incursion into Pleidian territory. Let them know we won't linger here . . . but would like to avoid any further confrontations. Send the message. I looked over to Mattis, "Hey, they can already see we're in trouble. We're not at war with the Pleidians . . . maybe they'll let us pass."

"And if not?" Mattis asked.

"We'll change course, if they let us, we'll fight if we must . . ."

I listened to LuMan's synthesized voice. He was, in fact, presently conversing with the Pleidian ships. Their own translation intercepts would have no problem converting English to Pleidian, and vice versa, the ChronoBot undoubtedly had the same capabilities. This Pleidian alien race had always interested me. Highly advanced and less warmongering than many of the other Major-League powers in the cosmos, they were amazing in a number of ways—for one thing, they glowed, giving them a kind of ethereal affectation. Something about their cellular physiology having light-emitting molecules—lumivale, similar to luciferin, which was found on Earth in such organisms as jellyfish and fireflies. Bipedal, tall, and typically thin, the Pleidian Weonans were a proud people who, for the most part, did not associate with any of their neighboring alien beings—they kept to themselves. Which, at the moment, was giving me pause.

LuMan turned in his seat. "XO ... the Pleidians have ordered us to halt any further advancement into their territory. Apparently, the decision to allow us temporary ingress into their space needs to be made higher up within their command structure."

Grimes, working both the Weapons Station and Helm, let out an audible breath. He shot me a pained expression.

"What is it, Grimes?"

"It's about momentum, sir ... I bring this three-kilometer-long dreadnaught to a standstill, in our current hobbled condition, there's no assurance we'll be able to get moving again. Not with our beat-to-shit, barely operational drives."

"Geez, Grimes ... how do you really feel?" Mattis said, heavy with sarcasm.

LuMan, with his face comprised of circular blinking sensors, stared back at me—clearly, he was waiting for a response for me to give to the Pleidians.

Shit! Do I relay to them the truth—just how damaged we really are and hope for a little sympathy? Or would showing them our vulnerable underbelly be a death sentence?

"XO, we're being hailed," LuMan said.

"I know ... I'm still *considering* what to say—"

"No, sir. We are being hailed by both the *Union* and the *Colorado* ... seeing our predicament, they had accelerated. Both are now within one-hundred clicks of the *Hamilton*."

One-hundred clicks was extremely close in terms of

proximity within the vastness of open space. I smiled. Sure, both ships were hardly in any better shape than the *Hamilton*, just the same, it was now a battle dreadnaught along with a small frigate and a destroyer, here to complicate things even more for the Pleidians.

Mattis said, "XO . . . don't think the Admiral would want us starting an intergalactic war here. With everything else going on. Just saying."

"I already know that, Alistair!" I snapped back.

A ruckus at the back of the Bridge stole my attention. *What now?* I wasn't sure if I was happy or dreaded seeing the person moving toward the Captain's Mount. I said, "Captain Tannock?"

"XO . . . Situation Report!" His eyes were focused, and he seemed somewhat more alert to his surroundings.

Wide-eyed, Lieutenant Pristy looked to the captain and then to me. I gave her a reassuring nod.

The captain had both weapons now, the *tagger* pistol and the deactivated plasma *shredder* rifle. His head was still bandaged, only now the small spot of blood on his forehead had seeped into a much larger rust-colored stain.

"Uh, yes, Captain, let me unfold the situation for you," I said. I proceeded to relay the course of events originally stemming from the Grish ambush. The total loss of the *Federal*, the *Republic*, the *Capital*, the *Austin*, and the *California*. That the Grish's two remaining warships had jumped away. Along with the *Hamilton*, The *Union* and the *Colorado*, although heavily damaged, survived the battle and are nearby. The staggering loss of life aboard the *Hamilton* having reached close to 2,200. The total fleet loss of life was in excess of 10,000. I relayed the onboard course of events—the three catastrophic deck breaches on Decks 12, 13, and 23—as well as the Deck 23 LabTech situation, the overheating of a Phazon Pulsar cannon on Deck 5—and the three compartments having been ready to explode and the use of the Hub Gunther to extricate them away from the *Hamilton*. I explained the slow repairs made to two of the *Hamilton's* three damaged reactors, how MATHR was still compromised, impacting a number of essential ship functions, including CIC weapons control, that all shields were only marginally operational, HyperDrive jump computations, to name just a few. Add to that, the *Hamilton* was extremely low on fuel, thus our attempt to refuel at potentially unfriendly Ironhold Station here within Pleidian Weonan space. And finally, I updated the captain on the presence of two nearby Pleidian Battle Cruisers—having ordered us to halt forward progress.

The captain, thoughtfully, rubbed at his chin. Clucked his tongue several times.

I said, "I expect their active scanners have conveyed our compromised situation. They'll probably want to board the *Hamilton*. That's what I'd do in their situation." I hadn't mentioned anything about Milo Wentworth's death and the possibility of a murderer being on board. That could come later when speaking within a more private location. I also kept our conversation with the Thine being from the verbal report—since much of that dealt with classified information—inappropriate to share here on the bridge.

The captain had remained calm and had seemed to be tracking along with my situational report. I was feeling optimistic—almost gleeful, that the weight of command was soon about to be lifted from my shoulders. There was just one problem. Surely, by now, the old man had spotted the shiny seven-foot-tall alien robot, LuMan, situated at the *Hamilton's* Comms Station. If that wasn't odd, what was? Why hadn't he blown his stack at seeing such a strange, uncharactcristic, anomaly?

I was aware by this point the Bridge crew was thinking along the same lines. Furtive glances were being made over to LuMan and then over to the captain—then to me. *Fuck!*

Out of breath and looking crazed, I saw Ensign Hughes entering at the back of the bridge. He looked about the space and then spotted the captain seated next to me. Hughes grimaced, then mouthed, *sorry XO,* and shrugged. He hurried closer and I took several casual steps backwards. He leaned in, spoke into my ear. "Sorry, sir . . . he was no longer buying the whole Wonkies bullshit. Demanded we abandon the search and he headed back here."

"That's fine. Hey, you went above the call of duty . . . maybe he's coming around." I said, optimistically.

The Ensign didn't look convinced. Being honest with myself now, I wasn't either. And the timing of the captain being here on the Bridge at such a crucial moment could have a devastating outcome. I turned to face the halo-display and saw that it was now a split-screen, with the two Pleidian Battle Cruisers occupying the left side, and, surprisingly, Admiral Block's craggy old face, on the right. He was looking at the Captain's Mount—more accurately, the man seated within it. The Captain was murmuring something incoherent and fiddling with the strap of his Shredder rifle.

I stepped up to the side of the Captain's Mount, "Admiral Block . . . um, have you been appraised of the current situation, sir?"

I waited while the comms interstellar signal pinged from one relay station to the next and then back again. "Yes, Commander Quintos . . . my feed had become active just prior to you updating the good captain there. The Admiral's eyes softened as he observed the captain—a captain clearly incapable of commanding a U.S. Navy warship. The Admiral now brought his attention back to me. "Commander Quintos, I would like to thank you on behalf of the EUNF, and the U.S. Navy. You have shone outstanding leadership qualities in the midst of most arduous of battle conditions."

I saw the expression on his face. I knew what he was about to say and wanted to scream for him to stop—to take some time to reassess—to find someone else far more capable, *and willing*, than me.

"Normally, this would take place in private. Perhaps the Captain's ready room. But we do not have the luxury of time. Commander Quintos. Unofficially, I hereby elevate your officer status onboard the *USS Hamilton* to Acting Captain and for you to remain the ship's skipper until you make spaceport upon reaching Earth, whereby the position will, most appropriately, be made permanent. Your ship's physician is being contacted as we speak, whereby Captain Tannock will be deemed incapable of further command due to medical circumstances."

I saw that smiles had appeared on the faces around me. Clearly, they were far more pleased with this outcome than I was. "Um, thank you, sir. I won't let you down."

"As for your decision to refuel at Ironhold Station there within Pleidian space, that is a risky one, but one I may have made myself. As for facing off with the two Pleidian Battle Cruisers... they will attempt to board the *Hamilton*, I have little doubt about that."

"Yes, sir ... agreed."

The admiral looked thoughtful. "I am not there. I cannot read the situation as you can. What I *can* tell you is that the U.S. Navy does not back down unless a situation is truly dire ... if there is no other choice. Captain Quintos, make the right decision. I would hate to see my faith in you has been mistaken. The lives of your crew and potentially those on Earth, depend on your actions here today."

Terrific, go ahead, Admiral, pile on the pressure. I nodded.

He took a thoughtful breath. "I will be out of pocket for the near term ... commanding the 7th Fleet, heading off to ..." he hesitated, looking as if he may already have said too much.

I said, "May I presume Exoplanet, Juno 5, sir?"

He looked surprised by my guess. He chuckled. "Ah, you've met my friend Coogong Lohp. All right then ... Help is on the way to you. But not soon enough to alleviate your current situation. Ensure you make contact with the *Prowess* and work out a rendezvous location as appropriate. That Carrier strike group has already embarked from the Lalande System."

"Aye, sir," I said.

"Godspeed, Captain." Prior to signing off, the Admiral glanced over to the robot sitting at the Comms Station. Looking somewhat concerned, he shook his head. The feed went black.

I was being hailed. Without looking at my TAC-Band, I said, "Go for X ... Go for Captain."

"God save us all. Do I really have to call you that?"

I recognized Doc Viv's voice within my ear comms. "Afraid so ... whatever you need, it'll have to wait. We have a situation on the bridge."

"Captain ... Galvin ... another body's been found. Looks like it's another murder. Very recent."

I closed my eyes and swallowed. "You haven't mentioned this to anyone else, have you?"

"No ... but, this will get out. The person that found the body ... someone here in the morgue ... it's only a matter of time."

I stared at the two battle cruisers up on the halo-display—my main priority at the moment. "Same cause of death?"

"Oh no ... not even close."

I saw Lieutenant Pristy's ears perk up at that. *Shit!* I raised a palm and made a no- big-deal expression—which did absolutely no good.

I said to the Doc, "For now, just keep him on ice. We'll

need to deal with Captain Tannock. I don't know what the protocol is for someone in his, um, condition."

She said, "The best thing, for now, would be to return him to HealthBay . . . sedate him. He needs rest. Once MATHR is functional again, she can provide a better assessment as to neurological damage and a long-term prognosis."

Once again, I was struck how dependent we all were on the ship's malfunctioning AI. "I'll have him delivered to you shortly," I said.

"Oh, and Captain? . . . I never said the murder victim was a man."

chapter 12

Captain Tannock put up no resistance being escorted by Ensign Hughes back to HealthBay. Watching him leave the bridge, I got the feeling the old man was, at some level, aware of his compromised condition—at the very least—that life for him may never be the same.

"Captain!" Chief of Security Mattis said, gesturing to the halo-display.

I said, "And where there were two . . . there were now five." I sat at the Captain's Mount. "Destroyers?" I said.

"Yes and . . . needless to say, Pleidian warships are highly advanced," Mattis said, "Strange since, word is, the alien race is archaic in other aspects.

"Such as?"

"Highly superstitious. Their belief in supernatural occurrences and the paranormal is commonly known."

Huh, not to me. "LuMan, open a channel. It's time I speak to them directly."

The robot tapped at the comms board, "Channel is open, Captain Quintos."

Up on the halo-display, a lone figure appeared. Dressed in a gray uniform not all that different than those of us on the *Hamilton*, his head and hands had the characteristic shimmering blue glow of all Pleidians. But the most distinctive aspect of the Pleidian physiology were their elongated doughnut-like heads, whereby a see-through open space encompassed most of the head. There was one eye on each far side of the face, if you could call it a face, and the mouth was almost human-like and could be found at the very bottom area of the head. I wasn't sure where the nose was. The Pleidian looking back at me now was completely hairless and his skin had the glowing bluish color. There didn't seem to be any sign of malice or animosity present on his face—but to be truthful, I'd have no idea how any Pleidian's expression would exhibit itself.

"It's like he has an aura," Lieutenant Pristy said under her breath.

"I am Fleet Commander, Twinwon . . . speak to me."

"Greetings. I am Captain Galvan Quintos of the Earth vessel, *USS Hamilton*. First of all, I would like to apologize for our presence here within Pleidian Weonan territory. As you have undoubtedly detected by now, our three starships have sustained heavy damage."

His only response was a slight tilting of his head.

I continued on, "Our fleet was on a diplomatic mission to Auriga Star System when we were ambushed by the Grish, a heinous action that destroyed five of our warships . . . over ten thousand lives lost in the battle. So, I assure you, we are not here to stir up trouble between our two peoples . . . we simply need to make our way home, safely, back to Earth."

His narrow strip of forehead creased with concern. "You say the Grish attacked you without provocation?"

"That is correct, Fleet Commander Twinwon."

"That was an egregious act of war, no doubt," he said, shaking his head. "Those foul beings straddle a dangerous line even with us of late. I do hope you were victorious . . ." he said, his words trailing off.

"I suppose we won the battle . . . undoubtedly, they will seek to remedy that . . . attempt to finish what they started," I said.

"And that is why you have chosen this precarious heading, knowing full well you would be met with far superior Pleidian forces?"

Even though the *USS Hamilton* was old, it was still a formidable warship—even in its current battle-damaged state. But this was no time to trifle or ruffle feathers. I said, "Fleet Commander, Twinwon, to be honest, with few options available to us, I was counting on the goodwill of your people. Please know, Earth has great respect and admiration for the Pleidian Weonan." He and I both knew I was piling it on here, but we were at their mercy. I wasn't above groveling a little to save the lives of those few of us remaining aboard our embattled, three, 3rd fleet warships.

Twinwon nodded, continued to assess me, but did not offer any kind of concession, just yet. He turned a shoulder to us and spoke to another crewmember who we could see via the opening in his head.

"That's so fucking freaky," I heard Ensign Hughes say under his breath somewhere behind me.

The Pleidians spoke amongst themselves for an extended amount of time. Finally, he turned back and said, "Captain Quintos, you may continue along your current trajectory within Pleidian space. Do not stray any deeper into our territory. Do not give us any reason to cause more harm to your vessels and crews." He inclined his head and said, "May you find truth, enlightenment, and harmony in your travels..."

I said, "Thank you, Fleet Commander Twinwon." His feed went black, leaving the wide view feed of the alien warships. Then, one by one, all five of the Pleidian vessels jumped away.

"Course, sir?" Grimes asked from the Helm Station.

"Take us deeper into Pleidian territory... Set a course for Ironhold Station."

Approaching HealthBay, I'd come to the decision that I would no longer be involved with Doc Viv's and Science Officer Stefan Derrota's murder investigation. As acting Captain, there would be little time now for such a distraction. And how certain could the Doc be that these *deaths* actually were murders, anyway? Hearing a noise behind me, I glanced back to see the towering robot had followed me here. I'd specifically ordered the ChronoBot to stay on the Bridge and man the Comms Station. I wanted to chastise the big bot but knew it would be a waste of breath. "If you're going to follow me around anyway, you may as well walk with me. So, hurry up!"

We entered HealthBay together.

"Damn it!" I said looking around the dimmed space. *Chaplain fucking Trent.* Then I spotted him at the far side of HealthBay. He saw me too, and hurried off, disappearing into an adjoining compartment or storage area. Tempted to track him down, I simply said, "MATHR, bring HealthBay illumination up to normal settings."

Nothing happened. I glowered in the direction of Chaplain Trent.

"Captain Quintos . . . it seems a new default illumination setting has been configured for this area of the ship. Password protected," LuMan said.

"How do you know that?" I asked.

"I have reestablished communications with your ship's MATHR AI. Would you like me to override those settings?"

"You can do that?"

Although the ChronoBot had no facial features, per se, I perceived an indignant response, "Of course. Your MATHR AI is rudimentary technology. I have reset the overhead illuminations to normal status and pass-locked the settings to exclusively yours and Doctor Vivian Leigh's voiceprints."

I stared at LuMan for a long moment. "Let me make myself perfectly clear here. In the future, you do not alter any ship settings . . . MATHR configurations, without my explicit orders to do so first. Is that understood?"

LuMan offered up that same indignant pose, and then said, "Yes, Captain Quintos, understood."

I made an abrupt left, heading down the narrow passageway toward the Surgery Center and Morgue areas. I'd deal with this quickly and get back to the bridge. The bad smell was still present, but somewhat better. I waved a hand approaching the Morgue and the double doors swooshed open. All the autopsy tables were occupied; several medical crew, along with robot counterparts, were busy attending to their work. I spotted Doc Viv off to our right. She gestured for me to approach.

"Oh good, we were just about to get started," she said, giving LuMan a discerning look. Clearly, she was still as uncomfortable with his looming presence as I was.

I heard the sound of motors and servos engaging, as the *cutter* robot moved in closer to the stainless-steel table. I stared at the sheet-covered body before us. "And who, exactly, is this?" I asked.

"I'll get to that. And that's one of the *strange* aspects . . . the body's been mutilated," Doc Viv said, looking somewhat confounded. "First," she gestured to her own forearm. "The TAC-Band controller . . . the little T-bead has been cut out. And none too gently, I'd say."

"So, you don't know who this—"

She cut me off, "No . . . MATHR would typically compare the DNA within the crew database listings . . . but even that seems to be beyond her capabilities right now," Doc Viv said. "Do you mind, we need to get started."

I gestured with an open palm to the sheeted body, "Let's go. Show me what you have."

The cutter pulled the sheet away with a quick flourish, exposing the lifeless body. She was lying on her stomach, oddly, and was fully naked."

"I have her turned over because I wanted to show you something from this perspective first," Doc Liv said, leaning over the body while glancing up at me. "You okay, Galvin? You look a bit piqued."

I continued to stare at the petite woman's form, my eyes settling on her brown hair. The unique way it was styled. Long, to the shoulder, on one side, buzz-cut short on the other. Her face was turned away from me, so I moved around the table, joining Doc Viv on the other side. I looked at her pretty, far-too-young face.

"Galvin?" Doc Viv said, now looking at me. "What is it? Do you know her?"

The tears flowed down my cheeks and I didn't care. *Who would do this? Who would snuff out this wonderful little fire-cracker?* I finally said, "This is Gunny Sergeant Zan Mattis . . . Chief of Security Alistair Mattis's daughter."

Viv stood up tall—her eyes closed. "Oh God, no . . ."

My sadness was already turning to anger—*no*—rage. *Who the fuck would do this?* I cleared my throat, "Tell me everything you know about her death."

Gently, Doc Viv reached over the body and turned Gunny's left arm to better expose her mutilated forearm. "As you can see, little care was taken excising her T-Bead device."

My stomach twisted at seeing the bloodied and torn flesh there. The exposed muscle, tendons, and ligatures within the gaping cavity.

"Perhaps it was removed to forestall identification. I don't know," the doctor said.

"And how you think she was murdered?" I asked.

Doc Viv used a gloved hand to move her hair away from the back of her neck. "See here?" she said pointing to a small blackened scorch mark. This was caused by a high voltage prod of some kind. I suspect this is what initially knocked her unconscious." The Doc motioned for the cutter to turn over the body. With indifferent functionality, Gunny Mattis was flipped over onto her back. I was struck, all over again, by her youth. The indignancy of her nakedness. Only now did I realize my fists were clenched—my knuckles going white as inner rage roiled up inside me.

Her eyes were open, her stare fixed and vacant. I brought my attention lower—between her small breasts, where her heart, undoubtedly lay beneath. "A knife wound?" I asked.

"Standard issue Ka-Bar . . . U.S. Navy combat knife," she said. Things are all over the ship."

"But the weapon wasn't found with the body?" I asked.

She shook her head. "She was murdered. Obviously. I estimate within the last few hours." She took the sheet from the cutter, and covered the body, then giving it a few pats. "Poor thing . . . so young. What a waste." Doc Viv looked up to me. "I'll tell Alistair about his daughter—"

"No, I'll do it. I knew her . . . I feel . . . a kind of connection to her."

"All right, Galvin. But look, you now being the skipper . . . our junior sleuthing, this needs to officially be turned over to Ship's Security."

"Yeah, well that's Alistair's department. And he'll undoubtedly want to take over the investigation, but he can't be involved. Navy protocol demands he step away from this. He'll need to mourn the loss of his daughter. Also, Ship's Security was hit hard with losses . . . the breach on Deck 13 took out everyone who was on duty."

"He won't give two shits about protocol . . . would you?"

"No, of course not. Just the same, he can't be involved. Not if we want any chance of making a conviction later when we catch the son of bitch who's murdering our fellow crewmembers." I looked at Doc Viv. "I'll make time. This is personal. And if the rest of the crew, who's already on edge, finds out there's a crazed murderer onboard . . . well, we'll have even bigger problems to deal with." I looked over to the ChronoBot, who had remained still and quiet throughout the discussion. "LuMan . . . we need your help. We need to find and apprehend this young woman's killer. I believe you have advanced sensors . . . an AI that is superior to that of MATHR, that you have enhanced deductive reasoning. Am I correct?"

"You are correct, Captain. I will assist you and the doctor in any way I can. With your permission, I will initiate a bioscan of the remains. Then, chemical and elemental analyses will provide more information. We must soon return to the scene of the murder."

I should have thought of that, myself.

"It's been sealed. No one's been allowed into that part of the ship where she was found," Viv said. "Oh, and we'll need to bring Stefan up to speed on this latest murder," she added, looking at the ChronoBot. "I'm sure Stefan, being the Science Officer, will make good use of whatever scans your robot provides."

My robot? I turned to leave, then turned back. "Hey, did Zan . . . um, suffer?"

"No, she was unconscious prior to being stabbed, killed."

That was at least something.

"And Galvin? I'm sorry, I'm sure she was a special young woman."

I left the Morgue, needing to get out of there. Heading back towards HealthBay, passing several medical attendants, it struck me that any one of them could be the killer. Hell, I may personally, unwittingly, even know the killer . . .

chapter 13

E ven with the capability to generate jump wormholes large
enough to transport spacecraft—travel between interplanetary spaceports usually required a good amount of standard
FTL space travel as well. Generating jump wormholes produced
high amounts of radiation and disrupted local quantum space
for weeks and sometimes months of time. For many areas of
the cosmos, wormhole generation was disallowed, mainly due
to overuse. And since jump wormholes were generated along
straight-line vectors, multiple jumps were typically necessary
in order to get from one location or another. So, space travel
was typically a long, arduous, monotonous, duty. And as much
as I complain about the *USS Hamilton*, the old dreadnaught
did have its positive off-duty virtues. A few of such virtues
included several dedicated open-space areas. Areas only a ship
this large could accommodate. These included the StarDome,
a diamond glass observatory situated mid-ship along the top
crest of the vessel. Also, there was Cherry Park, a one-hundred
meter-wide by two-hundred-meter-long cherry tree-lined

promenade amidst rolling grasslands—here, a meandering stream ran down its center. Overhead, a projected azure sky and heat-emitting yellow Sun slowly trekked across the celestial sphere each day from east to west. Setting late every afternoon, the Sun descended beneath a distant horizon into brilliant hues of crimsons blended with oranges and purples. Every day a different, unique, and breathtaking, virtual sunset. On any given day or night, you'd typically find off-duty crewmembers lounging here—often couples lying on blankets—nearby, open coolers stocked with beer or maybe wine. And for the ship's senior officers above the rank of lieutenant, such as Department Chiefs, the XO, and of course the Captain, there was the Sanctuary—two full acres of solitude. Here, there were five individual rustic log cabins situated within densely wooded patches. The *Hamilton's* original design architects had spared little expense and imagination creating ultra-real natural environments within a relatively confined space. Trees that looked to be five times the height they actually were. Air that smelled of pine and the ground a little dank and earthy. Here within the Sanctuary, far off distant vistas, spotted between the countless stout trees, seemed so very real, so very Earthlike.

I had sent word for Chief of Security Alistair Mattis to meet me. Since the battle with the Grish, all of the ship's open space areas were closed and off-limits to the crew. At present, I was walking along within the Promenade, the smell of cherry blossoms filled the air. To my right, the burbling creek eased some of the tension from my shoulders. Exhausted, I was operating on virtually no sleep for the past twenty-four hours—but

I couldn't put off what I had to do next. Up ahead, an arched Japanese foot Bridge spanned the flowing water. The Chief, busy like the rest of us, strode purposefully across the bridge— his expression one of mild irritation and maybe nervousness. He spotted me and offered up a half-hearted wave.

"As much as I like you, Captain . . . I'd prefer romantic walks in the park with my wife back home. What's this all about?"

I offered him back a brief compliant smile, but he could tell this was anything but a casual encounter. He fell into step next to me and we walked in silence for a while. I said, "Alistair, I have truly terrible news for you." I stopped and placed a hand on his shoulder. Our eyes locked. Unease and apprehension stared back at me. He said, "Oh no . . . not Zan . . . not my Zanny. Please, don't say it . . ." But he saw it on my face—that his worst fear was true. As his eyes filled with tears and his face distorted in agony, I pulled him close into a tight embrace. He sobbed for a long while—standing there by the meandering creek, beneath the pink and white cherry blossoms. In time, he pulled away wiping tears and snot onto the sleeve of his uniform. "Tell me how. Was it an accident . . . something resulting from the battle? Fucking old ship . . . it's a God-damn death trap!"

"No. She was murdered, Alistair."

"Murdered? I don't understand." Now anger was creeping into his anguish.

"We suspect it's the same person who killed Milo Wentworth . . . but we don't know anything definitive. We don't know why Zan was targeted. I'm so sorry," I said, knowing full well my words sounded hollow.

"Where is she . . . I need to see her body."

I shook my head, "She's with the Doc."

"Was she electrocuted . . . burned to a crisp like Wentworth?" He said, his voice cracking with emotion.

I stared at him, "Alistair, don't put yourself through—"

"Tell me! How the hell was she killed?!"

"Let me first tell you that she didn't suffer."

"Oh, is that supposed to make me feel better? Make everything all right? That there's an amiable killer onboard this ship?"

"No, of course not."

"What the hell are you doing to find this . . . this killer?" he asked, his voice getting louder.

"We've started an investigation, as you know."

"The three of you, Doc, Derrota, and you? This isn't fucking Nancy Drew time . . . there needs to be real, actual, investigators!"

I tried not to react. I knew he was dying inside. "Sure, we did have actual investigators. But you know better than anyone, they worked for you. But they're among the dead vented out on Deck 13. The ChronoBot is helping . . . it's collecting clues . . . making scans—"

"So, you're already pawning the investigation off on an alien robot we know nothing about? Tell me, how do you know it wasn't this ChronoBot who'd killed Wentworth and my Zanny?"

"That's highly unlikely."

The security chief closed his eyes and steadied himself for a moment. "I want to be a part of the investigation. And I don't want to hear any bullshit about me being too close to this." He looked at me with defiance in his eyes.

"Give yourself a few days. Maybe stay in a Sanctuary cabin. You need to allow yourself time to grieve, Alistair. But, yes, I knew you'd want to be involved and I'm fine with that."

We turned and headed back along the path the way we'd come. Up ahead on the little footbridge, Lieutenant Gail Pristy was waiting for us. Seeing us, she hurried to Alistair, and once more he broke down within the arms of a fellow crewmember.

I said to her, "Take him to a Sanctuary cabin . . . stay with him."

She nodded while saying soothing words and gently patting Alistair's broad back. I left them there wishing I could do more. Off in the distance, I saw a reflective glint of light. LuMan was there, waiting for me in the trees. I thought of Alistair's question, *how do you know it wasn't this ChronoBot who'd killed Wentworth and my Zanny?*

I didn't know. I didn't know much of anything right now and that was not a good place to be as the acting captain of this ship.

BY THE TIME I MADE IT TO MY QUARTERS, I WAS PRACTI-cally sleepwalking. The human body can withstand a lot of punishment, but two-and-a-half days without so much as a catnap had taken its toll. I contacted Lieutenant Pristy and ordered her to get some sleep and to make sure the rest of the daytime Bridge crew indeed had been relieved—also getting some well-needed bunk time. Typically, there were four, sometimes five, shifts onboard a warship such as the *Hamilton*—but with the death toll such as it was, most crewmembers were working double and triple shifts. Fortunately, not much happened during a night watch and the Bridge was no exception.

I waved the door to my quarters open, stepped in, and heard it swoosh closed behind me. Somewhere out in the passageway, I suspected was my lurking shadow, LuMan. At the moment, I didn't care. If the mechanical man wanted to play sentry and guard my door, that was his prerogative. I kicked off my boots and literally fell into my bunk. My TAC-Band was vibrating—had been, repeatedly, for the last hour or so. If there was an emergency that I was unaware of, Lieutenant Pristy would have informed me of such. Whoever needed to reach me would just have to wait until morning. I fell into a deep, albeit, restless, sleep.

I awoke sometime in the night, having to pee. Groggy, I swung my legs over the side of the bed and sat there a moment in the total darkness. That's when I realized I wasn't alone. Had the killer quietly entered my quarters? Was he here, somewhere close, and ready to strike with his electrical prod? Then realization hit me. I rubbed my forehead and stood up, "LuMan . . . what the hell are you doing in my quarters?"

"Staying close ensures your optimum safety, Captain Quintos."

I could almost make out the looming robot's silhouette

some ten feet away from me. "Beyond the whole creepiness of you watching me sleep, I insist on my privacy. You will not enter my quarters again without my direct permission. Is that clear?"

After a long silence, LuMan said, "There is a murderer onboard this vessel."

I said, "The very best way for you to protect me, and everyone else, onboard will be getting MATHR operational, whereupon she can tell a crewmember when someone has entered into their quarters without permission, such as you've done."

LuMan didn't answer.

"Why don't you make yourself useful. Get on over to the Bridge. Compile a full damage report for SWM. I'm not sure what's still operational and what isn't."

By the time I returned from the head, I was fairly sure LuMan was gone.

I WAS BACK, SEATED WITHIN THE CAPTAIN'S MOUNT BY 0600. LuMan had been there when I arrived, he was holding up one end of the fallen girder, while six SWM guys, including Lasalle, were straining to hold up the other. Several metal cables had been secured around it from above. I heard a motorized winch engage and saw the slack in the cables go taut. Slowly, the girder rose higher and higher, and soon, more SWM crewmembers from above were struggling to position the girder back into place. Sounds of mechanical whining wrenches filled the Bridge.

Lieutenant Pristy placed a mug of coffee on my chair's armrest, "Morning, Captain." She said.

"Thank you, Lieutenant, but you know ... I am perfectly capable of getting my own coffee. I don't know what was expected of you with Captain Tannock, but I'm used to fending for myself in that regard."

She smiled, "I was never expected, nor did I offer, to get Captain Tannock's coffee, sir. You just looked as if you needed it. And I wanted to tell you ... thank you."

"Thank you for what?" I asked.

She looked around to make sure no one was listening. She lowered her voice, "How you handle the delicate situation with Chief Mattis ... about his daughter's murder. You made an impossibly difficult notification ... as gentle and private as would be possible. Allowing him time within a Sanctuary cabin ... well, that was perfect."

I saw the concern on her face. It was no secret Gail Pristy was an emotional one—she cared—this Bridge crew was like family to her. This young woman was the central cog in the machine that kept everything going around here. She was irreplaceable to me and I was sure, the same to a good many others. I thought of the maniac out there, somewhere on the ship, killing the crew. I then pictured that once vivacious fireball, Gunny Zan Mattis. Then flashed upon her blue-tinged corpse lying upon the metal autopsy table—her lifeless unfocussed eyes. That was not going to happen to Gail or anyone else I cared about.

I said, "Gail ... it's you that I, that all of us, need to thank. You're doing an exceptional job."

Her face went pink, and she nervously smiled not knowing what to say.

"I want you to be careful ... be mindful of your situation moving about the ship alone."

She nodded, but now looked concerned. "Do you think ... I'm ... like in any specific danger?"

I shouldn't have said anything at all, and I now inwardly chided myself for scaring her. "No, no more than anyone else. I'm telling everyone to have heightened situational awareness when moving about the ship."

Looking mindful, she nodded. She headed off toward the tactical station and sat down.

I looked to my left and saw that LuMan was standing there. With a furrowed brow, I said, "I'm going to tie a bell on you."

He stared back at me blank-faced.

I said, "Looks like you got that girder back in place."

"You gave me orders. To compile a full damage report. I did so." He handed me a diamond glass tablet. I saw bulleted text points and numerous images glowing brightly from the quasi-translucent panel. I quickly scanned the information.

"I then issued a high-priority work order for SWM."

"I didn't ask you to issue a high-priority work order. Right now, Engineering and Propulsion require the highest priority for any new ship repairs. Without the ability to initialize a jump wormhole, or to maintain FTL speeds, we're easy prey . . . at the mercy of any number of enemy forces here within the sector."

LuMan said nothing.

I was grouchy and regretted taking it out on the mechanical man. "Why don't we tackle MATHR . . . maybe you can assist with getting her operational again." I looked to my left and saw Stefan Derrota there deep within the CIC. "Come with me.

We entered the CIC area whereby the Science Officer cut short a conversation he was having with another crewmember.

"Yes, Captain."

I said, "We need to get MATHR fully operational."

"We're working on it." He gestured to the adjacent, some-what smaller, compartment commonly referred to as MATHR's Den—a glorified server room. I could see there were at least three technicians in there now milling about with an assortment of diagnostics tools.

Derrota said, "Unfortunately, it'll take some time. We lost the specific people most capable of making the necessary repairs."

"How about we have LuMan here take a look?" I knew, as the acting captain, I had every right to order LuMan to jump right into the fray. But MATHR's Den was the Science Officers domain and stepping on his toes here would only cause more issues with Derrota later.

Derrota gave the robot a quick once over. "No offense, Captain, but do we really want to have alien tech messing around with the *Hamilton's* AI?"

"That's a fair question," I said. "But let me ask you this . . .

If the Grish come back with even a small contingent of warships ... what are the odds we could fend them off in our current state? MATHR manages most of the weapons systems, ship's shields, jump wormhole calculations, hell, there are few systems MATHR doesn't interface with either directly or indirectly."

"So, you're saying we're fucked either way," the Science Officer said with a wry smile.

"And we still need to review security feeds from throughout the ship. Can we do that with MATHR in her current state?" I asked.

Derrota shook his head while giving LuMan another sideways glance. "Alright, sure ... we'll have the ChronoBot take a look. But I would suggest he be supervised at all times."

"Agreed," I said. "Shall we?"

We move toward MATHR's Den and I felt heat emanating out from the compartment. Here, in the year 2170, advanced computer AI's are a synthesized melding of electronic circuitry as well as plug-in biological elements. Memory, it turns out, is best stored within chromosomal DNA arrays—where trillions of organic synapse firing strands interface directly to various mechanized system's components. Wet-matter fused with dry-matter—whereby ship's AI specialists must be both roll-up-the-sleeves machine techs as well as holistic, biotic, scientists.

I watched as Derrota spoke with the three techs. Each shot unfriendly glances toward LuMan. One of the men crossed his arms over his chest, clearly not pleased. The three took a step back and let us pass. Derrota guided us over to one of the five-foot-wide by seven-foot-tall AI access server cabinets. He motioned with one hand and two black-glass panels separated, exposing the AI's inner workings. Innumerable tiny lights glimmered on and off. Colorful hardwired cabling could be seen intertwined within a glistening wet red-meat-like substance adhered to a metallic substrate behind. The smell was somewhat sweet and took some getting used to. It was times like this I was forced to consider that MATHR was, at least at some level, alive.

Leaning over, hands on his knees, Derrota peered in at the ultra-complex looking workings of the ship's brain. I watched his face—his intense expression. I wasn't sure, but perhaps, earlier in his career, Derrota would have been better capable of making the necessary kinds of repairs this AI currently required. Perhaps, over time, along with his rise to the level of Science Officer, he'd spent more time administrating his team than actually doing any of the real hands-on work.

He said, "There are seventy other cabinets just like this one in here. To the untrained eye, they pretty much all look identical." He glanced back to LuMan, "So, tell me . . . robot, what am I looking at here? What aspect of the AI, specifically, does this block of organic bio-mechanics control?"

"You are looking at the Environmental Systems Control . . . this aspect of MATHR is currently functioning at optimal levels." LuMan turned, strode down the narrow corridor between the other identical server cabinets, and waved a mechanical hand. The black glass panels separated. "MATHR's cognitive issues arise, primarily, from this subsystem here."

Derrota stood tall, let out a breath, motioned to close the panels before him, and together we moved over to where the ChronoBot now stood. The Science Officer shook his head, "No way... why would the—" He stopped mid-sentence. I'd noticed it too. The smell was *off* here. Less sweet. Foul—*tainted*.

I asked, "What is this sub-system here? What aspect of the AI is this?"

About to answer, Derrota was interrupted by LuMan's electronically synthesized voice. "This is the Cordon Simplex Sub-system."

Derrota said, "Think of it like the thalamus area in a human brain. In humans, it relays sensory impulses from receptors in various parts of the body to the cerebral cortex. With MATHR, millions of ship-wide sensors are fed here and assessed for redirection to other neural subsystems. A kind of bio-junction."

LuMan pointed to an area low, about at knee-level, which was discolored—the bio-substance there no longer dark red, now more a rusty brown color. I said, "That area's been kind of cooked, eh?"

Derrota nodded, "Yeah... would never have thought to check the Cordon Simplex. Thinking about it now, though, it makes sense. This being damaged, MATHR would be getting inundated with massive amounts of unfiltered input."

By now, the three techs had joined us and were huddled together looking into the open cabinet. One of them said, "That's a week... maybe two week's grow."

I looked to Derrota questioningly.

He said, "We can grow many of our AI replacement parts here onboard. It's organic," he said with a shrug.

I pursed my lips, "Grow where . . . not up in LabTech, I hope?"

Derrota scowled. "Shit, that's exactly where we grow our replacements."

The same tech said, "We do have genetic-neutral patch sections similar to this in Cold Stores. So, we wouldn't have to start from scratch. Could shave a few days off the process."

Derrota further explained, "Each sub-system is grown to a specific genetic design formula. But it would still take a good bit of time, perhaps a week or more."

I said, "So, we're talking about continuing on without having a fully operational AI to control the *Hamilton*. There has to be a way to expedite things."

Derrota nodded, then looked up to the ChronoBot, "LuMan, are you capable of making the necessary alterations . . . do so any quicker?" He looked at me and then back to the robot, "I'm talking about the genetic code, manually altering the cellular machinery for the form, fit, and function of this subsystem. LuMan, here, would need to be able to read ribosomes . . . turn them into proteins. He'd need to work with the specific nucleotides and amino acids."

I said, "Ah . . . all this is way, way over my head. But I don't know if LuMan here has that kind of capability—"

LuMan interjected, "Be aware, my own internal AI brain is structurally organic, as well. Yes, I will bioengineer the replacement MATHR Cordon Simplex unit. This technology is rudimentary, far less sophisticated than that of my own."

I thought about that. Like MATHR, the robot was at least partially organic but had the bland disposition of a food replicator. Would it have been too much to ask for his alien *Sheentah* creators to have imparted some semblance of a personality?

LuMan continued, "I am equipped with an advanced genetic sequence viewer. Not to mention, my micron-sensor technology is beyond anything you have onboard. I will need a clean room environment to make the necessary alterations."

"So, if we get you this necessary, um, slab of meat from Cold Stores . . ." Derrota cringed at my choice of words. "Just how long would it take you to alter its genetic code. Make it usable specifically within this, um . . ."

"Cordon Simplex" Derrota, as well as the three techs, all said in unison.

"Yeah, Cordon Simplex? How long?" I asked again.

Without hesitation, LuMan said "Twenty-four minutes."

I could tell by Derrota's expression he had underestimated the ChronoBot.

I said, "Good. I'll leave you all here to work things out. Just contact me when you're ready to swap in the new . . . um, component."

I saw that Lieutenant Pristy was standing at the entrance, frantically waving me over to her. Approaching, I said, "What is it? What's happened now?"

chapter 14

Major Vivian "Viv" Leigh — Ship's Primary Physician

V iv watched as Lieutenant Gail Pristy emphatically motioned over to Gavin—who was somewhere farther inside the CIC and still out of her sightline. The two always seemed close. Viv contemplated their relationship, wondering if it was anything more than professional. Gail certainly was pretty, she thought, and she supposed more than a few men would be attracted to her wafer-thin form—her demure doe-like personality, which comes with being so young. What was Gail, all of twenty-two, twenty-three? Of course, senior officers conjoining with one's subordinates was against regulations on a Navy vessel, but it happened … hookups, trysts, whatever, the key was discretion—don't flaunt what goes on behind closed doors. Viv closed her eyes, regretting her own most recent actions—too much Tangarian Ale up on the StarDome

Lounge and an impetuous lack of discretion, not more than a week earlier. She glanced over to Lieutenant Wallace Ryder. They'd kept their distance from one another ever since—at her immediate realization that what had happened between them was a mistake. One she regretted. Especially since Wallace was Galvin's best friend here onboard the *Hamilton*. *Why should I care if Galvin learns of Wallace's and my brief hookup?* She knew why—she just didn't want to admit it to herself. She and Wallace had talked about it afterwards—she'd seen his disappointment as she implored him not to kiss and tell. She'd explained how caring for so many of the crew injured during the battle—a relationship was the last thing she could afford— not to mention a string of murder victims she couldn't talk about. Wallace had tried to look casual—smiled and shrugged it off as no big deal. The truth was, she didn't really know Wallace. Didn't know what he would do or say.

Galvin suddenly came into view within the CIC and she could hear him asking Gail, "What is it? What's happened now?"

That's when Galvin saw them all clustered together there. Viv stood within a group of about fifteen, those who Gail thought meant something special to Galvin. In addition to the surviving Bridge crew, there was Wallace Ryder, Chief of Engineering Craig Porter, Bay Chief Frank Mintz, Ensign Lucas Hughes, even Alistair Mattis had emerged from his self-imposed mourning to be here. Viv wondered why Gail had invited her too. It was no secret she and Galvin constantly squabbled. Or, maybe the young lieutenant saw something more beyond that?

Galvin, looking perplexed, cautiously made his way farther onto the bridge. "What is this? My birthday's not for a few months still, guys. Am I missing something here?" He looked from one smiling face to another, looking perplexed.

Both Gail and Stefan Derrota followed him in. Gail placed a hand on his upper arm, "Captain?" She held out a small black box in one hand.

Galvin looked at it, still looking confused. "Are you proposing to me, Lieutenant . . . you do know that would be highly improper," he said with a crooked grin.

Everyone laughed.

"Just open it," she said, her face flushing pink.

He took the box from her and did as told. Inside were two Captain's devices. Two reflective Silver Eagle collar pins.

Gail said, "It's official now, Captain Quintos . . . I've been instructed to convey to you, congratulations from High Command back on Earth . . . your official promotion to pay grade 06, with an officer's rank of Captain, has been approved. In Admiral Block's own words," Gail lowered her voice in an attempt to sound more like the admiral, "You are to wear these Eagles with pride starting today, and I expect you to behave with the decorum commensurate with such rank. I have high hopes for you, Galvin . . . Don't disappoint me."

Everyone applauded as Galvin studied the officer devices. Gail said, "The admiral would have joined us, at least virtually, but the 7th Fleet, of which he's commanding, is en route to some secret location."

Someone had produced a chilled bottle of champagne and small disposable cups. *Pop!*

Viv watched as Alistair wished Galvin congratulations, before quietly bowing out of the celebration and leaving the Bridge. Viv spoke to the others around her while keeping an eye on Galvin as he made his rounds between each of them. She watched as Galvin and Wallace shook hands and then Wallace leaning in and saying something into Galvin's ear. Viv wondered what was so private that Wallace would need to resort to whispering. She knew she was being paranoid—*God, I need to get a grip.* She stepped through the huddled bodies to interrupt Galvin, now talking to Ensign Hughes.

She said, "Hey ... I've got to get back to HealthBay, I just wanted to say congrats." She gestured to the still open box in Galvin's hand and grimaced. "You didn't notice, but they ran out of Eagles ... those, actually, are Silver Ducks ... I'm sure they're just as good."

Galvin looked at the box and saw they were, in fact, Silver Eagles. "Ha, you almost had me there, Doc."

She was surprised when he hugged her. He hadn't hugged anyone else, which made this even more strange and awkward. He stepped away looking embarrassed. She herself was surprised and a bit rattled. Not knowing what to say, she laughed, waved a hand, and turned to leave. She noticed Wallace Ryder was staring at her and not looking too pleased. *Shit.*

chapter 15

Captain Galvin Quintos

I watched as Doc Viv hurried from the Bridge. I had pulled her in for a hug without any thought. Only then, in the midst of it, did I realize what I was doing, but it was too late. I mentally chided myself—*clearly, I've made her uncomfortable! She couldn't get away from me fast enough.*

Somebody was talking to me.

"You listening to me, Galvin?" said the Chief of Engineering.

"Sorry . . . what was that, Craig?"

"Derrota says you may have MATHR up and running, or at least mostly up and running, soon? If that's true, I, too, should have some good news." I nodded, distracted, and looked for Derrota within the crowd. I turned to look back toward the CIC. He was gone. Undoubtedly, he'd want to supervise LuMan's work with the genetic coding. I said, "Yeah, let's cross our fingers ... we're trying something new."

Craig placed a hand on my shoulder to get my full attention. "Hey ... I'm telling you we've got FTL propulsion capabilities, at least partially, back online ... you should be doing backflips, Galvin."

I looked back to Craig, "Wait ... is that true? About propulsion?"

"Don't get too excited. But yes, the Alpha and Delta HyperDrives are slowly coming back online. HyperDrives Omega, and Beta, will take somewhat longer. We're being careful. It's a gradual ramping up process. So, yeah, FTL tests should be possible just as soon as MATHR is able to make the necessary flight calculations."

"And actual jumping? Are those HyperDrives capable of initializing jump wormholes?"

"Don't get greedy, Captain," he said with a smile. "We're making progress. I think they'll be operational. But that's not good enough. We'll need MATHR to help with further calibrations." He looked at me with more intensity. "Manufacturing jump wormholes is immensely complicated. Without MATHR's capabilities to run thousands, millions, of simulation jump scenarios beforehand would be suicide."

"That makes sense ..." I said, not knowing why he was giving me the third degree.

"Because it's not beyond the realm of possibilities that the *Hamilton* will soon be in another predicament where jumping away is our only option. And we're not nearly ready to try that yet."

I gave Craig as much of an assuring smile as I could conjure up. "I got it. Honest. Right now, I have two, monumental concerns . . . getting the ship's AI up and running and getting us adequate fuel so those HyperDrives of yours can, at the very least, get us moving at FTL." Actually, it was three concerns, I needed to find the sick fuck killing off my crewmembers, as well, but I kept that part to myself.

Having thanked my well-wishers, I ordered everyone back to their respective posts. Leaving Lieutenant Pristy to man the Bridge, I texted Derrota to his and LuMan's location. Apparently, they were up on high Deck 44, in an area of the ship I'd never been to. I found the two of them hard at work within a glassed-in clean room environment, not so different from the now destroyed LabTech area. Both were wearing pressure-sealed garments with fully oxygenated headgear. I was interrupted by a woman crewmember wearing something similar, "If you come with me, I'll help you to get properly outfitted, Captain."

Ten minutes later I was being guided through a series of decontamination zones and then an intermediary airlock. Stepping into the cleanroom, both Derrota and LuMan looked my way.

"Good . . . you're just in time," Derrota said, his voice sounding tinny and distorted coming through his helmet speakers.

On the pristine white worktable before them was a bright red section of organic material about two-feet wide by four-feet tall. It had the same colorful cables intertwining within the slab of meat that those housed within the various tall cabinets within MATHR's Den area.

I joined them at their side and looked down at the slab. "So, good progress then?"

Derrota's face, behind his helmet's faceplate, smiled enthusiastically. "If I hadn't seen it with my own eyes, I don't think I would have believed it possible. LuMan has been working with the specific nucleotides and amino acids . . . turning ribosomes into proteins, doing so on the fly! Recoding undefined DNA structures to the specific genetic design formula at astounding speeds."

Simplifying Derrota's scientific gobbledygook, I said, "So he's manipulating the genetics of this replacement Cordon Simplex."

"Yes, exactly!" Derrota said.

LuMan seemed to be grasping two silver chop-stick sized probes that moved around from one area of the organic material to another in a blur of fast motion. I then realized the probes were actually extensions of LuMan's own mechanical hands.

I took a moment to glance about the compartment. I wondered why I hadn't known about this section of the ship. What its purpose was since we'd already had something similar in the way of LabTech. "What is this place?" I said.

I noticed Derrota's near gleeful expression faltered some. "Well, it's a cleanroom environment. In some ways, it has even more stringent exposure ratings against contaminants than LabTech has . . . had."

"Okay, but that doesn't answer my question? What is this place, this cleanroom environment, used for?"

When Derrota failed to answer, LuMan answered instead.

"This area of the *Hamilton* was constructed fifty-two years ago, soon after alien microbial contamination had been detected onboard. It was necessary to prevent re-contamination."

"Alien microbial contamination," I repeated.

Derrota reluctantly said, "Yeah, biohazardous alien life was growing pretty much all over the ship. They started off microscopic but grew to the size of house plants. And these were smart house plants. Plants that could think and reason. Anyway, it was like a jungle had taken over the inside of the *Hamilton*. It took new methods derived from the Thine to contain the spread and eventually kill off the many thousands of these things. Once the contagion was properly dealt with, new protocols had to be followed, such as the implementation of redundant bio-barriers within the ship's air filtration system."

"This bio invasion took place on the *Hamilton* some five decades ago and this is the first I've heard of it?"

Derrota let out a breath that momentarily fogged the inside of his helmet's faceplate. "It's been kept a level 5 classified secret. If word had gotten out intelligent alien life once inhabited—"

"Hold on! Intelligent life!?" I said looking about the now seemingly highly confined space.

Derrota said, "At the time, the ship was unoccupied, for the most part arriving home, coming back from the Brigham

Flay quadrant . . . which I might add, is a section of space we no longer go anywhere close to."

"You said intelligent life. How do you know that?" I asked.

"There were four SWM guys doing maintenance onboard. All three were, um, infected by the spores."

It's like pulling teeth. "And . . . what? Their heads blew up, they grew new appendages out of their asses? They died?"

"Actually, no. All three are still alive," Derrota said, looking hesitant to get into this kind of classified information. Looking to have come to a decision he said, "As the ship's Science Officer, I'd been cleared to learn of this a few years back. And as Captain, I guess you too should know it, too. Apparently, they are being contained, within a certain high-security facility back on Earth."

"They must be pretty old, that having been some five decades ago, no?"

"Ah, well, in chronological terms, sure . . . but they haven't aged a day physiologically. But," he said holding up a finger to ward off any more questions from me, "As strange as that may be, perhaps more importantly, they are no longer the same crewmembers, the same people. They are *something* else. Something alien."

"What does that even mean? Something alien." I said.

"Just that . . . the crewmen they were, have been replaced by *other* alien consciousnesses."

"Good God, are they . . . dangerous?"

"No, not at all. They certainly wish to be released from their confined laboratory existence, but they understand. And they pose no danger of infecting those around them. The sprout-spores I mentioned are a separate aspect and are not a component of their host physiology. Any aspect of the initial sprout-spore aspect dried up and die after incubation."

My head was spinning. It was a lot to take in, but at least all that was in the past. *Or was it?* "So, I take it, this part of the ship was closed off for a reason? As some kind of safety measure, yes?"

"Totally unnecessary, but you know how Central Command can be."

Actually, I wasn't so sure. "At least we're safe inside these containment suits. If, by any infinitesimally small chance there were any of those . . . what did you call them?"

"Sprout-spores."

"That's right, sprout-spores. If any of those, say, had been hiding out here in this closed off part of the ship, we'd still be safe."

"Exactly," Derotta said with a comforting smile.

We both remained quiet for a few minutes while LuMan continued working. It seemed as though the ChronoBot was making good progress. But like a pesky gnat flying around within my head, something was becoming bothersome to me. Then I realized what it was. "Um, just saying . . . LuMan, here, isn't wearing a containment suit."

Derrota rolled his eyes, "Come on, Galvin, this amazing example of advanced technology doesn't require one."

I was a little taken aback at Derrota's total about-face on

LuMan, from being more than a little suspicious of him to now being his biggest advocate.

He continued, "In fact, LuMan here could exist quite easily in the extreme harsh temperatures within the vacuum of deep space."

"Yeah, I get that. But that's not what I'm talking about. LuMan's AI, is, at least in part, biomatter, right?"

That seemed to have earned a glance from LuMan in my direction. His chopstick probes suddenly became stationary.

Derrota said, "Well … LuMan is capable of running a myriad of self-diagnostic tests at any time. I'm sure he—"

LuMan raised one of his mechanical hands. "The captain is correct. I am initiating multiple analyses, now. A test that will search out any intrusive organisms that may have overted my standard operating detection protocols." LuMan then looked to Derrota, to me, and then down at the slab of meat on the table. "Both this Cordon Simplex biomatter as well as I, have, in fact, been compromised." The ChronoBot then did something totally unexpected, he laughed. "Oh my, this is quite strange. Ha … quite strange. What a chowderhead I've been."

Derrota and I looked from LuMan then back to each other. Not only had the robot laughed, which robots don't typically do, but gone was the electronically synthesized voice—he was now speaking with a fairly heavy Boston accent.

DERROTA, LUMAN, AND I QUICKLY MOVED OFF TO another area still within the cleanroom environment and were now seated within a long-abandoned office area. There was absolutely nothing remotely similar to how LuMan acted or spoke prior, to how he was acting and speaking now.

I said, "So, you have no memory of, um, what happened to you?"

"No! Look, I was swapping out a stack of environ-filters . . ." the robot looked around, "Yeah, right here on Deck 40." He pointed to a ventilation grate high up on the ceiling. "Up there." Seeing his own mechanical hand and the still protruding chopstick probe made him hesitate. I could tell he was having a hard time with all that was happening to him. All the indicators on his mechanical face were sporadically flashing on and off.

"Just try to relax. Um, what was your name? Back when—"

"Hey, buddy! It wasn't back when. It was like ten minutes ago . . . I woke up like this just now. A fucking tin man. I'm not human . . . I don't know what I am!" he looked down at himself. "Oh god . . . I no longer have a fucking pecker!"

About to tell him to take a few deep breaths, I caught myself. This was beyond bizarre, and I was having a hard time believing any of this could be real. How could LuMan, an advanced robot, now be acting human and talking like just any *guy* on the streets of Boston. It was almost comical.

"John Hardy . . . but everyone just calls me Hardy."

"Okay, Hardy . . . first of all, I'm truly sorry this has happened to you. There's been lots of advancements since you were—"

"Wait, what year is this?"

I was reluctant to tell him. Well, the year is 2170, Hardy."

"No. Not possible."

Derrota nodded, "Sorry. It's true."

"I've been what ... hanging out with mites and dust bunnies for like fifty-two frickin' years? I was forty-eight. I'm what, ninety years old now?" Hardy said looking at us.

My TAC-Band had been vibrating to the point of distraction, but I had purposely been ignoring it to concentrate on LuMan. Now Derrota's was going off too. We both glanced at our forearms.

"Shit, I need to get to the Bridge ... sensors have picked up an approaching ship."

Oddly, LuMan nodded, "Yeah ... it's a small gunship. I detect eighteen life signs onboard."

We looked at Hardy, *or was it LuMan,* for several long beats.

"Honestly, I have no flippin' idea how I know that. I guess, I still can access all my little robot parts?"

"Seems like it," I said. "Huh, interesting." I gestured toward the cleanroom. "So, the Cordon Simplex unit on the table in there. Is it still ..."?

"Viable?" Derrota said finishing my sentence for me.

"Hardy said, "Yeah, it's all ready to go, boys."

"What about any further alien contamination?"

Derrota said. "We'll still have to sanitize everything in this part of the ship, including that Cordon Simplex. Zap any remaining microbes hanging around."

✦ ✦ ✦

Prior to leaving for the bridge, I rattled off new marching orders for Derrota.

"Step one, immediately restrict any crewmember from entering Deck 40 and close off all the deck vac-gates up here. After that, fully extricate any of the remaining alien microbes in the area."

Derrota was looking more than a little overwhelmed. "Anything else?"

"Yeah, get that replacement Cordon Simplex Sub-system over to the CIC just as soon as you're sure it's safe. Can you do all that? I have to get to the Bridge."

"Of course, I've got this," he said, unconvincingly.

"Good." I gave LuMan one last glance and hurried away.

chapter 16

I reached the Bridge in time to see multiple zoomed-in video feeds up on the halo-display, all depicting a small alien vessel. I also saw that Chief of Security Alistair Mattis was seated at the Captain's Mount. Stepping to his right, I stood there a moment, "How you doing, Alistair?"

He let out a long breath and shrugged, "Awful. But sitting around that cabin all alone with my thoughts and memories of Zan was even worse." He stood and gestured for me to take his place.

After I took the seat, Alistair said, "My Sit-Report... we've been making slow but steady progress en route to that fueling station here in Pleidian territory..."

I said, "Uh huh, Ironhold Station."

"Well, at our still much-curtailed speed, we're still a half-day out from our destination. We suspect this is a sentry ship, maybe one of a number of them keeping guard around the station."

"Doesn't look like much," I said taking in what looked

to be a small ancient, rickety-looking, spacecraft. Its hull was streaked with rust and there were pock-marked dents and what looked like multiple welded on patch panels.

"Don't let the looks fool you, Captain. That's a mean little gunship. Two dorsal rigged railgun turrets, plasma cannons on port and starboard sides, externally mounted smart missiles . . . probably fusion-tipped. All I'm saying, in our condition . . . maybe best we do not engage. Especially if there are other similarly outfitted vessels in the vicinity."

"*Hamilton's* long-range sensors pick up anything?"

"MATHR seemed to have detected several nearby vessels, then there was nothing on sensors. Either our AI's shit the bed . . . again, or those ships have serious cloaking capabilities."

"Distance to that ship?" I asked.

Lieutenant Pristy said, "Thirty-thousand kilometers," Captain.

"It sees us?"

She said, "Oh yeah, without a doubt. And she's headed right for us, Sir."

I said, "Helm, go ahead and change course thirty-five degrees starboard. Instruct the Colorado and Union to do the same."

"Aye Captain," Grimes said from the helm station.

"Let's see what that sentry ship does now. Perhaps we can buy some time while we deal with our MATHR issues."

I got up and gestured toward the Captain's ready room. "How about we talk in private, Alistair?"

On the opposite side of the Bridge from the CIC was a

closed door that led into the ready room. I waved it open as we approached, and together, we went inside. I gestured with a palm up motion toward the door, for it to remain open so I could keep a line of sight into the Bridge.

Glancing around, I found the area had been purged of Captain Tannock's personal items. Along the far bulkhead wall was a large diamond-glass window providing an expansive and dramatic view out to the star-filled cosmos beyond. The well-appointed compartment was comprised of a large wood desk, void of anything on top of it except a floating halo-display monitor. The accompanying chair, of course, was empty, but I pictured Captain Tannock sitting there just the same. Off to the left, there was a seating area that consisted of a wine-colored leather couch and two matching armchairs. Mahogany bookshelves lined the wall opposite the window, and a plush Persian rug added to the ready room's warm and inviting ambiance.

"Nice digs, Galvin," Alistair said, glancing around.

And that they were—but this certainly didn't feel like they were *my* digs. Perhaps that would come in time. I proceeded to bring our Chief of Security up to speed on the course of other events that had transpired since his daughter's death. Although he was keenly interested in what we had been doing about the murders—more specifically, our lack of catching the murderer—he also seemed concerned that LuMan, already an alien presence here onboard the *Hamilton*, had been infected with some kind of alien microbe. We spoke for a long time, with Alistair reminiscing about Zan being a rambunctious child, the quintessential tomboy, albeit a daddy's girl, too. That she had followed in her father's footsteps—never wanting anything more than to join a crew on a naval warship. When two years prior, her orders had her placed upon the same vessel, the *Hamilton*, as her father, they'd both been ecstatic.

It took another two hours for Derrota, along with LuMan, to arrive on the Bridge, more accurately, into the CIC. As it turns out, advancements in microbial detection over the last fifty years had made the detection process a fairly simple one. Whatever alien microbes had been lingering around there in that part of the ship for the last five decades were easily found. LuMan/Hardy himself with his extended chopsticks had homed in on those hiding sprouts in a matter of minutes, whereby they were destroyed.

Derrota, investigating how the whole *Hardy* anomaly thing could have possibly occurred, was able to determine that LuMan's microbial infection contained hybrid chromosomal DNA strands. I mentioned earlier that, some fifty years prior, three SWM crewmembers had been contaminated, each of their minds replaced by microbial alien consciousnesses. Thought to be long gone—destroyed in the process—now it seemed one of those discarded human consciousnesses, *Hardy's*, had apparently somehow taken up residence within a long-lingering sprout-spore DNA, which had migrated into LuMan's Bio-mass AI.

My TAC-Band vibrated with a new message. Derrota and LuMan had arrived and were entering the CIC.

Both Alistair and I hurried from the captain's ready room,

back through the Bridge, and into the CIC and then into MATHR's Den area, catching up to Derrota and the robot. They moved directly to the cabinet with MATHR's defective AI bio-component. Derrota looked even more rumpled than usual, with his hair sticking up in odd places and the front of his uniform stained with something dark. LuMan was carrying a large enclosure I recognized as a CoolCrate, used for transporting temperature-sensitive items, such as one replacement Cordon Simplex Sub-system.

Before Derrota could wave open the cabinet's black glass panels, Alistair yelled out from behind me, "Hold on, there!"

"What is it?" Derrota said, looking annoyed. Then, seeing it was Alistair, said, "Oh, good to see you back at work, Alistair."

"Thank you, Stefan," Alistair said. "I'm sorry, but as the ship's Security Officer, and knowing what I know now, I can't allow for that component to be swapped out."

Derrota's brows knitted together. "There's absolutely nothing wrong with this component. It's been completely cleansed of foreign . . . alien, contagion."

I noticed Derrota's Indian accent had become even more pronounced as he got upset or irritated. While I could understand my Chief of Security's reluctance to introduce a possibly infected component back into our ship's AI, our Science Officer was uniquely aware of the implications if that had been the case. Derrota also knew just how dire a situation we were in, whereby Alistair had spent the last day and a half cloistered within a Sanctuary cabin. I looked to LuMan, hoping he'd have valuable input on the matter.

"LuMan? Your thoughts?"

The big robot stood there holding the large oblong CoolCrate in one of his mechanical hands. He teetered his teardrop-shaped head left and right several times in an attempted human kind of mannerism. "Christ, Captain . . . please, call me Hardy. I'm not this LuMan you keep referring to." His Boston accent had perked the ears up of Alistair who, up until now, had not had the pleasure of hearing it.

Hardy said, "I'd say, from what I've heard . . . you're pretty much screwed either way, right? The AI is almost worthless in its current condition. But, if the LuMan part of me didn't do a perfect job recoding the DNA aspects, well . . ." The robot attempted to shrug, failing miserably.

The three of them were now looking at me—clearly the decision was to be mine. "Go ahead and install the new component. But test the crap out of it, make sure it is fully operational before coming back online."

Derrota smiled, "Good decision, Cap. Just so you know, many of MATHR's functionalities will be offline while we make the swap."

"How long will that take?" I asked.

"Shouldn't be longer than a few minutes . . . maybe ten or fifteen at the most."

"Okay, get started."

I turned to see Lieutenant Pristy coming in from the CIC, "Captain . . . that gunship, it's closing in on us."

Before I could head back to the bridge, Alistair grabbed my arm, "Wait, Galvin . . . Captain, you sure you want to do this?

Installing a potentially infected sub-component into MATHR? Not to mention, involving an alien robot that has clearly been compromised? We're breaking so many security protocols I wouldn't know how to explain any of this if things go tits up."

"Right now, it's more about surviving the next few hours. Best you get to your station on the Bridge; I have a feeling you'll be needed there soon."

I came around the corner into the Bridge to see the dirty face of a grungy-looking humanoid looking back at me up on the halo-display. Everything about his appearance screamed storybook pirate—as if a character from a book or movie had transitioned into real life. Although he didn't have an actual eye patch, he did have a wicked-looking scar that sliced down from his forehead, dissected his drooping left eyelid, and continued on down onto his cheek. I noticed his long, greasy-looking black hair was loosely tied into a ponytail, which only enhanced the whole pirate ensemble. *So, this is one of those Pylor fellas.*

Now, him seeing me in turn, a rogue smile exposed two rows of crooked and discolored teeth.

I was annoyed that someone on the Bridge had opened the channel without my permission.

Looking frazzled, Lieutenant Pristy said, "Not sure how, but they were able to hack in ... open our end of the comms channel ... sorry, sir. This is Captain Rye of the *Blight*—"

"You will stand down and prepare to be boarded, Captain Quintos," the Pylor captain said with a smirk that I wanted to backhand off his grimy face. "And before you start making idle threats, be aware of the fact, you no longer have control of your on-board weapon's systems. Your smart missiles are offline, your Phazon Pulsar cannons, are offline, Rail Gun batteries, are offline . . . need I go on?"

"Three, no four . . . no five, more gunships have just uncloaked in close proximity, Captain," Lieutenant Pristy said, from her tactical station.

Captain Rye continued, "Now, I know what you are thinking, our little ships don't look like much. Rattletrap clunkers, right? But looks can be deceiving, I promise you that. There again, you would have already known that if your Main Artificial THought Resource—I believe you refer to it as MATHR—perhaps if MATHR was functioning properly, things would be different right now, but, alas . . . that is not the case. In other words, I own you, Captain. I own that battered Earth dreadnaught along with what little crew survived your battle with the Grish."

I smiled as if I didn't have a care in the world. That this was all little more than a pesky nuisance. "Give us a minute to discuss our . . . options."

There was laughter from Captain Rye, as well from his unseen Bridge crew behind him. "You have no options here Quintos. Prepare to be boarded."

Through gritted teeth and under my breath, I said, "Somebody get this fucking comms channel closed!"

Three seconds, later the feed on the halo-display went black.

I turned to see Alistair, leaning over the comms station.

He looked at me, wearing a triumphant smile. "I hacked their hack, but it's a stopgap measure."

I nodded and tried to think. "How much of what he said was true ... about our weapon's systems being offline?"

Lieutenant Pristy looked over to Alistair for confirmation, then said, "All of it. These Pylors aren't just pirates, sir ... they're cyber-pirates as well. Although, MATHR in her current state would have offered little resistance to their incursion."

"Captain! We're being hailed." Pristy said.

"Our Pylor friends will just have to wait—"

"No sir, it's Lieutenant Brian Giar of the *USS Colorado*."

The *Colorado* was our lone destroyer which had sustained two breached decks and other significant damage. "Put Lieutenant Giar through," I said.

The feed came alive on the halo-display, whereby we could see the young officer standing upon his Bridge, looking more than a little distressed. He, along with those I could see behind him, were rhythmically swaying back and forth due to the ship's RTM malfunction. Lieutenant Giar's plastered down hair was wet with perspiration and dark sweat circles had formed beneath his armpits.

"Captain! Enemy vessels have initiated a target-lock on the *Colorado* ... while, somehow, our shields have been hijacked ... they're down, they're all down! We're defenseless, little more than sitting ducks out here, sir."

"Stay calm, Lieutenant. We've been in contact with the, um, enemy. They want the *Hamilton*. That's their prize here. They're using your vulnerability to make their point."

"Well, I think they've made it, sir. What are we to do? Our weapon's systems are operational, but who knows for how long?"

Lieutenant Pristy interjected, "We're getting similar reports coming in from the *Union*, sir."

"Lieutenant Pristy, we need a better field of view . . . deploy video/sensor array package."

"Drones being deployed now, sir."

All eyes were now on me—like so many laser beams burning holes into my flesh. *Fuck!* I was in way over my head and all too soon, everyone would become aware of that.

"Captain? Orders?" Grimes said from the weapon's station.

From the tactical station, Lieutenant Pristy yelled out, "Tracking . . . Smart Missiles have been fired, sir! They're inbound to the Colorado."

chapter 17

I sent a desperate glance toward the CIC in hopes of seeing Derrota and or the robot emerging with good news about their MATHR repairs.

"Both the *Colorado* and the *Union* reporting their weapons have gone offline," Grimes announced.

"Orders, sir" came the question again, this time from Lieutenant Pristy.

The halo-display now showed multiple video feeds depicting the *Hamilton*, the *Union,* and the *Colorado*, as well as the now eight Pylor gunships. Bright blued tongues of thruster fire revealed where the inbound smart missiles had progressed along their trajectory toward the *Colorado*.

"Can we intercept those missiles using Phazon Pulsars?" I asked.

"Possibly. Better if we had MATHR . . ." Grimes said rapidly tapping at his console. "Four missiles . . . it'll be close. Manually implementing firing barrage now."

The halo-display suddenly lit up with multiple pulsing

streaks of Phazon Pulsar fire. Simultaneously, there were three deep-space explosions.

"Three enemy missiles atomized." Lieutenant Pristy said but her words were cut off by a much larger explosion up on the halo-display. The lone remaining smart missile had found its target—flames had momentarily engulfed the aft end of the *Colorado*. Now atmosphere and debris were venting out into space.

I was beyond angry and I had never wanted to kill someone like I did at that moment. "Fire everything we have at those enemy ships! Rail spikes . . . Phazon Pulsars!"

"*Hamilton's* weapon's systems have been taken offline . . . all of them, Captain," Grimes said sounding defeated.

Up on the halo-display, a new video feed emerged—it was Captain fucking Rye. Smiling and casually leaning against a vertical support strut, he was conversing with another of his Pylor crewmembers. Periodically they both shot glances toward their own display and their view into the *Hamilton's* bridge. Clearly, they were well accustomed to this scenario. I wondered how many other warships had fallen prey to these vile marauders.

Looking pleased with himself, Captain Rye was talking again, but this time to me. "Captain Quintos, please . . . let's dispense with any more of this drama. There need not be any further loss of life. I promise you, captain to captain, that the crews of your three vessels will not be accosted in any way. But those vessels are already mine. Your vessel is already mine. You must know that by now."

I stood and straightened my shoulders. I blinked my eyes and took in a deep breath. I conveyed the look of a proud but defeated human officer. "What guarantee do I have that my crews will be unharmed?"

"Uhh . . . none. But you can trust me . . . I promise. Honest!"

Genuine laughter came from the Pylors behind Rye.

I nodded and looked to be contemplating his ultimatum. Dragging out the seconds into minutes since I had tapped out a clandestine message on my TAC-Band to both Bay Chief Frank Mintz and Lieutenant Wallace Ryder. About now, over one-hundred Arrow Fighters would be emerging from both starboard and port-side bay ports—unseen and undetectable. For as the *Hamilton*, *Union*, and the critically damaged *Colorado* had not undergone the latest Thine technology upgrades, which will be a space-port process, all of the Arrows most certainly had.

"If I didn't know better, I'd say you were stalling, Captain Quintos." Rye smiled and shook his head in bemusement as a father would to a rambunctious child. "Perhaps another demonstration is in order. The *Colorado* is little more than scrap metal anyway. We would have made a hefty profit on it, but for demonstration purposes, I have no problem eviscerating that ship and all those still clinging to life onboard her."

Now, let me tell you that the beauty of the modern-day Arrow Class Space Fighter was her mighty battle capabilities in comparison to her relatively small size. Each was factory-configured with a two-pilot cockpit design but required only one pilot to operate them. Weapons systems included both spike railgun turrets, plasma cannons, not to mention twelve smart-mini-missiles. But perhaps what made the little fighters most dangerous was their speed and agile maneuverability. Their nested G-force dampening systems could counteract pilot-crushing inertia gravitational forces up to twenty G's—making the phrase "turn on a dime" as close to a reality as physically possible. And, at the moment, the absolute best feature of the *Hamilton's* Arrow Class Space Fighter was its total independence from MATHR. These fighter's AI's were both smart and totally self-contained.

My TAC-Band vibrated just prior to me hearing Ryder's voice via my inner ear implants. "Please tell us we can commence firing on these ass-hats, Captain ... a little whoop-ass payback is in order, wouldn't you say?"

I said to the Pylor captain, "I'm going to give you one opportunity to surrender, Captain Rye ... do so now or pay the consequences."

He looked back at me with both surprise and disbelief. After a long beat, he looked up while tapping his chin several times, feigning that he was giving the idea full consideration. "Uhh, no—"

And before Rye could say another word, I said, "Take them out, Ryder ... take them all out."

Lieutenant Pristy had rearranged the halo-display and, although the enemy could not, we here on the Bridge could see each of our bright red Arrow Fighters just now breaking formation and coming in for their individual attack runs. My eyes were locked onto Captain Rye. Someone off to his right spoke in a curt, excited, tone. Rye's eyes narrowed. His bemused expression was now gone. The feed into his ship went black.

Since the attack on the eight Pylor gunships had occurred all at once, all the vessels had been caught off guard. Which meant that not a one of them had had time to re-cloak themselves. Not one of them had had time to jump away or fire weapons. Three of the Pylor ships blew up almost immediately. Overconfidence had allowed them to drop their shields. The five remaining gunships took another few minutes to destroy. The last to go up in an abrupt ball of fire was none other than Captain Rye's.

A foot to my left came a loud, "Fucking A! Suck that you piece of shit!"

The Boston accent was unmistakable. There stood Hardy, the seven-foot-tall gleaming metal robot—a clenched fist still held suspended up in the air. "Frickin' brilliant, Cap . . . frickin' brilliant!"

Derrota was there, too, and he was smiling. There was a smear of blood on the Science Officer's chin and I could smell a long day's sour body odor, but he was looking pleased with himself.

"MATHR?" I asked.

"She's just completed her last round of self-tests . . . MATHR should be fully operational within minutes."

Cheers went up around me from the Bridge crew. Alistair said, "A little late, but welcome news just the same."

I looked over to the looming tall robot. "Thank you,

Hardy . . . excellent work. You and Derrota may have helped save what's left of our fleet."

"Don't mention it, Cap . . . my inner LuMan did the mental grunt work . . . I just coached him along."

Lieutenant Pristy said, "Lieutenant Giar is requesting assistance. The *Colorado* is a total loss. Would like permission to transport remaining crew over to the *Union*."

"Permission granted."

"Also, Bay Chief Mintz would like to know if our Arrows are to RTB."

RTB was standard for Return to Base—a phrase used even here in deep space. About to affirm the order, I changed my mind. "Have Bay Chief Mintz maintain an escort squadron. Keep them on rotation until further notice or notice that we're making preparations to jump."

"Aye, Captain."

"What's our ETA on reaching Ironhold Station?" I asked.

"Now that we'll be able to push into FTL speeds . . . I estimate by this time tomorrow," Grimes said from the Helm station. "Our biggest hurdle will be fuel, sir. It will be close."

I continued to stare at the still-venting *Colorado*. One more 3rd Fleet U.S. Navy vessel that had reached the end of service. *And then there were just two . . .* "Instruct Lieutenant Randy Cobb of the *Union* to maintain close proximity to the *Hamilton* from this point on."

My TAC-Band began to vibrate. It was Doc Viv. I answered her call, hearing her voice through my auditory implants. "Quintos . . . um, I think you need to see this."

"See what?" I said, just loud enough for her to hear.

"Get over to Coogong Lohp's quarters. I'm there now."

"This can't wait?"

"Not really . . . and bring the robot."

I ARRIVED AT COOGONG LOHP'S QUARTERS TEN MINUTES later, with Hardy close in tow. Twice in the elevator, I'd had to tell the chatty ChronoBot to be quiet—that I needed time to think.

We found the hatch door to Coogong Lohp's quarters half-open, held there in place by ankle-high viscous material that had oozed out into the passageway—which I assumed to be Ambiogel. I used the toe of my boot to confirm the stuff had hardened and that I could walk on it without sinking. I shouldered sideways inside and found Doc Viv waiting there for us. By her somber expression, I could tell things were not good. She shook her head, "Who would do such a thing?"

I assessed the situation. The glass wall was fractured with most of the glass lying broken on the mound of dried Ambiogel. Perhaps the wall had been struck by a hard object such as a hammer. An avalanche of the brown gook had poured out along with poor Coogong Lohp—whose remains were scattered about the deck.

"He's been chopped up," I said without thinking. I saw Hardy was kneeling down over one of the larger sections of the white worm—a part that comprised some of the head area. Doc Viv gave me a chastising glare.

"Sorry Hardy . . . I know LuMan and Coogong Lohp were, uh, close."

There was the sound metal against metal—like that of a stiletto knife being deployed. The robot had extended one of its chopstick like probes and was inserting it into the worm-like flesh. Doc Viv and I exchanged a wary glance.

She said, "Our Cutter Bots are equipped to do an autopsy back at the morgue . . . if you can wait."

Hardy poked and prodded into a few more locations before looking back to us. "LuMan, understandably is concerned. LuMan and the Thine had been inseparable for many years."

"So, LuMan talks to you?" I asked.

"Not really *talks* to me. It's more like he updates me. Informs me. It's all pretty unemotional . . . more matter of fact, if you ask me. Me? I'd be Curled up in a corner balling my eyes out. As for doing an autopsy, apparently, Coogong Lohp's not as dead as he looks. All, or most of these chopped up segments will regrow into individual sentient beings. Thine cells have cellular regenerative properties."

Doc Viv said, "Hold on . . . just stop. Why has the robot been talking like a Boston longshoreman? And, who the hell is this Hardy person?"

I stared back at her.

She splayed her hands, "What? I've been in surgery for the last five and a half hours. A passing-by crewman reported the death of Coogong Lohp to HealthBay—"

Hardy said, "Not dead . . . just minced."

"Whatever! He looks to be as good as dead to me," she said.

It occurred to me then that Doc Viv had been out of the loop for a number of important recent events including the discovery of still alive alien sprout-spores up on Deck 44, the infection of LuMan's AI biomatter by one John Hardy's DNA memories—an SWM guy who had lived some fifty years ago, the most recent attack by marauding Pylors, and the subsequent loss of the *Colorado*. My TAC-Band had started to vibrate, which I ignored.

Doc Viv continued to stare at Hardy as he inserted his probe into another worm section.

I said, "Let me bring you up to speed on a few things, Doc, okay? Everything will make a whole lot more sense if you just give me five minutes."

"Can you stop doing that?" she said to the robot. "I don't remember the ChronoBot being this annoying." She put her attention back onto me. "Yes, sure, tell me what I've missed."

I told her in as much detail as I could manage. With each new incident explained, she shook her head in bewilderment.

"Space battles ... alien sprout spores?" She closed her eyes for a moment, taking it in.

Hardy suddenly stood, then turned to face us. "You know ... this hack job took place even prior to the murder of Gunny Zan Mattis. The spreading, creeping, movement of the Ambiogel must have activated the hatch door somehow."

I hadn't wanted to make the mental leap that this killing was related to that of Milo Wentworth and Zan—but it most probably was—*of course it was.*

An announcement from above and spilling in from the

outside corridor filled the confined quarters. "CAPTAIN QUINTOS, YOU ARE REQUIRED ON THE BRIDGE ... CAPTAIN QUINTOS, YOU ARE REQUIRED ON THE BRIDGE."

Doc Viv looked up, "MATHR's back online?"

"Oh yeah, that's another recent occurrence."

"So, we should be able to review ship-wide security feeds, right? Maybe catch the killer in the act?"

I checked my TAC-Band. It was Lieutenant Pristy. "I have to go, Doc. Let's talk later. You have this, um, all handled?"

"Yeah, I'll have med tech collect all the, uh, pieces here, and get them to HealthBay."

I HURRIED FROM THE THINE'S QUARTERS AND RAN FOR THE bank of elevators. Like a faithful Labrador, I heard the heavy pursuing footfalls of the robot somewhere behind me. Obviously, LuMan still had a strong influence over its alter-ego, Hardy.

By the time I'd reached the bridge, I was out of breath and expecting to see another alien warship up on the halo-display. Instead, Lieutenant Pristy was getting to her feet. She gestured to the hatch door leading into the Captain's ready room. "You have high-priority interstellar communications, as well as a visitor, waiting for you inside."

chapter 18

I waved the door open and entered the Captain's ready room. Right off the bat, two things caught me by surprise. First was the projected face of Admiral James Spinker, hovering over the desk, and second, was Chaplain Thomas Trent sitting within one of the leather armchairs. While Spinker looked annoyed, Chaplain Trent had the smug expression of the cat who'd swallowed the canary.

My previous dealings with Admiral Spinker had been limited until now since he was high up brass—even Admiral Block's direct superior. Spinker was what was called a Sector-level Admiral and oversaw the military goings-on for all fleet assets within his territory. He was a *pinchy* long-faced man, and what receding strands of combed back dark hair he had left, glistened with some kind of gel. His mouth was small and pursed—had always reminded me of a tightly clenched anus. When he spoke, if you looked close enough, you could see tiny little teeth, like a rodent's teeth, within.

"It's about time you arrived, Mr. Quintos." The admiral's

eyes went to my Captain's collar Eagles. He made a face as if he'd just eaten a bug.

"Admiral . . . good to see you, sir. I'm surprised, Admiral Block—"

"Silence! This is not a social call. As for Admiral Block, I suspect he is no longer among the living, nor any of those fine men and women amongst the 7th Fleet." Again, his eyes flicked down to my Captain's Eagles.

His words had hit me hard. Admiral Block had been a key ally, and dare I say, friend to me for a good many years. Sadness gripped my heart and I found myself speechless.

"Are you paying attention to what I'm saying, Quintos? Get a grip young man, you are in enough trouble as it is!"

For the first time, Chaplain Trent spoke up. "This is what I was talking about, Admiral . . . a total lack of decorum. A clear indication this young man is not ready for leadership."

Ah, so that was why Trent was here—his cozy relationship with Captain Tannock. And having lost influence since the captain's head injury, Trent had been relegated to doing those mere trifling things commiserate with being a ship's chaplain.

"You have some serious explaining to do, young man," Admiral Spinker said, "If what the good Chaplain here tells me is true, I have a good mind to relieve you of your Captain's duties."

I thought he was finished talking, but he held up a slender finger to stifle me. Looking down at a tablet, he began listing off my egregious missteps.

"With the attack of the Grish on the 3rd Fleet and Captain Tannock's being injured, you immediately took command."

"As the ship's XO, I was next in line—"

"Did I say you could interrupt me, Mr. Quintos?"

"No, sir. Sorry, sir."

"Upon taking command of what remained of the 3rd Fleet, instead of immediately jumping away in accordance with regulations commiserate with such dire battle situations, you made the decision to stand and fight."

"The Grish had instigated overlapping saturating gravfields . . . jumping away was impossible—"

"Silence!"

I had to literally bite my tongue not to dispute the things the Admiral was saying.

"Instead, you came up with the hairbrained idea to utilize ship's weaponry that has been deemed unsafe, hell, *dangerous* . . . and again, against regulations! Bowlers for God's sake. Bowlers, Quintos?!"

"Yes, sir."

The Admiral's glare was so intense I had to look away. Glancing over to Trent, it was clear he truly was in heaven. He made no attempt to hide his bemused smirk.

"Let me go on. By some miracle, you escaped having the 3rd Fleet totally annihilated when remaining Grish warships jumped away. Lucky, for you, I should say."

"Sir . . . can I just ask one question here?"

His brows knitted together. "What is it?"

"Have you read my complete situation report? The one

submitted to Admiral Block, or are you basing all your findings strictly on the biased observations of Chaplain Trent?"

"You will not disparage the good Chaplain. In my years of service, I have known few men of such high integrity and sense of honor."

Hmm, Not to mention you, Captain Tannock, and Chaplain Trent here all graduated from the Naval Academy together—you have been besties for almost half a fucking century.

"Sorry, sir. Please . . . continue."

"No. But in due time I will get to your report . . . perhaps you haven't considered how busy I am of late. Are you unaware that we are at war, Mr. Quintos?"

I wanted to say, *you mean, like having lost over ten thousand good men and women within this embattled 3rd fleet?* But held my tongue.

The Admiral cleared his throat. "I could go on and on . . . like you having sent the injured Captain Tannock on some kind of spiteful fool's errand to get him out of the way." He shook his head. Swallowing, his enormous Adam's apple bobbed within his thin, elongated neck. "You neglecting to make timely repairs to the *Hamilton* while taking her, along with the *Union* and *Colorado,* into off-limits Pleidian Weonan territory!" He looked at me with condemnation, "Is starting a war with the Grish not enough for you? Do you need the Pleidians joining the fight against us as well?"

By this point, I was beyond angry, beyond frustrated. I was even beyond picturing myself dismembering Chaplain Trent limb by limb. Obviously, Trent had cherry-picked what stories—what lies—he wanted Spinker to know. *Fuck! I never wanted this job in the first place.*

"I want the *Hamilton* and *Union* back here in Earth's high orbit immediately. You have passengers onboard that vessel that must ... I repeat, must be returned safe and sound as soon as possible."

If he was talking about Wentworth and Coogong Lohp, well, that ship had already sailed. That was the problem, though, when you get incomplete and totally biased information from this kind of blowhard—someone as morally corrupt as Trent. At this point, I wasn't going to mention anything about the onboard murders. Or any of the long list of other things I'd taken it upon myself to do. Things I'm sure the Admiral would more than frown upon—like blowing away a good portion of the *Hamilton* to extricate it from an over-heating Phazon Pulsar cannon platform.

"Sir, at this point my main objective is locating fuel. If and when that happens, we will make haste back to ..." I stopped mid-sentence. "Sir, were we not ordered to intersect with the previously deployed Space Carrier, Prowess, and her strike group coming out of the Lalande System?"

The Admiral's shoulders noticeably sagged. "Like that of the 7th fleet ... there have been heavy losses incurred with fighting the Grish. Clearly, they have been planning a multi-thronged attack on Earth for some time ..." His words trailed off and he seemed to be momentarily distracted.

"Perhaps you are right, sir ... maybe another officer would be better suited for this command."

"Just shut up, Captain Quintos."

It was the first time he'd referred to my actual rank.

The admiral continued. "At least for the time being, we are stuck with one another. But hear me loud and clear . . . you are being watched. If you want to salvage what's left of your career, you'll be mindful of your future decisions. Get the *Hamilton* and *Union* repaired and fueled, do what you have to do . . . and get back to Earth. Her very survival may be at stake."

Chaplain Trent stood, not looking very happy. "Admiral . . . we spoke about this. Quintos has to go. Anyone would be preferable to him, captaining this ship."

"You mean . . . someone like you, Trent?" I said.

Brooding, his lips made a tight line and his nostrils flared. "Well, yes . . . perhaps. I am an officer in good standing."

"Yeah, an officer who is neutered . . . one who cannot give orders to crewman above the rank of deck swab."

"Enough!" Admiral Spinker barked. "Captain . . . you will show the Chaplain his due respect. And Thomas, please . . . show some support. Nothing's going to change while in the midst of war . . . no matter what your personal issues with the man are."

Trent glowered at me. Obviously, he had envisioned a different outcome here.

BOTH DERROTA AND DOC VIV WERE STANDING OUTSIDE the ready room door when first Chaplain Trent and then I, stepped out onto the bridge. Trent acknowledged the doctor with a cordial bow of his head while ignoring Derrota completely—apparently, I wasn't the only one on the chaplain's shit list. We waited until he'd left the Bridge before talking. Acknowledging the two of them, I said, "What's up?"

Doc Viv said, "MATHR . . . she's up and running."

"I already know that," I said.

Derrota, who really needed a shower, shave, and change of clothes, said, "We need to check the security feeds."

"Or had you forgotten there's a murderer onboard picking off crew and passengers one by one," the doctor added.

I gave Doc Viv a wary look, but she looked as if she already regretted her words.

"Sorry . . . that was a bitchy thing to say. It just seems that every minute that goes by, we're chancing he'll strike again. I'm sure you had a perfectly fine reason to be chatting with the Chaplain—"

"Chatting with the Chaplain? Is that what you think I was doing in there?"

She shrugged.

"It's actually none of your business, but I was in a virtual conference with Admiral Spinker, doing my best to hold onto my job. Seems the good Chaplain has lodged a formal complaint about my conduct as the commanding officer of the *Hamilton*." I held up a palm to keep her and Derrota from saying anything. "I'm dealing with it. What exactly do you need from me right now?"

Derrota said, "Your approval. MATHR requires a

Captain-level, along with the Chief of Security's, authorization for the viewing of archival security feeds."

I wasn't aware of any such regulation. In fact, it made no sense at all. It struck me then that my *shadow* was nowhere to be found. Not that I missed the seven-foot-tall robot, but I found it interesting since he had insisted so adamantly to be my protector as long as the murderer was still at large.

Doc Viv must have noticed my wandering gaze and said, "LuMan—"

Derrota corrected her, "Hardy... he likes to be called Hardy, now."

"Fine, the robot said he'd be right back and not to let you leave the Bridge before he returns."

"I rolled my eyes. "Let's take care of that authorization before anything else happens. Lead on, Stefan."

"Good, Alistair is already waiting for us," Derrota said.

Within a small adjoining compartment to MATHR's Den, sat the Chief of Security, Alistair Mattis. He was seated at a console and before him was a curved wrap-around view-display. No less than two-hundred thumbnail-sized video icons were on the left, while a full-frame video feed was in the process of playing on the right. I recognized the overhead view of that particular compartment. It was the Zone E Gymnasium. Mattis was in the process of rewinding and replaying the same clip over and over again. On the screen, his daughter's lifeless body was being tossed into an out-of-the-way alcove. As if on cue, the three of us leaned in to get a closer view. Although there was no mistaking the young woman was indeed Gunny

Zan Mattis, the other person kept to the shadows and was little more than a dark form. There was a running timecode displayed on the bottom right of the video clip.

I said, "Authorization from a Captain-level?"

Mattis glanced up to me and then to Doc Viv and Derrota, apologetically. "I'm sorry. I just needed some time alone ... you know, to see ... my daughter."

Doc Viv placed a consoling hand on Mattis's shoulder, "It's fine. I'm sure this must be terrible for you."

I said, "So, what have you discovered so far?"

"I've just gotten started. Sorry, but I went right to where my daughter was discovered. She was already dead. Her body tossed there, in that dark alcove. It's evident the killer is aware of the overhead camera and stayed, for the most part, out of view."

"Carrying a lifeless body around a ship would not go unnoticed. What about the other feeds? Like from the Gym's entrance out in the passageway?" Derrota asked.

Alistair didn't answer right away. He was angry and clearly doing his best not to come unraveled. He tapped at one of the icons on the left, which brought it to full size on the right. "The timecode corresponds to right before the clip I just showed you."

"But there's nothing but static?" Doc Viv offered, saying the obvious.

Alistair tapped on another icon on the left. "Here is the feed from right after the killer deposited Zan inside the gym."

Again, it was all static. Alistair sat back in his chair and swung around to face us. He looked defeated. "He wanted us to see Zan being thrown into that alcove as if she was just so much trash. But he didn't want us to see him arriving or leaving."

"So . . . what? He had access to MATHR to mess with . . . like erase ship-wide security feeds? I thought the ship's AI had been completely down, inaccessible," I said.

"I thought so, too," Alistair agreed. "What this *does* show us, though, is that our killer is a techie . . . knows his way around both MATHR and rudimentary programming."

"That and the ship's layout . . . I couldn't tell you where any of the security cameras are on this ship," Doc Viv said. "There must be hundreds of them."

"Hundreds in each Zone . . . and combined, thousands of cameras situated all over the ship," Alistair said.

I had a bad feeling in my gut. "We've had three murders—"

"That we know of," Doc Viv interjected.

"That we know of. How about we check the closest camera feed to Coogong Lohp's quarters?"

"Alistair nodded and was already bringing up a new set of icons on the left side of the display. "This is the Zone D subset of feeds. Give me a second while I find what we're looking for."

I stood back and arched my back trying to relieve a kink.

"What the hell?" Doc Viv said looking past me out into the CIC.

I turned in time to see him coming our way—all seven-foot-tall of him. Only now, Hardy did not look the same as he had the last time, I saw him. Now, he was fully dressed in an oversized gray SWM jumper. Still wasn't large enough to fit his enormous frame—whereby several inches of reflective metal ankles were exposed between the tops of his boots and the bottom of his pantlegs. Sleeves only reached to his mid forearms. The jumper material across his wide upper torso looked to be stretched as tight as a drum.

He came to a stop within the open doorway. He filled the space and his head barely cleared overhead. But none of that was as disconcerting as what was showing on his robot face.

Doc Viv placed a hand over her mouth, and I could hear her holding back a laugh.

Derrota said, under his breath, "How the hell did he do that?"

Apparently, Hardy now had full control of all the little sensor lights upon his robot face. Typically, they had been flickering on and off within a full circle. Only now, just two remained upon the upper portion of his face, at the ten o'clock and two o'clock positions—like two little eyes. Below, a series of only six or seven of the sensor lights remained on—creating a kind of happy-face smile.

"That's not the least bit creepy," Alistair said from behind us, peering up at the robot.

Hardy said, "What did I miss?"

Only then did I notice the robot had his *John Hardy* I.D. along with *SWM Supervisor*, embroidered onto the upper left breast of his jumper.

chapter 19

Doc Viv said, "How about the feed from where Milo Wentworth was killed ... where he was electrocuted? That would have happened not long after the battle with the Grish."

"Where exactly was the body found?" Alistair asked.

"Aft ... near Hold F14, right outside an access crawlspace. Like the Gym alcove, it's still taped off as a crime scene, as far as I know," the doctor said.

It took a few moments for Alistair to find the right clip. "I think this one is it," he said bringing up a dimly lit feed from a narrow passageway that showed inset metal ladder rungs leading up to a circular maintenance tube. Alistair said, "All non-critical area feeds are motion-activated ... like this one."

The video clip seemed not to be active or a still image. I was about to say something and then saw a shadow move across the scene.

"There he is! There's Wentworth!" Doc Viv said.

The tall well-dressed negotiator was walking backward into frame. His hands came up, a gesture of *stay back* or *I'm no threat to you.* In a fast blur of motion, another figure was visible. He was holding an object in his right hand.

"Is that a knife?" Alistair asked, to no one in particular.

"No, too bulky. Looks more like a wrench or some other kind of tool," I said.

The figure continued to advance on Wentworth.

"Why's the image of the other guy so blurry and dark?" Doc Viv asked, just before I was about to ask the same thing.

Alistair said, "It's not the feed camera . . . has to be some kind of distortion generator. Something the killer has on him that would hinder any of the ship's security camera's getting a clear image of him."

"So that's why the Gym image was so poor," she added.

The figure, the killer, was suddenly upon Wentworth. He grabbed a fistful of hair at the back of the negotiator's head and was angling his face upward—as if to force him to look toward the ceiling. The blurry distortion was now surrounding both the killer and Wentworth. The still-unidentified tool still grasped within the killer's hand began to strobe and flash—like arcing bolts of emitted electricity.

I think the killer is wearing oversized rubber gloves," Alistair said.

Reflexively, Doc Viv brought both hands up to her mouth. "Oh, my God!"

I, too, was startled as I watched the killer shove the electrified tool down into Wentworth's mouth and drive it deep down into his throat. Wentworth's body, clearly being electrocuted, went rigid. Then, his limbs began to flail and contort uncontrollably. His head was the first body part to erupt into flames, which was soon followed by his torso and then his arms and legs.

Quiet until now, Derrota said, "I guess we can rule out his death as being a battle-related injury."

I watched as the killer withdrew the murder weapon from Wentworth's now charred corpse and backed out of frame. Smoldering dark smoke continued to rise off of what was left of Wentworth.

"Whoever did this, knew how to disable the smoke detection sensors in that part of the ship," Alistair said.

"Hmm," the robot said.

We all looked over to him.

"You have something to add?" I asked.

"Uh . . . can you wind this video clip back? To right before the killer jams that thing down the guy's gullet?"

Alistair did as asked, pausing the video at the point where the killer was fully in frame, right before he attacked.

"There . . . on the deck," Hardy said pointing a reflective metal finger at the display.

We all leaned in to see what he was referring to,

"I don't see anything," Derrota said.

"I don't either," I added.

Doc Viv brought her face within a few inches of the display. "Wait. There's something gray or white there. Maybe a powder of some sort left by the killer's right foot?" She stood back and gazed up at the robot, "How the hell did you even see that?"

Hardy said, "I've always had good eyesight. As a kid, I

could make out who's fishing boats were who's ... even miles out into Boston harbor."

I exchanged a look with Derrota. Neither of us commented on the robot's ridiculous statement.

Doc Viv said, "Do you know what the substance is?"

"I believe so. I will need to collect samples from that passageway, as well as from the gym, to confirm my assumptions. There was a similar white substance found within Coogong Lohp's quarters."

"Dare I say it?" Derrota said. "That, perhaps, we have our first clue?"

I said, "Let's not get ahead of ourselves. Hardy, I want you to take Ensign Hughes with you. Do an analysis of the other two crime scenes. Make sure you get everything you need, images, samples, all of it."

"Yeah ... I would prefer not to leave you alone. It's that inner LuMan part of me. He's pretty adamant you are to be protected 24/7."

I raised my chin—gesturing toward his jumpsuit. "You're wearing standard Ship Wide Maintenance overalls. Even have your I.D. and ship's job position embroidered there on your chest. So, you want to be a crewman on the USS Hamilton, Hardy. Am I right?"

"That's right, Cap ... it's all I've ever wanted to be, to be honest."

"Then you better start following orders ... and that means right now."

The big robot got the message and immediately nodded

his oddly shaped head. "I'll find the Ensign and head on out, then." He suddenly stood up tall and saluted.

About to tell him he didn't need to do that, that saluting within the confines of an already underway vessel was not appropriate, but I saluted back instead anyway. The robot spun on his heels and trudged out.

Doc Viv gave me a quizzical look. "Why have Ensign Hughes tagging along with him?"

"Just for now. A few hours. To be honest, I'm not one-hundred percent sure the killer isn't the robot. He certainly is technical enough to distort the camera feeds. Would know how to alter MATHR programming..."

"So, that's how it's going to be? Not trusting one another?" She asked.

I shrugged. "How about we just do things in pairs from now on... take the guesswork out of the equation. At least for now." I placed a hand on Alistair's shoulder, "You holding up?"

He didn't answer right away. "There, back in the gym. He'd tossed Zan's body like it was nothing. Meaningless. I've never wanted to kill someone. I'm not a violent person. But I want to kill that... that monster. Kill him with my bare hands." Alistair clenched and re-clenched his fists several times.

"For now, how about we all get back to work? I'm sure each of you has a long list of things to do before end of shift." I checked my TAC-Band. We were already well into the evening shift. "Nix that, everyone should get a good night's sleep. Tomorrow we'll be closing in on Ironhold Station."

* * *

I SPENT ANOTHER HALF HOUR WITH DERROTA WITHIN THE CIC as he demonstrated how MATHR was, in fact, now fully operational. My main concern was her ability to oversee the *Hamilton's* weapon's systems—that she could calculate smart-missile trajectories, as well as ensure the ship's shields were operational and could dynamically vary power accordingly across the hull in times of battle. She seemed to be operating nominally. Leaving the CIC, I spent another half-hour on the Bridge, speaking with each crewmember to address any issues or concerns they may have. As always, my rock and right hand, Lieutenant Pristy, went through a checklist with me of tomorrow's hot list of items I needed to address. I told her to get some rest and let Lieutenant Barkley, a tired-looking middle-aged crewmember standing at her tactical station, to do his job. She said she needed just a few more minutes and she'd get out of there.

I left the bridge, intending to head to my quarters. But I wasn't tired; I was too wound up with all the day's events. What I needed was a little downtime—some time alone. Without much thought, I headed aft and upward within, fortunately, one of the less rickety rattletrap elevators. The elevator doors opened to darkness beyond and the soft fragrances of rose bowers, wisterias, and lilacs, but the most prominent scent here in Cherry Park was, of course, the perpetually-blooming cherry blossoms. Normally, the park would have stayed open—even though it was close to midnight according to the *Hamilton's* simulated Earth's Eastern Time zone stings. But with the recent space battle, not to mention a killer running around causing havoc, the park was closed and off-limits to the crew. *Rank has its benefits; I have the place to myself.* Heading into the park it took a while for my eyes to adjust to the darkness. Minimal indirect lighting was provided for maintenance and other personnel so they could navigate the numerous paths and natural terrain areas. Once beyond the one-hundred meter-wide by two-hundred-meter-long cherry tree-lined promenade, I found the hidden stone path I was looking for. Softly illuminated by traditional Japanese tōrō lanterns made of stone, the path eventually led to another, far more intimate garden area called a Korakuen. *Korakuen*, in Japanese, comes from the word kōraku and derived from a poem by Fan Zhongyan. It refers to the phrase, *later pleasures*—in turn, which stems from *hardship now, pleasure later.* Upon entering the hidden garden, I immediately felt the tension in my shoulders begin to wane. This area was based on the more spacious grounds of the outer Japanese garden of Kanazawa Castle— constructed in 1871 by the ruling Maeda family over a period of nearly two centuries. I took in the variety of traditionally pruned trees, rolling hills with flowering plant life, whereby the colors were muted by the limited evening light. I listened and heard the welcoming sounds of trickling brook waters nearby. The air here was warm and humid. This place was all about the three individual hot spring ponds nestled into a rocky land- scape that you would swear couldn't have been made by man. The farthest, and most secluded of the three hot spring ponds, was my favorite. As with natural landscapes, one had to climb and navigate rock outcroppings, get around barberry and boxwood shrubs, before accessing the river rock beachhead. Here, near-total darkness comforted me. Although I knew hot steam was rising from the pond, all I saw was the sporadic glint of light upon the placid water. I undressed, tossing my clothes upon the nearby boulder I had used for this same purpose many times before. The smooth river rock tickled the soles of my feet as I gingerly stepped from the beach into hot springs water. I walked out until my feet could no longer touch bottom and floated there while the heat continued to relax every muscle in my body. Leaning back, I let my legs rise and I floated there in the stillness for several minutes. I cleared my mind and concentrated on the slow rhythm of my breathing. In time, I paddled over to the far side of the pond and found the submerged rock there that made for a perfect submerged seat. About to drift off to sleep, I heard *something*. Perhaps a branch from a nearby tree had dipped into the water, or rock had rolled into the pond from one of the steeper shoreline boulders. Already discounting it, my eyes grew heavy again—sleep was calling to me. Then ripples in the water gently caressed my chest and I knew, without any doubt, I was not alone in the pond.

"Hello . . . is someone there?" *Of course, someone is there, you idiot.* I could hear soft breaths, not six feet from where I was seated. My heart began to race. *How could I have been so stupid?* There's a murderer loose onboard this ship and here I sat, naked, defenseless—ripe for an easy kill, just as Wentworth, Coogong Lohp, and poor Zan Mattis, had been.

I stared into the blackness, listening, trying to pinpoint exactly where the killer was located. It occurred to me that the killer could have come up at me from behind—wrapped his hands around my throat, or garroted me, or thrust a knife into me, far more easily than climbing into the water with me.

The whisper was so faint, I almost missed it. A woman's whisper. She repeated the words. "*Stop worrying, Galvin ... no one's here to hurt you ...*"

I squinted my eyes and only now saw that she was treading water right in front of me. I couldn't see the features of her face—I had no idea who she was. Her hand found my knee and she came closer. Her other hand found my thigh and she came closer still.

"*Stay or go ... it's up to you ...*"

I didn't know what to say. All I knew was that I desperately wanted to know who she was. I felt her pull away and I said, "Stay ... I want you to stay."

The woman stayed motionless for several long moments, as if weighing a decision in her mind. Slowly, she came closer again. Her hands now planted on my knees, she pulled herself up and out of the water. With the strength and grace of a gymnast, she positioned herself onto my legs—her face mere inches from mine. I felt her warm breath. I saw the glint of light in her eyes and on her skin. I reached out for her, placing my hands upon narrow hips. She pushed my hands away. Her whisper was huskier now, "*No ... touch me and I'll be gone ...*"

Her lips found mine soft and gentle as the ripples in the pond. The tip of her tongue flittered and probed as she pressed her body into me. Without thinking I placed a palm onto her left breast—round and firm—she pushed my hand away.

"*Don't touch.*"

I did as I was told.

As we made love, or more accurately, as she made love to me; I no longer tried to discover her identity. Even without seeing her face, I knew she was beautiful. I knew her body was lithe and firm and wonderful. Her skin was smooth and youthful and her long, wet hair draped below the rise of her breasts. Erect nipples rhythmically moved across my chest as the water around us lapped at our bodies. The once placid pond had turned choppy with waves, slapping at the surrounding shoreline.

With a departing kiss on my cheek, and with no further whispers, she was gone. She had left just as quietly and unobtrusively as she had arrived. As my breathing returned to normal and the steaming waters around me settled to glass—I wondered . . . had I fallen asleep? Had she come to me in a dream? Only then did I hear the distant whisper, *"Just stop worrying, Galvin."*

chapter 20

The Killer

He kept out of view, as motionless as a statue, within a maintenance closet recessed into the starboard side bulkhead. The door had a convenient eye-level metal grate—enabling him to see crewmembers moving within the passageway. The hour was late, but the killer was accustomed to waiting—to being patient. He checked the time on his TAC-Band. *Christ, her shift should have ended an hour ago*, he thought. There again, he knew the young woman was dedicated. A zealous twit who, undoubtedly, would hate to disappoint her Captain. The killer, like most others, suspected she held special feelings for Galvin. A kind of pathetic puppy love for her new captain. The killer smirked.

He heard the distant sound of an elevator car arriving. The doors clattered open and he heard approaching footsteps. He pressed his face against the grate to see who was coming, but the angle wasn't quite right yet. Then he heard her voice. She was talking on her TAC-Band—probably to a girlfriend. He figured she was using her audio implants, because he could only hear one side, her side, of the conversation. Eventually, she came into view, slowed her pace, and then stopped.

"No, I didn't say anything to him . . . it's not my place to say anything . . . It doesn't work that way on the Bridge. Yes . . . I guess . . . Maybe. My day off's Saturday, but I might work that shift. I know, I know . . . I'm sorry. I mean it, I'm really sorry."

The killer rolled his eyes. *God, bitches sure like to talk, yap-yap-yap, fuck, they never shut up!*

Lieutenant Gail Pristy smiled. She turned, looked up as if she was looking right at him. She laughed and leaned her slight frame against the far bulkhead. "Oh, by the way, I watched that movie you told me about . . . the one with the steamy shower scene . . ."

The killer reminded himself he was, indeed, a patient man. Soon, the pretty Lieutenant would finish her stupid frivolous call and go inside her quarters where he would use his electronic passkey. Perhaps she would be in the midst of undressing, or taking a shower or just slipping beneath the covers of her bunk. It made no difference—he'd end her life tonight in a totally unique, and creative, fashion. But perhaps he'd have a little *fun* with her first. That would be new for him. He felt a stirring at his crotch at the thought of what was to come. He adjusted his privates to accommodate the growing snugness in his trousers. Who would have thought, at this late stage, he would have found his true calling in life? Sure, he'd known since childhood he'd had certain, unnatural *proclivities*. So, *w*hen the opportunity presented itself several weeks past, a posted Interstellar DarkNet open contract, one paying top dollar to take out that Wentworth character and the disgusting alien maggot, Coogong Lohp, he'd jumped at the opportunity. Everything had been anonymous—that's how things worked on the Interstellar DarkNet. What he hadn't expected was the total thrill—the exhilaration he'd experienced completing these murders. But there would be no way he could stop now. And hell, there was nothing in the contract that said he had to stop with the two, right? If anything, his employer should be paying extra for the chaos and misdirection he was now causing. He let himself replay the murder of the other young woman—Zan Mattis. What commotion her death had caused. The emotion, the despair he glimpsed on Galvin's face. It was almost worth it just to wipe that typical smug smile from his lips. After tonight, Captain Galvin Quintos will be a truly broken man.

The killer watched as the pretty officer, finally, motioned at the door to her quarters to slide open, and walk inside. The door slid closed. Now, he would wait. He let his mind wander—he thought about home.

He had grown up in Emporia County, Virginia. Most of the families in the county there were farmers but his father, Charles, the principal of Greenville, High School, was a vengeful-angry man and was despised by pretty much everyone—everyone except his mother. She, Judith, on the other hand, had loved him. She was kind and beautiful. That was, until the accident. The killer thought about that. He'd been about eight or nine at the time. Story was, a hit-and-run driver nailed her as she was halfway into a crosswalk—leaving his thirty-two-year-old mother a bedridden, life-long quadriplegic. Turns out, the speeding driver was one Lorn Platt, a gargantuan four-hundred-pound fatty who owned the town's only dough-nut shop, which was aptly called *Chubby Nuts*. Apparently, he'd been late opening the shop that morning and was speeding through town like a bat out of hell. A couple months later, Lorn disappeared. Then his shop burned to the ground. The rumor was that Lorn had committed the arson himself, then fled when the cops had determined he'd been the hit-and-run driver. The killer thought about that now and smiled. How wrong they had been. Nope, it had been his father, Charles, who'd torched *Chubby Nuts* to the ground. That, and had cut Lorn's throat from ear to ear using a seven-inch boning knife. The killer knew this as fact—he'd seen it take place with his own two, young, eyes. Had even helped his father load the big man's carcass onto a hover-dolly, elevated it up-up-up, and roll Lorn into the bed of their family's vehicle. The killer was all too well aware how his not-so-typical upbringing was now influ-encing his current actions. He thought about Lorn Platt, he was fairly certain his body was still buried beneath that rusted out old school bus near the edge of town, within the confines of *Taylor's Junk and Scrap*.

The killer checked his TAC-Band and nodded. It was time. It was *killing time*. He cracked open the closet door and checked the passageway. He peered up and saw the security camera high up there—a camera that was fully operational since MATHR was now up and running again. No matter. With his trusty phase-emitter device powered on and secured to his belt, he would be showing up as little more than a dark, out-of-focus shape. He was anonymous. Tonight would be special. He'd brought along something of nostalgic importance. Sheathed, he reached across his torso and touch the handle of his father's old boning knife. Yup, the passageway was empty. He moved quickly across the passageway to the door of pretty young Gail Pristy. He electronically unlocked the door, and waved it open, entering her quarters. The darkness within called to him—*it was killing time.*

chapter 21

Captain Galvin Quintos

At 0630, Hardy and I entered the Bridge together. The robot was still talking, rambling on and on about Boston's new Fenway Park being a far cry to the original structure built back in 1912. But I wasn't really listening. My mind was still replaying the course of events of the night before within Cherry Park. The woman in the pond. *Who was she? Do I know her—do I interact with her on a daily basis?* On my way in, I'd scanned the passageways, the elevator, for female crewmembers that would match the same physical criteria— athletic build, long hair, erect nipples—and no, of course, that last physical characteristic would not have been easily visible beneath a uniform—but that's where my mind had gone. Hey, I'm human.

My TAC-Band began to vibrate as I approached the Captain's Mount. Mattis and Derrota were huddled together, speaking in low tones. Seeing the dire expressions on their faces, I ignored my TAC-Band. Both turned as Hardy and I approached. Evidently, something was wrong—very wrong. I shot a quick glance around the compartment. The other Bridge crew were busy at their respective stations, but enough stolen glances in my direction only exasperated my unease. That's when I noticed the one Bridge station that should have been occupied. I mentally reviewed today's duty roster. *She's always on time. No, she's always early* ... Before anyone could speak, I said, "Where's Lieutenant Pristy?"

Wide-eyed, no one spoke for several seconds; it was as if their collective tongues had ceased to work properly. My heart was already thundering in my chest and each consecutive beat pounded in my ears like a kettle drum. My anger flashed. *No* ... *not Lieutenant Pristy. God, please no, not Gail* ...

A hand lay heavy on my shoulder which I realized was that of Hardy's.

"You should answer your TAC-Band, Captain. It is the doctor."

I stared at the towering robot dressed in his too-small maintenance uniform. *He knew. Of course, he knew.* He was tied into MATHR and every other aspect of the *Hamilton*.

I saw Doc Viv's face icon looking up to me from my wrist. I answered the incoming call.

"Where the hell have you been? I've been hailing you for the last ten minutes!"

"Tell me what's happened, Doc ... is it Lieutenant—"

She cut me off, "Just get over to HealthBay." She cut the connection.

I shot a desperate look at my Bridge officers, who had yet to speak. I sprinted for the exit.

Out of breath with my chest heaving, I arrived at HealthBay to see many of the previously filled beds now empty. Although some of the injured crewmembers had succumbed to their injuries, most had recovered enough to continue their convalescence within their own compartments—still, some others were already back on duty. But none of that was of the slightest interest to me at the moment.

A medical assistant must have picked up on my despair. "Sir, Doc Viv is waiting for you inside." The woman's eyes looked tired and lifeless. She gestured to the side door off to my left. A door I had become all too familiar with of late, one I knew that lead down a narrow passageway into the ship's morgue.

I said, "Thank you." Hardy had entered HealthBay behind me. "Stay here . . . give me some space."

"But . . ."

"Just back off, Hardy . . . please." I left the robot and the medical assistant with her tired lifeless eyes and motioned the door open. As quiet and tranquil as HealthBay was behind me, here, there was much commotion. Doctors and medical techs bustled from one compartment to another. A Cutter Bot with its bloodied appendages patiently stood still as a maintenance worker made repairs within an open access panel. I continued down the passageway, twice, having to sidestep to let hurrying medical staff move past. I reached the double-doors leading into the morgue. I stopped, took in a deep breath, and slowly let it out.

"Damn it, Quintos! Where the hell have you been?"

I turned to see Doc Viv standing halfway down the passageway. She was wearing bloodstained scrubs, her hair hidden beneath a surgical bonnet. Her eyes, irritated, then softened as she glanced up to the large Morgue sign above the doors. The doctor offered up a half-smile, "She's not dead, Captain Quintos."

Only then did I remember this passageway also serviced HealthBay's Surgery Center.

She gestured with a tilt of her head, "Come on . . . I'll take you to her."

I FOLLOWED DOC VIV INTO WHAT WAS CALLED THE Advanced Care Zone, or ACZ. Here, there were six individual treatment alcoves—each with a myriad of high-tech life support and monitoring equipment. Four of the six alcoves were occupied—each had a projected 3D floating human-looking avatar that slowly rotated above their beds. Each avatar was virtually tethered to various continuously updating metatag text blocks, unique to each patient's medical condition.

Lieutenant Gail Pristy's treatment alcove was the last one on the right. She was awake and sitting up in bed—watching her own avatar slowly spinning around and around. She was wearing a HealthBay gown, which was hanging open at her left shoulder where bright white bandages drew my attention. There were multiple purple bruises all around her neck. Her eyes widened and she smiled seeing my approach.

"Captain... I'm sorry... I know I'm supposed to be on duty—"

"Hey, hey... none of that." I placed a consoling hand on her arm. "Just tell me you're okay."

"I'm okay. Thanks to Doc Viv, here."

The doctor was standing directly across from me now on the other side of the bed. "She'd lost a lot of blood. It was touch and go for a while... needed surgery to repair a nicked subclavian artery—"

"Wait... I don't know what happened. I don't know-how she was injured," I said looking from the doctor and then to Pristy.

"No one told you? What, have you been hiding under a rock somewhere?"

The lieutenant flushed, "It's okay... how would he have known?"

I could see Doc Viv's irritation with me hadn't diminished.

The lieutenant continued, "I was attacked last night."

"Where? When?"

"For God's sake, let the girl talk, Quintos!"

"Well... I'd just gotten off shift. It had been a long day. I remember debating if I had the energy to even brush my teeth."

I nodded, wanting her to hurry up and just get to it.

"But I did... I always brush my teeth. Anyway, I got

undressed, told MATHR to turn out the lights, and crawled into bed. I don't even remember falling asleep . . . I must have zonked out as soon as my head hit the pillow."

"What happened next, Gail?" I prompted.

"I woke up with him on top of me . . . like straddling me. His legs pinning my arms to my sides." Her face flushed again. "He had one hand around my throat. I couldn't breathe . . . couldn't scream out."

I felt the anger, the rage, building inside me, but I kept my expression neutral. I needed to hear everything she was saying.

She swallowed and sniffed. The memory of what had happened to her was obviously painful. "I knew, without a doubt, it was him . . . it was the killer." Gail looked at me, her expression intense, "I tried to see his face. Even as he was choking me . . . I tried to see him. But it was too dark."

"What happened next, Gail . . . tell me the rest."

"I heard a sound. Like metal sliding against metal. A sound I've heard in action movies. I knew it was a knife being pulled from a, um . . ."

"A sheath?" I said.

"Yeah! That's the word. He was going to stab me. Why would he do that, Captain? He was already choking the life out of me!"

"I don't know. He's a sick fuck. How did you . . ."

"Survive?" she said.

I nodded.

She gave me a devious smile. "I shot the motherfucker." Her face reddened again.

I'd never heard her swear before that moment. "What?"

"Ever since I heard what happened to Zan, I've kept a charged tagger under my pillow. It took me a while to get an arm free. Then to reach under my pillow and get ahold of the pistol. I think he was raising the knife to stab me. It may not have been a direct shot ... maybe a hit him in the arm or shoulder because he still stabbed me. I heard him yell something. Felt him tumble off me ... he was cursing. But I could smell burnt flesh ... I'd gotten him. It took me a minute before I could say anything ... to call out to MATHR. I passed out ... then woke up here in HealthBay."

Both the Lieutenant and Doc Viv were looking at me. I said, "Gail, you showed amazing bravery. I can't tell you how impressed I am." I gave her arm a squeeze. "Okay, I need to go. You take all the time you need to recover.," I hurried out of the ACZ, ran down the narrow passageway, and arrived back in the HealthBay. Hardy was there, right where I'd left him. I said, "Come with me!"

WE ARRIVED AT THE HATCH DOOR TO LIEUTENANT PRISTY'S quarters just as Derrota and Mattis were getting there. I'd messaged them both en route. What I hadn't expected was Doc Viv, breathing hard, jogging up behind me—sans stained scrubs and surgical bonnet.

"What? You thought I wouldn't want to be here? Like I'm not a part of the team?"

I didn't bother answering her. I turned to Hardy, "This is a crime scene. There has to be evidence . . . DNA, something that can point us to the killer."

Hardy was wearing his lit-up smile again. He raised one mechanical hand and out slid a chopstick probe, "Cap . . . I am ready to go to work."

"Yeah, that's not the least bit creepy," Doc Viv said.

"Please, stay back . . . best not to corrupt the crime scene." The robot said, waving the hatch door open and stepping inside. The four of us followed him in but stayed back close to the entrance. I'd never been in here prior to this moment. Lieutenant Pristy's compartment was clean and minimally decorated. A few pictures hung on the bulkheads—mostly images of horses and pastoral ranchlands. I remembered her mentioning she'd grown up on a farm somewhere in the Midwest. We all knew she loved anything to do with riding and taking care of horses. Personally, the big animals made me nervous.

Hardy moved about her quarters with measured efficiency. He had both of his chopsticks out and was testing—sampling, the air, the linens on her bunk, even the deck plates.

"What are you detecting?" I asked.

Hardy didn't answer right away. He continued doing his analyses all the way into the adjoining head area. He emerged sometime later, his face now showing two tiny lit eyes and a small line for a mouth. This was obviously his serious expression. "This compartment has been . . . sanitized."

"What do you mean, sanitized?" Derrota said.

"Your killer must have returned. Come back once

Lieutenant Pristy was taken to HealthBay. All organic matter has been *doused* with a molecular deadening field."

I looked at him, not understanding.

Science Officer Derrota said, "It's like a tagger gun, only it's used in the lab . . . mostly for scientific utilization. Like when foreign organic material would interfere with a specific experiment. Allows for a kind of clean slate test environment."

"And he used it here? In Gail's quarters?"

Derrota nodded, "Must have."

I looked to Hardy. "You're telling me there's not one organic DNA molecule still lingering in this room?"

"Nope . . . lots in the head from Lieutenant Pristy. You four gasbags are pouring tons of organic material out into the air, but I've already accounted for that."

"Who would even have access to such equipment? Better yet, know how to use it?" I asked, making no attempt to hide my growing frustration.

Both Doc Viv and Alistair Mattis shook their heads, looking baffled.

"Me, for one. I have access to molecular deadening field equipment, and know how to use it," Derrota said.

I looked at the disheveled and overweight science officer and discounted there being any possibility of him being the killer.

Doc Viv said, "What we do know, is that Gail nailed him pretty good with her tagger. She'd smelled burning flesh. And let me tell you, even a minor strike from a plasma pulse would need medical attention. Not to mention the fact that he will be in a serious amount of pain."

Mattis said, "So what do you suggest, we examine every crewmember for that kind of injury? That's over fifteen-hundred people."

"Not true," she said with an *I-know-something-you-don't-know* kind of smirk. "Gail already assured us it was a man. Not a woman, who attacked her. That cuts down the possibilities since the ratio of men to women crewmembers is about two men to every one woman onboard the *Hamilton*."

"There's another problem with your . . . assessment, Doc," Derrota said.

"What?"

"There's a lot of men crewmembers that were injured during the battle with the Grish."

"But not that specific kind of injury . . . I don't remember treating anyone with a plasma shot from a tagger. I think we should concentrate on those people, men, that would have the kind of technical know-how . . . education, to pull something like this off. Remember, he's hacked into MATHR multiple times already without leaving a trace."

"There can't be many onboard that fit's that criteria. Again, I would be your best candidate to be your killer," Derrota said. He looked to the rest of us. "What . . . you don't think I'm *bad-ass* enough to pull this off?" he said, his Indian accent somehow making his proclamation even more ludicrous.

Mattis said, "MATHR can generate the list of crewmembers that meet that criteria in no time at all."

"Let's not involve the ship's AI, since the killer seems to have senior officer level access to her." At that, Mattis looked up and his brows furrowed together. "This conversation will need to be scrubbed from her memory banks. I'll take care of that."

Hardy said, "I've sent an encrypted file to each of your TAC-Bands. The list of crewmen that fits the bill."

I'd forgotten Hardy, actually, LuMan, was a highly advanced AI, that most likely exceeded the capabilities of MATHR. "How many are on the list?" I asked.

"One-hundred-and-eight meet the criteria you specified. But I believe the list can be pared further down."

"How, exactly?" Mattis asked.

"From Lieutenant Pristy's description of the assailant—"

"Hold on ... you weren't even in the room when she described him to me," I said.

Hardy transformed his lit sensors into a ridiculous frowning face. "Uhh ..."

"You listen in ... through MATHR ... through the ship's PA system?" Mattis said getting angry.

Hardy shook his head—adamantly denying the accusation.

"Then how, Hardy? Tell us!" I ordered.

"Well ... I may have, inadvertently, opened your TAC-Band's comms channel while I was waiting in HealthBay ... I was bored."

"You get bored?" Doc Viv asked.

I said, "Let me make something perfectly clear here, Hardy.

You are never, ever, permitted to infringe on my, or any crew-member's, privacy. Do you understand?"

Hardy nodded. "Yes, it won't happen again. Boy scout's honor." He held up a mechanical hand with three fingers extended.

"Fine. Now, back to the list you say you've pared down."

"I believe, according to the Lieutenant's description—and the apparent agility demonstrated by the killer—there is a high probability that less than forty crewmen are a good match."

"And you sent this abbreviated list to our TAC-Bands?" I asked. But I noticed Derrota, Mattis, and Doc Viv were already scrolling through the information on their respective wrists. Doc Viv looked up, her eyes finding mine. "You know, the four of us are on this list . . . as well as other people we know and trust."

"Everyone gets checked out. No exceptions. I'd suggest all TAC-Band ship-positioning-locations should be mapped in accordance with the various murder locations too, but the killer is technical enough to get around that kind of thing. Let's break the list down into four groups, our names included in those groups."

Doc Viv said, "Maybe we should talk to the, um, . . . *suspects*, in their quarters, when they're off duty. Certainly not in front of their peers. Plus, we may find evidence there too."

"You think the killer's going to just leave a murder weapon lying around their cabin, out in plain sight?" Mattis said.

"No, probably not. Okay, so maybe Hardy comes along with us on these visits."

"Well, that will slow things down a bit," I said thinking about it. "Doc's right, visits should include Hardy." I looked to the robot. "I know you're a big fella, Hardy, but can you protect any one of us, if things get physical?"

"Me ... probably not. LuMan, on the other hand, is a battle-bot like you wouldn't believe."

"Okay, Hardy, go ahead and organize visitations over the next few duty cycles for us and our assigned group of crewmembers—"

Suddenly, the ship's emergency Klaxon was blaring above us. Doc Viv placed her palms over her ears. MATHR's voice came over the speakers, "EMERGENCY PROTOCOL, EMERGENCY PROTOCOL, CAPTAIN QUINTOS, PLEASE RETURN TO THE BRIDGE ..."

WITH THE EXCEPTION OF DOC VIV, WHO'D HEADED BACK to HealthBay, Derrota, Mattis, Hardy, and I entered the Bridge as a group. Up on the Halo-Display was a highly magnified view of Ironhold Station. That and no less than fifty various kinds of spacecraft within close proximity to it. I noticed out of the corner of my eye; Ensign Hughes's had extricated himself from the Captain's Mount. Sure, he was a junior commissioned officer within the Navy ranks, but he knew I didn't like him to sit there.

"What do we have, Mr. Hughes ... you took the mount, you can provide the sit-report."

"Yes sir, um, well ..."

"Now, Ensign," I said, taking the seat.

"We're approximately eighty-thousand clicks from Ironhold Station, sir."

"Have we been detected?"

"No sir . . . no passive or active sensor scans coming our way have been detected."

"And those crafts? Threat assessment?"

"Looks to be a combination of trade or commerce vessels and warships not dissimilar to those we encountered earlier."

"Pylor warships," Mattis said.

"Exactly," the Ensign confirmed. "Although, there are several larger warships . . . five light battle cruisers and two destroyers . . . or their best adaptation of those. They're all junk-yard rebuilds as far as our passive sensors can determine."

"Can you zoom in any farther on the station itself?" I asked.

"We're pretty well maxed out, in that respect."

"My sensors are superior," Hardy said. "Mind?" he said gesturing toward the CIC. "I'd need to synchronize to the *Hamilton's* sensor arrays."

I made eye contact with Mattis. He shrugged, "We stopped paying attention to Navy protocols when we let the ChronoBot repair the Cordon Simplex Sub-system."

I said, "Go ahead Hardy, do your best."

chapter 22

As we waited for Hardy to do his magic, I kept coming back to the fact we were deep within Pleidian Weonans territory. Why would they allow these Pylors to have refuge here? With those Pleidian' s high-tech warships of theirs, they could have atomized Ironhold Station in minutes.

I saw Hardy coming out of the CIC. Joining us, he said, "All synced up."

Mattis took a seat at Lieutenant Pristy's tactical station and began tapping at the console. The feed up on the halo-display suddenly altered magnification. We were now looking at a zoomed-in crystal-clear view of the rusted-out shell of Ironhold Station with what must have been many years of add-on and makeshift enhancements.

"Good job, Hardy," Derrota said. "Interesting, the scale of the station is larger than I'd thought. Maybe one-fiftieth the size of Earth's Moon."

I watched as a beat to shit looking spacecraft approached and then docked into an external port fixture. The magnified view changed again—this time panning near the top section of the station where a slew of communication dishes and other kind of antenna were fastened.

"Hold on," I said. "Go back and elevate the feed higher up there on the station."

Mattis did as asked.

"What the hell are those?" Derrota said taking a step closer to the halo-display.

"Those cables encircle the entire top of the station," Mattis said. "And I think we'll find the same thing at the bottom of the station sphere." Mattis altered the feed and sure enough, another cable was there as well. It drooped and swayed, affixed every few hundred feet or so.

"I'd guess both cables to be around fifty to seventy-five kilometers in total length," Derrota said. "But all those hanging . . ." he said pointing.

Derrota was referring to what must have been untold thousands of hanging skeletal remains. What was unique about these skeletal remains were the skulls. They were elongated ovals—like charms on a necklace, the cables ran in and out through the skull openings.

I said, "We've seen those stretched doughnut-shaped heads before."

Derrota added, "Yeah, the Pleidians."

"Explains why these Pylors have been allowed to stay here unrestrained."

We all looked at Mattis. He continued, "Remember, the Pleidians take supernatural occurrences and the paranormal very seriously. My guess, they don't want to chance angering some deity or hellion conviction."

Hardy said, "LuMan's memory archives has a bit more ... and you are correct. The Pleidian Weonans are a Polytheism society. The belief in many gods. Not so different than Earth's early Greek or Roman societies. The Pleidians, polytheistic, culture, even to this day, is obsessed with demonic and ghostly forces. Their gods, as well as a few of their supernatural beings are larger than life. But perhaps it is the malevolent beings, the demons, that instill the most fear and trepidation into the psyche of their culture as a whole."

"So, you're saying these are a kind of talisman? Like to ward off the Pleidians?" Derrota asked.

"That's about the size of it," Hardy said.

I sat back and considered the situation. I said, "MATHR ... connect me to Chief Porter."

The halo-display segmented in half showing a view of Engineering on the left and the Ironhold Station on the right. Hardy, looking distracted, came into view. "Chief here," What can I do for you Captain?" his voice resonated within the confines of the bridge.

I said, "So, last I checked we're well into the *Hamilton's* fuel reserves."

"Have to admit it, didn't think we'd make it here with what we had in the tank. But you've done a good job, Cap ... stayed below the speed limit ... no fancy driving."

I smiled. Not everyone on the Bridge would have a clue as to what Porter was referring to—being those old 21st century gas-powered automobiles. "Look, MATHR's back up and running. You've had time for further repairs ... please tell me we now have jump capacity."

"Sure ... but manufacturing a jump wormhole takes more than MATHR's advanced mathematical computations ... it takes a shitload of fuel. And that we don't have. But if you're not too rough with our HyperDrives, once the tanks are topped off, they'll perform well I'm sure."

"Good to know. Captain out." The feed slid away.

I said, "MATHR ... connect me to Bay Chief Mintz."

Mintz's craggy old face appeared up on the halo-display. "It's about time you rang in!" he said.

Behind him was the expansive flight bay. A sea of red spanned the background—over one-hundred Arrow Fighters primed and ready for battle. I could hear their noisy combined engine noise. Clearly, Mintz had been paying attention to our situation here, in close proximity to Ironhold Station. It was one reason why the chief was so indispensable—he anticipated imminent orders with preparation and action. I remember our biggest issue had been finding viable pilots with the Grish destroying Flight Barracks C and some five-hundred pilots reduced down to one-hundred and twenty-two. I said, "Battle orders coming soon. Hang tight. And you let me know if I'm needed ... think I still know my way around an Arrow's cockpit," I added.

"Will do, Captain ..." the flight bay feed slid away.

I turned my attention to the weapon's station, where

Crewmember Grimes sat at the ready. "Talk to me, Grimes . . . weapons and shields"

"Shields are up and operational over all sections of the hull, Sir. There is the issue of hull damage from that Phazon Pulsar cannon platform area . . . there's a vulnerability there. Let's hope it's not easily detected. As for weapons systems, all remaining Phazon Pulsars are operational, all Rail Gun Cannons are operational, and we have ample spike munitions reserves. Smart Missiles, operational, near full-stock reserves throughout ship-wide magazines." Grimes offered up a crooked smile. "Captain, the *Hamilton* is battle-ready."

Chief of Security Mattis said, "Lieutenant Cobb of the *Union* has moved into position at the far side of the station per your earlier orders. She too is battle-ready but running on fumes. Without fuel from that station, neither of us will make it out of this system."

"Then let's just hope everything goes as planned," I said.

Over the last few days, I'd been stealing time, two hours here, three or four hours there, shuddered within the Captain's ready room. Where at first, I had felt I had been intruding into Captain Eli Tannock's personal space, it was now becoming more and more my own. A quiet refuge to think and plan. Over the years. having been one ship or another's XO, I had been involved with numerous tactical attack plans. Now the responsibility of success or failure would rest upon my shoulders. The buck would stop with me. And this was exactly why I'd avoided further advancement—too much gut-wrenching pressure. Let someone else, all the captains and admirals, fight off the urge to throw up or crap their pants. No thank you. Yup, now it was all on me. There was nothing simple about space warfare—including the incredible speeds in which enemy craft can travel, or the vast distances, sometimes tens of thousands of kilometers, between combatting warships. Now, add the complexities of storming a fixed position, most likely a highly fortified, space station—one that we cannot afford to be destroyed in the course of battle. Well, this was going to be supremely difficult. Although the success of the operation ultimately rested on my shoulders, that didn't mean I hadn't brought in any help. Lieutenant Wallace Ryder had spent hours with me talking about our Arrow attack strategy—he would be leading the three Arrow fighter squadrons for this mission. Another resource I'd brought in, actually had him shuttled over from the *Union*, was Sergeant Max Dryer. Typically, the *Hamilton* would have had its own onboard contingent of Marines—often as many as five-hundred strong—but the higher-ups had seen fit to curtail the fleet's troop levels. The original mission to Auriga Star System was supposed to be little more than a diplomatic show of force—there was little danger of any enemy contact—*or so they'd thought*. Fortunately, the *Union* had deployed with a small contingent of seventy-five Marines of their own. Only forty-two had survived the battle with the Grish. Now, these men and women would have the responsibility of taking the station once Ryder did his job with the spatial attack. I liked Sergeant Max Dryer, who preferred me to call him simply Max. Maybe forty, he was as seasoned a soldier as any I'd ever met. A little over six feet tall, he wore his copper-colored hair in the high and flat-top style. His face was a splattering of countless freckles—giving him a somewhat boyish appearance. I'd discovered through our talks, that this solid block of a man started each day doing what he called his Up-3's. Three-hundred pushups, three-hundred sit-ups, and three-hundred pullups. Of course, later, after practice maneuvers with his forces, he'd go to the gym and get a more thorough workout. The guy was a machine. Just listening to him had me committing to myself to a more in-depth physical workout plan of my own. But that would require we first survive what lay ahead. Max and I discussed the mission objectives once his forces would land—his attack to take full control of Ironhold Station and doing so with a paltry forty-two Marines. Together, we had come up with a number of solid strategies, but all had their weaknesses. Weaknesses that could get the fuel reserve tanks within that station, destroyed.

I said, "Hardy, with those advanced sensors of yours, how much detail can you now gather on the internal layout of that station? The sooner we get that data over to Sergeant Dryer, the better. He's requested two days to run practice simulations. With your readings, more accurate holographic models can be made, which could save lives, not to mention the entire mission."

"I currently have eighty-six percent of Ironhold Station mapped. I would have had closer to one-hundred percent by now if I hadn't detected several, um, anomalies."

I didn't like the sound of that. Hardy's faux expression

now had the addition of arched eyebrows, giving him a look of surprise.

"Just spit it out minus all the dramatics."

"I guess you could say I've discovered I have kinfolk aboard that station."

Derrota said, "Like from Boston … human relatives?"

"Oh, no … I was speaking more from the LuMan perspective."

That got all of our attention—and not in a good way.

"Please tell me you're not referring to other ChronoBots," I said.

Hardy stayed quiet. After several moments he began to tap one foot and, making a small 'o' with his faux mouth lights, began to whistle.

"That's not funny. Save us the comedian act. This is serious. How many are there?" I said.

"Three. Well, two fully operational, one is being repaired. The Pylors work them hard. There should be laws protecting—"

Mattis said, "Hardy! Three, or even two, ChronoBots changes everything. No matter how much Max trains his Marines, going up against ChronoBots makes for an impossible situation! I don't even know if your kind can be destroyed."

chapter 23

I ordered both the *Hamilton* and the *Union* to fall back another two-hundred-thousand kilometers. The last thing we needed was for a Pylor scout ship to stumble upon us and screw up our small advantage for making a surprise attack.

Sitting at Tannock's desk, which was now *my* desk, I was getting caught up on the ever-present paperwork that comes with being a warship's skipper. And since there was no XO, that I could pawn any of this on to, I was stuck. The EUNF—U.S. Navy had an official form, for everything. A crewman has a request for personal leave, there's an SP-NAVCOMPT 3065 form for that. Something needs to be repaired. There's an SP-NAVCOMPT 5501 form for that. Food stores running low and needs restocking? There's an SP-NAVCOMPT 8666A form for that. Just because the *Hamilton* was damaged and readying for battle, it didn't mean things could slide, at least for very long—this was the monotony that comes with the job. A lot of the Captain's job was to review requests, ensure there wasn't waste or obvert graft going on before I digitally signed my John Hancock.

My TAC-Band vibrated, and I saw Doc Viv's face. The icon image of her showed her smiling. That, and her hair was down—a curtain of golden locks that fell well below her shoulders—probably below her breasts, although the icon didn't show that much of her. I answered her hail. "Go for Captain."

"Want to see something . . . really weird?"

I glanced to the virtual stack of paperwork on my hovering holographic display that was just waiting for me to get to. "You know, I am the captain of this dreadnaught. Have important senior officer duties to—"

"Hey, no skin off my nose. Just thought you might like to see something."

"I'll be right there," I said, practically jumping out of my chair.

I ENTERED HEALTHBAY WITH ALL BEDS SEEMINGLY VACANT and was glad for it. I wandered through the various main compartments comprising the hospital section, just to make sure I didn't miss anyone still recuperating—and it was definitely empty. I remembered signing off on multiple requests for R&R. During this respite, the bulk of the medical crew was on well-deserved leave. I knew Doc Viv's office was over near the surgery center, but I didn't find her there. Then I heard distant talking—*no*—laughing. I crossed over the narrow passageway into the Advanced Care Zone and found two crewmen, both asleep in their beds. Strangely, Lieutenant Pristy's bed was not only empty, but all made up. Again, I heard laughing. I found another door I hadn't noticed before, beneath a sign that read, Pediatrics & NICU. I was fairly sure there weren't any babies, or even expectant mothers, currently onboard the *Hamilton*. I waved the door open, stepped in, and saw a group of five crewmembers huddled around what looked to be an infant's incubator. *Maybe I was wrong, maybe someone did have a baby.* I saw Doc Viv and three of her medical techs, as well as Lieutenant Pristy, who was dressed in her uniform.

"Adorable! I just want to grab one of them and take it home with me to my cabin," the oldest of the med techs said.

Doc Viv said, "They're not pets, Angie."

Lieutenant Pristy said, "Why are they blue?"

Doc Viv was the first to see me approaching. "Hey there, Quintos . . . come see our newborns."

Lieutenant Pristy smiled, "Captain . . . look, they are sooo cute." She shuffled over to her right, so I'd have enough room to squeeze into the huddle. I really hadn't known what to expect in the incubator, but this was the farthest from my mind. Within a murky watery solution were six bright blue organisms about the size of your standard American frankfurter. Frankfurters with happy faces. The six of them swam and scurried about, bumping into the glass enclosure and each other. Tiny squeaks, what I figured were the equivalent to the yipping of puppies, only added to their adorableness.

"What do you think?" Doc Viv said above the med tech's ohs and ahs.

"Yeah, most definitely cute. But what the hell am I looking at? I'm thinking I probably should know something about any alien species onboard my ship."

"This is re-gened Coogong Lohp … or what was left of him."

"Really? These happy little wieners are baby Thine?"

The doctor nodded. "And you want to know something even more crazy?"

She didn't wait for my reply. "Each of them, even at this early developmental stage, is more intelligent than any human alive."

As if on cue, one of them wiggled up and away from the fray—stuck its head out of the gunk, which I assumed was a weak solution of Ambiogel. A tiny Thine face looked up and seemed to have found mine in return. A rapid series of squeaks and clicks emerged from the organism's tiny mouth before it submerged itself again back into the muck. I glanced at my TAC-Band as it vibrated, seeing that the text translation application had been triggered. I had to read the message twice. *Oh, so good to see you, Captain Quintos. My father's memories of you are positive. He held special affection for you …All right, I have to go now … time to play!"*

Feeling somewhat special, I held my TAC-Band out for the others to read.

All five looked and smiled appreciatively. Then they all laughed—showed me their own TAC-Bands. Each of them had multiple translated messages from the little hot dogs.

Lieutenant Pristy patted my shoulder, "You're still special,

Captain. Yours was the only message that referred to Coogong Lohp . . . their father."

"Mine said I had beautiful eyes," one med tech said.

"Mine said I radiate bliss," Angie said.

Stepping back from the incubator, I eyed Doc Viv and gestured for her to join me. Except for several wayward strands, her hair was all tucked back within a scrubs bonnet. Walking next to me, I said, "What are you going to do with them?"

She shrugged. "I guess we should return them to their home planet of Morno . . . to be with other Thine?"

"Or I guess you could ask them?" I said.

Another thought occurred to me, "You haven't seen Ensign Hughes lately, have you?"

She shook her head. "No. He's not a patient here, I know that much. Why? How long has he been missing?"

"I wouldn't call it missing. A matter of hours, maybe a day. Truth is that the kid's not that noticeable. Anyway, it's probably nothing. MATHR doesn't know . . . but I'm sure Lucas knows how to ghost his TAC-Band . . . so maybe he's taking some R&R."

"Which you would have had to approve beforehand."

I didn't say anything to that.

"Let's not jump to any conclusions," the doctor said, but her concerned expression revealed she already had. She pursed her lips, "Couldn't Hardy detect, like in two seconds, where the kid's run off to?"

"Good idea. I'll ask him when I get back to the Bridge."

"Back to the Bridge?" She repeated, now looking over my

shoulder. "Ahh, he's lurking around outside this door. The big robot has a fairly unique sound when he walks. Not to mention the deck plates clatter under his weight."

"It's weird, huh? I've told him too many times to count that he can't be following me around like this. I have no damn privacy."

"Well, I'll let you know if I see Ensign Hughes." With that, she turned and returned to the huddled group.

I said to her back, "You can tell the Lieutenant that if she's healthy enough to gawk at the hot dogs, she well enough to return to her post."

Doc Viv waved a hand in the air but didn't turn around.

chapter 24

Just as the Doc had mentioned, Hardy was waiting for me outside the Pediatrics/NICU door. Before I could yell at him, he said, "I, too, do not register young Lucas's whereabouts."

Ignoring my urge to reprimand him for eavesdropping on my conversation with the doctor, I let the gravity of the situation with Ensign Hughes sink in. As I stormed out of HealthBay, I said, "How is that possible? You can provide the internal detailed layout of that space station hundreds of thousands of kilometers away, detect the specific whereabouts of those onboard, but can't locate one measly crewman here, right under your nose?"

"And that is a clue unto itself, Captain."

I spun around to face him out in the main passageway. I was angry—furious—I considered punching this solid metal seven-foot-tall robot for no better reason than he was the closest thing around. "What does that even mean?"

"The Ensign, being dead or alive, my inner LuMan's sensors

would be able to detect Lucas Hughes' DNA signature and do so easily."

I tried to control my breathing. I liked Lucas. The kid was a bit of a misfit. But he was also funny, loyal, and I knew that one day, he'd make a fine senior officer. *He can't be dead. The fucking killer can't have taken another person I care about.* I said, "So? What . . . Lucas is being held in some kind of a sealed box onboard the ship, or was shoved out an airlock and is floating somewhere out in space?"

"Both scenarios could be strong possibilities," Hardy said.

I thought about something. With hands on hips, I began to pace. I always think better when I pace.

"Captain? What are you thinking?" Hardy asked.

I held up a finger and continued my back and forth trek from one side of the passageway to the other. "I hadn't interacted with the first victim, Wentworth prior to his murder. He meant nothing to me."

"Okay . . ."

"But I had just interacted with Coogong Lohp. As with Zan Mattis. And his fourth murder attempt, Gail Pristy." I looked up to Hardy. "Tell me, what are the odds of that?"

"Of what?"

"That I would be some kind of common denominator?"

The robot attempted a casual shrug, but it didn't quite work. "Without giving you a number that would mean little to you, let me just say, the odds are beyond the realm of coincidental. You had had recent interactions with Zan Mattis, Coogong Lohp, Lieutenant Pristy, and Ensign Hughes. With what I have now obtained from MATHR, reviewing hundreds of security feeds, crewmember TAC-Band location logs and such, I do not see the same level of intimate interactions taking place between anyone else onboard the ship."

"Yes! Not a coincidence," I said.

"Not a coincidence," Hardy said back.

"So, this has to be personal . . . personal to me."

"Seems so. Well, with the one exception of Wentworth. You're sure you'd never met him, correct?" Hardy asked.

"Correct. I can't explain that part. Anyway, our list of current suspects . . . can you now narrow it down to just the people onboard that I've had, or have, a personal relationship with? Those I have a history with?"

"Done. Whittled down to the list of suspects based on your assumptions. I sent it to you and the rest of the team: you, Doc Viv, Science Officer Derrota, and Security Chief Mattis."

I felt my TAC-Band vibrate. I read the now truncated list and didn't like what I saw. There were less than ten names.

"Hardy . . . have you had the chance to analyze that white chemical substance found on the passageway at the gym near Zan's body, and within Coogong Lohp's quarters?"

"Yes. I've been meaning to tell you about it. Could be a substantial clue. Organic in nature. By mass, it is 17% nitrogen; of which is about 80% uric acid. 10% protein, 7% ammonia, and 0.5% nitrate. There are elements of phosphorus, calcium, and slight amounts of magnesium."

Feeling victorious I raised my fist into the air. "Yes!" But my self-congratulations quickly faded, my smile evaporating. *Could it be true?*

"Captain?" Hardy said. "I still have yet to do comparison modeling with other areas of the ship."

"You won't have to. I know what that white powdery stuff is. And I know who the killer is."

"That is excellent! So, why the long face, sir?"

"Because that white powder is nothing more than good old-fashioned bird shit . . . specifically from a Scarlet Macaw found deep within the jungles of the Amazon. The killer had tracked it from the deck plates within his quarters. Which means, the killer is none other than Chief Craig Porter . . . who just so happens to be a good friend of mine."

Hardy said, "Interesting. The data works . . . yes." He stopped talking. "I'm sorry. I know from personal experience, losing a close friend is a gut punch. It's awful. Hell, I woke up in this tin can of a body having lost every friend I ever cared about . . . the fact that it happened over a half-century ago made that discovery no easier."

I wasn't really listening to Hardy—my mind was still reeling about this latest revelation. It took several beats longer for his words to register. It was true, Hardy had lost so much, more than I could comprehend, yet, here he was. Doing his job, or at least what he perceived what his job to be. He hadn't complained. He hadn't folded under the weight of what must have been feelings of overwhelming loss.

"I'm sorry, Hardy. I've been calloused . . . indifferent to your personal situation. Please forgive me. And let me assure you, you haven't lost every friend you've ever had."

Hearing my words, Hardy went quiet. I could tell the sentiment had struck home with him.

Then I rolled my eyes, "You just had to go and ruin it, didn't you?" I said, staring up at the robot's face. Faux dripping tears streamed down from his equally faux eyes.

"Sorry. That was not an attempt to make light of your sentiments. Thank you, Captain. That means a lot to me."

I huffed out a breath. "Okay. Look, I need you to contact the others who've been helping with the investigation. Have them meet me in my ready room right away."

IT TOOK ANOTHER TWENTY MINUTES TO GET EVERYONE assembled—which gave Hardy time within the CIC to scan and remove any security feeds of our recent conversations concerning the identity of the murderer. Having a killer onboard the *Hamilton* was bad enough, having a killer onboard with nothing to lose, well, that would be much worse.

While Derrota, Mattis, and Hardy were now standing around my desk, Doc Viv sat across from me in one of the high-backed armchairs. "I just can't believe it. Craig. Come on, he's one of your best friends. Sure, he's a bit of an idiot sometimes . . . definitely could use a primer in political correctness . . . but a murderer? And why you?"

Hardy said, "The facts, the evidence, speak for themselves.

As for why he'd want to kill people associated with the captain, that's anyone's guess."

Doc Viv shot an angry glance toward the ChronoBot. "Have you even ever met him?"

"Please. Let's not bicker amongst ourselves here," Derrota said. "What is most important is the safety and wellbeing of young Lucas Hughes. We must be extra careful not to jeopardize his safety any further. We must find him . . . save him."

Mattis made a face, "I can't be the only one who thinks the kid is probably already dead . . . right?"

"You're not helping any, Alistair," Doc Viv said. She looked over to me. "You're the damn Captain, what do you suggest we do?"

I thought about that. "We must assume Lucas is still alive. So, whatever we discuss must be contained to those of us in this room. If it gets out . . . about Craig Porter . . . about Lucas Hughes, things could easily go from bad to worse."

"So, it's up to the mere five of us? To find them?" Doc Viv said, sounding skeptical.

"Basically, yes."

Doc Viv looked up to Hardy, "I know you don't know where Lucas is, do you know where Craig is? Is he showing up on any of your fancy sensor readings?"

"Neither of these individuals are showing up on my scans. If, in fact, they were still onboard, it would take a high-level of technological know-how to accomplish such a feat. Does that sound like your friend?"

I threw up my hands, "I don't know. Of course, it's possible. He's the damn Chief of Engineering."

Mattis said, "This is crazy. We're about to raid that fortified, weaponized, Ironhold Station. We're talking about a mission that could easily fall apart. Any number of things could, and probably will go wrong. Hey, I like the kid as much as anyone else, but do we really want to be dealing with all this now?"

Derrota said, "You've never liked young Lucas. You've told me you think he's annoying. What was the phrase you used? A stumbling pumpkin?"

"A bumbling bumpkin," Mattis corrected.

I stood up, raising my palms to stifle them. "Of course, the mission tomorrow is of the utmost importance. It fails... we don't make it home. The ship gets boarded and we all become slaves to the Pylors. I get it."

They all just looked at me.

"In any event, if there's one thing I've learned over the years of being an XO, and now a CO, is that problems don't arise in convenient, self-contained one-after-another timeframes. They come at you at different times. Sometimes they overlap. Sometimes they hit you in the face all at once and from all sides! Hey, we're all senior officers here, right? Isn't high-pressure multitasking what were trained for? What we excel at?" I looked at my TAC-Band. "We attack Ironhold Station first thing tomorrow. How about we spend the rest of the day saving the life of a twenty-three-year-old young man?"

Everyone nodded.

"Good. With the exception of Hardy who'll be just fine on

his own, the rest of us will break up into two-person teams. We search the *Hamilton* from stem to stern … every damn inch of her if we have to."

Making a faux raised eyebrow expression, clearly, Hardy did not like the idea of being separated from me. Well, he'd just have to deal with it.

"Uh huh… Search a three-kilometer dreadnaught, seventy-five decks in what? Three or four hours?" Mattis said.

"Why are you always such a defeatist?" Doc Viv said. Then, seemingly remembering the man had just lost his daughter, she cringed. "God. I'm sorry, Alistair. That was uncalled for."

"He's right," I said. "The killer, Craig, would not be keeping Lucas out in the open where any crewmember could stumble over him. We'll be searching areas of the ship that are hidden, even those off-limits. Everyone needs to be armed with a tagger at the minimum. And we stay in contact with each other."

chapter 25

Major Vivian "Viv" Leigh — Ship's Primary Physician

Derrota and Mattis paired up and were already squabbling as they left the ready room. Quintos had assigned them to search the forward zones of the *Hamilton*. Hardy, who would be taking the ship's mid-zone sections alone, lingered for a moment looking ready to protest.

"Go, Hardy. If there's any trouble, you'll be the first one I contact," Quintos promised. "Think about it, without me slowing you down, you can cover a lot more of this ship in a fraction of the time it would take the rest of us."

Hardy stared at Quintos and then over to Doc Viv.

Quintos said, "By the way ... do you, um, does LuMan, have any kind of built-in weaponry?"

The ChronoBot extended both of his arms, causing his already too short jumper sleeves to recede higher. In unison, chrome weapon barrels snapped up and into place—one on each of his mechanical forearms. "Mini plasma canons ... far more effective than your standard-issue taggers, or even your shredder rifles."

"Good. Let's hope you won't need to use them. Now go ... find Lucas." The ChronoBot left the ready room, leaving Quintos and Doc Viv alone. They looked at each other for an extended moment. Quintos looked as if he wanted to ask her something but had changed his mind.

"So, you ready to do this?" She asked, getting to her feet.

Seeing her already wearing a holstered tagger, he opened the bottom drawer of his desk and retrieved his own tagger and holster. "Ready."

Two and a half hours later they were tired and feeling overwhelmed by the daunting size of the ship. They had started their search in Craig Porter's compartment where Doc Viv had ignored Quinto's warnings to keep her distance from the cranky bird, Millie. Subsequently, she now had a bandage wrapped around her right hand forefinger. Moving on, together they had ventured up and down a dozen access ladders, looked within countless cubbyholes, nooks, niches; most seemingly provided little real purpose. Periodically, Quintos checked in with Derrota and Mattis—who sounded just as tired as the two of them were—and had not found anything yet. Hardy, still searching the mid-ship zones, as expected, was moving much faster than the rest of them, but also hadn't found anything of importance.

From what Quintos mentioned, they were currently

searching as far aft a location on the *Hamilton* as was humanly possible. They were within a cramped meter-tall crawl tube situated just inside the ship's enormous, external, aft exhaust nozzles. Both of them had set their TAC-Bands for optimum illumination. Doc Viv, crawling on hands and knees, was making slow progress in front of Quintos.

"And this leads where, again?" she asked.

"To a kind of junction area that services all four of the aft exhaust nozzles. It's called the Pinion Reconcile Cabin . . . all big ships have one. Allows for the nozzles to be manually calibrated in one direction or another. If one nozzle is misaligned by even a centimeter, the *Hamilton* could go off course by thousands, if not millions, of kilometers."

"Hmm, how interesting," she said sarcastically. "Well, I think you should have gone first," she added.

"Why's that? You're doing fine."

"How about because I'd rather you not be staring at my ass like you've been doing for the last ten minutes."

He said nothing.

"I think I see something up ahead," she said extending her TAC-Band out in front of her. "Most definitely a compartment of some kind . . . looks like there's a light on in there."

"Maybe I should have gone first. Just be careful."

"Yeah, I'll crawl more carefully," she said.

"Smart ass."

"Dumb ass," she said back.

The closer they got to the end of the access tube, the more nervous Doc Viv was getting; she knew she might be dropping in on the killer. When she reached the opening she said, "I don't see anyone." She crawled out and stood up.

"If you take a step to either your left or right, I'll be able to join you in there."

She did as she was asked, and Quintos extricated himself from the tube and stood tall to the left of her. Together, they took in the compartment. Rectangular in shape, it was about ten meters from port to starboard side and about four meters deep, forward to aft. There was a double-wide hatch door to her left—which made the whole crawling through the access tube avoidable—but her eyes went directly to the black object situated at the middle of the compartment.

"Does that kind of thing typically come standard within a ship's Pinion Reconcile Cabin?" Doc Viv asked.

"Nope," he said.

She glanced about the rest of the compartment. The farthest aft bulkhead was a myriad of blinking lights, display meters, and various sized metal crank rings, all duplicated within four separate sections that undoubtedly coincided with the four HyperDrive exhaust nozzles. There was a shredder rifle propped up in one corner along with another object that looked like a kind of Billy club, about a half-meter long with two pincher-like metallic contacts protruding from one end. Quintos picked it up to examine it.

"Careful . . . you don't want to end up like Wentworth," she said. She pictured the killer, Chief Craig Porter, shoving the business end of that thing deep into Wentworth's open mouth. *Certainly not the most comfortable way to die.*

Continuing on, Quintos stood before a low bunk along the starboard bulkhead wall. He said, "It's made proper. I could probably bounce a coin on this tightly-tucked blanket."

At the end of the bunk was a neat stack of clean overalls and a big water jug. Three cups were lined up on the deck. She watched as Quintos used one end of the shock club to open the lid of a nearby portable toilet unit. He grimaced.

Doc Viv came over to look. Inside she saw loose windings of used and discolored bandages.

He said, "Looks like Gail was a better aim than she thought."

"Yeah, a regular Annie Oakley." She turned to assess the entire compartment again, "My quarter's never been this tidy," she said.

They turned their attention back to the black box. About a meter-and-a-half high, it came up to about waist level on Quintos. Doc Viv rapped her knuckles on it. "Thing is solid . . . extremely solid. Like it was forged from heavy cast iron."

Quintos was examining a series of horizontal seams that ran from side to side. He said, "Perhaps this thing folds down somehow . . . would explain how it was transported into this compartment."

She moved about the exterior, "Come on, help me think. Lucas might still be in here . . . and running out of air. We have to do something. Like right now."

Together they looked for a way to open the thing. But there wasn't a latch or even visible hinges for a door. Quintos used the end of the shock club to tap on its top and then they listened. *Nothing.*

She placed an ear on the cube. "I don't hear anything inside."

Quintos hailed Hardy on his TAC-Band. "How long would it take for you to get to us?"

"Give me ten, Cap ... on my way."

They sat on the bunk in silence for five of the ten minutes. Quintos eventually said, "Something's not right."

"With what?"

"With this compartment."

"Well yeah, there's a big metal box or cube thing in the middle of it."

"No, beyond that."

She shrugged. She heard the ChronoBot making his way through the access tube. It would be a tight fit, and they heard Hardy mumbling a series of crude curses. Christ, nobody could swear like a Navy guy.

The robot finally emerged and stood up to his full height. Without even glancing their way or taking in the rest of the compartment, Hardy strode over to the black cube. He tapped a metallic finger onto its top. "Solid."

"We already know that," Doc Viv said. "Can you open it or not?"

Hardy strode around its perimeter. "This is called an *Isolation Encase* ... made by the Grish and used for quarantining alien prisoners. Explains why my, LuMan's, sensors couldn't get past the surface. Made from Germorian Ore ... Nothing gets through this material. Sensor scans, sound waves, not even extreme temperatures ..."

Hardy seemed to have found what he was looking for. He knelt down, ejected one of his long chopstick probes, and placed its tip halfway down on one of the sides. "Requires an eight-billion character transmit code ... easy peasy."

Almost undetectable, there were a series of faint metal clicks and then on the opposite side of the cube from them, the Isolation Encase door popped open.

Doc Viv said, "Oh God, let Lucas still be alive in there!" she hurried around to the now opened side. She leaned over and peered in. Her eyes went wide, and her jaw dropped open. She looked over the top of the cube to Quintos, "He's alive. You already knew ... didn't you? Knew who'd be in here."

Quintos nodded and got to his feet. "Uh huh. This compartment, way too neat. And Craig's never made his bunk since I've known him."

"Well, don't just stand there, help me out of this fucking thing!"

Hardy and the doctor helped Engineering Chief Craig Porter unfold himself from the cube's interior and stand upright. He arched his back and stretched his neck. "Thank you ... I was running out of air. Thought I was a goner," he said, his voice cracking with emotion. Turning to face Quintos, the Chief's eyes were now welling up with moisture.

Quintos opened his arms wide, "Hey buddy, come on ... bring it in." They embraced for a long time—long enough for his uncontrollable sobs to eventually slow and then stop. Doc Viv looked away, not wanting to intrude on the two friends' moment. Separating and stepping back from Quintos, the chief looked embarrassed.

As if only now remembering, the chief said, "Hey . . . it's the kid, Ensign fucking Hughes. He's the one that put us in that box; he's your killer."

"Us?" Quintos repeated.

"Yeah. he shoved the both of us in there together. Opened the door every so often to give us some fresh air. Could hardly move. Tight as a camel's arse in a sandstorm." He glanced over to Doc Viv, "Sorry, that was crude." He wearily eyed the shock club Quintos had set down on top of the cube.

"Chief! Who else was captured?" she said, exasperated.

"Oh . . . sorry, it was an SWM guy. Nice guy—"

"Who is it, Craig!" she said.

"Um, Black guy, talks with a deep southern accent."

"You mean, Crewman LaSalle?" Quintos asked.

"Yeah, that's it, LaSalle. Good guy. Been onboard the *Hamilton* forever. A real history buff . . . and knows more about this ship than anyone I've ever met."

Quintos looked as if he was about to go ballistic. He clenched and released his fists several times. "I like LaSalle. Fits . . . another person I'd had close contact with of late," he said, "Where's Lucas taking him, taking Crewman LaSalle? Did he tell you?"

"Sure . . . the kid told us everything. Probably figured we'd be dead soon anyway . . . a real chatty Cathy, talked to us as if we were the best of buds." Porter gestured to the side of his head. "He's fucking crazy, you know. Totally flipped his lid."

Doc Viv was clearly getting annoyed with Porter. "Chief! Please concentrate... two things... where is Lucas taking LaSalle and why is he killing people?"

"I think he's taking him pretty far forward... like to the ship's bow. Lucas likes to leave the bodies where they can be discovered later, he told us. Makes sure he's not anywhere near them when they're found."

"So, nothing more specific on the location?" Quintos asked.

Porter thought about it. "I need some water; can I get some water?"

Doc Viv retrieved one of the three cups on the deck and tipped some water out from the large jug. "Here you go."

The Chief guzzled the water down, then said, "Thanks."

"Come on, Craig, where did Lucas take LaSalle?" she asked.

"All I remember is he mentioned something about the spot would be appropriate. Like how the Zan girl's body had been tossed into the gym, her being a muscular gym rat and all. And the worm alien being killed in his specially outfitted quarters... and having that brown muck seeping out into the passageway. Lucas said he liked giving his locations a lot of consideration."

"So, back to where he's taking LaSalle. What's near the bow of the ship that would be *appropriate* for LaSalle, specifically?"

"Hold on," Quintos said looking thoughtful. "Craig, while LaSalle was here with you, did he talk about Alexander Hamilton at all? Like, a historical reference, that kind of thing?"

"Yeah! He did. And Lucas found it interesting, asked a ton of questions. Wanted to know all about some inscribed brass dedication plaque... there's a quote from—"

Quintos cut him off, "From Alexander Hamilton. It's mounted on Deck 1 near the bow's apex."

Quintos looked to the robot, "Go Hardy! Fast as you can. And contact Derrota and Mattis on the way, they may still be close by there." Hardy left the way he'd come via the access tube.

Craig helped himself to another cup of water. He then said, "The kid didn't, you know, come right out and say *why* he was on a murdering rampage . . . it took him a while to open up. Eventually, he shared how he was hired by the Grish. Hired to kill both Wentworth and the maggot-looking alien."

"Coogong Lohp," Doc Viv impatiently corrected him.

"Yeah, Lohp, that's right. Apparently, Lucas liked to hang out on the Interstellar DarkNet, like, *a lot.* He bragged about his mad tech skills, that nobody had a clue what he knew, what he was capable of. That he had hacked MATHR every which way possible. Could do it in his sleep. That's he now controlled, commanded, the *Hamilton* even more than you did, Galvin." Craig shook his head, "God, the kid's obsessed with you, man. Anyway, a few weeks back, he'd stumbled across this secret Grish DarkNet posting. It was like a contract hit type thing, to kill both negotiators onboard the USS *Hamilton* and do so prior to the meeting in the Auriga Star System. Lucas said he'd been reluctant at first. It would change the course of his life . . . change everything. But realizing he was in a prime position to take on the job, he eventually agreed even before finding out how much it paid—which was about seven million dollars. Half upfront and half upon completion of the job."

"God, he really shared all this with you two?" Quintos asked, looking astonished.

Doc Viv said, "Let's keep going. Okay, so that explains the death of Wentworth and Coogong Lohp ... why all the others?"

The chief made a bewildered face, "I asked him the same thing. Kid had a hard time answering at first. Then he was amused, sort of creepy. He said he really liked it, liked killing Wentworth and Coogong Lohp. Said he felt he had a knack for murder."

Craig made eye contact with Quintos. "He said that you had ruined his life. That you'd ruined his chance with her because she was in love with you. That you'd taken her away from him."

"What?" Quintos said.

"Lucas wanted revenge, wanted you to feel the kind of pain and loss you'd put him through," the Chief continued. "Hell, I didn't know who he was talking about at first. Thought it might be the doc here, but then thought she might be, you know, a little long in the tooth for the young man."

"Screw you, Craig, I'm not even thirty yet ..." she stopped herself, realizing she was arguing to be the center of attraction for a serial killer. "Just go on, Chief."

"It became evident that Lucas was in love with Lieutenant Pristy, both being young, close to the same age. And it's obvious to everyone that Gail's crushing on the new Captain here."

"Wait ... Lucas tried to kill her, kill Gail in her cabin!" Quintos said.

"Yeah, well, I guess he figured if he couldn't have her, no

one would. I think this was all more about making *you* suffer, Galvin. Like I said, the kid's obsessed with you."

Doc Viv said to Quintos, "Gail's in love with you?"

He looked confounded by the question. "No! I don't know . . . she's like a kid sister to me. Can we get back to the matter at hand?"

chapter 26

The Killer

Ensign Lucas Hughes stopped to wipe the perspiration from his forehead with his sleeve. Feeling nauseous and unsteady on his feet, he leaned against a nearby bulkhead. Wet with still oozing pus, his uniform continued to chafe against the infected burn area where his upper shoulder met at the crook of his neck. *How could you fucking shoot me, Gail?*

"Son, you need a doctor," LaSalle said.

"I'm fine . . . and I'm not your son. Keep your ass moving, grandpa." Lucas directed the barrel of his tagger toward LaSalle's chest, "Go!"

Surprisingly, the old SWM crewman looked concerned—even having been locked within that cube for hours on end—even being zapped with the cattle prod a number of times, albeit on its lowest setting.

Reluctantly, LaSalle turned and headed off again, his broad

shoulders nearly touching both sides of the utility egress passage that ran below the *Hamilton's* lowest deck. Lucas liked that few people knew about this hidden walkway, one which—according to LaSalle—ran the entirety of the ship. Here, where metal ventilation ducts hummed and vibrated overhead, and where a wall of stacked plumbing pipes gurgled and swished with the sounds of recently flushed toilets and the flow from untold shower drains. Multi-strand laser-fiber braid crisscrossed all around the confined space like some kind of insectile webbing, making an already dark and creepy section of the ship all that much more menacing.

Lucas checked the status of his modified TAC-Band. Actually, it was the embedded T-bead, just below the skin, that he'd modified. It was amazing what information was available on the Interstellar DarkNet. This particular hack allowed for his TAC-Band to project a virtual head-to-toe energy dampening cocoon. One that made him undetectable to both MATHR's scrutiny, as well as virtually all other sensor scans—including those emanating from that ridiculous fucking robot.

Lucas steadied himself and headed after the maintenance guy.

"Young man, why don't you tell me where we're going. Take it from me, there is nothing down here . . ."

"Shut your trap, old man. I already know there's nothing down here. But it allows us to keep heading forward unseen, right? But I imagine we'll need to get on up to Deck 1, soon. Then, you can show me that dedication plaque you told me about."

"And that's where you'll kill me?"

"Well, I'm certainly not inclined to drag your dead carcass all over the ship. Uh, no thank you. But come on, you have to admit . . . won't it be a righteous kill location for you? You being such an aficionado of everything Hamilton and all?"

LaSalle didn't answer for a while. He then said, "What happened to you, boy? What made you want to kill and cause so much pain?"

Lucas thought about the question. It was a fair question, considering it directly affected LaSalle's future. Lucas was aware he was a borderline sociopath, but watching his father kill Lorn Platt, helping him burn the Chubby Nuts doughnut shop down to cinders—wouldn't that have an effect on any young mind? But wasn't it important for one to know themselves? Embrace one's inner essence?

"Just keep moving," Lucas said, sending a glance over his shoulder, thinking he'd heard something behind them. Sure, he wasn't detectable, but LaSalle *was*, now that he was out of that Grish Isolation Encase—something he'd special-ordered via the Interstellar DarkNet over a year ago, without having a clear intention for its use.

Up ahead, LaSalle was yapping about something again.

"I'm sure you know that then-Vice President Aaron Burr, had shot Alexander Hamilton. It took place in Weehawken, New Jersey on July 11, 1804. What you may not know is that just three years earlier, another Hamilton had died under almost identical circumstances, and on the very same patch of land. Like his father, Philip Hamilton was quick to anger, easily provoked. It had happened in 1801, where the 19-year-old had a deadly run-in with one George Eacker, a prominent Democratic-Republican lawyer. It was on July 4, that Eacker delivered an Independence Day speech in which he not only denounced Alexander Hamilton but asserted that the former Secretary of the Treasury was plotting a violent overthrow of President Jefferson. Father and son, seemingly both destined to the same fate."

"You tell me one more stupid Hamilton story and I swear I'll cut out your tongue and let you drown in your own blood."

"Copy that, Ensign Hughes," the older man said.

"How much farther before we reach the bow?" Lucas asked.

"We'll be reaching the end of this maintenance egress pretty soon. We'll have to ascend up to Deck 1. There are a few forward hold areas we'll need to pass through, but these are holds that are currently off-limits."

Lucas made a face, "So, what ... this creepy corridor of yours is off-limits, too. Who gives a shit if those holds are off-limits."

LaSalle said, "The battle with the Grish ... thousands onboard the *Hamilton* perished that day. All were heroes as far as I'm concerned."

"Whatever ... that's old news."

"The dead, the bodies, they're being stored within those temperature-controlled holds."

Lucas attempted to pull the soggy collar of his uniform away from his inflamed neck. He said, "Just show me the way. And put a cork in it ... no more bullshit historical trivia."

"It just seems this is as good a place as any if you're going to kill me anyway, son."

"Don't tempt me," Lucas said, considering doing just that. He certainly had things to do, like head back to the Pinion Reconcile Cabin, drag Chief Porter out of the cube; he'd be running out of air soon. Doc Viv would be next on his list. He looked forward to ending her. Thinks she's so smart. Lucas chuckled. Quintos will lose everyone he cares about; only then would he kill Chief Porter—do it in a way that looked to be self-inflicted. Lucas thought about that. There'll need to be a suicide note. Of course, Chief will have to cop to all the killings—be apologetic for being such a homicidal maniac. Only then would he kill Quintos. Yeah, after he'd suffered enough. Maybe make him disappear out an airlock. He thought about Gail, again. *I forgive you . . . I still love you.* Yes, perhaps it was best she'd survived. He'd been far too impulsive. *Hell, there's no reason she and I can't still be together . . .*

A metallic *clang* rang out from somewhere within the dark recesses behind then. Lucas doubled his pace. Up ahead, he saw LaSalle waiting for him by the inset rungs of a ladder. They'd reached the end of the utility egress.

"Get on up there . . . chop, gramps."

While LaSalle climbed, Lucas kept a wary eye on the way they'd just come. There was definitely someone back there.

Lucas holstered his tagger and headed up the ladder. With every overhead reach, pain coursed through his neck and shoulders. *Note to self, have the doc fix me up before I kill her . . .*

Nearing the top of the ladder, Lucas retrieved his pistol

while holding on to the ladder with the other. "If you're planning on doing anything stupid up there, remember I still have my tagger. Step away ... don't even think about kicking me in the head."

He listened, then heard the sound of a pipe or something metal being dropped onto the deck. Taking care not to fumble his pistol he climbed up the last few rungs. He saw LaSalle waiting for him in some kind of maintenance room. A small workbench was nestled into a cubbyhole with a pegboard mounted behind it. A variety of tools hung down from little hooks. Nearby, a crowbar lay upon the deck plates where LaSalle had tossed it.

Lucas said, "I'm impressed. I didn't think you had it in you to crush someone's skull." With effort, he extricated himself from the vertical crawlspace. "There again ... in the end, you didn't actually have the balls to do it, did you, now?" He gestured with the tagger, "Let's keep moving."

Together they headed forward. Lucas was glad they were done navigating that below-deck passageway; having to sneak around like some subterranean vermin was unsettling. He thought about the sounds he'd heard off in the distance. They had to keep moving—*faster.*

LaSalle stopped in front of him. He entered an access code next to a closed metal hatchway. A pleasant-sounding tone preceded the sound of a latch mechanism releasing. The hatch door slid sideways. It was like getting hit in the face by a fucking Siberian winter gust. Lucas breathed in the frigid air and regretted it. "Christ on a stick! What is that smell?"

LaSalle glanced back, "Show some respect, young man. The men and women at rest in here gave their lives in service to Earth's United Nations Forces, Space Navy."

The hatch door slid shut behind Lucas as he stepped farther into the large hold area. Blue tinted lights from overhead gave the teeth-chattering cold compartment an artic, glacier-kind of ambiance. Up ahead, he watched LaSalle's dark form wade through a waist-high mist. It was then he noticed the bodies. Metal racks on rollers that easily reached twenty-five feet high. Countless corpses were wrapped and stacked all around them. *And I thought the sub-deck passageway was creepy.*

By the time they'd reached the opposite end of the hold, Lucas was shivering uncontrollably. LaSalle, waiting for him, didn't seem to be as affected by the cold.

"What? You have antifreeze in your veins?"

"No, I feel the cold. But your physiology was already compromised with that infected burn. There's another, even larger temporary morgue hold we must cross before we reach the bow. Perhaps we should turn back."

"Just keep going, I'm f-f-fine," Lucas said having to hop from one foot to the other to keep his circulation moving.

LaSalle entered the appropriate hatch access code and soon the two of them were hurrying forward—moving in between rack after rack of bodies. Lucas, feeling sleepy, was aware that it was the onset of hyperthermia. He was tempted to stop, to lay down on the deck, and be done with it all. Along the way, he'd spotted several open racks—hell, he could crawl into one and let the cold and darkness take him.

"It's right up ahead," LaSalle said, his voice sounding coarse. Lucas didn't have the fortitude to even raise his head. He simply followed along in LaSalle's wake through the mist. Then he heard a hatch door slide open and felt two hands ushering him out into the warmth.

They'd made it. Not twenty feet in front of them, Lucas could see the rounded contours of the ship's bow. And there, at the vanguard of the bow was the Hamilton's dedication plaque, made of tarnished brass. The thing was big and impressive:

U.S. Space Vessel Dreadnaught No. CV-3

HAMILTON

HULL N<u>o</u>. 656

BUILT IN 2110 BY JOHNSTON SHIP BUILDING AND SPACEPORTS, LTD.

"Give all the power to the many, they will oppress the few. Give all the power to the few, they will oppress the many."

LaSalle, with his back to Lucas, stood before the plaque and read the quote aloud.

Lucas, just now able to flex his fingers, found the butt of his holstered tagger, and drew the weapon. He pointed it at LaSalle's back. It was then that he noticed there were two other egresses to this location on the ship—one from a corridor on the left and another on the right.

"We didn't have to walk through those two iceboxes, did we?"

LaSalle turned to face him. "No. We didn't."

"You thought I wouldn't make it? Thought I'd die trying?"

LaSalle shrugged. "In your condition, I am surprised you are standing here with me now."

Lucas had to give the old coot his due; it wasn't a bad plan, but it would take a hell of a lot more than that to bring him down. "I'd ask you if you had any last words before you, you know, die ... but I'm afraid you'd spew off another Hamilton rant, and I just couldn't take it. So, goodbye, Mr. LaSalle." Lucas raised the barrel of his weapon and—A gust of chilly air raked against his back. He hadn't heard the hatch door slide open behind him, but apparently, it had.

LaSalle's eyes were no longer looking at Lucas, or the tagger held within his right hand. Instead, the man's eyes had settled on something behind—something standing a good bit taller than himself. "It's that fucking robot, isn't it?"

LaSalle's expression did not express any form of pleasure at knowing what was to come. Lucas felt the weight of the large heavy palm atop his head—felt mechanical fingers encompass his cranium like a tight-fitting cap. In the split second that it took Hardy to unilaterally constrict his five digits—crushing young Ensign Hughes's skull—he thought of Gail . . . *there's no reason she and I can't still be together . . .*

chapter 27

Captain Galvin Quintos

I later learned that Doc Viv and I had arrived last on the scene, several minutes after Derrota and Mattis, and well after the ChronoBot. I hadn't been here before—had never laid eyes on the 2110 USS *Hamilton's* original launch dedication brass plaque. As interesting as that would normally be, my full attention was currently on the body of the young man sprawled out on the deck. Head bowed, as if in prayer, SWM Crewmember LaSalle was kneeling next to the corpse.

Doc Viv hurried to his side and checked for a pulse at the side of young Lucas Hughes' neck. She gave it a moment or two before looking up to me. She shook her head. She then took a closer look at the Ensign's injuries. "Good God, his skull's been completely crushed. How . . ." her words trailed off as her gaze settled onto the robot. "Really? Was it really necessary to kill him?"

The robot continued to stare down at the body. When he spoke, I was surprised to hear the ChronoBots original synthesized LuMan voice. "An assessment of the situation called for immediate action. An action, I alone, was capable of making." LaSalle let out a defeated breath. "He's right. Lucas was about to shoot me. I had mere seconds, if that, to live. The robot saved my life."

I continued to stare at Lucas's body. What a waste—what a total fucking waste. I'd liked the young man. "Did he say anything to you, about the murders? Like why?"

LaSalle said, "Sure. Rambled on and on about all sorts of things. Some made sense some didn't. The boy was clearly disturbed. A psychotic killer. One thing was for sure though, he had it in for you, sir. Seems you'd stolen the love of his life . . . that Lieutenant Pristy on the bridge—"

"This shit again?" I said cutting him off at hearing the same crap Chief Porter had recounted to us earlier. "Look, my relationship with Lieutenant Pristy is, and has always been, strictly professional."

"And perhaps thou dost protest too much?" Doc Viv said under her breath.

Ignoring her, I stood and assessed the robot. "And what's the story with you? What happened to Hardy?"

"Hardy was incapable of taking appropriate action."

"Is he coming back?"

The ChronoBot hesitated. When he spoke again, it was with Hardy's now-familiar Boston accented voice. "I'm here . . . although, perhaps I shouldn't be, Captain. I couldn't do it.

Couldn't kill the young Ensign. Even knowing what he'd done. Knowing he was about to shoot LaSalle here . . . I was a coward when it counted. If it wasn't for LuMan . . ."

"You're no coward, Hardy. Hell, I'm not so sure any of us would have been able to do what LuMan had done. We all liked Lucas."

"Oh, I could," Mattis said with true venom in his voice. "If I had a tagger right now, I'd shoot the murderous shit again. He took my Zanny from me . . . from all of us. What he got was more than appropriate." The Hamilton's Chief of Security spit a loogie at the dead Ensign. He turned and strode away.

I felt my TAC-Band begin to vibrate. I saw the other's TAC-Bands had also begun to flash and vibrate.

"Go for Quintos," I said.

"Captain! You're needed on the Bridge."

WITH THE EXCEPTION OF DOC VIV, WHO'D STAYED BEHIND to deal with having Lucas's body transferred up to HealthBay, the rest of us rushed to the Bridge. I was surprised to see Lieutenant Pristy back at the Tactical Station. Grimes was at the Weapons console. Crewmember Don Chin, one of the original Bridge crew who had been injured during the battle with the Grish, was now manning Comms. The Asian man was capable of doing miracles with the ship's communications and it was good to see him back at his station.

I took my seat at the Captain's Mount and took in an

innocuous-looking starfield up on the halo-display. The one bright spot was a distant Ironhold space station.

Hardy, who was now standing several feet to my left, jerked his head—first to the left and then to the right. It was as if he was hearing something the rest of us were oblivious to.

"What is it?" I asked.

"We have company."

"Yup, he's right," Lieutenant Pristy said.

The forward halo-display changed perspective. It looked as if we were looking out into deep space with the twinkling of a million distant stars. The magnification level increased again, once, twice, thrice...

"Holy shit," Derrota said.

We were now looking at a distant line of pristine white warships—way too many warships.

Lieutenant Pristy said, "We're using the ChronoBots' enhanced sensor capabilities to boost MATHR's sensor range. This is as close a view as I can manage. Those warships are approximately five-hundred-thousand kilometers out from our current location. Pleidian Weonan fleet assets. The fleet is comprised of twenty-three warships... they are armed and ready for battle."

"Yeah, but still... they keep their distance," I said. "And we'll be taking advantage of their superstitious ways." I flashed back to the untold thousands of hanging skeletal remains that encircled Ironhold Station. Cables woven in and out of those open skulls—and like charms on a necklace—they hung there lifeless and foreboding.

It reminded me of how early American Indians would avoid venturing into sacred burial grounds at almost any cost. Obviously, having deep-seated superstitious beliefs shrouded in the occult was powerful, no matter the species.

"This does complicate things, Captain," Mattis said. "Even if we're successful with the Pylors ... with taking that station. When the Pleidians warned us to leave their system, they'd left little doubt what repercussions we'd face if we ignored them."

"I know that. And I know we can't deal with two highly capable forces simultaneously. So, the Pleidians will just have to wait their turn."

"And if they don't?"

I didn't answer. My silence was enough of a response. *If the Pleidians do get involved, then we're probably all dead.* Instead, I looked around for Ensign Hughes, who'd typically be the one to make the announcement. My heart sank remembering the young man's recent fate. I said, "Grimes, how about you bring the *Hamilton* to Battle Stations status ... trigger MATHR to make the announcement. And hail the *Union*, inform Lieutenant Randy Cobb that it's GO time."

I hailed Lieutenant Ryder on my TAC-Band. Sounding annoyed, he said, "You know you have three full wings sitting here in flight bay awaiting your orders ... are we doing this, or what?"

"Sorry, needed to deal with ... some issues."

And, yes ... we're most definitely doing this." In the background, I heard more Arrow fighter engines coming to life.

Ryder must have signaled his pilots to ready their craft for flight.

"Your pilots have the station armament strike locations?" I asked.

"Thanks to the intel your robot provided, yes. Plus, the fact that they're not, for the most part, hidden. Mostly rail and energy cannons. The real danger lies with the station's security patrols. Those jalopy-looking craft are anything but innocuous . . . we found that out. As discussed, each of our three wings has its orders. Wing one, take out Ironhold Station's defenses and ready the target for our Marines' landing crafts. Wing two, get after those enemy security patrols. And the third wing will hang tight with the *Hamilton,* protect the mothership at all cost."

"Copy that, J-Dog . . ." I said, referring to his call sign, short for "Junk Yard Dog" . . . a moniker he had earned more times than I could remember. Lieutenant Wallace Ryder was as laid back as anyone you could imagine. But once he was seated within that cockpit, he became someone else completely— vicious, unyielding, and downright mean.

"Hang tight, we'll be moving into position soon . . . your teams will take flight on my command."

"Roger that, Captain," he said, cutting the connection.

I hailed Sergeant Max Dryer. "It's GO time, Max . . . tell me you're ready."

"We're ready . . . packed into four Ploppers. All bunched up like sardines in a can."

Ploppers were basically ruggedized shuttlecraft, capable of land and water landings, each with a passenger seating capacity of twenty. Since no one would be sitting, the seats had been removed allowing another five fully geared up Marines to be jam-packed inside.

"Captain... We've left room for your robot. Awaiting status on it joining us."

Why did everyone refer to Hardy as my robot? "Him, not it," I said.

"Well, this mission falls apart without him, getting onboard and going up against his three brethren within that station. I did a little research on those machines. They're advanced Sheentah technology... Captain, these things are made for war, made for killing. Thing is, Sheentah stopped making them some three-hundred years ago. Did you know that it, *he*, is that old?"

"Yeah, I've heard that," I said.

"Did you know these robots were outlawed by the Intergalactic Oversight Commission decades of years ago? That they have a tendency to go on rampages ...like uncontrollably?"

"No."

"Hey, we need him. Just thought you should know."

I looked over at Hardy. Even though I was using my audio implants, he was undoubtedly listening to our conversation. Hardy played by his own rules. "I'll take care of it ...he's on his way." I cut the connection.

Hardy turned to face me. I said, "You need to get yourself on that Plopper, Hardy. We already talked about this."

The ChronoBot's face was a mixed jumble of blinking,

meaningless lights which was a nice change. A display of faux emotions was the last thing I wanted to deal with right now.

"It's not me, Captain. I take orders . . . I do what I'm told."

I raised a brow, "And?"

"And LuMan will not budge. His loyalty to Coogong Lohp, and subsequently, to you, is basically hard-wired into his core being. You can order him to go until your face turns blue . . . but he's evaluated the danger of this mission. He will not leave your side until we're clear of this station and those enemy crafts."

"He's told you as much?" I asked.

"Yeah, sir . . . I guess you could say, we talk."

I had an audience of three. Derrota, Mattis, and Lieutenant Pristy. Each clearly had their own opinion and looked to be bursting at the seams to share their thoughts.

"Lieutenant?" I said.

"The Marines will just have to manage without the ChronoBot . . . it's probably good he's here protecting you."

I turned my attention to my Chief of Security, "Alistair?"

"No. We hold back . . . clearly we are not prepared to advance on the enemy."

"Hold back for what? We're out of fuel . . . we're out of time!"

Mattis tilted his head, "Let's take a day and think about this plan. We're rushing things."

I turned to my Science Officer, "Stefan?"

Derrota looked up to the robot and then off to the halo-display. "I'm sorry, Captain . . . you're in a real pickle. No disrespect intended, but the mission relies more on Hardy than it does you, no?"

"True."

"Maybe you should go along with the robot. Let him go on the mission, you tag along?"

"That's crazy! He belongs here, on the bridge." Lieutenant Pristy said.

I smiled. Derrota had come to the same conclusion I had. I said to Hardy, "Would that be acceptable to LuMan? Me coming along where he can keep an eye on me?"

Hardy did one of those unsuccessful shrug things. "He doesn't like it. Does not like the idea of you placing yourself in even more danger."

"So, tell him I'm going anyway. I've already decided. He's welcome to stay here and watch the action from the bridge. To hide where it's safe."

Hardy said, "I don't need to play *inbetweener*, sir. He hears you loud and clear. LuMan is not happy. Not so sure that's what you want."

"This is beyond stupid. A captain belongs on his ship," the lieutenant said, repeating her objections.

Hardy said, "LuMan will join you. Join the contingent of Marines."

"Good!" I said, standing up. "I'll stay in constant contact via comms. I'll be leaving the Bridge in excellent hands . . . the three of you will work together." I placed a hand on Derrota's shoulder. "Stefan . . . I want you seated upon the Captain's Mount. You'll be my acting XO."

I heard Lieutenant Pristy's audible *huff.* She crossed her arms over her chest and narrowed her eyes. Clearly, she felt that she should be the one to take that seat, but she'd chosen to be protective and motherly. She cared too much for my welfare versus that of the ship and crew. Mattis had shown hesitancy and lack of fortitude. Only Derrota saw the situation and understood the only real solution. Would I be breaking protocol? Going against orders? Probably. But that had never stopped me before.

IT HAD TAKEN ME ANOTHER TWENTY MINUTES BY THE TIME I'd stopped by the armory, gotten outfitted with the appropriate combat suit, helmet, and Shredder rifle. I had a holstered tagger on my thigh, and a Ka-Bar knife secured at my hip. By the time Hardy, no longer wearing his ill-fitting overalls, and I arrived on the flight deck, the noise from so many idling spacecraft had reached a near-deafening level.

Bay Chief Frank Mintz, an unlit stub of a cigar in his mouth and a tablet in one hand, greeted us. "It's about fucking time! You do know we're burning fuel... that there's good reason for not filling this bay with exhaust fumes, right?" He tapped his tablet onto the brim of my battle helmet. Me being the ship's skipper made no difference to him—which I actually appreciated.

"Sorry, Chief. How about you just show me the way to Plopper 3, and we'll get this show on the road?"

His creased and worn face didn't look pleased. "You

shouldn't be going on this mission, Galvin . . . your days of this kind of shit are supposed to be behind you. I suggest you stand down, young man."

I wasn't new to the Chief barking orders at me—mostly back as an Arrow pilot, under my call sign, *Brigs*. On three occasions, I'd spent time in a ship's brig for not following direct orders to drop pursuit of an enemy craft—to RTB—*return to base*. The moniker, *Brigs,* had stuck after that last three-day stint behind bars.

Having to hunch over, Hardy led us beneath one scarlet-colored Arrow fighter after another. We found Plopper 3 at the back of the pack—a beat-to-shit looking craft that showed many years of battle wear. Blackened strike craters scarred the hull plating; plating that had been weld-repaired so many times the armored shuttle didn't look so different from any of those Pylor gunships we'd soon be tangling with.

Beyond, I saw both Plopper 1 and Plopper 2, looking equally battle-worn, all sealed up and ready for flight. Plopper 3's dual-purpose gangway/rear bulkhead was splayed open for us like an extended tongue. We hurried up the ramp and into the cabin where no less than twenty-five Marines stood waiting. Similar to my own sealed combat suit made of hardened alloy kamacite and a helmet faceplate configured with diamond glass, the Marines had a few added necessities geared for battle situations, such as shoulder-mounted auto-tracking Phazon Pulsar weapons. Although, my suit had—as theirs did—the latest enhanced Thine technology stealth capabilities.

The Marines, having been rowdy, loud, and excited to

finally be on a mission, suddenly quieted down, first seeing the seven-foot-tall ChronoBot with its reflective metal surfaces, and then me, the Ship's Captain with my faceplate's tint-level set to fully transparent.

Sergeant Max Dryer pushed his way through the tight throng of soldiers. He first eyed the big robot and then me. He said, "Welcome aboard, Captain. My Marines are ready when you are."

"Thank you, Max . . . say hello to Hardy here. He'll be tied in via comms throughout the assault."

Hardy said, "Hey, man."

Max looked surprised when the robot held out a fist for him to bump. Max hesitated, then bumped knuckles.

Max asked, "Any last-minute intel or orders, sir?"

"Your HUD should have all the latest mission parameter updates. But let's review one more time. Max, there are currently one-hundred-forty active life-signs on that station. Your seventy-five well-trained Marines should manage that near two-to-one odds ratio, I take it?"

"*Pfft*, that won't be a problem, sir."

"Good."

Via selecting Lieutenant Pristy's tiny face icon at the bottom of my HUD display, I brought her into the open-channel conversation. "Lieutenant, can you display for us Ironhold's tactical targets?"

A 3D rotating model of the station appeared upon our HUD displays.

I said, "Once the station's armaments have been destroyed

by Ryder's Arrows, our Ploppers will set down upon the pre-determined LZs." I watched as key enemy life-sign locations moved about as tiny red icon people. "As you can see, most of the enemy are clustered together. Your three teams will be entering the station here at the top, here at the middle, and here at the mid-level or equator, of the station."

All this had been gone over a number of times before—I wanted this one last review to ensure we were all on the same page. If Max, or any of the other team commanders, had any questions, this would be the time to speak up.

"The ChronoBots, sir . . ." he said. "Your ChronoBot—"

"You can call me, Hardy." The robot said.

"Sorry, yes . . . Hardy, you and six Marines are taking responsibility for those assets, correct?"

"Affirmative," I said.

We saw the enemy ChronoBots had been differentiated on the 3D model as bright blue, larger, icons. Max continued, "Two of them are clearly posted to their most valued locations; the station's Central Command Terminal, here, and the Fueling Depot here . . . locations we are keenly interested in capturing with minimal damage."

"Correct," I said. I saw Max looked hesitant to say something else. "Spit it out, Sergeant. This is no time to hold back."

He looked at Hardy. "No insult intended, but are you certain, um, Hardy here is up to the task. Even with six Marines, and yourself, those ChronoBots will not go down easily."

I, too, turned my gaze to Hardy.

Hardy said, "LuMan assures me, there is little comparison

between himself and those three older version models, one of which is in such disrepair it squeaks when it walks and has a limp. I assure you, Sergeant Dryer when the time comes . . . those broken-down heaps won't know what hit them."

Max slowly nodded. "This is your operation, Captain. And no disrespect intended, but I sure hope you know what you're doing." He shouldered past several Marines, moving farther aft. He slapped at a big red button, and immediately, the gangway began to elevate upward and soon closed, making a vacuum-sealed *thunk* sound.

chapter 28

I said into the open mission channel, "Lieutenant, go ahead and jump the *Hamilton* into position when ready." Prior to leaving the bridge, I'd contacted Chief Craig Porter, who'd assured me that he was no worse for wear after the whole kidnapping ordeal. He also assured me Engineering and Propulsion were mission-ready and there was just enough fuel for a short jump. Running on fumes, there would be no opportunity for any kind of dry run. This would either work or it wouldn't. Like so many other less-than-optimal factors with what remained of our battle-damaged fleet, we were now operating on a wing and a prayer. I knew at this moment, there within the CIC, MATHR would be making her complex computations to manufacture a jump wormhole—the bending of space/time to correspond to our predetermined embarkation point. The Lieutenant, always thinking ahead, had provided the visuals to our HUDs. The formation of a manufactured wormhole never ceased to amaze me. It was both beautiful and awe-inspiring. I watched as the confluence of brightly colored prismatic spatial distortions formed into a yawning wormhole mouth, with a slightly narrower throat beyond, taking shape, as well. Although it wasn't visible, I knew another mouth was forming at the opposite jump location. Now, seeing the fully formed jump wormhole, without something, a reference, to compare it to within the vastness there in open space, it was hard to tell just how large it was. But taking into account the size and mass of the *Hamilton*, I knew it was colossal. And that it took immense amounts of energy to both form the thing—as well as keep it open.

We all felt it at the same time; a slight tingle upon our flesh, like a static electric discharge. Our breaths caught in our collective chests. *We'd just jumped.* Our HUD displays showed the now not-so-distant rundown looking Ironhold Station with its rust-stained hull plating and ad hoc additions. Still, it would be a grave mistake to underestimate this space station's true capabilities.

"J-Dog... deploy your Arrows... I repeat, deploy your Arrows," I said.

I saw that Doc Viv's small icon was requesting admittance to the row of other mission-critical icons at the bottom of my HUD. *Shit.* I really didn't need another lecture from her or anyone else about why I shouldn't be off on another dangerous mission. Reluctantly, I accepted her virtual request. Her icon enlarged to a full view feed. I now realized this was a pre-recorded and personal video communication to me.

"I just wanted to wish you luck, Quintos... please come back to us. Godspeed." The clip had halted on a particular frame where her pretty face looked both concerned and bemused." Her lips were partially pursed, and I wondered if she was in the process of throwing me a kiss. Nah, no, perhaps she was still talking when she cut the feed. I jostled forward—someone had tripped and fallen into me, maybe a Marine who hadn't found his space legs yet.

My HUD display now showed an external view of the *Hamilton*. A steady flow of Arrows was streaming out of the port side flight bay—like a volcanic eruption of bright red lava fragments spewing out into space. It took less than three minutes for the three Wing collectives of eighty-five fighters each to clear the ship and head off to their assigned objectives—about two-hundred-and-sixty Arrows in total. Again, I was hit from behind; one more Marine losing his balance.

J-Dog's voice crackled over the open channel. He was leading the Tango Wing, heading off toward the Ironhold Station, where their attack sorties would soon commence. "Captain ... we have a problem. Over."

"Already? What is it? Over."

"I'm hearing chatter that you and your robot aren't getting much respect from our Marine compatriots in there."

I looked about the Marines packed within the cabin, taking in their stoic and determined-looking faces behind the myriad of faceplates. "Uh ... no, not real sure what you're talking about, J-Dog. Over."

"Captain ... someone, and I won't say who, stuck some kind of 'Kick My Ass' sticker on to both yours and Hardy's back. Over."

I gestured for Hardy, who I knew was listening, to spin around. Sure enough, there was a yellow sticky note adhered to the middle of his broad back: 'Kick My Fat Ass.'

Fuck! I peeled it off. I turned around and pointed over my shoulder . . . "Hardy, get that sticker off my back, will you?"

The entire cabin exploded with laughter. Obviously, the Marines had been joined into the open channel.

"Ha," I said. "You wait . . . revenge will come when you least expect it. And it won't be pretty."

The Marines were still chuckling, and I heard J-Dog laughing too. I said, "Hey . . . J-Dog, good luck out there. Go blow some shit up, okay? Over."

"Roger that, Brigs."

I liked that he'd used my call sign.

I watched in relative silence as Tango Wing was soon buzzing all around Ironhold Station like angered bees around a hive. Only these *bees* could fire off mini-smart missiles toward their intended targets. I counted five explosions, solid hits to the station's defensive weapons, before Ironhold's energy shielding came online. It was actually visible—a kind of shimmering wavering distortion field. Now, the trick for the Arrow fighters would be to temporarily breach the shielding with bursts of rail spike munitions just prior to deploying a missile. The timing had to be right—just perfect.

Having caught the Pylors off guard was an advantage we'd counted on and had achieved. Security patrols were being called in to help defend the station. The Pylors were also deploying their own fighters from several newly-open bay locations. It wouldn't be long before the *Hamilton* would come under attack; few battles are won by just playing defense. Bravo Wing would be ready for them when they came.

Lieutenant Pristy appeared on my HUD, "Captain, two things . . . they're already trying to hack into MATHR, again, and we're being hailed by the enemy. One who calls himself, um, Cardinal Thunderballs. That's a rough translation I think . . . he's human or humanoid."

"Thunderballs?"

She looked distracted—undoubtedly, she was juggling ten different emergencies at once. She had little time for my adolescent humor. "Do you want to talk to him or not, sir?"

Max was back at our side. He and Hardy were both nodding their heads.

Hardy said, "With a name like Thunderballs, he probably walks bowlegged."

"This coming from someone who no longer has a set of those," Max said.

"True enough." Hardy conceded.

"Just put him through, Lieutenant," I said.

He appeared in a darkened compartment, the background behind him a myriad of pipes and junction boxes—perhaps some kind of plumbing service area. And perhaps done intentionally to obvert any real intel we could have picked up from the feed. I would guess he was about thirty-five or forty. Not a bad looking character, yet, in a word, the guy was beyond *hairy.* Long dark locks fell over one shoulder, while his goatee was neatly trimmed. From his splayed open white button-down shirt collar, was a billowing, massive, thatch of dark brown hair. Wearing short sleeves, his exposed arms were equally hairy—like two thick well-manicured topiaries of hair. To say this guy was proud of his *hairiness* would be an understatement.

"Captain Quintos, I presume?"

His view of me would be somewhat distorted—he'd be seeing my face in a reverse helmet cam feed. "Yes, and you wish to be addressed as Cardinal . . . Cardinal Thunderballs?" I maintained a straight face, but Hardy was making it difficult, having now donned a blinking, faux ear-to-ear smile.

He ignored my question and offered up one of his own, instead. "This is not neighborly . . . not in the least. You have come to take what is not yours, Captain. But I get it. You need fuel. That Exotic-Derivative Antimatter Proton goop to replenish those nearly depleted reactors of yours, yes?"

"Well, we did ask nicely," I said. "Instead, your Captain Rye tried to abscond with my ship. Now, *that* was not neighborly."

Cardinal Thunderballs let loose with an easy, contagious, laugh. Even those large brown eyes of his conveyed real humor and no malice. "Yes . . . Captain Rye. Want to know a secret?" He didn't wait for my replay. "Even though we are, were, of the same clan—you would call us genetic cousins—I despised him."

"So . . . perhaps we can put this disagreement behind us? Be willing to discuss selling us some fuel—"

His smile now gone, he waved away the request as if

swatting away a pesky fly, "No. It may take some time, but eventually, we will take possession of that big ungainly ship of yours, Captain. Those of you that survive our onslaught, will be sold off into lifelong servitude. Understand, Captain . . . we have debts of our own to pay. Responsibilities. Not to mention, our reputation to uphold." He looked as if he was considering something else. "I would be willing to let you leave here . . . you and I having now gotten off to what seems the foundation of a good friendship."

"You mean leave here and take our chances with the fleet of Pleidian Weonan warships nearby?"

Between thumb and forefinger, Thunderballs twisted the end of his goatee, "So you see them there . . . waiting."

"We do."

"Yes, a formidable show of force, I must say."

I said, "And you know as well as I do, without refueling, we'd be destroyed within minutes."

He tried to look sympathetic to our plight, but it came across looking more conniving than anything else.

"Look, Cardinal Thunderballs . . . right now, my duties require my full attention. Perhaps we'll meet again. Goodbye." I cut the connection.

I'd been listening to the open channel all during my brief discussion with Thunderballs. All three Arrow Wing formations were now fully engaged by enemy craft. I hailed Ryder, "Talk to me, J-Dog. Over."

"Little busy right now. Over."

I waited a full minute before hearing him come back online,

"These rogue pilots don't have our training. And their gunships don't have nearly the technology of our Arrows. Unlike our earlier encounters with the Pylors, there's no cloaking technology on these birds. But hell, these pilots do have tenacity. Giving us a good run for our money. Shit! Hold on . . ."

Lieutenant Pristy must have deployed sensor-drones because I was now seeing a zoomed-in feed of a lone Arrow fighter in the midst of a spatial dog fight. J-Dog was being pursued by two enemy gunships and they were gaining on him. I smiled, knowing the exact tactic J-dog was about to employ. I looked at the overall HUD mission timer. It was time. J-Dog's Arrow suddenly disappeared. All the other Arrows at about this time would be engaging their cloaking systems as well. I thought of my friend and piloting mentor, Clive Barkley, and what he called his ten *Battle Decrees of Success*. This particular battle decree was number 5 . . . *Always keep your opponent off guard.*

I changed the setting of my HUD visuals. Now updated, I had the ability to decipher the faint outline of J-Dog's cloaked Arrow as it finalized a reverse barrel roll maneuver and fell in right behind his two pursuers. His railgun cannon came alive—sending hundreds of explosive spikes into both gunships at once. In the span of three seconds, they became little more than shredded fragments.

Good job, Ryder, I said to myself. Turning my attention back to the *Hamilton,* I said, "XO, status of the battle?"

Derrota's voice came back an octave or two higher than usual. He was nervous and feeling out of his element. "Mattis is in the CIC... those clever fuckers are trying to breach MATHR... and making a good run at her, I may add."

"We can't lose the ship's AI, Stefan... not if we want to survive this battle," I said. "Talk to me about damage reports."

"The *Hamilton* is taking damage. Shields are holding, but it seems the Pylors know about that weakened hull area where the Phazon Pulsar cannon platform had been jettisoned. Shielding there is insufficient."

I was watching multiple HUD feeds at once of the battle in play. "Use your resources, Stefan. Have Lieutenant Pristy concentrate more of Charlie Wing assets there—"

Derrota cut me off, "Captain... you put me in this chair for a reason, so let me do my job. Don't you have a siege on a space station to attend to?"

"Point taken. Just keep me apprised. Captain out."

Ryder's icon flashed. He was requesting a private conversation. "Go ahead J-Dog."

"I just wanted to give you an update... we have all but a few of the station's weapons taken out."

"Excellent!" I said. But I didn't see the point of the private comms channel.

"Galvin, there's something strange about this station. About Ironhold."

He'd used my first name, this told me he was talking to me as a friend and not so much as a superior officer. "Can you be more specific? What do you mean by 'strange'?"

"That's just it. I can't put my finger on it. Anyway, be careful. I don't like the feel of this place."

"Noted," I said.

Ryder said, "Okay ... the last of Ironhold's cannons just went down. My job is done here."

"Copy that, J-dog ... go ahead and RTB."

Over the open channel, I said, "Commence second phase assault. Plopper pilots, bring us onboard the station."

All three Plopper pilots came back with a "Copy that, Captain."

We had less than a minute before we'd be touching down at our predetermined LZ. I said to the ChronoBot, "You know, there can't be any kind of disconnect between you and LuMan. There's far too much at stake for that. Can't have a repeat of what happened with Ensign Hughes."

"There will be no disconnect, Captain."

"Maybe it would be best if you just took a back seat to LuMan for the duration—"

"If that's what you are ordering me to do, I will comply. But I think there is value in my not doing that."

Other than Hardy being a good guy, a personality I liked and respected, I didn't see any advantage of his involvement with the mission. LuMan was the warrior here. The one that would be operating on raw programming.

He said, "Even more than LuMan being an updated version of the three other ChronoBot's, I am the de facto difference that can bring home a win for us."

Hardy had always come across as a confident personality, but this was taking things to the extreme.

"Captain ... I hate to lose."

"Join the club . . . me too. But—"

"No . . . I mean I really hate to lose. Ever since I was a kid, I'd do just about anything to win, to come out ahead. Sports . . . I played baseball in high school. Pitcher with a golden arm. Got a full-ride scholarship. I was unbeatable."

"What happened . . . injury?"

"No . . . I'll tell you sometime."

"Fine, but if I see a problem, I'll be ordering you to step back."

"Understood."

I turned to Max, "Sergeant . . . who are the six Marines you've selected to babysit us?"

chapter 29

Max gestured to a group of five Marines clustered together off to our right. It may have been my imagination, but they seemed to be bigger and meaner looking than any of the others.

"I only count five jarheads, Max... you trying to short-change me here?"

Max took several steps over to the hulking soldiers, now joining them. Max said, "And then, there were six."

He introduced them to us one by one. He placed a hand on the shoulder of a smiling Latino Marine, "This here is Magnet."

Hardy said, "Why's that?"

Magnet answered for himself, "Because women... any woman, is irresistibly attracted to me." When he smiled, I noticed one of his front teeth was polished gold.

Max said, "This here is Grip."

Grip, who was Black, reached out to shake hands, which wasn't appropriate, but I took his hand anyway. Immediately,

I regretted doing so. His grasp was like a vise. "Okay, okay! Christ, you nearly broke my hand!"

"This here is Wanda . . . just Wanda."

She stared back at me with such intensity it made me nervous. "You have a problem with a woman on your squad, sir?"

Grip said, "Careful, that bitch can kick your ass back into yesterday."

"I warned you about calling me that, Grip. I won't warn you again."

The staredown lasted several uncomfortable seconds.

Wanda was easily six-five and two-hundred pounds of sinewy muscle. I saw she had bright blue eyes and several strands of aqua died hair within her helmet. Breaking the tension, I said, "No, man or woman . . . it's good to have you as part of the team, Wanda." She actually scared the shit out of me. *Never get on this Marine's bad side.*

"Now, these two mountain-sized Marines we call Ham and Hock. And yes, identical twins," Max said. "They don't say much. But you won't find any two leathernecks more loyal. They'll follow you down to hell and back, Captain."

"Two dimwits with half a brain each . . . but, yeah . . . they'll go the distance." Magnet said.

One of the twins said, "Captain . . . it's real good meetin' ya'."

I said, "You boys from Arkansas?" recognizing the distinct southern twang.

"Yup . . . both of us are."

I sent a glance over to Max, who shrugged apologetically.

"How can we tell who's Ham and who's Hock?" Hardy asked. "You both have the same DNA markers, look the same to me . . ."

"I've always just been known as Ham—"

I said, "No, I mean how do the rest of us tell you apart? Do you have any distinguishing marks?"

Max said, "Your HUD can differentiate. That, and they have different tattoos on their chests. And no, you don't want to ask about those."

Both twins hucked and snorted.

"See, Hock's combat suit . . . his left arm? He has a red stripe there on his sleeve. Ham, on the other hand, has a blue stripe."

I heard the Plopper's engine start to whine into a higher cadence and felt the landing thrusters engage. A moment later, the shuttle touched down.

Max yelled out, "It's showtime Devil Dogs . . . stand ready!"

With the exception of Hardy and I, everyone else pounded a gauntleted fist against their chest plates in unison. "Fight for honor . . . Die for Earth!"

About to tell Max to get that ramp down, Hardy took hold of my arm, "Captain . . . we were wrong. *I* was wrong."

All eyes locked onto the ChronoBot.

"There are more life forms on this station than previously detected . . ."

"How many more?"

"Like, three times as many."

I considered sending out an abort order over the open channel.

"Wait." Hardy looked up and to the side. He scratched at his chin, looking contemplative.

"Hardy! Enough of the antics."

"Sorry. Hmm. Oddly enough, the other life forms are not humanoid, they're Pleidian Weonans. My sensors are picking them up now. Like the device Ensign Hughes had used to block his whereabouts on the *Hamilton*, the Pleidians are each wearing something similar.

I considered the new information. "Are they here voluntarily?"

Hardy shook his head, "No way ... my guess, the way they are all grouped together throughout the station, they're prisoners."

The ramp was almost down. Over the open channel, I said, "All squads ... engage the enemy ... Go! Go! Go!"

We stormed out of the aft section of the Plopper. Each combatant knew where to go and what to do. Their individual HUDs provided their mission parameters: who were their fellow squad members, their direct squad leaders, along with their precise positioning within Ironhold Station. Each combat suit had limited AI capabilities, but much of the updated information we were getting was streaming in from MATHR, back on the *Hamilton*.

Far more detail of the structure's environment was now available to us. It occurred to me that Ironhold Station was truly immense, and not anything like what I'd expected. The ramshackle outside exterior was a ruse . . . what I was looking at now was a modern high-tech facility that made the *Hamilton* look like something out of the dark ages. Most surfaces were coated in a kind of smooth rubbery white material. There wasn't a scuff mark or smudge to be found. *Almost sterile.* And there were no light fixtures here—the rubbery material emitted its own bright white illumination. Hardy, being seven feet tall, could have had two more of him stacked above his head. Looking at a diagrammatic view of the station, I could make out where the big fuel storage tanks were located. Up until now, I wasn't one-hundred percent sure they were actually here.

Up we trudged within the gradually elevating corridor. Our first destination: one of the larger compartments on this deck, situated about a half-mile ahead. Virtual icons on my HUD showed both humanoid and Pleidians lifeforms milling about there. I said, "Hardy . . . are they tracking us? Will we have any element of surprise?"

"Affirmative, they are indeed tracking us. And no, there'll be no surprise on their part."

I felt my hands sweating within my gauntlets. A bead of perspiration was making its way down my back. Then I saw movement on my HUD. The blue icon of the ChronoBot was on the move—headed our way. There were four humanoids following close behind. *Good, I like those odds.*

I found myself now directly behind Hardy. I hadn't noticed, but his dual forearm canons had deployed at some point. Listening to the open channel, others in the Marine squads were just now meeting resistance throughout the station, coming under attack. I maintained a passing interest with each of the various skirmishes going on, but I needed to keep my eye on the proverbial ball here. There was a ChronoBot headed our way with intent to kill us—to defend its home ground.

Even Hardy's heavy footfalls were silent on this strange surface. Other than what we saw on our HUDs, we'd have little warning of an opponent's attack. Hardy, moving farther out in the point position, was leaving myself and the six Marines running to catch him.

Because of the curve of the corridor, we had a limited view of not much more than fifty or sixty feet up ahead. But according to our HUDs, by now we should be close.

Max, striding in lockstep off to my left said, "You trust in this robot's, um, combat readiness?"

"Honestly? I haven't witnessed him in action, yet."

"You know, we've based the success of this operation on that robot's touted capabilities."

"Well, Hardy's all we've got."

"He shits the bed, this assault will come to an end really quick," Wanda said from behind me. She added, "Cap . . . best you keep back when the shooting starts."

At that precise moment, the enemy ChronoBot came into view and I almost dropped my shredder. It didn't look much like our own Hardy ChronoBot. For one thing, it had lost its mirror-like luster. It had far fewer tiny blinking lights on its face, but most importantly, the robot had been fitted with all sorts of ad hoc weaponry. Like our Marines, there were swivel-mounted shoulder cannons and added similar thigh-mounted cannons, and the robot was holding a gargantuan energy weapon within its grasp.

His arms extended; Hardy fired off the first bolts of plasma fire. In turn, the enemy ChronoBot fired a nanosecond later. That's when I went down like a sack of hammers.

Lying there on my back, stunned—breathless, and probably dying, I realized that out of our seventy-something invading combatants, I'd been the first casualty. Doc Viv will take delight in rubbing my dead nose in that fact—I'd had had no business being here in the first place.

"Get up, Captain . . . your suit absorbed the strike. You're perfectly fine," Wanda said while taking a knee next to me. She raised the barrel of her shredder and fired off a series of shots toward the enemy. Together, each taking an elbow, her and Max hefted me onto my feet while errant plasma bolts flashed overhead. I noticed the Pylors wore similar advanced combat suits to that of our own—which was just one more unexpected complication I hadn't counted on. Max handed me my shredder, which I'd apparently dropped when hit.

At present, Hardy and the enemy ChronoBot were dominating the corridor, thrashing about as sounds of *clanging* metal smacking against metal filled the space. Hardy took two solid punches to his face, which staggered him. I raised my shredder and tried to get a bead on one of the Pylors farther beyond. I fired three consecutive shots and missed with each. A sideways glance by one of the twins, Ham or Hock, *who knows*. Shit, I was quickly losing what little self-respect I may have had before leaving the Plopper.

The brawl between the battling bots was intensifying. We didn't have time for this. I was on the verge of giving Hardy the order to back off and let LuMan step in when I saw something. Hardy was acting less and less like a robot. He was getting irritated. Getting mad. Hardy got in a good kick to his opponents' midsection, toppling the ChronoBot over backwards.

"Get up powder puff. You fight like a god damn wussy ... You're a disgrace to our kind." Hardy loomed over the still-struggling-to-rise robot. He waggled his fingers toward himself—Bruce Lee style. "Come on, you're embarrassing yourself."

"What's a wussy?" Wanda said.

"I think a cross between a pussy and a wuss," I said.

The enemy ChronoBot, having only partially risen, could do nothing to thwart what came next. Hardy, taking its head within his two mechanical hands, lifted the now flailing robot up and off his feet. With a dramatic show of strength, next came a twisting torque motion—and off came the ChronoBot's head. Down clattered the headless body.

You could hear a pin drop. But Hardy wasn't done yet. Palming the head in one hand, he turned his attention to the stunned Pylors standing beyond. With the grace and fluidity of a Nolan Ryan and the raw power of a Mark Wohlers, Hardy wound up and fired off a wicked pitch for the record books. In a blur of motion, two of the Pylors were decapitated, and a third nearly lost an arm. Plasma bolts now shot from both of Hardy's forearm cannons. He kept firing until the four bodies were little more than smoldering husks.

"What do you think, Max ... Hardy up to your standards now?" I asked the sergeant without looking at him.

"Uh, yeah ... guess he'll be okay."

I did a quick HUD review of our combined ongoing offensive. Twenty-seven Marines had lost their lives so far. Clearing the station had not progressed nearly as quickly as I'd hoped. And based on the trouble we'd come up against, this was going to be a long haul.

I heard Max in a heated discussion over the open channel. ChronoBot number two had ten Marines hunkered down three decks above. I heard the exchange of plasma fire and then the sound of a man's painful howl. Twenty-eight now dead.

chapter 30

We'd need to ascend several decks up. We hurried past the decapitated robot, and then the decapitated Pylors, in search of an elevator that, according to our HUD's diagrammatic view of the station, shouldn't be too much farther up this corridor. Between Derrota's incoming hails concerning the *Hamilton's* failing shields, and from Mattis, concerning the Pylors' impending infiltration of MATHR, and Lieutenant Ryder, giving me updates on our three Arrow Wing squadrons (now, down from three to two squadrons), it was clear to me, Derrota, my acting XO, might not be quite up to the job. Everyone's transmissions were still coming to me.

"We're here," Hardy said, gesturing to just one more bulkhead coated with that same white rubber stuff. I cut my conversation with Derrota, telling him to utilize his team more, Lieutenant Pristy and Mattis, for starters.

I looked at the bulkhead and made a face. "I don't see an elevator or lift . . . just a bulkhead."

Hardy said, "Different technology here, Captain. Where

we're used to automatic sliding hatch doors that are easy to spot, here, onboard this station, they are impossible to see with the naked eye. In fact, we have been passing by dozens of entrances to various compartments."

"Huh." I turned and looked back the way we'd come seeing nothing but pristine smooth surfaces. "And you can see them . . . the doors or access points?"

"You can too if you know what to look for. I have altered our view of the diagrammatic station schematic. All hatchways, doorways, accessways, are now displayed in bright yellow."

Sure enough, I now saw hundreds of bright yellow indicators on my HUD. And ten feet in front of me was a double-wide set of doors with what looked to be a vertical duct shaft that spanned the entire station.

Ham, or maybe it was Hock, said, "Maybe we should try knocking."

I said, "Hardy, can you get that door open? Control the lift?"

Max said, "My Marines are dying as we stand here holding our dicks . . . can we move things along?"

Hardy stepped closer to the blank wall, raised a hand, and placed it on the surface at about chest level. Immediately, the previously solid-looking wall split apart revealing the interior cabin of a lift car.

Grip said, "That' some cool tech. Without Hardy here, we'd be up a creek without a fucking paddle."

"Let's go!" I said ushering everyone in. At least inside the car, there were actual, visible, controls. There were touch buttons with unrecognizable symbols on them. Hardy tapped on one of the buttons. The door closed, more like flowed back together again, resealing itself. The car began to ascend upward.

In stark contrast to the *Hamilton's* lifts—clattering, jostling, seemingly medieval in comparison—Ironhold's lift system was both smooth and quiet. There was a tinkling sound of bells prior to the lift doors spreading open. According to my HUD, there should be no one directly outside in the corridor, a corridor that should look identical to the one we'd just left several decks below. Hardy moved out first, with the rest of us following, weapons raised at the ready.

Max was on the open comms channel talking to the team leader of the Marines pinned down by the ChronoBot. "We're on our way, Jordy . . . just hold on!" Max was already sprinting down the corridor. While the rest of us hustled to catch up, Hardy was abreast of him within three strides and then passed him by.

We heard their energy blasts before seeing anything. Then we saw stray plasma bolts striking the curved nearby bulkheads and, surprisingly, being absorbed upon impact. Coming around the bend, I saw Max up ahead—he was laid out flat on the deck. With a quick check of my HUD, I saw that his life signs were still present, although they were weak. Wanda slowed and took a knee next to him, while the rest of us continued on. The corridor up ahead opened into a circular chamber where tables and chairs, of course, all the same, pristine white, were situated. All along the surrounding bulkhead were integrated glowing blue panels. This was a kind of mess hall and the panels were access portals to meal replicators; we had something similar, far less advanced looking, onboard the *Hamilton*.

The enemy ChronoBot was identical to the one on the lower deck—with the exception that this one still had its head attached. No less than a half dozen Marines were laid out on the deck. All were dead. Farther on, tables had been upended, making a barricade of sorts for the remaining ten stranded Marines to take shelter behind. Whatever that white rubbery shit was coating everything here, it had saved their lives to this point.

I was thinking this was going to be a repeat of what happened down below, where the two mechanical gladiators would turn their attention exclusively to each other and battle it out. Via my HUD, I was surprised to see Pylor combatants making their way through another access corridor—one that emerged into this mess hall. Startled, hearing a noise from behind, I saw Wanda struggling to support a now conscious Max.

I said, "Ham ... Hock, don't just stand there with your thumbs up your asses, give her a hand."

Hardy and the other ChronoBot had already engaged each other. Once more, metal clanged against metal. Hardy had already started in with the name-calling.

"Grip, Magnet, you're with me," I said, heading off toward the other corridor. Until Hardy had the other robot down for the count, we needed to stop that approaching band of Pylor combatants.

Turning the corner into the other corridor, I saw Wanda was now with us, too. It would be ten against four. I didn't like the odds. And like every other corridor on this damn station, there'd be nothing to take cover behind. Then I thought of something. I hailed Hardy.

"A little busy here right now," he said.

"I know. Sorry. Listen ... can you see where we're at?"

"Of course. You're about to come head-to-head with more bad guys."

"Yeah, exactly. Can you, um, do your magic and open some of the invisible hatch doors along here, right where we're positioned?" I heard Hardy reel off a slew of graphic insults and more sounds of clanging metal. "Hold on."

All at once, four doorways *flowed* open upon the previously smooth bulkheads on both sides of the corridor. I yelled, "Take cover!"

No sooner had we each ducked into an opening, the enemy rounded the end of the corridor. "Let them get closer," I said, smiling to myself. *They won't know what hit them.* Then, I saw movement on my HUD. I looked back the way we came. *No fucking way.* Ham and Hock, with a barely conscious MAX supported between them, had entered the corridor—the three of them would be easy targets in a matter of seconds.

Wanda said, "Those fucking twin morons. Captain ... permission to just shoot them myself?"

It was tempting.

Max seemed to have wakened up enough to realize their dire predicament. He untangled himself from Ham and Hock, and in a hoarse voice said, "Turn around ... back the way we came."

They'd almost made it. But they were easy targets as the enemy continued around the bend with guns blazing. Running, they'd somehow reached the mess without all being killed. While Ham and Hock dove left, Max dove right, out of sight. "Fire!" I yelled letting loose with my own shredder. Wanda, Magnet, and Grip followed suit. All ten enemy combatants were caught off guard. And with nothing to hide behind, our weapon fire made fast work bringing them down. Several had tried to retreat the way they'd come, but it was a lost cause. Checking my HUD, no life signs remained. I wasn't above patting myself on the back for a job well done and was in the process of doing just that when the little hairs on the back of my neck began to bristle. Someone, there in the darkness behind me—within a compartment I'd had no time to look into prior to engaging the enemy, was there. Lurking. *Fuck.*

I didn't turn around. At least, not right away. How I instinctively knew it was Thunderball, I have no idea—but I knew it just the same. I also knew there were weapons trained on my back. So, when I did finally, slowly, turn around, I smiled making sure I looked as harmless and cordial as possible. And there he was, Cardinal Thunderballs himself. Him, and no less than ten of his fellow armed Pylor marauders.

I heard the door reseal itself behind me. My HUD connection to the open mission channel displayed a 'disconnected' icon. So, not only was I physically disconnected from my team, I'd lost the ability to communicate with them, or anyone. I opened my faceplate and I noticed a nauseating scent permeating the air, something both sweet and musky.

"Captain Galvin Quintos . . . I am so pleased to meet you in the flesh."

His men wore combat suits while he was dressed in plain clothes, albeit fancy ones. He wore the same open-collared dress shirt I'd glimpsed earlier back on the *Hamilton* and had the same thatch of chest hair billowing forth like unruly shrubbery. A kind of cape or cloak—I'm not real sure what the difference is between the two—hung from his shoulders and obscured most of his arms. His trousers were snug, almost like tights, and he wore knee-high polished boots. There was no immediate tie-in to his surname, Thunderballs, no gargantuan bulge there between his legs.

"It is so rare that I have guests these days . . . please, lower your arms." He took several strides forward and extended a hand. "I believe this is your custom on Earth. To, what is the phrase? Shake palms?"

"Shake hands," I corrected, taking his hand in my combat suit's far larger gauntlet. It was like shaking the hand of a small child, and by the momentary tightening of his smile, I could tell he regretted the whole hand-shaking greeting thing.

"I must give credit where credit is due, Captain," he said. "Although you are not the first to breach our defenses, even to land upon this station . . . you *are* the first to best even one of our ChronoBots. Besting two of them, most impressive."

I hadn't known Hardy had taken down the second ChronoBot, and Thunderballs must have picked up on my surprise.

"Ah, that's right, you have been disconnected from your

compatriots. You didn't know." He let out an audible, regretful, sigh, "Alas, you also do not know what happened next ... just moments ago. That the rest of your team, mere feet from where we are standing now, were defeated ... I am sorry to say, many more of my men had arrived. A blaze of crossfire had put your team at a great disadvantage. I assure you, they died bravely ... honorably. And just now, having remotely brought down her shields, your ship, I am sorry to say, will be boarded within the hour."

Was that really possible? How the hell would he know what had transpired out in that corridor? On the Hamilton? As if reading my thoughts, he turned his head just enough for me to see the small apparatus protruding from his left ear; some kind of comms device.

"I'm sure you have many questions. Like what is to become of your Marines still alive on Ironhold Station. And what is to become of that great dreadnought of yours? And her crew? All will be answered in time. First, walk with me. As I said, I have so few guests these days." He shot a disgusted look to the armed combatants surrounding him, "And let's just say, establishing strong friendships here has been difficult." He smiled broadly, "Yes, I decree you and I will become the very best of chums."

"Well, you can never have too many friends, I always say ... um, can I call you Cardinal?"

"Please do. If I can call you Galvin."

I nodded.

"And yes, realistically, I know ... right now you want to kill me with your bare hands. Or perhaps pull that knife at your hip and drive it into my heart." He shook his head. "This too shall pass. I can tell . . . like me, you are a survivor, Galvin."

It took all of my will not to reach for my knife, or the tagger, still holstered on my thigh. Thunderballs spoke over his shoulder to one of his subordinates. I didn't recognize the language in which they conversed. But what it made me realize was that this Pylor leader had been speaking near-perfect English to me and had done so without the use of a translation device.

All but three of his guards suddenly turned and hurried off. Then, one of those who remained confiscated both my knife and my tagger.

Thunderballs broad smile returned, "Please, come this way, Galvin."

We walked together within the now brightly illuminated compartment, one just as nondescript as any of the various corridors I'd encountered thus far. Approaching a bulkhead, an opening formed and soon there was a door entrance before us. Thunderballs stood aside and gestured for me to proceed. "Please . . ."

Crossing through into what I assumed would be one more sterile white compartment, I was surprised by how wrong I was. It was like walking into something from a storybook. Roughly hewn timber beams crossed overhead while the surrounding walls were gray stacked stone. There were several colorful hanging tapestries depicting variations on old eighteenth-century equestrian fox hunts. Across the room, flames danced within a fireplace large enough for me to stand tall within, with room to spare. Above, a large painting of a woman wearing a kind of shimmering green pantsuit dominated the entire rock chimney. She wore a serious expression—a woman with muscular, broad shoulders. I leaned in—squinted my eyes. Her upper lip could have definitely used a little grooming. Glancing to my right, I saw Thunderballs looking up at the portrait with adoring eyes.

"Your mother?" I asked. I supposed it could have been his father but kept those thoughts to myself.

"Alexandria LeCorpus . . . yes, my beautiful mother."

I turned my attention to our surroundings, at all the work Thunderballs had put into this transformation. The expansive interior of a grand English manor came to mind, but yet, different. An alien version of something *Earthly*, that just missed—was off in a kind of way I couldn't quite put my finger on.

"Makes you feel homesick, Galvin?" he asked looking pleased with himself.

"Mm . . . you have no idea."

"I have been enamored with Earth for most of my adult life. What a messy, self-centered, contentious, world you come from, Galvin."

"I can't argue with that assessment."

Thunderballs continued, "Yet . . . there is an interesting dichotomy, the humans on your world have a great capacity for compassion and creativity, as well. Nothing about Earth can be taken at face value . . . oh such wonderful, wonderful, chaos!"

We traversed through more rooms, a sitting room, an

immense kitchen and dining area, a music room with various instruments, such as an old-fashioned grand piano and an upright harp. We continued on through an archway and into a narrow stone passageway. Here, flames danced upon lit wall torches and hardwood flooring had given way to worn cobblestones. I wasn't thrilled with the direction this tour was going. I was tempted to jump the Pylor leader from behind, but the three guards following behind us would kill me before I could get my hands around his neck.

I said, "Cardinal . . . can I assume you, too, are Human?"

"Oh, yes, well, both Human and Clarmonian. I was born on Clarmon . . . one of a small cluster of planets within what you would call the Orion constellation." He turned to look back at me. His eyes filled with adoration once more, "My mother was Human. She spoke of Earth often . . ." Thunderballs continued down the hall—quiet for several minutes. Walking within the wake of his sweet, musky, cologne was taking its toll on me.

"Where, exactly, are we going?" I asked.

He spoke over his shoulder, "Where all your questions will be answered."

Thunderballs slowed to a stop in front of an immense timber door. One of the Pylor guards came forward from behind with key. Unlocking the latch, he swung the door open upon ungreased hinges.

Thunderballs motioned me inside, "Please . . . I wish to introduce you esteemed Empress Shawlee Tee, of the Pleidian Weonans people."

chapter 31

And here she was. I saw her there, standing mournful at a porthole window—she'd been looking out into the dark vastness of lonely space beyond. She wore a simple long white gown that bunched at the floor and hid her feet from view. She literally glowed a pale blue. Like that of Fleet Commander, Twinwon, her head was oval in shape—the center of which was an open void. Large, wide-set eyes now assessed those of us who had intruded into her solitude.

It was then that I remembered something about the Pleidian Weonan's Empress having been captured and taken prisoner, some years prior. Not an elected official, she'd been born into the esteemed position. She was royalty. And as long as she remained alive, her people could not, *would not*, elevate another to be the next Emperor or Empress. And now, I knew the real reason that fleet of Pleidian Weonans warships had kept its distance. Not for any mystical or superstitious reasons, as we'd assumed, but because the one person this society cherished most was their young female leader.

Her eyes scanned the faces before her. Then, seeing Thunderballs, the hatred she held for him was undeniable. She spoke in her native tongue as my audio implants translated her words. "What do you want ... why do you disturb me?"

"Now Empress, how it pains me, such cold receptions I must endure." Thunderballs placed the palm of his hand over his heart. "Do I not nourish you ... keep you safe and in good health?"

She glowered back at him.

"How rude of me. You have a guest, Empress." He gestured toward me. Empress Shawlee Tee, this is Captain Galvin Quintos, of a great warship called the *USS Hamilton*."

"So, what ..."

"So ... please, you will do me, uh ... a bit of a favor," Thunderballs said.

She closed her eyes. Clearly, Thunderballs had requested *favors* from her before.

"Oh, nothing like that, my sweetness ... what I request is, simply, for you to speak with the good captain. Explain to him the futility of resisting my orders. Perhaps you can tell him your own, unique, predicament."

Empress Shawlee Tee crossed her arms over her chest; she was clearly humiliated. My TAC-Band translated my words for me, "I'm sorry, Empress ... I'm not here to cause you any more grief. I, too, am a prisoner."

Her nod was almost imperceptible. "You're from Earth." She'd said it more like a statement than a question.

"Yes."

She let out a resigned breath. "Three cycles ago . . . about four of your Earth years, my family and I were en route to the Amoroah Nighn System . . . one of the many Pleidians' colonial outposts. There for Holiday. My royal StarClipper and our accompanying security fleet stopped off here. Ironhold was a Pleidians refueling station. Although, it currently looks nothing like it had back then." She sent another hateful glance toward Thunderballs. "It resembles a derelict floating junkpile now. Anyway, we were ruthlessly attacked just as the station's shields were lowered and we had set down. Countless Pylor pirate ships streamed in from all directions. Energy weapons blazed . . . missiles exploded." She hesitated, before continuing. "Most of the crew of my security fleet is now long dead. Most of those Pleidians inhabitants upon this Ironhold Station are now dead. All but a few of my immediate family members are now dead. Those that do remain are only alive for one reason . . . to keep my people, the Pleidian Weonan, from storming—or outright destroying—this station. I wish they would attack . . . I would gladly die for that to happen. But no . . . that is not to be. So, we remain hostages. And as a reminder to my military forces of the seriousness of Pylor ruthlessness, Captain . . . and undoubtedly you have noticed this . . . the dead of my people . . . all strung together like vile decorations—those that encircle the outer hull of this station."

Thunderballs feigned the clapping of his hands, "Wonderful, Shawlee . . . thank you for that heartwarming recollection. His smile vanished and his eyes turned to cold dark ice. He was upon her in a flash. One hand taking hold, slipping through her open skull structure and clasping it in a grip that made the Empress grimace. I moved to help her but found two sets of Pylor hands holding me back. Thunderballs wrenched her head backwards even farther to where she was now looking straight up toward the ceiling.

"You're hurting her. Stop it!"

He let go of her but continued to stand close to her. He used a forefinger to trace the inner contours of her face. Thunderballs continued speaking, so quietly that I had a hard time hearing him.

"Captain, I have brought you here so you can see, for yourself, that I do not jest, I do not exaggerate when I tell you that the survival of the *Hamilton's* crew, any of those captured Marines of yours still alive on this station... all depends on what you do next."

"Yeah, about that, Thunderballs," I said it with an appropriate tone and seriousness in my voice. "I am a mere cog in a much larger machine. And let me tell you, U.S., Navy Fleet Admirals cannot, will not, be threatened or give in to terrorism; that just won't happen. Even at the hefty price of losing the *Hamilton* and her crew."

"You say that now. Of course, you would say that now. I anticipated as much."

"We have a phrase back on Earth that conveys so much with just two simple words."

Thunderballs raised his brows.

I said, "Fuck... you."

"No need to be crass, Captain, No, you will order your

Bridge crew to surrender. And you will order those very few, still-surviving Marines onboard this station to stand down." He took a step closer to me—the smile had returned to his lips. "I will leave you for a spell with the young empress. Ask her what it is like to watch as, one by one, crewmembers—and later family members—were executed in that chamber not far from here. Ask her how long it took before she was begging to contact that fleet of warships out there . . . commanding them to stay back. Not to attack."

The Empress's shoulders slumped as she stared down to the ground.

"You have one hour before the executions begin. First up, the one you call Max. You know Max, copper-colored hair, face full of freckles? As we speak, more cable is being strung along the outer hull of this station. Max's body will be the first human to ever adorn Ironhold Station. A kind of honor, don't you think?"

Thunderballs and his three Pylor guards left, locking the door behind them.

She said, "I am so sorry, Captain. He is beyond evil; he will take everything sacred from you. And in the end, you, too, will do as he asks."

"Nah . . . I wouldn't be so sure of that, Empress. You know, a lot can happen in an hour." I took off my helmet.

She looked at me—a calculating expression that said, *can I trust him?*

chapter 32

Doc Viv

The battle klaxon continued to wail from somewhere high above her. The constant strobing alarm reverberated within her aching head. Beneath her feet, HealthBay's deck plates vibrated as each of the *Hamilton's* big weapons fired off one energy pulse after another. The entire ship shook as Pylor missiles continued to pummel the ship's weakening shields.

"No! Make a paramedian incision, here... you'll need to open him all the way up." she said sternly to the Cutter Bot. The surgery center was already at max capacity and she knew the passageway outside was stacking up with more of the injured and dying. She checked the patient's life support and monitoring readouts. The virtual 3D floating human-looking avatar had stopped rotating above the operating table. A lone metatag text block blinked on and off: PATIENT DECEASED ... PATIENT DECEASED ... PATIENT DECEASED.

"Alright, it's too late for this pilot. Bag him up and send the remains down to cold storage on Deck 1." She peeled off her gloves and deposited them into a biohazard bin.

"Bring in the next one!" She ordered. Moving to a small counter, she washed her hands and then placed them under the warm beams of high-intensity germ-killing light. Behind her, she heard another hovering gurney being positioned into place. She snapped on a pair of clean gloves and turned around.

"Okay, who do we have—"

"Hey there, Doc," Lieutenant Wallace Ryder said with a crooked smile.

She gave his body a once-over, her eyes coming to rest on a charred area just below his left hip. "Ouch . . . bet that hurts like a son of a bitch," she said, returning his smile. "Pulsar blast?

"Yeah . . . my ship and suit took the brunt of it, though. Hey, all in a day's work, right? I've had worse."

"Yes, you have, and this isn't the first time I've had to put you back together again." She glanced around the compartment; spotting what she was looking for. "You, Cutter, get over here."

The Cutter Bot traversed through scurrying medical staff, taking up a position on the other side of Ryder's gurney.

She said. "Your medi-hands clean? Disinfected?"

"Affirmative," the bot replied.

"Get him turned onto his side . . . No! Christ, with the injury side up."

Ryder winced, then smiled at hearing the doctor's bossy tone.

"What?" she said.

"I don't know... you're just funny. Even when you're yelling at a bot."

She leaned over and took a closer look at his injury. The flesh on his hip was in pretty bad shape. Some of it would need replacement. Without looking at the bot, she said, "Inject local area with Torcain... he's in enough pain as it is. Clean the wound and this area here is to be incised down to the subcutaneous layer. I want all this dead flesh here cut away. Anything black and crusty gets removed. Disinfect, then spray in a generous amount of AugmentFlesh. Then, bandage the wound."

"Affirmative," the bot said and immediately got to work.

She gave Ryder a squeeze of the shoulder, "You'll be fine. Sorry, but you won't be cleared to fly for a few days."

"Uh huh, that won't work. I need to get back out there, Viv."

She knew things were bad. "What's going on out there?"

"Seems like a load of Pylor fighters came out of nowhere. We thought we had the upper hand, but we were being overrun." He looked to her, "The *Hamilton* is taking a beating... again. Poor ol' gal never seems to catch a break. I'd like to get out there... unfortunately, it doesn't look like time's on our side."

She nodded not knowing what to say to him. To the Cutter, she said, "Put a vac-seal on the bandage when you're done. Then release him."

Ryder took her hand in his and spoke with just above a whisper, "Hey... what happened to us, Viv?"

She saw the pain in his eyes. *Strange...* Bar none, there was no one aboard the *Hamilton* who played the field like Ryder. An infamous playboy—a history of breaking many a young woman's heart. Some of whom, nurses and doctors, were right here in this department. *So why me?* She wondered. It had only been that one night. Was little more than a tryst and a mistake at that.

"We talked about this, Wallace," she said. "Can't we just move on? I love being your friend—"

His expression turned serious, "It's him, isn't it?"

Looking confused, she said, "Huh? Who?" But of course, she knew the 'who' that Ryder was talking about. Her mind flashed back to that darkened Japanese garden, the steam rising above the hot spring pond nestled there within that rocky landscape. The feel of Galvin's tongue in her mouth, the joined rhythm of their movements, and the sound of water lapping up on the shore. She would not tell Ryder. Nor would she tell Galvin that it had been her who he had made love to that night. So easily, Galvin could break her heart. No, she'd been down that road before.

"Look, Ryder . . . I don't know what you think you know. but take it from me, I'm simply not in a place where any kind of relationship would work for me. So, how about you shut up and let the Cutter do its job?"

She left him there before he could object further. Once more, she peeled off her gloves and discarded them into a biohazard-bin. She felt a hand on her shoulder and spun around. More than a little surprised she said, "Captain!"

It was Captain Eli Tannock. Strange, she hadn't thought

about him in days. Figured he had been cloistered within his quarters in that persistent mental fog. But right now, his eyes looked sharp—his keen intelligence apparent.

"Hello, Vivian . . ." he said.

"Um, what . . . what are you doing here? Are you okay?"

"I'm good. And I need you to do me a favor?"

"Of course. Anything, Sir."

"I need you to clear me for duty."

Fuck. "Sir, I can't do that. Maybe when we reach port again. A new assessment can be made. What you've been through . . . your injuries—"

"You will. You must, Vivian. Mr. Derrota, I'm sorry to say, is not capable of skippering this ship. And Captain Quintos, unfortunately, is not here. Without my experience at the helm of the *Hamilton*, she will be lost . . . perhaps it may already be too late."

"Captain, Sir . . . Quintos is still the skipper. I'm not going to get in the middle of a turf war. He's done an amazing job taking up the reigns since your accident."

"Agreed. Although, I'm somewhat surprised. Vivian, I'm not looking to be reinstated as Captain."

"What are you asking, then?"

Tannock seemed momentarily baffled by the question and then smiled. "XO . . . I'll take over as Quinto's' XO."

"Really? You'd do that?"

"Sure, I would. And only for the limited duration of this battle. I'm not at one-hundred percent, but I'm good. More than adequate get us through this battle. An asset that's required right now."

She looked into the Captain's eyes, weighing the decision. What limited reports she'd gotten about the course of the battle had been sketchy. Things were not going well. Derrota and Mattis were overwhelmed and bickering like a couple of old schoolmarms. Lieutenant Pristy had been furious when Quintos had passed her over for the job. But as sharp as she was, Viv agreed, the Lieutenant was still too young, too inexperienced to be XO.

"Captain . . . you're putting a shitload of responsibility in my hands. I'm the ship's primary physician, yes, but this decision is way over my pay grade."

"And yet, it is yours to make."

She looked at him with discerning eyes. "What year was the Hamilton launched?

"Twenty-one ten," he said.

"What's Alexander Hamilton's inscribed quote on the dedication plaque?"

Retrieving the mental information, Tannock's eyes looked up and to the right. "Give all the power to the many, they will oppress the few. Give all the power to the few, they will oppress the many."

Her eyes narrowed as she continued to assess him. His cognitive abilities seemed sound. But was it temporary? Could he lapse right back into befuddlement at the worst possible moment, there, on the bridge? She saw that two more gurneys were being pushed into the surgery center, critical patients needing surgery. She needed to get back to doing what she could for those lives. "This better not come back on me." Her face went stern, "Don't even think about screwing with me, Sir. If and when this battle ends, you step down."

"Agreed. I am cleared for duty?"

She raised her chin, "Yes, but only if Derrota agrees to it. I'll message him ... that you're temporarily cleared for active duty."

AT THIS POINT, LIEUTENANT GAIL PRISTY NO LONGER waited for direct orders coming from Derrota. He was clearly overwhelmed. She deployed the last of the sensor drones since most of those previously deployed had been destroyed. One by one, new video feeds came alive on the halo-display. She'd wanted to get visuals on the *Hamilton's* mid-section, where the Pylor fighters had been concentrating most of their near-constant barrage.

MATHR's voice was a near-constant, overhead. *Hull breach ... hull breach, Deck 5, Deck 11, Deck 29 ...*

Pristy turned to the Captain's Mount, which, again, was empty. She spotted both Derrota and Mattis, off to the right. They were engaged in another contentious dispute.

"Absolutely not ... I will not give that order. Captain Quintos, Galvin, will make contact soon," Derrota said.

Mattis shot a hand toward the halo-display, "We're out of time! Can't you see that, Stefan? Surrender now and maybe, just maybe, we save the lives of what's left of the crew."

"I'm in command, not you," Derrota said. "Why don't you concern yourself with what's happening there within the CIC . . . keep MATHR from being hijacked!"

"There's nothing more we can do to in that regard. Cyber firewalls are being obverted just as soon as they're put up," Mattis said, sounding defeated. "It's just a matter of time now . . ." he added.

Lieutenant Pristy saw him enter the bridge. Was he the man he'd been prior to the battle with the Grish? No. But he looked a hell of a lot better than he'd been a few days ago. Captain Tannock approached the Captain's Mount. His head's bandage was gone—remnants of AugmentFlesh still clung to his forehead.

Before taking a seat, Tannock said, "Science Officer, Derrota . . . I need your verbal affirmation."

"Sir . . . what is this all about?" Derrota said, looking apprehensive.

"That as of this moment, I am taking back command of the *Hamilton*. Let me get us out of this mess."

It was Mattis that spoke up first, "Captain, unless you have been cleared—"

"Check your TAC-Bands . . . see the message from Doctor Leigh. People, we have zero time to waste here."

Pristy checked her messages and saw that Doc Viv had, indeed, cleared the captain for duty . . . but for duty as an XO, not Captain.

Immediately, Derrota and Mattis began to bicker again.

"Stop!" she yelled before she'd consciously realized what

she said. "Stefan, Alistair, put a sock in it. Captain, sit down, and take command. Get us out of this fucking mess!"

She caught Grimes, sitting at the helm station, holding back a smile.

Captain Tannock continued to stare at Derrota. "I still need your affirmation, Stefan."

Derrota glanced toward the halo-display and then to Pristy. She nodded, "It's time, do it."

Derrota said, "You have my affirmation, Sir."

Tannock sat down. "Someone tell me the last time we had contact with the Union?"

"Four hours and ten minutes ago," Pristy said.

"Who's in command?"

"Lieutenant Randy Cobb."

"Hail the Union . . . get him on the horn."

It took several moments before Cobb's face appeared on halo-display feed. "Cobb here . . ." He saw Captain Tannock sitting at the Captain's Mount—confusion turned to comprehension. "Captain . . . we're taking it from all sides here. Shields are down to thirty percent. Rail spikes are depleted . . . most of our Phazon Pulsar cannon platforms have been taken out—"

"Just tell me about propulsion, Cobb . . . tell me you can get that ship of yours over here."

"Sir . . . sure, we can make that maneuver. But what's the difference? We'll get our asses handed to us wherever we go within this part of space."

"I'm not accustomed to having my orders questioned, Lieutenant. But if you must know, I've chosen to save the

Hamilton over the *Union*. Although the *Hamilton* shields are down along our portside midsection, they're holding everywhere else. All our damage is occurring along that one stretch. Get the Union over here now, and cozy right up to us."

Cobb stared back at Tannock. "That's one hell of a good idea, Sir. The Union will take the place of your mid-ship shields. Consider it done, Captain. Cobb out."

chapter 33

Captain Galvin Quintos

The hour was nearly up. The Empress and I, seated next to each other on her bunk, spent the time talking. She asked me to call her Shawlee, and she called me Galvin. I learned of her home and her family. Learned of a world far more advanced than Earth with a people that were both spiritual and reclusive. In turn, she asked about Earth and my own family and upbringing in the small town of Valentine, Nebraska. She was genuinely interested in my personal life and laughed easily hearing about my childhood dog, Gomer, who obsessively tried to mate with every farm animal for miles around. I did my best to keep her mind off the current situation. It was clear, at some point of her abduction, she'd given up hope. Yet, if she was going to survive whatever came next, I needed to show her there was light at the end of the tunnel—even if I wasn't so sure that it really was there.

"Galvin . . . can you promise me something?"

"Sure. As much as I can."

"If I am to die here . . . and you survive—"

"That's not going to happen—"

"Let me finish. You will not kill Cardinal."

That floored me. After what she had been through. The loss that she'd endured. How was it possible she wanted mercy for such a despicable piece of shit? "Empress . . . Shawlee, Thunderballs is responsible for the death of untold hundreds of my people. As we speak, he is attacking my ship. He has to die, preferably with my hands wrapped around his throat."

The corners of her mouth turned upward. "I have no affection for this Pylor monster, I assure you of that, but my people have suffered much. The love that the Pleidian Weonan people hold for their Empress is probably not something you would understand. I'm not so sure I understand it myself. They will need what we call *Settlement.* Atonement for what they have endured."

"He needs to die, Shawlee."

"Of course, you would see it that way, Galvin. But what must occur will happen on my homeworld of Weonan. He will be tried and convicted. And he will be sent to the garden world of Cincree, where he will live out the rest of his life caring for our Pleidian sick and impaired."

"That's your idea of justice?"

"No, that's our idea of redemption and elevation of spirit." She stared back at me, the smile still present on her small lips.

"And what . . . I have to make you this promise right now?"

"Yes, please."

"Fine. I promise I'll do my best. But if it comes to self-defense, a he-or-me situation, I'll choose me."

"Understood."

Sounds were coming from outside the door. I was already regretting my promise to the Empress. Thunderballs and his Pylor guards were coming for me.

"I don't suppose you have anything I could use as a weapon. A fork, or a spoon, preferably a knife?"

She looked about her small cell. "I have nothing. I am not permitted to have eating utensils."

God, I hate that Pylor shit. I stood, crossed over to where the door was. I backed up so I'd be out of sight when the door opened. *If I could get the jump on one of them—one of their weapons . . .*

But the door didn't swing open as I'd expected. I heard the shouted demand, "Stand back!" right before it crashed open and slammed down hard onto the cobblestone floor. The Empress screamed and pulled her legs up off the floor and into herself—hell, I think I may have screamed myself.

Hardy entered with all the grace of a bull in a china shop. His pristine mirror finish was now anything but that. Blackened scorch marks pocked much of his torso and his four mechanical appendages.

Seeing the towering robot with his faux smiling face, Empress Shawlee Tee screamed bloody murder.

I rushed her side and took her into my arms. "Hey, hey . . . it's okay. The robot's with me."

"Her face was buried into her hands. "No!...ChronoBots! They're horrible...killing machines...killed so many of my people."

I glanced up to see Hardy looking horrified with a new faux face I hadn't seen before. "Shawlee, this is Hardy. He's with me...one of my crew and he's good. Um, part human."

I saw an eye peek out from behind one of her hands. She looked up at the towering robot. "Part human? Are you insane? How would that even be possible?"

"Yeah, I know...even sounds absurd to me. But, do you trust me?"

She didn't answer. It took a few moments before she nodded.

"We have to go, and I need you to be brave. Can you do that?"

Her hands fell away as she took in the robot once more. "I can be brave."

I said to Hardy, "Tell her you won't hurt her."

I heart soared at seeing a cluster of impatient Marines standing at the door's open threshold.

Hardy lowered down to one knee so he could look at the Empress face-to-face. His Boston accent was as prevalent as ever. "My name is John Hardy...I used to be human, like the Captain there. But that was a long time ago. I would never hurt you, Missy, I promise."

She covered her mouth with one hand, "You really are a machine person...that's beyond strange."

Hardy held out one of his massive mechanical hands to her. "We must go, now."

I said, "Is there anything in here you want to bring with you? You're not coming back here. Ever."

"No! There's nothing for me here."

"Hardy, keep her safe." I left the Empress's cell and greeted my awaiting team of Marines. All but one; Magnet wasn't here among them. Someone handed me a shredder rifle.

Max said, "We lost him right after you went missing."

"Killed by the Pylors?" I asked.

"No, we literally lost him. He's somewhere about," Wanda said.

"Our HUD sensors are all F-ed up ..." Grip said, eyeing the Empress. "you know, she's pretty in a weird, alien kind of way."

"Shut up, cretin ... she might hear you," Wanda scolded. She plucked my helmet off of the bunk and handed it to me.

"Max, give me a quick sit-report," I said. "Took you a while to find me."

As a group, we moved back through the creepy passageway, then convened in Thunderball's fancy English manor. The kitchen seemed as good a place as any to hold up. Cupboards were flung open and plundered, the dual refrigerators were raided. With the exception of Hardy and the Empress, who was too nervous to eat, everyone drank and chowed down. In between bites, I had Max update me.

Apparently, Max's Marine's had spent the better part of two hours looking for me after I'd been grabbed by Thunderballs. Since all comm signals had subsequently been blocked between individual Marines, as well as with the *Hamilton*, Hardy had been tasked with finding a creative way to reestablish some kind of communications. As it turned out, he'd recently discovered an alternate TAC-Band text messaging frequency that was not being blocked by the Pylors. This was also how he'd pinpointed where I was being held. Contrary to Thunderball's dire description of my invading Marine's near-total annihilation, they had actually prevailed, accomplishing much of what they'd been tasked to do—taking this station—but at a heavy cost. Close to thirty fine Marines had lost their lives fighting the Pylors. Approximately forty-five Marines were still active.

The Empress looked out of place and scared. In a barely audible voice, she asked, "Are there any of my people . . . still alive here?"

Max said, "Yeah, several teams have found and set free a number of hostages. Not sure the exact number. But rest assured, we're keeping them safe."

Moisture filled her eyes, "It's been so long. Can I see them now?"

"As soon as it's safe to do so, I assure you," I said.

Max turned his attention back to me, "By the way, Plopper 1 is toast . . . destroyed. Suppose we can catch a ride on Plopper 2 when it's time to bug out of here."

"Two questions," I said. "First, what's the status of Ironhold's fuel tanks . . . considering that's what we're here for?

And second, where's Cardinal Thunderballs now? Any of our teams encounter him and his guards?"

"He's been spotted. Problem is, he knows all the secret Ironhold passageways and hiding places. Not to mention, he's got that third ChronoBot along with him, providing excellent defenses."

"Hold on ... I thought Hardy destroyed that one, too." I glanced toward Hardy, who looked as though he'd been through the wringer. I wasn't sure, but he looked to be sulking.

"They've come up against one another twice now. Talk about fireworks ... we all just get the hell out of the way," Grip said.

"Cap ... that ChronoBot ain't like the other two. Bigger, meaner, and smarter ... a real smart bot," Hock said.

"Yeah, real damn smart," Ham agreed.

"And the *Hamilton* ... what's the status there?"

Max shrugged, "Hardy's TAC-Band messaging thing doesn't seem to extend off of this station. So, what're our orders, Captain?"

"We need to re-establish normal comms back to our ship," I said to Hardy. "Is there, like, a central communications terminal onboard this station? One that's responsible for blocking our signals?"

Hardy seemed to snap out of his funk, "Yes, two decks down. But with the exception of the refueling tanks, the station's Comms Hub, is the most highly defended ... has the most still-active combatants."

"Then that's where we'll make our next advance. Max, get

busy on your TAC-Band... get the rest of our forces down there." I moved closer to Hardy, "Undoubtedly, Thunderballs and his pet robot are squirreled up there. You have until we reach that Comms Hub to come up with a way to defeat that ChronoBot. You still up for this? Maybe time to call up LuMan?"

"No. That Twat-bot's all mine."

chapter 34

We headed off together, this time Max taking point. The Empress, with Hardy as her protector, stayed within the middle of the group. It bothered me that Magnet had not been located yet—that we didn't have a way to key into his whereabouts.

Something else that I'd learned: all of the station's lifts had been disabled. Fortunately, there were multiple inter-deck stairwells—but unfortunately, they'd be perfect for staging enemy assaults and picking off Marines like fish in a barrel. We were just half a flight down when we had to skirt several dead Pylor bodies.

I said, "Your handywork?" to Max.

"Actually, "Ham's . . ."

I looked over my shoulder to the twin behind me, "Good work."

"I'm Hock." He gestured with a thumb over his shoulder. "That's Ham."

The sounds of distant weapon fire suddenly rose up from

below. I looked over the banister to the pristine white open, winding, stairwell below. I could just make out flashes of energy fire—some of which was unmistakably that from shredder rifles.

I said, "Double time it! We've got Marines in trouble down there."

It wasn't long before we heard running footsteps. Looking over the banister, I saw a contingent of seven armed Pylors headed upward. Neither Thunderballs nor his robot was among them. It was Max and me at the lead, so I signaled those behind us to hang back. Max and I descended the steps two at a time while staying close to the wall. With all the racket the Pylors were making, I was fairly certain they were clueless as to our presence within the stairwell. They were just around the bend when Max tapped my shoulder and gestured to hold up. He crouched and I followed suit. Both of us raised our shredders and waited. I appreciated Max not given me a hard time about putting myself, the captain of the *Hamilton*, in unnecessary danger. The first two of the Pylors came around the bend, I pulled my trigger, nailing the one on the right; Max got the one on the left. Both had been clean shots to the neck area, right below the lower ridge of their helmets—a known weak point to any combat suit.

Max said, "Nice shot, Cap."

We stood and took advantage of the mayhem caused by two dead bodies falling backward onto the still-advancing Pylors—then we continued with our relentless downward firestorm. We watched as enemy combatants tumbled lifeless ass-over-teakettle down the stairs. Only one of the Pylors had gotten a shot off and I thanked my lucky stars that we'd been spared, only to notice that Max was wavering where he stood. Behind his faceplate, I saw a man in pain.

"Where you hit, Sergeant?"

"Foot."

"Foot? How the hell could you get hit in the foot?" I asked looking for a blast mark. He lifted his left boot higher and sure enough, there was a charcoaled patch on his heel. "Wow. Must have tagged you right when he was tumbling backward, and you were taking a step. Hurts, huh?"

"I'll be fine ... just need a second."

I signaled the others it was clear to keep moving. I got beneath one of Max's arms with a shoulder and said, "Sorry ... we can't stay here."

Down we continued, although, now at a slower pace. We reached the location where the Pylors and Marines had skirmished earlier. Three Marines lay dead on the steps.

Max said, "Let me try to walk ... or at least hobble."

We checked the faces of the dead; I didn't recognize any of them.

Grip leaned over each and then said, "Yeah, I know these guys ... they'd come in on Plopper 2. Jenkins, Gomez, and Combs."

Hardy said, "We can get to the Comms Hub from this level." He moved forward through the crowd, stepped over the bodies, and joined Max and me. The ChronoBot scrutinized the curved bulkhead wall before placing his mechanical palm upon it. A small opening appeared and soon there was a full-sized doorway large enough for us to cross through.

The passageway was identical to any number of the others I'd seen, with the exception this one wasn't empty. I stopped in my tracks as I stared into the barrels of no less than thirty shredder rifles. Someone said, "Friendlies . . ." and they lowered their rifles in unison. It was then I noticed those behind the Marines. An equal number, thirty or so, of Pleidian Weonans—those that had no doubt been hostages here on this station.

A scream from behind me caused my heart to miss a beat. The Empress had come through the open door. Now charging, she knocked both Max and me aside. Arms outstretched she weaved her way through the perplexed looking Marines. Heartfelt cries filled the passageway as the Empress was enfolded into the arms of her fellow Pleidian hostages.

One of the Marines approached, "Sure glad to see that you guys are still among the living, Sarge," he said.

Max grimaced, having mistakenly put weight on his injured foot. "Thompson. Who all do we have here . . . and who're we missing?"

"Missing?"

"Yeah . . . the other teams."

"This is it . . . all of us, Sarge. With the exception of your team, we all combined a while back. This is all who are still alive. The good news, we've pretty much cleared out all the Pylors."

I let that sink in—so far, we'd lost forty-five Marines on this mission. I wondered how the Arrow wings were faring out beyond this structure. Was the *Hamilton* even still in one piece? I thought about Doc Viv and did my best to nudge her face from my mind.

God, how had we—no—*I*, how had I so greatly underestimated the ferocity of these Pylor bastards? Admiral Spinker's orders had been simple; fuel up the *Hamilton* and the *Union* and get ourselves back to Earth. Help protect our home planet. What a clusterfuck this had turned out to be. *I should never have been promoted. I have no idea what I'm doing here.*

"Captain ... there's a problem getting us to that Comms Hub," Hardy said.

I tore myself away from my self-incrimination, "Your sensors not picking up anything new?" Checking again, I confirmed a minimal amount of information was coming into my own HUD—what little being displayed was practically useless.

"I believe we're close, but this Pylor's jamming technology is impressive. Beyond anything Humans, Pleidian Weonans, or Grish could unscramble, perhaps even the Sheentah. Thinking about it, though, the actual jammer itself could be anywhere. Not necessarily within the Comms Hub."

"So, you're saying we're screwed, and you've sent us on a wild goose chase," Wanda said. "You know, this deck alone spans, like, miles and miles."

Hardy remained silent.

How am I going to check in with the Hamilton? "Okay, new plan ... Max, you'll be sending a squad down to those fuel tanks. There'll be an adjacent docking platform down there on the outside of the station. Your Marines will need to get things prepped and ready to fuel up the *Hamilton* and *Union* once they arrive here."

"How you going to contact the *Hamilton* to bring them over? We just talked about this . . . comms are jammed."

"I'll have to go fetch them," I said.

Everyone just looked at me.

Max said, "Undoubtedly, those enemy gunships are out there blasting everything and anything in sight! A slow Plopper wouldn't last two minutes . . . be blown to kingdom come."

Wanda made a face, "Yeah, that won't work. It's a stupid idea."

I smiled at her frankness. "I won't be piloting one of our remaining Ploppers. Hardy and I will be heading over to Ironhold's flight bay. With any luck, there'll be a gunship or a fighter for us to abscond with. You give me something fast and maneuverable, I'll get us over to the *Hamilton*."

"And the rest of us . . . and all the hostages?" Wanda asked, still looking skeptical.

"You'll all head back to Plopper 2 and 3. Pilots are still there, waiting. Get everyone onboard and be ready to am-scray out of there on my command."

"On your command? The comms are jammed," Grip said, adding his two cents to the conversation and sounding annoyed.

"We'll figure something out. Just be ready."

"There's just one little problem with your plan," Wanda said. "Thunderballs and his ChronoBot . . . they could surprise anyone of us, either the team heading down to the fuel tanks or those of us heading to the Ploppers. Without Hardy, here, for protection, we're going tits up."

"I'm the one Thunderballs blames for upending his way of life. Vengeance is a powerful emotion. No, I'm the one he'll come for. With Pylor's technology, I'm betting he's tracking my TAC-Band. Knows where I'm at right now. He'll be watching and he'll see where I'm headed off to." I looked over to the robot. "Not to put undue pressure on you, Hardy, but you'll need to confront that ChronoBot one more time."

"And kick its ass this time!" Wanda said.

I nodded. "Okay, we all have our jobs to do. Let's head out."

"Wait!"

I turned to see Empress Shawlee Tee, with two other of the hostages, both male, heading toward us.

"Empress, Shawlee, I need to go. Time is—"

"We will be accompanying you. You made me a promise, Galvin."

"And I'll keep that promise if I can. But this will be beyond dangerous . . . something Hardy and I have to do alone."

"No. Cardinal Thunderballs must remain alive, and I will ensure that is the case."

Sure, I could argue with her, physically restrain them, but I decided—with time being such an issue—to allow the three Pleidians to come along. As it happened, we passed by what Hardy said was the station's Comms Hub, with its dead bodies strewn everywhere along the passageway. Most were Pylors that had lost their lives defending their post. Hardy did a quick check of the equipment inside, conveying his belief that Ironhold Station's capability to communicate to the outside world was still intact, although we already knew that signals were still being jammed from an unknown location.

We continued on, Hardy in the lead, the Empress Shawlee Tee and her two cohorts in the middle, and me bringing up the rear. Each of us was armed with shredders and each uneasy as to what lurked around the next bend, or even behind any adjacent bulkhead.

We descended two different stairwells and made our way closer to the exterior of Ironhold. Hardy confirmed we were approaching the perimeter hull.

I said, "I don't suppose there's a porthole window...be nice to get a visual of what's going on out there."

"No porthole windows. There are strategically placed video displays to the outside, but—"

I finished for him, "...but the those, too, are currently being jammed."

Shawlee said, "How is it such an advanced ChronoBot as yourself has been so easily outsmarted? The Pylors are smart enough, but ChronoBot technology is extremely advanced."

I'd been thinking something similar but didn't want to kick someone when they were down.

Hardy stopped, then slowly turned to face the Empress. He'd put on his creepy big smiling face. "Exactly."

"You want to expound on that, big guy?" I said.

"Well, not only has the station's communications been taken down...my own internal comms, as well as some of my most basic functionality, has been affected. I'm having a hard time remembering the layout of this station. Even, where we just came from."

"Terrific . . . that's encouraging," I said.

"No, you're not getting my point," Hardy said. "It's not the Pylors who are jamming things, it's Thunderball's ChronoBot."

"Are we heading in the right direction? Are we close to the station's flight bay?" I asked. "I could swear we've been down this same corridor more than once."

"How do you know the other ChronoBot isn't sending you around in circles? You said it yourself, your most basic functionality has been affected," the Empress added.

Hardy seemed to be considering that. "Perhaps . . . it is time LuMan takes a more *prominent* role from here on out."

The Empress looked from Hardy then back to me. "I don't understand. Who is LuMan?"

"It's a long story," I said.

I knew that Hardy hated relinquishing his dominant state over to the base robot. Perhaps he felt he'd be relegated to living the rest of his life in the background.

"If it could help, do it. Perhaps you're interpreting things, indicators, differently than how LuMan would."

"I get all my information from LuMan . . . but yes, maybe having one too many interpretations going on *has* been a problem. I'll be taking a back seat until further notice." The robot's demeanor immediately altered. The ChronoBot stood taller, more rigid. His face, with all its blinking sensor lights, no longer made faux expressions. It was evident, LuMan was back in control.

I said, "LuMan?"

"Yes Captain," came the electronically synthesized voice.

"Can you get us to the station's flight bay? If not, bring back Hardy."

The big robot neither said nor did anything for a good ten seconds or so. He then turned to face the passageway's bulkhead. He placed a mechanical hand upon the surface, spurring an opening there. It grew in size and soon there was a new door. LuMan said, "There is a sixty-two percent likelihood the flight bay will be found using this dedicated stairwell. Even though well hidden, blocked from all sensor access."

"How'd you find it, then?" I asked.

"I was temporarily able to block all of my incoming signals. Within less than the span of three nanoseconds, I brought up a more detailed schematic of the station."

"Clever," I said. "Well, daylight's burning . . . let's get going." I gestured to the ChronoBot to get moving. One after another, we followed LuMan through the doorway. This stairwell seemed to be more like service stairs. There were no bulkheads and the cool rubber coating on everything was missing—we could see the inner superstructure, the inner bones, of the station. Here, our footsteps clanged and echoed noisily as we descended. It seemed like an hour before we'd reached a kind of metal scaffolding that took us around in a circular direction. It was so narrow, the robot had to turn sideways and side-shuffle along the way. LuMan stopped when we'd reached what seemed to be an impassible dead end, a wall of vertical metal struts. I looked up into the skeletal insides of the station and cringed. We were truly sitting ducks here. *Was this the plan all along?* Had LuMan's already dubious capabilities been pirated by the other ChronoBot? Had swapping Hardy for LuMan been a terrible mistake?

I realized I'd been hearing something. Earlier, as we'd descended, it had grown louder and louder. I huffed. "That's engine noise."

"Are you sure, Captain?" the Empress said.

"Yeah . . . I'm a pilot. I've spent a good part of my life hearing sounds like that. LuMan . . . any way you can break through those struts there?"

"Affirmative."

We all stepped back and let LuMan go to work. Whatever kind of metal comprised these struts, it was incredibly strong. LuMan's internal servos whined with strain as he pulled and pried at girders that had little give to them. Then, suddenly, there was the sound of something cracking—something snapping. LuMan pulled a length of metal-free and tossed it over the side of the scaffolding and went to work on the next one. It took him close to twenty minutes to breach an opening large enough for us—and him—to squeeze through. The noise of multiple spacecraft engines increased tenfold. Loud enough to hide all the noise LuMan had been making.

I yelled, "Let me take a peek out there first!" I squeezed by the others and LuMan, sticking my head out through the opening. It was a large open space, but still not even a quarter the size of the *Hamilton's* flight bay. There were eight gunships throttled up, but not one of them was in good shape. Smoke billowed up from several. Each showed signs of recent battle damage. Pylor flight crews were running around, looking harried. From my position, I didn't have a good angle to see out through the flight bay doors. I needed to get a status of the battle taking place in space . . . perhaps even get a glimpse of the *Hamilton,* if it was still there. The closest gunship, this one not fired up, was about thirty feet away.

"Stay here . . . back in a flash," I said. I took another quick glance around before making a mad dash across the open flight bay. I reached the gunship without getting shot, ducked beneath its port-side wing, and took refuge behind a landing strut. My view to open space beyond was now unobstructed. What I saw took my breath away.

chapter 35

Brilliant crimson and emerald streaks of light flashed by upon a canvas of twinkling stars and inky blackness. As much as the battle inside Ironhold Station was coming to an end, outside was a far different story. Dodging and weaving Pylor gunships were battling an equal number of nimble Navy Arrows. But all of that paled in comparison to the roaring battle at a distance beyond. The *Hamilton* was taking a beating. The *Union* was saddled up right next to her, and I immediately knew why: to protect that vulnerable flank where her shields had undoubtedly become ineffective. Still, countless explosions erupted all around the two Navy vessels—most were impact blasts hitting their shields, but not all. The two vessels were taking a terrible beating. *I need to get out there ... I need to get into that damn fight.*

Thinking about it now, beyond the threshold of this flight bay was a raging battle that still required much direction. It would require an admiral, of sorts, giving commands. And it was then I realized why Thunderballs had not laid in wait for me, hadn't tried to finish me and my team off once and for all. It was because he was fighting, directing, a different battle . . . this one, this amazing conflict here, beyond the hull of this station.

Two more gunships suddenly appeared at the entrance to the flight bay—where they breached a shimmering energy containment field—one that maintained the bay's internal atmosphere. The gunships showed recent battle damage but seemed flight-capable, just the same. Landing, they skidded to a stop where crews quickly approached. The Pylor vessels were coming and going from this bay to get a quick fix that would enable them to return to the fight, or perhaps have weapons magazines replenished with rail munitions.

This flight bay was a crucial component to the battle-readiness of the Pylor space offensive. Right now, the most effective means to alter the outcome of this conflict lay right here. I scanned the underbelly of the gunship above me. These vessels were a good bit larger than our Navy Arrow fighters—perhaps thirty feet long and twelve feet wide. Could easily hold ten or more. The reason I couldn't, at first, find the underside access panel was because it was directly over my head. A glowing light blue touch panel indicated I'd need to enter a code to gain entrance. *Shit*, I'd need LuMan for that. Looking back to the torn away bulkhead opening from where I'd emerged, I saw a number of faces looking back at me. Remembering that our TAC-Bands still, partially, worked, I sent a simple test message.

NEED JUST LUMAN -- GET OVER HERE!

The big robot, without Hardy's more human awareness, stomped across the open deck as if he owned the place with no attempt to be even the slightest bit stealthy. Amazingly, the ChronoBot ducked beneath the gunship's underbelly, reached where I was hunkered down, all without having been noticed.

"Can you get this hatch access open?" I said.

It was difficult, LuMan being so large, for him to crane his head up around to see the touch panel. One of his chopstick probes emerged from one hand. He touched it to the device and hatch access slid open a metal ladder extended down. I said, "Can you do some kind of diagnostics on this craft... determine if its flight-ready?"

LuMan tapped some more on the touch screen. "The vessel has not been deployed to the battle for a reason."

Great, a smart ass ChronoBot. "So, this gunship can't be flown ... that's what you're telling me?"

"No. I have determined there is an electrical malfunction with the vessel's navigation system."

"Can it be easily and quickly, fixed?"

A moment passed while LuMan tapped some more on the panel. "Done. The damaged circuit area has been bypassed. The vessel is now operational."

"Good job. Okay ... let's get everyone over here. You may need to help cover their dash over here. But don't shoot unless I say to."

I messaged Max:

COME ON OVER -- ONE AT A TIME.

The Empress was the first to sprint across the open bay followed by the two other Pleidians.

"Head on up the ladder," I said to them.

Next came Ham and Hock, not coming one at a time but side-by-side and looking as noticeable as a parade float. *Shit*, they'd grabbed the attention of a repair crew working on an adjacent gunship. Above the racket of so many spacecraft engines, I heard the piercing sound of an alarm klaxon. *Shit! Shit! Shit!*

Ham and Hock reached the gunship's underbelly.

"Up the ladder, move it!" *Idiots!*

No sense in hiding anymore, everyone was looking at us. Fortunately, a repair crewman wasn't typically armed. I moved out from beneath the gunship, stood, and frantically signaling the others. "Get moving! All of you! Hurry!"

Wanda, Grip, and then Max bringing up the rear, were hot-footing it across the flight deck. Halfway across it looked like they'd make it. But that's when the deck plates beneath my feet began to rumble and vibrate. A series of bright plasma bolts were streaming in from somewhere off to my right—from deeper within the flight bay.

"Move it!" I yelled.

The three of them ducked as more plasma fire tore into the deck mere feet away. Wanda dove beneath the gunship, while both Grip and Max stopped, took a knee, and returned fire. I still didn't know who was firing at them.

Then I did, as Thunderball's modified ChronoBot came into view holding an energy weapon almost as big as he was. I turned to LuMan. "It's your turn at bat, LuMan. Not to put too much pressure on you . . . but you need to take out that damn robot . . . that, or we're all screwed."

LuMan needed no additional prompt, heading off in the direction of his rapidly advancing opponent. The barrage of plasma fire ceased. I caught sight of both Max and Grip, stopped halfway on their way over to the gunship, and watching as the two seven-foot-tall machines drove toward each other like two speeding locomotives on a collision course.

I yelled, "Max! Grip! Get moving!"

Whatever happened between the two mega-bots, was out of our control. I needed to get this bird fired up and readied for a battle of our own.

As soon as Max and Grip had scampered up the ladder, I followed them up and inside. Outside the gunship, I heard the familiar sound of hardened metal clanging against metal.

The inside of the gunship was pretty much barebones. A hold area aft with few accoutrements—no seats, just drop straps, which everyone had taken a hold of. I said, "Anyone here have any kind of flight experience? Any at all?"

No one said anything for a few beats. Surprisingly, it was the Empress who eventually spoke up.

"I do, Captain . . . I was flight-certified to pilot my family's royal StarClipper."

"Good enough . . . you'll be my co-pilot. Come up to the cockpit."

We took our seats and I surveyed the controls in front of me. Although similar to any other small spacecraft I'd piloted over the years, the placement of controls was all off. And because my TAC-Band and even my optical implants were still being interfered with, *jammed*, I was on my own to figure things out.

"Captain, if I may . . . I can explain what's what here."

She pointed out what the various Pleidians readouts were, how the hand controls worked, how to engage the weaponry, and most important at the moment, how to fire up the engine drive and lift thrusters. I initiated the power-on sequence, took hold of the controls, and said, "Can you kick in those lift thrusters, Shawlee?"

She smiled and did as asked.

The view out the wraparound view-window before us was of the flight bay's open bay doors, providing a view of the space and the ensuing battle beyond. As the gunship rose five, ten, fifteen feet off the deck, I attempted to pivot the gunship around on its axis. Instead, the nose of the craft suddenly dipped and the gunship careened hard into the flight deck with a resounding *Clunk!*

Nervously, the Empress glanced my way. Her expression conveyed; *Does he have the slightest clue what he's doing?*

I said, "I got this . . ." with far more confidence than I was feeling. I got the ship leveled out and attempted to swing it around one more time. Pivoting counterclockwise, the view before us changed from the flight bay opening to other nearby gunships, and the far side bulkhead. I continued the pivot until we'd swung around a full one-hundred-and-eighty degrees and were facing into the back of the flight bay. And there they were below us—the two battling ChronoBots.

From behind us, Max said, "Looks like your bot's getting his ass handed to him." Irritated, I glanced back. The cockpit was small but evidently large enough for everyone who'd been standing in the aft hold area to squeeze in to watch the spectacle before us.

Wanda said, "I feel kind of sad and embarrassed at the same time."

ThunderBall's ChronoBot had LuMan laid out on his back and was repeatedly punching him in the head—which in turn, was thwacking it down onto the deck. I grimaced with each strike. *Get up LuMan!*

"Boy's down for the count, Captain . . . Hope you have a plan B. Maybe we just leave him . . . skedaddle out of here?" Max said.

Sure, if it was just LuMan down there getting his ass handed to him, maybe. The cost of battle. But Hardy was there too. A human consciousness. Dare I say, even a friend?

I'd made a grave error, letting LuMan take control. What I needed to do was get Hardy back in the driver's seat. But how? Message him via my TAC-Band? No, I think he'd need a verbal command. "Shawlee? Is there an external public address system . . . a way to broadcast externally?"

She scanned the dashboard before us. "Uh, maybe . . ." She used a forefinger to trace the various complex-looking readouts and touch buttons before us. "Maybe this . . ." She tapped at a button. One of the smaller display screens scrolled a message of alien symbols and characters.

"That's it . . . just key that button on your hand control when you speak."

"Thanks." I let out a breath, swallowed, and pressed the button.

"LuMan." The ChronoBot's name broadcasted and echoed loud outside into the flight bay. I said, "LuMan . . . this is Captain Quintos."

Thunderball's ChronoBot had gotten a hold of LuMan by his neck with one hand and a leg in his other. In a kind of weightlifter's clean jerk maneuver, he had LuMan up off the deck, raised up high over his head.

"I'm sure he knows who you are, Captain . . . Christ! Just get to it!" Wanda spat.

"LuMan, I order you to relinquish control and let Hardy take over."

But LuMan was already being hurled into the air. He landed hard and rolled several times on his side. He didn't move. Didn't so much as twitch.

"Oh God, I can't watch this," Grip said.

I knew what was coming next. Thunderball's ChronoBot took one, two, three fast strides forward, then, letting his trailing leg extend even farther backward—getting a full extension—he was all set up for one, final, colossal, kick to LuMan's perfectly positioned head.

I clenched my fists. I clenched my teeth. I really didn't want to watch this. I saw the Empress cover her eyes with one hand.

And then, at the last moment, LuMan moved. He had timed it perfectly. Sat up, positioned his hand out in front of himself, and caught the ChronoBot's incoming foot. Everyone in the cockpit gasped in unison. I leaned forward, seeing LuMan's face, it was evident who I was now looking at: Hardy was back. And a big, stupid, faux smile was spread across his robot face.

chapter 36

Hardy stood while still clutching the other ChronoBot's foot. Unable to keep its balance, the Pylor ChronoBot slammed down onto its back. Immediately, all of its energy weapons came alive—forearm cannons, shoulder-mount cannons, and two more that had ejected out from its thighs. Hardy was being bombarded with enough plasma fire to take out a small battleship. But he continued to hold on to his opponent's foot. His exterior was glowing now—a red-hot broiler you could cook a steak on.

"He has to be close to overheating . . . shit, maybe start to melt," Wanda said.

Hardy, slowly at first, began dragging the other ChronoBot away.

Max said, "What's he doing?"

"I have no idea," I said.

No longer firing its weapons, the Pylor ChronoBot had begun to flail about—desperately reaching and clawing the deck for something, anything, to grab onto. But Hardy didn't falter or slow—in fact, he'd picked up a bit of speed. As the two robots disappeared beneath our gunship, I manipulated the controls and pivoted the craft another one-hundred-and-eighty degrees to face forward again, toward the open bay doors and open space beyond.

Below us, I could see pilots and flight crew personnel had stopped what they'd been doing to watch the show. Hardy was running now, the sound of his powerful legs thundering down onto the deck with each stride heard above the ambient engine noise, the still blaring klaxon, and now the coaxing cheers coming from the people standing right behind me.

At about sixty feet from the bay's entrance, the Pylor ChronoBot became airborne. Still flailing, still reaching for something to grasp, but it was futile wasted energy. Even before Hardy had initiated his next move, I knew what was coming. I turned and caught Max's eye. "You ever watch the Olympics? Track and field events, Max?"

"Oh yeah . . . I especially like the hammer throw."

We both laughed.

Hardy was already mid-way through his first three-hundred-and sixty-degree running spin.

"That takes some bad-ass skills to move like that. For a robot, not bad," Grip said.

"Nah . . . that's all Hardy's skill," I said.

Still advancing while spinning his captive around and around, building incredible momentum, Hardy was now approaching the bay's separating energy field.

Wanda said, "Wait for it . . . wait for it . . . and . . ."

Timing it perfectly, Hardy released his hold on the ChronoBot's foot. And like an Olympians hammer throw release, the robot shot out through the flight bay's opening. The energy field shimmered with the disruption. Appendages flailing, the Pylor ChronoBot had been catapulted out into the still-raging space battle. Then, to everyone's dismay, there was an explosion of epic proportions. A white-hot ball of flame characteristic of a small but powerful antimatter disruption.

"What just happened?" Ham said.

"Yeah, what just happened?" Hock said.

I said, "Well, boys, that's what happens when two fast-moving, high-mass objects collide in space . . . in this case, a Pylor gunship having collided with a ChronoBot."

The Empress, who had watched the transpiring events in silence, let out a unique whoop sound. Fists raised over her head, she laughed, "That was spectacular!"

A warning alarm suddenly erupted within the cockpit. "Everyone back in the hold area! We're taking fire from below!" I yelled. I spun the gunship around while feeling with my fingers for the weapons controls. I found them but wasn't sure which were for rail guns and which were for plasma cannons— so I triggered both.

"You're shooting too high!" both Max and Wanda yelled behind me; both had obviously ignored my order to go aft.

"I already know that. Just shut up and let me do what I do." I accelerated the gunship forward while dipping the nose of the craft down thirty degrees. I'd notice earlier the rail gun had done far more damage to the flight bay's surrounding bulkheads, and now triggered that weapon exclusively. One parked gunship after another was torn apart. Having their shields down during maintenance, disintegrating hull fragments spewed into the air as if the gunships were little more than exploding toys. I continued to unleash relentless hellfire until there was nothing left to shoot at. The atmosphere within the bay had turned dark and cloudy—clusters of debris swirled upon invisible currents of air.

Wanda said, "Okay... If you're done with your macho rampage... you'll notice our comms and HUD functionality is back online."

I'd had my faceplate retracted. Lowering it, I saw all the little indicators and readouts back where they were supposed to be. Taking out the Pylor ChronoBot had done the trick. I watched as one facial icon after another took its place at the bottom of the HUD. Several, those who had not survived, were dimmed and had a red line angled through them. I also noticed that close to two-hundred comms messages had been left for me, all of which were of the highest priority level. But, with what lay ahead, I wouldn't have time to listen to any of them. I found a relatively open area on the deck and set the craft down.

"Somebody open up the side access hatch back there, and let Hardy in."

The was a lot of clattering as the robot came aboard, then came the congratulations by one and all. Hardy poked his war-torn face in, "Thank you, Cap. Your faith in me means a lot."

"It's me who should be thanking you, Hardy. Good job.

Excellent job. Now tell everyone back there to grab a strap . . . this ride's about to get a whole lot rougher."

I glanced over to the Empress who was quiet and looking introspective. "You holding up okay?"

She nodded. "I can't believe we're doing this . . . you're doing this. I honestly didn't think I'd ever get off this awful station. I owe you my life . . . my people will learn of the sacrifice you, all of you, have made today."

I'd come here to steal fuel from the pirate Pylors, not to save the Empress and the other hostages. But I wasn't about to say that now. "You're welcome. Now hold on, we're not out of trouble yet."

"Where are we going now?" She asked.

"Well, now that the station's been cleared of enemy Pylors, I can tell the *Hamilton* to make its way over and get fueled up. We'll get you and your people onboard where you'll be safe."

"I just want to go home, Galvin . . . can you contact the Pleidian Weonan fleet?"

"Of course, as soon as possible, I promise," I said. First, I needed to hail the *Hamilton*.

"Captain Quintos?"

I recognized Crewman Grime's voice. "The one and only. Grimes, I'm not getting a visual."

"Yes, sir . . . much of our comms have been taken out by the Pylor gunships. Audio is all we've got going right now."

"Fine, let me talk to my XO, is Derrota—"

Grimes cut me off, "Sorry, sir . . . um, well . . ."

"Grimes!"

"Sorry sir, Captain Tannock has retaken the Captain's Mount and is currently in command of the *Hamilton*. Um, so, do you want to speak with him?"

It took me a moment to wrap my head around what I'd just heard. "That's fine, put me through." *Did Tannock made some kind of miraculous recovery? Is he back in charge—is he my superior again?*

Captain Tannock's voice came on the line, "Captain Quintos! Status... we haven't heard from you, anyone on mission for close to eighteen hours. What the hell is your status? Would it have been too much to ask that you make contact!?"

"We ran into a bit more trouble than expected. Thunderballs was a far more cunning leader than anticipated, commanding nearly twice the number of forces than ours. Oh, and did I mention there were three weaponized ChronoBots? Or that the young Pleidian Weonan Empress, among others of her kind, were here on Ironhold... being held hostage. Which, by the way, was the real reason that the Pleidian fleet hadn't attacked the station for the last few years. So, yeah... I guess we had our work cut out for us, sir."

There was a pregnant silence before Captain Tannock spoke again. "So, Ironhold Station has—"

"Has been cleared and is currently being prepped for the *Hamilton* to come over and dock."

I waited—not sure if Tannock's continued silence was a sign of his disbelief in my report or if, perhaps, his mental state was once again impaired.

Tannock finally said, "That's commendable, sir ... quite commendable."

Wait, he just called me "sir." What the hell is going on here?

He continued, "Captain Quintos, I have Lieutenant Pristy waiting to speak with you. She'll set up the logistics concerning the *Hamilton's* and *Union's* refueling process."

chapter 37

Lieutenant Pristy came on the line, "Captain . . . I can't tell you how happy I am . . . we all are, to hear you are alive."

She sounded relieved. Relieved and stressed. "Are we on a closed channel, Lieutenant?"

"Yes, sir . . . just you and me on the line."

"What the hell is going on? Where's Derrota? Why's Tannock taken back the Captain's Mount?" I waited for her reply, but it didn't come right away. "Gail!"

"Oh, sorry, sir . . . it's just that . . . they're leaving . . . bugging out."

"What? Who?"

"The Pylor gunships. They're leaving the system as we speak."

I tried to make heads or tails of the gunship's display and sensor readings when I heard Hardy's voice from behind me.

"It's true, Cap . . . all enemy craft, some fifty-six gunships in all, have left the system."

"I thought I told you to stop eavesdropping on my private comms conversations!"

"Oh ... yeah, forgot. Never happen again, sir. Over and out," Hardy said. He was undoubtedly lying.

Before I could continue my conversation with Lieutenant Pristy, static-filled my helmet. Then I heard an all-too-familiar voice.

"Well, well, bravo ... a job well done my friend. So, I must give credit where credit is due."

"Thunderballs ..."

"Now please, I so prefer that you call me Cardinal, Galvin."

"Uh huh."

He continued, "You know this isn't over, right? Sure, for the moment you can revel in your minor victory here, but I, as we speak, am making plans for the future. Plans that involve you and all those onboard the *Hamilton* that you care so much about. I believe you humans have a saying; revenge is best served cold. What a wonderful idiom, or is that a cliché? ... Hmm, English is such a wonderfully expressive language. What you don't know, Galvin ... is that I made one last transmission to Fleet Commander Twinwon."

"Good for you."

"Yes, but not so good for you. You see, I informed him that with your clumsy invasion of Ironhold Station, you systematically murdered all the hostages. You murdered the Pleidians Weonans', dear Empress. Just maybe, Twinwon might have let you escape here with your tails between your legs, but ...

no longer. They will be coming for you. They will settle for nothing less than total restitution."

Shit! That was unexpected. "You think this is all a game, don't you, Thunderballs? I assure you, it's not. We'll find a way out of this. As for you . . . next time, you won't get away so easily. There again, I guess cowardice befits you." I knew those words would strike home. Calling him a coward had triggered something. So, I beat the point home even farther, "So here's a new game for you . . . Hide and go fuck yourself." I cut the connection.

I sat back and let out a long breath. I suspected I'd have to deal with Thunderballs again. Until he, or I, was dead, this wouldn't be over.

"Captain?" Lieutenant Pristy said.

"Sorry . . . we were interrupted by—"

"Cardinal Thunderballs. I heard. We all did."

Christ, what's with my conversations never being private these days? "There, on the Bridge?"

"No, sir . . . it went ship-wide."

I just shook my head. None of this was worth fretting about right now. "Talk to me about my XO. Where's Derrota? Is he okay? What's the status of the *Hamilton* and *Union*? And why the hell are we all reporting to Tannock again . . . just days ago he was drooling into his soup."

She laughed out loud at that and I was reminded how much I liked this young officer. How much her friendship and trust meant to me.

Her voice lowered conspiratorially, "Captain . . . you're

reading this all wrong. Science Officer Derrota wasn't ... um, let's just say, he's not built for command when things get stressful. Without you here, and the *Hamilton* operating with such a limited officer crew ... options were limited."

"What about Mattis?"

"He refused, and had his hands full dealing with multiple Pylor breaches into MATHR."

"Okay ..."

She said, "So Captain Tannock, apparently, has been steadily recovering. Not to the point of where he was ... but still, better. He went Doc Viv and talked her into clearing him for active duty again."

"And she signed off on that?" I said, loud enough to surely get the others' attention, even aft.

"Well, I guess that's that. Any specific orders I should be aware of?" I engaged the lift thrusters and brought the gunship fifteen feet off the deck. I gunned the throttle and we shot out into open space. Sure enough, there were no enemy vessels anywhere in the vicinity, though I did see several Arrow fighters on routine patrol.

"Captain ... he hasn't taken back the captaincy ... he's your XO. And you know what, thank God he was here and of a right mind enough to fend off the Pylors."

"He's my, our, XO?"

"Yes."

"Oh."

"And, he's awaiting *your* orders. Apparently, the Pleidian

Weonans' fleet, specifically Fleet Commander, Twinwon, is readying to attack us."

"Well, if anything they should be throwing us a damn parade for saving those hostages ... saving the Empress!"

Empress Shawlee Tee was staring at me with rapt attention—taking in every word I said.

"Remember, none of us on the *Hamilton* knew anything about there being hostages. Captain, XO, Tannock knew nothing about hostages. And apparently, that was not something Fleet Commander, Twinwon was willing to share. What he *was* willing to share in a conversation with Tannock not more than an hour ago, was that our ships will be atomized just as soon as we attempt to leave the system. And Twinwon's cut off all communications. XO Tannock has attempted, multiple times, to hail the Pleidians."

That coincided with what Thunderballs told me. His lie about us killing off the hostages. *Shit!* "So, even having the Empress here to attempt communications—"

"...would go unanswered," the Lieutenant said.

"Damn ... okay, one thing at a time. We need to get both the *Hamilton* and the *Union* fueled up. I'm assuming you have established contact with other teams on the station?"

"Affirmative. Grimes is currently talking to the pilots of Plopper 2 and Plopper 3, both vessels are lifting off now ... headed back to the Hamilton. Max's squad of Marines is finished prepping the fuel depot. Everything's a go."

chapter 38

Approaching the *Hamilton*, I saw the far smaller *Union* slowly pulling away from that massive dreadnaught's vulnerable starboard side.

Wanda, from behind and looking forward through the cockpit's window said, "She's unrecognizable... oh, my god, look at her..."

Both warships had been battle-damaged to the point neither vessel would have any kind of future deployment. I was fairly certain that both vessels would be decommissioned, broken apart, and sold off for scrap.

Huh. Only a week earlier, I couldn't wait for my new orders to come through—an XO post on that Light Battleship, the *USS Truman*, as it was coming out of Earth's Lunar Halibart Shipyards. But now, seeing the old girl, hundreds of tiny sparks erupting where her shields had been penetrated by smart missiles and rail munitions, with multiple plumes of atmosphere escaping all along her hull—I was suddenly struck with conflicting emotions. I no longer wanted that other post. I no longer wanted that XO position . . . I wanted to remain Captain of the *U.S.S. Hamilton.* I thought about my Bridge crew, and how they had become more than just that. They were my family. And I thought about Doc Viv. I honestly didn't know how she felt about me. But I knew how I felt about her. This was my crew. These were my people. Unfortunately, if the collective *we,* somehow, could get ourselves out of this mess, we'd all be assigned other posts—on other Navy warships. Earth was in danger, perhaps under attack at this very moment. No, my time with this old broken-down warship and her crew, one way or another, would soon be over.

I got clearance from Bay Chief Frank Mintz to proceed for landing within the *Hamilton.* I slowed our approach and piloted the gunship in through the open bay doors. The separating energy field shimmered as we transitioned from open space into the familiar cavernous flight bay.

Within minutes, we'd landed and were all filing out of the gunship. To my surprise, there was a small welcoming party waiting for us. I saw Science Officer Derrota, Chief of Security Mattis, Lieutenant Pristy, and Engineering Chief Craig Porter. Also there, Captain Tannock. As we approached, they applauded us.

Lieutenant Pristy broke ranks with the others, ran over to me and gave me a hug. "Captain! I thought for sure you were dead. That you were all dead. We were losing that battle . . . all I could think about, dread, was when Thunderball's boarding party would come. That we were all destined to become Pylor hostages."

"Well... fortunately, a few things ended up going our way. But much of all our thanks should go to Hardy, here. He battled three ChronoBots and saved our bacon." Hardy beamed with the praise.

Captain Tannock stepped forward and held out his hand. I took it and was about to thank him for stepping in at such a crucial moment, but he spoke first.

"Captain Quintos... over the years you and I have had our differences."

"That's maybe an understatement," Derrota mumbled.

Tannock looked tired and frail, as if the previous hours had taken what little life force he had left in him. He motioned with his chin, "I need to say something to you and if I wait, I may not ever have the chance."

"Okay..."

We stepped away from the others. "I owe you an apology, Quintos."

"Not at all, sir."

"Shut up and listen to me. I'm done. My time commanding Navy warships is over. I know that and I'm okay with that. But I wanted to acknowledge that your unconventional leadership style, your total disregard of regulations, may actually be one of your most valuable assets. If the EUNF—U.S. Navy, hell, Earth, is going to survive these next few years, it's going to take brash and independent officers such as yourself. So, good job today, Captain Quintos." He squeezed my shoulder and smiled. "One more thing... I was given this one last opportunity to be that officer, that man, I used to be. I thank you for that. Now, I'm quite tired and need to lie down. Go . . . be with your crew." He waved to the others and, with effort, stood erect as he made his way toward the exit of the flight bay.

By the time I returned to the others, Doc Viv, dressed in her typical scrubs, had arrived and was speaking to the Empress and the other two Pleidian Weonans. I'm sure HealthBay was once more packed with the injured; her being here was a statement by itself. She glanced my way and saw that I was staring at her. Without acknowledging me, she ushered the three aliens away. I'm sure they were suffering from malnutrition and a slew of other ailments.

The Empress then turned back to me, "Later, Galvin . . . please come find me, at your hospital facility."

"I will, Shawlee."

Doc Viv shot me a crooked smile before the four of them headed off.

I turned to the others. "I appreciate the welcoming party, but isn't there a Bridge missing its crew right now?"

Porter said, "About that . . . The *Hamilton* is finished. Reactors are caput, drives are caput . . . any kind of propulsion for the Hamilton is a thing of the past. The old gal has fought her last battle."

I looked to the others, Lieutenant Pristy, Derrota, and Mattis. They all looked as if they'd lost their best friend.

"And the *Union?*"

Derrota said, "She's beat to shit as well . . . but she'll get us home . . . once she gets fueled up."

That's something, at least.

Lieutenant Pristy shook her head. "I'm not so sure about that. When Captain Tannock spoke to Fleet Commander Twinwon that last time, it was clear, they would be coming for us. As far as he's concerned, there's no reason for him to allow us to leave the system. I'm actually surprised that the fleet of Pleidians warships hasn't moved to finish us off already."

I watched as Plopper 2 and Plopper 3 entered the flight bay, engaged their landing thrusters, and setting down.

I said, "The Pleidians know we're down for the count . . . no longer a real military threat." I rubbed my chin and tried to think of a way to communicate to Fleet Commander Twinwon, and to do so before he sent a barrage of smart missiles our way.

Just then I saw a lone Arrow fighter enter the flight bay and watched it circle overhead and then set down next to several other Arrows in a row not far from where we were standing. To my surprise, it was Lieutenant Wallace Ryder who was now climbing down from the cockpit.

Ryder was making his way over to us and looking as tired and battle-worn as I felt.

"Captain?" Lieutenant Pristy said. "What are you conjuring up in that head of yours?"

She was right, I was thinking of something. A totally ridiculous, impossible, idea. Even before Ryder could speak, I spoke first. "Ryder . . . I have two questions for you."

"Good to see you too, buddy."

"One . . . " I looked over his shoulder toward the back of the bay. "That Hub Gunther mining vessel. Is it still operational?"

"Sure. Think so."

"Good, and two ... what's the maximum haul rating of that beast?"

"I have no idea ... but it's considerable."

I said, "It'll have to be."

WHAT CAME NEXT TOOK A TOTAL OF SIX HOURS. TWO OF those hours were spent getting all remaining crew personnel, including all the injured from HealthBay, off of the *Hamilton* and onto the *Union*. We'd used all available shuttles on both vessels for that colossal endeavor. No one was happy about it, least of all Doc Viv and her staff. It took three hours to bring the Union over to Ironhold Station, having her depleted fuel tanks filled to the brim. During the last hour, I sat upon the *Union's* Bridge Captain's Mount, having taken command of that vessel. Lieutenant Randy Cobb, the warship's previous CO, had gladly transferred that responsibility over to me, then taking on the role of XO.

The *Union's* far smaller Bridge was currently fully manned, having both *Union* Bridge crew and *Hamilton* Bridge crew working together. My eyes were on the halo-display and the multiple feeds generated from recently deployed sensor-droids.

Lieutenant Pristy sat at the tactical station, where she said she'd feel most comfortable. Derrota and Mattis stood at my side, their attention also locked onto the halo-display.

Derrota said, "I'm sorry, Captain ... but this idea of yours ..."

"I know, far-fetched."

"I was going to say *moronic*."

Chief Mattis huffed, "I have to admit it, he's right. This will probably end up being a futile waste of valuable time. We should just make a run for it."

Lieutenant Pristy said over her shoulder, "Jumping isn't an option, according to Craig. *Union's* jump drive's too damaged."

Trained on the exterior of Ironhold Station, four separate video feeds displayed the progress of seven volunteers wearing spacesuits. The team included SWM Crewmember LaSalle, Sergeant Max Dryer, both Ham and Hock, Wanda, and Grip. But the one doing much of the heavy lifting was none other than Hardy. Between the seven of them, they were disconnecting most of the connection points of the lower encircling cable. A cable that still had the hundreds of Pleidian skeletal remains dangling from it. Having already completed this same task with the higher cable, they were almost done.

Another skeleton, its skull fracturing, broke free and floated away into the darkness of space.

"This is fucking creepy," Wanda said, using a power tool to disconnect another connection point. "That's the last of them. Leaves you four to stay attached."

I said, "Good job, Wanda. Hardy . . . you ready?"

chapter 39

"Ready as I'll ever be." The ChronoBot was holding the free end of the heavy metal cable. A cable, floating untethered, that had been cut but was still close to five miles long.

I watched as Hardy, with cable in hand, jumped from his perch on the station, out into open space. He hadn't needed to jump far, though, because the aft section of the Hub Gunther was no more than twenty feet away. Hardy bicycled his legs, making it look as if he was running the distance. *Smart ass.* Reaching an aft support cowling, Hardy grabbed hold and was now standing upon the Gunther. He began his work to attach the cable so it would be directly across from where the other cable had been affixed, earlier.

"Done and done," Hardy said standing tall and looking directly into one of the sensor-drone cameras.

"Good work, everyone," I said. "Now get back to the *Union.*"

There was a nearby shuttle waiting for them. I watched

as Hardy leapt back over to the station, and the group—far too slowly for my taste—made their way to the shuttle's open hatch.

I said, "J-Dog . . . you ready? Over."

"Roger that. Over."

Lieutenant Ryder was seated within the cockpit of an Arrow fighter, mere feet off the port side of the pilotless Hub Gunther. In addition to piloting his own craft, Ryder would be remotely piloting the Gunther vessel as well.

Mattis said, "The cables won't hold . . . they'll snap like little threads pulling a bowling ball."

I didn't bother answering him. It would be close, I knew that. The mass of Ironhold Station was nowhere near that of a small moon, since much of the materials that comprised it were light composites. And much of the interior was open—just atmosphere. Still, we were talking mass that weighed millions of tons. The problem wouldn't be so much towing Ironhold Station through space; it was getting the thing moving from a dead start. Newton had understood the three basic laws of motion. (1) Objects in motion (or at rest) remain in motion (or at rest) unless an external force imposes change. (2) Force is equal to the change in momentum per change of time. For a constant mass, force equals mass times acceleration. (3) For every action, there is an equal and opposite reaction. The *Union's* version of MATHR had done all the calculations. So theoretically, what I had in mind *was* possible.

"Throttling up now," J-Dog said.

The Hub Gunther's main engine suddenly came

alive—evidenced by a tongue of bright blue flames shooting out from the vessel's aft section. The Gunther began to sway back and forth, and it was visibly starting to vibrate.

"As I said, futile," Mattis said.

I gave it a few more moments before saying, "J-Dog...talk to me. Over."

"Throttling up to ninety percent. Over."

The Gunther's back and forth swaying increased as did the vibrations.

"J-Dog... push it to one-hundred percent. Pedal to the metal."

"Good way to blow the drive, Captain. Thing's already overheating. The ship wasn't designed to tow a damn space station...just saying."

Now the swaying had become exaggerated back and forth swings, the vibrations so great that the Gunther was little more than a blur on the halo-display.

No one said anything. I might have seen the station tremble, there again it might have been hopeful thinking.

Lieutenant Pristy said, "Did you see that?"

"You saw that too," Derrota said.

J-Dog said, "We have movement... three feet... ten... twenty...one hundred..."

We all saw it. Ironhold Station was indeed picking up speed. I glanced over to our resident pessimist, Mattis, and raised my brows.

"I may have spoken too soon," he said.

We watched as the Hub Gunther, the Arrow fighter close

at its side, and the immense trailing space station headed off toward the distant fleet of Pleidian Weonan warships.

"Well I still don't get the point," Mattis said. "What do you expect the Pleidians to do?"

It was Derrota who answered before I could. "They will think it totally bizarre. Ridiculous, even."

"Exactly," Mattis said.

"And it will convey a message. That we are delivering Ironhold Station back to them. It's a gesture," Derrota said.

Twenty minutes later, J-Dog was back on the line. "Approaching the Pleidian Weonan fleet . . . they're all lined up just as before. Initiating maneuver two, now. Over."

The maneuver he was referring to was the process we'd worked out by which he'd bring the station to a standstill— right in front of the alien fleet.

He'd slowed some and was in the process of making a tight U-turn. While the Arrow was already heading back slowly from the way it had come, Ironhold Station's forward momentum had it continuing in its same trajectory. It took just moments for the slack in the five-mile-long cables to go taut once more. The space station suddenly spun around, as the connection points were still facing forward.

J-Dog's broadcasted voice filled the bridge. "Throttling up again . . ."

Mattis said, "What happens if Ryder can't stop the forward momentum? That the space station ends up careening into a few of those Pleidian warships? Do you think that's the kind gesture they'd warm up to?"

All my attention was on the halo-display. The Hub Gunther was throttling up again, straining to slow the massive space station.

"Throttling up to one-hundred percent. Getting a few new warning lights. Over," J-Dog said.

"Best you put some distance between you and the Gunther, J-Dog. Get out of there before it blows. Over."

Earlier, Ryder had mentioned that he didn't have a lot of faith in the quickly slapped-together remote piloting mechanism they'd rigged. Distance could be an issue.

"I've come this far . . . think I'll see this through. Over."

I said to no one in particular, "Who's hairbrained idea was this, anyway?"

No one spoke. No one looked away from what was transpiring up on the halo-display.

Lieutenant Pristy said, "It's definitely losing some of its speed now."

Derrota said, "Will you look at that, Captain . . . it's really slowing!"

I didn't speak right away. I didn't want to jinx anything. But sure enough, Ironhold Station was doing just that. Ninety seconds later, the space station was at a complete standstill.

"Good work, J-Dog . . . go ahead and RTB. Over," I said.

"Copy that. Over"

Lieutenant Pristy said, "That was close. Too close. Twenty-eight miles. That's the narrow span of space between the Pleidian fleet and Ironhold Station."

From behind me, I heard Hardy's Boston-accented voice,

"I bet Fleet Commander Twinwon will need to change his shorts after that white knuckler."

Everyone laughed, though nervously.

"And what now?" Mattis asked.

Lieutenant Pristy said, "Oh my . . . four, seven, no ten, of the Pleidian warships are bringing their weapon's systems online, sir."

As if on cue, I noticed that Doc Viv, along with Empress Shawlee Tee at her side, had entered the bridge, making their way over to me. The Empress was now wearing a formal gown of sorts. She wore makeup and looked like a new person. Even her blue-hued illumination seemed to have brightened some.

"Welcome, Shawlee," I said,

"Thank you, Galvin," she said, nervously looked about the Bridge and then up at the holo-display. "They haven't reached out . . . tried to contact you?"

"Not yet."

"They still may fire on . . . destroy your vessel."

"That's a distinct possibility."

"You must initiate the hail," she said.

"We've opened a channel to them a number of times—"

"They are waiting for you to do so once more."

"So be it," I said. "Grimes . . . open a channel to Fleet Commander Twinwon . . . see if he wants to talk to us."

"Aye, sir . . . opening a channel now."

Lieutenant Pristy had cleared all other feeds from the halo-display, which was now black.

We waited.

"No answer on the hail, sir," Grimes said.

Hardy said, "Hail them again, maybe Twinwon was using the facilities, or taking out the trash. You never know."

Grimes waited for my nod, then did as asked.

The halo-display suddenly came alive and there, looking more than a little pissed, was none other than Fleet Commander Twinwon.

"You have mere moments to live, Captain Quintos . . . best you make this count."

I didn't speak. I didn't need to, for the fleet commander's eyes had settled onto the Empress standing at my side.

His mouth opened, but no words spilled out. Others behind him moved into view, their mouths also agape.

Shawlee smiled, "Ah, Fleet Commander Twinwon, would you be so kind as to shut down your weapons systems? These humans have saved my life . . . and the lives of many of the hostages."

He finally found his tongue, "Is that really you, Empress Shawlee Tee . . . truly, you?"

She laughed. "Yes, good sir . . . It is I."

Twinwon's gaze now turned back to me. He placed a hand on his chest. "Captain Quintos . . . on my behalf and on the behalf of the Pleidian Weonan people, I apologize."

I got to my feet and said "Apology accepted. All I ask is safe passage out of your Pleidian space. With a promise not to bother you again."

"No . . . no, that will not do, Captain. Not remotely."

"Um, I'm sorry?" I said, seeing that things may have just made a turn for the worse again.

"The Pleidian Weonans are great builders of StarCraft's . . . you will allow us the privilege to repair your dreadnought . . . the vessel you call the *USS Hamilton*. And you will come to our world where a proper show of gratitude can take place."

"Thank you, but—"

"I am not finished, Captain . . . you humans have demonstrated a level of courage and honor I had not thought possible. As the highest-ranking Weonan Fleet Commander, I do not have ultimate authority. That said, I do have significant Parliamentary influence. And perhaps, with the assistance of the Empress here, we can discuss a treaty, a kind of war pact. One between Earth and Pleidian . . . between Humans and Weonans. It is time we teach the Grish a lesson, no?"

I was speechless. Not only would the *Hamilton* be transformed, but perhaps enhanced into something even better than before. And if what Twinwon said could be believed, Earth's prospects for survivability was looking a whole lot better. I realized that I'd yet to answer him. That, and now everyone was looking at me.

Doc Viv raised a hand . . . "Hi, Doctor Vivian Leigh here . . . He sometimes gets like this. Yes. The answer is, most definitely, yes."

The End

Thank you for reading *USS Hamilton - Ironhold Station*, book one in this new series. If you enjoyed this book, PLEASE leave a review on Amazon.com—it really helps!

To be notified the moment the next and all future books are released, please join my mailing list. I hate spam and will never, ever share your information. Jump to this link to sign up:

http://eepurl.com/bs7M9r

Acknowledgments

First and foremost, I am grateful to the fans of my writing and their ongoing support for all my books. I'd like to thank my wife, Kim—she's my rock and is a crucial, loving component of my publishing business. I'd like to thank my mother, Lura Genz, for her tireless work as my first-phase creative editor and a staunch cheerleader of my writing. I'd also like to thank Sarah Mayor for her fine work editing the manuscript as well. Others who provided fantastic support include Lura and James Fischer and Stuart Church.

Made in the USA
Monee, IL
03 May 2023